COMMAND LAUNCH

"Target bearing four four degrees . . . Range five thousand five zero zero yards."

The pings became louder.

Boxer hit the GQ button.

The men of the *Shark* responded instantly.

Boxer dialed in a change of speed from twenty to ten knots.

"Target bearing four four degrees . . . Range five thousand . . . Speed now two zero knots."

Boxer pursed his lips. The captain of the *Skoryy* would in a matter of moments decided to attack, or turn away.

"Two ASW rockets launched," the SO reported. "Four four degrees speed five zero knots."

"AUTO NAV off," Boxer said. "Helmsman come to course three zero zero." He spun the electronic speed selector to twenty five knots.

The *Shark* slashed through the water.

Boxer glanced over to the men at the CIC. Grim faced, they studied the GDT, fixing the position of the target as the SO called out its bearing, range and speed.

Suddenly the muffled sound of two explosions rolled over the *Shark*.

"Target bearing forty seven degrees . . . Range three thousand two five zero yards . . . Closing fast."

MORE THRILLING READING!

THE LUCIFER DIRECTIVE   (1353, $3.50)
by Jon Land

Terrorists are outgunning agents, and events are outracing governments. It's all part of a sequence of destruction shrouded in mystery. And the only ones who hold key pieces of the bloody puzzle are a New England college student and an old Israeli freedom fighter. From opposite ends of the globe, they must somehow stop the final fatal command!

THE DOOMSDAY SPIRAL   (1175, $2.95)
by Jon Land

Alabaster—master assassin and sometimes Mossad agent—races against time and operatives from every major service in order to control and kill a genetic nightmare let loose in America. Death awaits around each corner as the tension mounts and doomsday comes ever closer!

DEPTH FORCE   (1355, $2.95)
by Irving A. Greenfield

Built in secrecy, launched in silence, and manned by a phantom crew, *The Shark* is America's unique high technology submarine whose mission is to stop the Soviets from dominating the seas. As far as the U.S. government is concerned, *The Shark* doesn't exist. Its orders are explicit: if in danger of capture, self-destruct! So the only way to stay alive is to dive deep and strike hard!

DEPTH FORCE

BY IRVING A. GREENFIELD

ZEBRA BOOKS
KENSINGTON PUBLISHING CORP.

ZEBRA BOOKS

are published by

Kensington Publishing Corp.
475 Park Avenue South
New York, N.Y. 10016

SECOND PRINTING: APRIL 1984

Printed in the United States of America

1

"Stand by to surface," Commander Jack Boxer ordered from the command center in the control room.

His order was immediately relayed by Bill Harris, his exec, to the diving officer, who in turn passed it on to the boat's duty section.

Boxer's gray eyes were riveted to the navigational clock on the instrument panel to his left where degrees, minutes and seconds of longitude and latitude were digitally displayed in large green numbers.

"Forward and aft diving planes up fifteen degrees," Boxer said. "Blow forward ballast . . ." "Blow all main ballast." His finger pressed the klaxon horn's button twice.

Again Harris repeated the captain's orders.

The bow of the long killer submarine, *Sting Ray,* began to tilt upward.

Boxer glanced at another digital readout that gave him the speed of the *Sting Ray.* The boat was doing twenty-five knots. Suddenly a bell rang. He shifted his eyes back to the narclock. A red digital readout appeared directly above the green.

"Two minutes and counting to surface," Boxer said. Automatically he scanned several other readout devices that indicated everything from the revolutions per minute of the boat's turbines to the ambient temperature of the water through which they were moving. His eyes flicked over the depth gauge. They were thirty meters below the surface of the North Atlantic. Even as he watched the depth gauge readout the *Sting Ray* had risen three meters.

"Target bearing fifty-seven degrees, distance seventy-hundred yards. Speed twenty knots," the sonar officer reported; then less formally, he said, "Probably our Russian trawler friend."

Boxer grinned mischievously. "I sure as hell would like to circle back under that son-of-a-bitch and surface aft of him." He looked at Harris as he spoke. "You'd think that in all this big ocean that Ruskie captain could find something else to do than shadow me. He might even do some fishing."

Harris grinned back. "Just doing his job."

"Target bearing fifty-seven degrees, six-thousand-five-hundred yards, speed fifteen knots," the sonar officer said.

Boxer looked up at the red NC readout. Forty-two seconds were left until the boat surfaced.

"I sure hope the sun is shining," Harris commented.

"Out there this time of year?" he asked; then answered, "I doubt it." The red digital readout on the NC reached 2.0.0. At the very instant the green number read the *Sting Ray*'s exact position in terms of latitude and longitude. A buzzer sounded.

"Surfacing completed," Boxer announced. "All stations secure from surfacing procedure."

Within moments all station officers reported secured.

"Deck section topside," Boxer ordered.

"Target bearing fifty-seven degrees, five-thousand yards, speed twelve knots," the sonar officer said.

Box grabbed for his winter parka as he passed a rack of heavy weather gear and hurried up the narrow ladder wells leading to the top of the sail. Mahony, the helmsman, preceded him and cracked the hatch; then opened it. Instantly a gust of fresh, pungent sea air rushed into the sail. Even as he bounded up to the bridge, Boxer took several deep breaths. The fresh air felt good in his lungs and against his face. But the moment he stepped onto the bridge, a cold slashing rain brought tears to his eyes. He switched on the intercom and said, "This is the captain, the bridge has the con." At the same time he looked toward the approaching Russian trawler. She was beginning to turn to the north. The *Sting Ray* had surfaced just inside the twelve-mile limit, that invisible barrier marking the sovereignty of the United States.

Boxer flicked a switch that connected him with Lieutenant Mark Bander, the boat's communications officer. "Mark, have you got our Ruskie friend's operating frequency?" he asked.

"Yes, sir."

"Send this message."

"Copying, sir."

"From Captain Boxer, of the *Sting Ray* to Captain—get his name out of our index—of the Russian trawler *Norvigrod*—Thanks for the company. Best of luck . . . Commander Jack Boxer, U.S.N. . . . Then send the same message over the scatter band frequency the Ruskie ships use to communicate with Moscow. . . . Someone there should burn his butt."

"Yes, sir," Mark laughed.

Boxer pushed the switch back to his *off* position and peered forward, looking for lights of New York City, which lay directly in front of him. But in the quickly fading light of December 10, 1995, with a heavy sea running and a misty rain falling the odds were against him seeing them now. Maybe later, when they were only two or three thousand yards out, the lights of the Verrazano Bridge would come into view.

"Mister Cowly," Boxer said, addressing a jg lieutenant next to him, "pass the word to rig boat for surfacing running."

The young man managed to stammer, "Aye, aye, sir."

Within moments the sail and that portion of the *Sting Ray*'s hull riding above the water were brightly illuminated by high intensity lights recessed in the deck and sail and protected by ten inches of special glass.

Boxer flicked another switch. "Mister Mallon," he said, speaking to the engineering officer, "slow one-third ahead."

"Aye, aye, sir," Mallon answered; then in a more familiar tone, he asked, "How's the weather up there?"

"Not much to talk about," Boxer answered. Like his exec, Bill Harris, Mallon was an old friend. This was the sixth patrol the three of them had made together in the *Sting Ray* and other nuclear submarines.

"Are you going to stop off for a couple before you take off?" Mallon questioned. By now Boxer's post-cruise stop offs with the crew at the Wardroom cocktail lounge for a couple of rounds had become a tradition with the men of the *Sting Ray*.

"Sure," Boxer said, somewhat puzzled. Mallon was the only officer aboard the boat who hadn't joined them. In the past, as soon as the boat had been docked, he'd run to his pretty wife, Lucy, who'd been waiting for him in their antique yellow Volkswagen Bug. "But isn't Lucy—"

"She won't be there," Mallon said tightly.

"Oh!" Boxer exclaimed: Mallon's marriage had ceased to be, just as his had five years before. "We'll go together."

"Thanks," Mallon said.

That was the end of the conversation. Boxer shook his head. Mallon and Lucy always had seemed to be the perfect couple. . . .

"Target, bearing ten degrees, range three thousand yards, speed twenty knots." A moment later the same voice announced, "Target outward bound."

At the same instant Boxer saw the green lights marking the graceful catenary of the Verrazano Bridge. He touched Cowly on the arm and pointing to the lights said, "We're almost home, Mister Cowly. . . . After we're berthed and liberty begins, you might consider joining me and the rest of the crew at the Wardroom outside of the base. It's easy to find. Just ask anyone."

Cowly grinned. "I already know the place."

"Good," Boxer answered. The invitation was tantamount to telling the young officer he was more than satisfied with his performance and would request him the next time he took the *Sting Ray* out on patrol.

For the next few minutes on the bridge, Boxer had no need to speak to anyone. The crew of the *Sting Ray* was a highly efficient machine, a human counterpart to the one they manned. The boat had been designed to hunt and destroy other submarines. And for the past three months it had patrolled its assigned sector of the South Atlantic with the vigilance of the mythical Cebrus, keeping track of every Russian, Red Chinese, Cuban or any submarine from the Communist bloc of nations that ventured into its domain. It operated at a depth of four hundred meters. Its ultrasensitive electronic detection devices could pick up and track six different targets simultaneously over a distance of fifty nautical miles from itself. Its torpedoes were guided from the *Sting Ray*'s fire control center until they were within one hundred meters of a target; then the torpedo's own sound-detecting devices were automatically activated, and no matter what evasive action the target would take, the torpedo would find and destroy it.

At the end of each patrol, Boxer was secretly pleased that he didn't have to use the awesome power at his command. And this time, as he stood on the *Sting Ray*'s bridge watching the lights of

New York manifest themselves through the curtain of rain, was no exception. Digging into the pocket of his parka, Boxer pulled out an old pipe and tobacco pouch. After several tries, he managed to light the pipe. But it didn't stay lit very long.

The *Sting Ray* slid past Coney Island. The wind had dropped off but it was still raining. On his starboard side, Boxer could make out the stream of eastbound traffic on the Belt Parkway in Brooklyn. The way the *Sting Ray* was illuminated the drivers couldn't avoid seeing it.

Suddenly the buzzer sounded and the green light flashed on the small control panel in front of Boxer. He pushed a switch into its ON position. "Boxer here," he said.

"Sir, message from base," Mark Bander responded.

"Go ahead, read it."

"First message — Welcome Home. *Sting Ray* will berth on the south side of pier ninety, Stapleton, Staten Island. A six knot current running north, directly offshore and a east nor' east and sixteen-knot wind."

Even as Boxer heard the conditions of the current and wind, he had a mental picture of how he'd work the *Sting Ray* to her berth. But he'd have very little to do with the operation. The actual placing of the boat alongside the pier would be accomplished by the Short Distance Navigational Computer.

"Second message — From Admiral Richard Stark, Chief of Naval Operations, Washington — Commander Jack Boxer, 101-21-9483, captain of the USN Submarine *Sting Ray* is hereby ordered to report to my office 1000 hours 13 December 1995. Signed Admiral R. Stark."

"Now that's something I didn't expect," Boxer commented. "But thanks anyway." He flicked the switch back to its normal position. Since he couldn't even begin to guess why the CNO wanted to see him, he wasn't going to waste time trying to come up with a reason. . . . Boxer lit his pipe again; this time he had better luck with it.

The *Sting Ray* passed under the Verrazano Bridge.

"Captain to crew, stand by to initiate docking procedure," Boxer said, activating several switches on the control console in front of him. "Mister Cowly, take the con please."

Cowly hesitated.

"Mister Cowly, you have the con," Boxer said, remembering how frightened he was the first time he brought a submarine dockside. Then in a less formal voice, he said, "You know the drill backward and forward."

Cowly took a deep breath, nodded and stepped up to the control panel. "Nav. station coordinates please." The exact position of the *Sting Ray* came up on a small video screen. "Nav. section, the exact coordinate of Pier Ninety, please." Another set of numbers appeared on the screen. "Comp. section, I want the course and speed that will place the boat alongside the pier." A third set of numbers appeared on the screen. "Transfer course and speed to Nav system."

"Course and speed transferred to Nav system," a voice answered over the intercom.

The *Sting Ray* began to slow down. When she was still some distance from the pier, she executed a port side turn and continued to move slowly forward.

Suddenly the lights on the pier came on.

Boxer puffed on his pipe: so far Cowly was doing just fine. A few more years' experience and he'd become a first-rate officer.

"Target two hundred and eighty-five degrees, range five zero-zero yards and closing fast," the sonar officer announced.

Cowly glanced at Boxer.

"Target two hundred and seventy-five degrees, range four zero-zero yards and closing fast."

Boxer continued to puff on his pipe. If Cowly didn't—

"Mister Mallon," Cowly said, taking the *Sting Ray* off the Nav system and opening communication between the bridge and the engine room, "full speed ahead on starboard engine one and two, half speed reverse on port engine one and two."

"Target two hundred and seventy degrees, range three seven-five yards and closing fast."

"Helmsman, hard to port," Cowly said.

"Aye, aye, sir," the helmsman answered.

"Target two hundred and seventy degrees, range two five-zero yards."

The *Sting Ray* began to respond to the combination of the helm and the torque produced by its engines: she began to turn to her portside.

10

"Target two hundred and ninety degrees, range two zero-zero yards and closing fast."

The boat continued to drop off to the port side.

Cowly called for an increase of speed on the two starboard engines. "Helmsman, hold her steady at three hundred fifty-eight."

"Aye, aye, sir."

Everyone on the bridge could see the target: it was the *Mary-Ann*, a large white ocean-going yacht. Boxer guessed it was at least a hundred feet long with a twenty-five-foot beam.

"Target three hundred and fifty degrees, range one zero-zero yards and closing fast."

"Full speed ahead," Cowly ordered.

"Target three hundred and forty degrees, range five-zero yards and closing fast."

"She's going to ram us!" Cowly exclaimed.

Boxer jumped forward and hit the red crash button: the shriek of a klaxon sounded. "Now hear this," Boxer yelled over the intercom, "Now hear this — Rig ship for collision. . . . Rig for collision . . . We're going to be rammed! Hold fast! Communications: send a Mayday."

The *Mary-Ann* was almost on them.

"Target three hundred degrees, range two-five yards and closing fast."

Boxer looked out over the bridge. There was nothing he could do to prevent the disaster. The *Sting Ray* was moving fast, but not fast enough. "Hold on," he said to Cowly. "Hold on tight!"

The *Mary-Ann* slammed into the stern of the *Sting Ray* with the sound of a jack hammer; then followed the scraping and screeching of torn metal.

The *Sting Ray* slowly rolled to her portside and righted herself, while the crushed bow of the *Mary-Ann* lay over the starboard side of the boat.

Boxer felt as if something had tried to tear his arms out of their sockets. "Damage control," he shouted. "Damage control, what do we have?"

"Engine room on fire, sir," Barker, the damage control officer answered. "We're taking water fast. Pumps operating but too much water is coming in."

"Casualties?"

11

"Can't get through because of the fire."

"Get that fire out!" Boxer shouted.

Boxer looked up at the *Mary-Ann*. Several men and women were looking down at him. "I want a boarding party," he said tightly. "An armed boarding party to go aboard that fucking yacht and find out what the hell is going on."

"I'll take it," Cowly said.

Boxer nodded. "If one of those bastards gives you trouble," Boxer said. "Put him under arrest."

"Damage control to bridge," Barker said.

"Go ahead," Boxer answered.

"The A-power has shut down. We're on emergency diesel, as of ten seconds ago."

"What's the state of the fire in the engine room?" Boxer asked.

"Can't get to it."

"I'm going below. Send Mister Harris to the bridge. He'll have the con."

"We're beginning to make some headway with the flooding."

"Good," Boxer answered, watching Cowly on deck below him. The boarding party was ready to go aboard the *Mary-Ann*.

Harris came up through the hatchway.

"How bad is it down there?" Boxer asked.

"The engine room caught it," Harris said. "I don't think we'll—" He hesitated. "We'll have at least five dead, including Mallon."

Boxer nodded and hurried down into the hull of the boat. The blowers and air purification system kept the smoke down to a minimum but the stink of the fire was everywhere.

Boxer made a quick tour of the boat. The crew, grim-faced and sweating, were at their stations.

Harris's voice came over the intercom. "Several officers from the base are coming aboard. Admiral D'Arcy, base CO is with them . . . a New York fireboat is standing by. . . . Police and Coast Guard craft are also standing by."

"Have the admiral and his party escorted down to me," Boxer said. Then he spoke over the MC system. "Now hear this. . . . Now hear this. . . . This is the captain speaking. . . . The *Sting Ray* is in no danger of sinking and as of this moment we've maintained nuclear integrity. . . . Our engine room is still on fire, but we hope to have that out shortly. . . . Continue to be calm. . . .

12

We'll tie up sometime tonight, even if we have to row the *Sting Ray* to the dock."

The men smiled but none of them laughed.

Harris came on again. "Captain, the *Mary-Ann*'s owner wants his yacht pulled free of the *Sting Ray*."

Damage control came on again. "Sir," Barker said, "the fire in the engine room is out."

"Good work!" Boxer exclaimed.

"Sir, I think you should come aft."

"Yes, I'll be right there."

"What about—" Harris began.

"Tell the owner of the *Mary-Ann* that if he so much as moves the *Mary-Ann* a millimeter, I will personally kill him," Boxer answered; then he went aft to the engine room.

The stink of burnt oil and burnt flesh hung in the air. There were five bodies—or what was left of them—sprawled grotesquely on the deck. The *Mary-Ann*'s bow was wedged into the hull of the *Sting Ray*. Boxer guessed it had sliced through an oil line. The oil had caught fire and had exploded.

He bent over the charred remains of one of the men. A portion of the upper face had been burnt away, revealing the skull.

"This area," he said in a choked voice, "is off limits to everyone until the medics remove the bodies." Then he stood up and walked quickly back to the command center.

Admiral D'Arcy and his two aides were already there. The admiral was a man in his mid-fifties. A former fighter pilot and carrier task force commander, he knew very little about submarines and the men who sail them.

Boxer saluted him. "Sir," he said, "heavy damage in the engine room and five dead."

D'Arcy pursed his narrow lips. "My aides told me that you took evasive action but the *Mary-Ann* followed you?"

"Yes, sir."

"I would like your sworn statement and those of the other officers on the bridge at the time of the collision."

"Yes, sir."

"Is there anything you want done?" D'Arcy asked in a somewhat less formal tone.

Boxer shook his head. "No sir. . . . The *Sting Ray* will come in under her own power. We have sufficient emergency power to do that."

D'Arcy nodded. "I'll speak to the CNO. Your departure to Washington will be delayed a few days. There'll have to be a formal inquiry."

"Yes, sir."

"I have had my office issue a formal statement to the press and the TV stations. . . . I would prefer it if you and the other members of the crew did not make any statements about the accident to reporters."

Boxer nodded. The admiral's suggestion was really an order, though he couldn't state it as such. "I'll pass the word," Boxer responded.

"Well, Captain, I don't want to take up any more of your time."

The two men saluted and D'Arcy and his two aides retreated up the companionway into the sail.

A few minutes later Boxer accompanied a team of medics from the base into the engine room. Mallon was his friend but the bodies were so badly burned he couldn't tell which one was Mallon. . . . Boxer stopped himself from taking a deep breath. He didn't want to fill his lungs with the stench of burnt flesh. He stood by and watched while each of the bodies was placed in a gurney and a white canvas tarpaulin was placed over it. He wondered if Lucy would claim Mallon's body, or would she let the Navy bury it? The question bothered him. It made him wonder what his ex-wife Gwen, would do? But his situation was very different from Mallon's, or was it? He really didn't know anything about —

"Ready to bring the bodies topside, sir?" the chief in charge of the medics said.

Boxer nodded and followed the sad procession out of the engine room and on to the deck. It was still raining. The bodies were put aboard a launch for their last voyage. . . .

As soon as the bodies were gone, Boxer ordered the rest of the engine room section to begin cleaning up. Then we went topside and boarded the *Mary-Ann* and went into the lounge, where Cowly had gathered the yacht passengers and crews.

Immediately, a short dapper-looking man with a light blue ascot around his neck, a gray moustache and gray wavy hair approached him. "Are you the ranking officer aboard the submarine?" He spoke with a pronounced Spanish accent.

Boxer waved him away. "Mister Cowly," he said, spotting a table on the other side of the spacious room. "I'll use that table there. Have one of your men go back to the boat, pick up a tape recorder, and enough tape for several hours of taping."

"Yes, sir," Cowly snapped.

Boxer crossed the room, eased the table away from the wall, placed a chair on either side of it; then he sat down behind the table and looked at the people who were looking at him.

All of them were tan. The women were beautiful. Both the men and the women were well dressed. "I'm Commander Boxer, captain of the *Sting Ray*."

"I must protest —" the man with the gray moustache said.

Boxer glared at him.

"My name is Julio Sanchez," the man said. "My lawyer has already been summoned and will be here in a few minutes."

Boxer nodded. He recognized the name. Julio Sanchez, a Colombian, was reputed to be one of the wealthiest men alive.

"You have no right to take statements from anyone. The Coast Guard will do that," Mr. Sanchez said.

Boxer tuned him out. He watched one of the other men take a cigarette from a gold case and hand it to a woman, then light it with a gold cigarette lighter.

She raised her head slightly and blew smoke into the air; her eyes locked with Boxer's.

Her long strawberry blonde hair was held in place with a simple dark green head band. Her nose was slightly upturned. She had lovely lips, a graceful neck and she wore an apple green jump suit which accentuated her svelte body.

She flashed a smile.

Boxer looked away.

A few moments later the sailor returned with the tape recorder and tapes.

Once again Sanchez stepped forward. "These people are my guests," he said. "None of them had anything to do with the accident."

"Mister Sanchez," Boxer replied brusquely. "I want their statements. The sooner I start the sooner I'll finish."

"None of you," Sanchez said, addressing his guests, "are obligated to say anything without—"

Boxer stood up. "If you interfere, Sanchez," he said in a low angry voice, "I'll have you put aboard the *Sting Ray* and held under armed guard."

"You wouldn't dare—"

"Mister, I have five dead. One of them was a good friend of mine. So don't tell me what I'd dare do."

The guests began to whisper among themselves.

"It was an unfortunate accident," Sanchez said.

"It was not an accident," Boxer said tightly. "I was on the bridge. The *Mary-Ann* was deliberately rammed into my boat."

Sanchez ran a white linen handkerchief over his forehead and said something in Spanish. The captain of the *Mary-Ann* answered him.

"What was that all about?" Boxer asked.

"If you send two of your men with my captain they will bring the two guilty men back here."

"Mister Cowly, I ordered you to have everyone aboard in this room." He was angry with Cowly for not carrying out his order.

"The two men are in the engine room," Sanchez said. "Everyone else is here."

"Mister Cowly, take another man and go with the captain," Boxer said.

"Aye aye, sir," Cowly answered.

"Do you know what happened, Mister Sanchez?" Boxer asked.

"Yes," Sanchez answered calmly. "We were having our last party aboard the *Mary-Ann*. My first officer, Luis Revera, and the helmsman, Juan Diaz, were on the bridge. Both men were drinking and doing some smoking."

"Drinking and doing some smoking," Boxer repeated. He didn't have to ask what the men were smoking.

"Si . . . yes. By the time I noticed something was wrong, it was too late. The *Mary-Ann* couldn't be stopped or turned."

Boxer's eyes went to slits. "Smoking and drinking, eh? Tell me, Mister Sanchez, what were they really doing?"

Sanchez shrugged. "They were only playing, Captain. Having fun."

16

"What?" Boxer roared. "Playing with the lives of my crew. . . . Playing with my boat?"

"I understand—"

"You understand nothing," Boxer snapped, turning his back on Sanchez.

"Well, Captain," a woman said, "now that you know what happened and who was responsible, you no longer have a reason for holding all of us here."

Boxer slowly pivoted around.

"It's really very tiresome to be forced to stand here," the woman continued.

It was the woman who had caught Boxer's eye for a few minutes before.

"I'm Tracy Kimble," she said. "A reporter for the *Washington Globe*."

"A reporter, eh," Boxer responded. "What kind of reporter are you, Ms. Kimble? Don't tell me. Let me guess. . . . Yes, you're a crack foreign correspondent."

"I write the society column," she answered proudly.

"Sorry, I don't bother reading such drivel," Boxer said.

Tracy flushed. "Captain, I'm certainly not interested in knowing the kind of drivel you do read but I would like to go to my cabin and pack my clothing."

"You and everyone else here will be free to go when I tell you to go," Boxer answered.

"Aye, aye, sir." Tracy saluted, bringing snickers from the other guests and open laughter from Sanchez and several members of the *Mary-Ann*'s crew.

Cowly returned with Revera and Diaz, who were having difficulty keeping their eyes open and walking without staggering.

"Take them aboard the *Sting Ray*," Boxer ordered.

"Captain," Sanchez said. "I can't let you do that. The *Mary-Ann* is registered in Colombia and those men are Colombian nationals. . . . You don't want to embarrass your country, do you?"

Boxer knew that if he didn't take the two men, they'd be on their way back to Colombia the moment the *Mary-Ann* docked.

"I have many friends in Washington who would be very upset if you—"

"Take the men aboard the *Sting Ray*, Mister Cowly," Boxer said sharply.

"I hope you know what you're doing, Captain," Sanchez said.

Boxer didn't doubt that he was breaking the law. But he wanted the men responsible for the deaths of five of his men.

"You're putting your career on the line," Sanchez said smugly.

Boxer nodded. He knew that better than anyone else in that room. Sanchez probably had the political clout to force him to resign from the Navy.

"I promise you that the men will be properly punished," Sanchez said. "You have my word on that."

"Punished by whom?" Boxer asked. "By you, Mister Sanchez?"

"Yes."

"No, Mister Sanchez. You don't represent the law. The men will be tried or set free by my government. Not by you. . . . Take them aboard the *Sting Ray*, Mister Cowly."

"Aye, aye, sir," Cowly answered, saluting smartly.

2

Boxer sat alone in a booth. Unaware that he was the only customer left in the Wardroom, he stared down at his Glenlivet and soda. The *Sting Ray*'s crew had gone their separate ways. Those who were lucky enough to have their families living in the city, joined them. A few others went into Manhattan to find pleasure for the night. But everyone had been ordered back aboard the *Sting Ray* by 0830. As a result of the accident, all leaves and three-day passes had been cancelled. Though the crew, with the exception of those on the duty detail still aboard the *Sting Ray*, had come to the Wardroom, they had stayed only long enough to toast their dead shipmates. . . .

Boxer took a deep breath and exhaled slowly. He had been the last one to leave the *Sting Ray* after she was berthed. It took several hours to fill out the necessary accident forms and a few minutes to remove the log tapes from the boat's recording station. These constituted a complete operating record of the *Sting Ray*. They automatically recorded the boat's vital functions and provided an accurate record of the way the crews functioned at their duty stations. They were equivalent to the black box recorders used on aircraft. The tapes would give the board of inquiry a moment-by-moment breakdown of everything that had happened aboard the *Sting Ray*. Boxer pursed his lips. Everything that could have been done to avert the crash had been done. He would have given the same orders that Cowly had and the results would have been the same: five men dead and a destroyed engine room. The only difference would have been that he would have been giving the orders: he would have had the con, not a junior officer.

Boxer finished his scotch and looked around for a waitress to bring him another.

"Closing time," the barkeep called from behind the bar.

Boxer looked at the clock above the mirrored bar. 2:15. He glanced at his own watch. 2:15.

"Can't sell ya another drink," the barkeep said. "It's after two."

Boxer nodded, stood up, put on his coat and hat and walked over to the bar. "How much?" he asked. Traditionally, he picked up the tab for the entire crew.

"It's on the house," the barkeep said.

Boxer raised his eyebrows.

"Saw what happened to your boat on the tube," the barkeep explained. "It's a tough rap . . . Even saw you, when you came off the boat."

Boxer nodded. "Thanks for the drinks. I'll pass the word to the crew. They'll appreciate it." He turned to leave.

"Wait a minute, Commander," the barkeep said, "there's no law against having a drink with a friend . . . One for the road." And he poured a shot of Glenlivet for Boxer and for himself. "To the guys who weren't here," he toasted.

"Good men," Boxer said lifting his glass. He wanted to say more, but his throat tightened; he couldn't get the words out. Tomorrow the pain would be worse. He'd have to write the letters to the next of kin. Letters to explain—What? A dumb accident. The scotch went down easily and filled Boxer with warmth. In the mirror behind the bar he saw the reflection of the telephone on the opposite wall. It was one of the open acoustical stations. Suddenly he wanted to be with Gwen, his exwife.

"Mind if I take a couple of minutes to make a call?" he asked.

"Here, Commander, use this phone," the barkeep said, placing a cordless phone down on the bar and walking away.

With his forefinger, Boxer punched out Gwen's telephone number. He usually saw Gwen and his son, John, a day or two after a patrol ended. He'd call ahead to give her time to cancel any appointments she might have made. Sometimes he'd really feel as if he were still married to her, especially if he'd spend the night with her.

The phone rang three times before Gwen answered. Her voice was throaty with sleep.

"It's Jack," Boxer said.

20

There were a few moments of silence.

"Gwen?"

"Yes," she answered. "I saw you on TV . . . Thank God you're safe."

"I'm sorry I woke you," he said. "Is John all right?"

"Yes . . . yes . . . He's fine."

"Good," Boxer responded. "Good." Then he said, "I know it's after two in the morning but—" he stopped and took a deep breath. "I want—I need—"

"Don't say it, Jack," she said.

"For Christ's sake, why not?" he flared.

"Because," Gwen answered softly, "I have someone here."

Boxer clenched his teeth together. He felt a sudden twist in his groin; then it was gone.

"Jack," Gwen said, "I didn't know about the accident until after the theater."

"Is John there?" he asked tightly. It was a stupid question: Gwen wouldn't have a man sleep over if John was there.

"He's at my mother's," she answered.

"I'll call him in the morning," Boxer said.

"Don't be angry," Gwen told him.

"I'm not," he lied. "I'll call you when things straighten out." Before she could speak, he hung up. She didn't belong to him any more. She was free . . . "Thanks for the phone," he called out.

The barkeep waved to him.

Boxer turned and walked out on the street. It was still raining. He buttoned and belted his coat. Rather than spend the night at the BOQ, he returned to the *Sting Ray*.

Boxer went straight to the bulkhead door of the engine room. Men were still working. Most of the charred paint had been scraped away and a temporary steel patch already had been welded into place where the boat had been holed by the *Mary-Ann*. But sufficient damage had been done below the water line and to the turbines that would require the *Sting Ray* to be dry docked for several months in order to make the repairs.

Suddenly one of the seamen saw him. "Atten-hut!" he called.

"Carry on," Boxer said, noting that several of the men were from other duty sections. That kind of camaraderie was part of what being a submariner was all about. The men who served on the boats were tight. "I'll be aboard tonight," Boxer said. "If you men need anything, give me a squawk. Okay?"

"Aye, aye, sir," the men answered in unison.

"I'll have the cook do up some steaks, a few pies and ice cream." Boxer said.

"That'll be just fine," Peterson, one of the engineering chiefs, said.

"Goodnight, men," Boxer said.

"Goodnight," each man answered in turn.

Boxer walked slowly along the passageway to his cabin. The fire's stink was still in the air, even though the blowers had been steadily sucking in fresh air for several hours. The smell reminded him of letters he had yet to write to the next-of-kin of the men who had been killed. All of them would be difficult to write. But the most difficult would be to Lucy, Mallon's wife. Boxer grimaced and opened the door to his quarters: a cubicle large enough for a bunk, a closet to hang his clothes, a chair, a small desk and two shelves above the bunk. Nothing was wood. All of the furniture, walls, and the ceiling were painted a light blue. A red leather-framed picture of Gwen, John and himself was next to the radio on the shelf directly above his bunk. On the other shelf there was a dogeared copy of the King James Bible — not that he was a religious man — but he enjoyed the eloquence of the language. For the same reason, he had a complete collection of Shakespeare's plays and sonnets. There were several other books: some fiction, detective and suspense novels, but mostly non-fiction, mainly about history. Boxer was an avid and eclectic reader.

For several moments he looked at the photograph. Gwen was a beautiful woman, with long blonde hair, a classic face, full, high breasts and flaring hips. He pursed his lips. "Well," he said aloud, "you have your damn freedom, all right!" Then he undressed down to his skivvies, took a towel and went to the shower.

A short time later, when Boxer was back in his cabin, he lay down on the bunk, reached up, turned on the radio and found a station playing classical music. Closing his eyes, he put his hands behind his head. For the first time since the crash, he realized how exhausted he was. Every part of his body ached, especially his neck and shoulders. Just as Boxer was about to fall asleep, he had a fleeting vision of Gwen's naked body in the arms of a strange man and then he saw the bow of the *Mary-Ann* slicing through the hull of the *Sting Ray*. . . . "No," he shouted, "No!" He bolted up in a cold sweat. Trembling, Boxer stared at the ceiling until he drifted off to sleep again. . . .

The proceedings of the board of inquiry were held in a long narrow room on the second floor of the administration building. Two windows overlooked the Narrows, where the water and sky were gray with the promise of more rain. It was quickly established by statements from the crew of the *Sting Ray* that they had been following the routine procedure for docking at the time of the accident. And it was admitted by the various members of the *Mary-Ann*'s crew and the guests aboard her that the *Mary-Ann* had struck the *Sting Ray*. The last guest to testify was Tracy Kimble.

When Boxer heard her name called, he swiveled around to look at her.

"Here, your honor," she called out. "Or is it here, your admiral?" She walked toward the front of the drab room with complete nonchalance. "You are an admiral, aren't you?" she asked, directing her question to the officer heading the board.

Admiral D'Arcy cleared his throat but didn't answer.

Boxer sat on the aisle and when Tracy passed him their eyes met. She flashed him a smile and went on, leaving him with the intense awareness of her physical being. She wore a simple green dress with a princess collar and a musky perfume that lingered in the air long after she passed.

After she was sworn in, Admiral D'Arcy asked her to state her occupation and explain how she happened to have been aboard the *Mary-Ann*.

"I write the society column for the *Washington Globe*," she answered. "I was aboard the *Mary-Ann* as a guest of Byron Hayes, who in turn was a guest of Senor Sanchez. Byron Hayes, as you probably know, is an actor."

"And where were you at the time of the accident?" one of the board officers asked.

"In the main salon . . . We were having a party when the accident occurred."

"Did you sense anything was wrong before the *Mary-Ann* struck the *Sting Ray*?"

She shook her head. "No. Everything seemed fine to me."

"Had you been drinking before the accident?" another officer asked.

"Yes. It was a champagne party."

"We understand there was a sharp exchange between Commander Boxer and—"

"He was rude, pompous and dictatorial," Tracy answered. "The guests aboard the *Mary-Ann* were not responsible for the accident."

Boxer flushed.

"Are you aware that the accident cost the lives of five members of the *Sting Ray*'s crew?" Admiral D'Arcy asked.

"So Commander Boxer informed the guests of the *Mary-Ann*, when he came aboard and took—or should I say illegally placed the guests and the crew under semi-arrest."

"Hardly semi-arrest, Ms. Kimble," the admiral chided.

"You tell me what it was with armed men watching your every move?" And before he could answer, she asked, "Also, Admiral, tell me what right did Commander Boxer have to seize and remove two members of the *Mary-Ann*'s crew?"

"Those men are in Federal—"

"That is not the question I asked," Ms. Kimble shot back. "I want to know the specific law that gave Commander Boxer the right to take two foreign nationals off a ship of foreign registry?"

Boxer couldn't remain silent. "If it please the board," he said, getting to his feet, "I request permission to answer Ms. Kimble."

"Permission granted," Admiral D'Arcy responded.

A momentary smile touched Tracy's lips, as Boxer took a few steps forward. He felt as if she were telling him not to put his proverbial foot in his mouth. He was sweating so profusely he could feel the droplets skid down his back. "Ms. Kimble—"

"You may call me Tracy, Commander," she said, now smiling broadly.

"All right, Tracy. Isn't it true that Mister Sanchez—"

"Senor Sanchez," she corrected.

Boxer took a deep breath and slowly exhaled. She was cool, almost to the point of being frigid. Suddenly he wondered what she'd be like in bed? "Isn't it true, Tracy," he said, thrusting that question out of his thoughts, "that Mister Sanchez advised me that Luis Revera and Juan Diaz were on the bridge of the *Mary-Ann* at the time of the accident with the *Sting Ray* and didn't he say both men had been drinking and smoking?"

"He did say something about that," she answered. "But he didn't specify what they were drinking or smoking . . . You assumed that—"

"I assumed, Tracy," Boxer said with unmistakable anger, "that whatever they were drinking or smoking, they were responsible for killing five men." Then addressing the board, he added, "sir, it is bad enough when the usual hazards of the sea are out of control and cause the death of our men, or if a mechanical failure does the same. But when death is caused by negligence, either by those of us who are in command position, or from others, who in civilian life hold the same position, then that responsibility must be met. They must be held accountable for their activities. Both Diaz and Revera are guilty of no less a crime than murder. In other circumstances, had I seen them just after the commission of a similar crime on the streets—say in a hit-and-run situation—then I would do everything in my power to stop them from escaping, which was what I did. Had I left them aboard the *Mary-Ann*, the moment she docked, they would have vanished. As captain of the *Sting Ray* and as a citizen, I could not let that happen."

For a moment there was absolute silence in the room; then the men of the *Sting Ray* began to cheer.

"Order," Admiral D'Arcy shouted, rapping his gavel several times. "Order, I say. . . ."

The men quieted down; then fell silent.

The admiral did not reprimand the men of the *Sting Ray* for their outburst. "Thank you, Ms. Kimble," he said. "You are excused. And then you, Commander Boxer." Then looking at his watch and comparing the time it had with the time shown on the wall clock above the door in the back of the room, he said, "As of now, fifteen hundred hours, this board of inquiry is adjourned until eleven hundred hours tomorrow morning." And he rapped his gavel three times.

The TV cameras were waiting just outside of the room where the board of inquiry had been held and as soon as Boxer stepped out into the hallway, they bore down on him, thrusting their microphones in front of him.

"Will you give us a statement, Captain," the red-headed, on-the-spot reporter, for station BSC asked. He was nattily dressed in a brown Harris tweed sports coat, matching tan shirt, brown tie and slacks.

"I have nothing to say," Boxer answered.

"What do you think the finding of the board will be?" a woman from station IPW asked, grim-faced.

Boxer ignored the question and tried to move out of the blaze of the TV lights.

"Captain," the man from station CBJ said, "we were told from an unofficial source that the officer who was killed was a good friend of yours."

Boxer stopped, wondering how they managed to find that out.

"Was he a good friend?" the reporter pressed.

"Yes," Boxer acknowledged, "he was."

"Have you ever had an accident before while commanding a submarine?" the woman asked, moving closer.

Boxer realized he was trapped. He wasn't going to be allowed to get away without making a statement. Just as he was about to speak, Admiral D'Arcy and the other members of the board came out of the room.

"Do you think the Navy will try to hang you for the accident?" the BSC man asked.

The admiral stopped and looked straight at Boxer, waiting, it seemed, for his answer.

That he might be held culpable for the accident hadn't entered Boxer's mind. It was Navy policy to convene a board of inquiry whenever there was an accident at sea.

"Senor Sanchez is a very powerful man," the same reporter said, "and he is already saying, or at least intimating, that though the *Mary-Ann* struck the *Sting Ray*, you exercised poor judgment by allowing a junior officer to be in command when the weather was so bad."

Boxer's heart began to race. Suddenly he was angry and that was the one emotion he couldn't afford to have.

"Let me put the question another way," the reporter said. "If there was the opportunity to replay the event, would your actions change?"

Boxer rubbed his chin. The bastard had just pinned him to the wall. If he answered no, then he'd be saying he was willing to accept the casualties, something no sane man would do. But if he admitted to the charge, he'd be agreeing with Sanchez.

Suddenly Admiral D'Arcy stepped forward. "Gentlemen," he said, drawing the lights, cameras and reporters to himself, "if I may be permitted to comment on the question."

"Why certainly, Admiral," the reporter answered.

"It's Navy policy to teach young officers by allowing them to take full responsibility for their actions. Mister Cowly had command of the *Sting Ray* at the time of the accident."

Boxer's face became flushed; Cowly was going to be the sacrificial lamb. No way was he going to allow that to happen, even if it meant scuttling his own career. "Admiral D'Arcy," Boxer said, becoming the focus of activity, "Lieutenant Cowly was not responsible for the accident. The men on the bridge of the *Mary-Ann* were, to use Sanchez's own description, were 'playing'."

Admiral D'Arcy frowned.

"Only a miracle could have prevented the accident," Boxer said.

"Then it will be your work, Admiral, and the work of the other members of the board of inquiry to decide whether or not the officer in command of the *Sting Ray* at the time of the accident should have been able to pull off that miracle," the reporter from station BSC said.

"Yes," D'Arcy said with a nod. Then he turned around and walked away.

"Thank you, Admiral, and Commander Boxer for your comments. This is Roberto Suarez, live from the naval base on Staten Island. Now back to station BSC."

Boxer started down the corridor. His defense of Cowly could very well cost him his career.

Harris and several of the officers and men from the *Sting Ray* caught up with him. "We're going over to the Wardroom for a few drinks, Captain," Harris said. "Com'on and join us."

"We'll do the buying this time," Cowly told him.

Boxer smiled. "Thanks, but I think I'll go into the city for a few

hours. Have a good dinner. See a show. You know, play the tour-
ist."

"You sure?" Harris asked.

"I'm sure," he answered. Then looking at the men, Boxer softly
said, "Thanks guys, thanks." And he walked away.

3

Boxer was escorted into Admiral Stark's office by a lovely looking lieutenant-junior grade, who said in a southern drawl, "Commander, the admiral is expecting you all."

Boxer noted the name next to the photograph on the plastic ID badge was Cynthia Lowe. He thanked her and wondered how anyone would be able to keep his mind on his work with a woman as beautiful as her close by? Then he suddenly realized that because of the inquiry, he hadn't been with a woman since the *Sting Ray* returned. He hadn't had the desire to go looking for one. He hadn't even bothered to phone Gwen after his first call. Other than the other night when he went into the city, he hadn't left the base.

"Make yourself comfortable, Commander," Lowe said. "The admiral will be with you in a moment or two."

Boxer nodded, sat down, but was prepared to stand the moment the admiral entered. He glanced over his shoulder and with pleasure he watched the rolling motion of Lowe's buttocks under the tight blue skirt she wore. When she finally closed the door after her, Boxer examined the room.

The admiral's flag was to the left of the desk. The walls were decorated with photographs and paintings of several famous ships. Some were from the days of sail; others from World War II. And a few were from today's Navy. A large window framed a portion of the sky and a large plot of grass, which was now brown. The office had a few other amenities that come with the rank; such as brown wall-to-wall carpeting, a large color TV and a small bar.

Suddenly the door opened and the admiral stepped into the room.

Boxer stood up and faced the door.

"No formalities," Stark said, coming toward Boxer.

They shook hands.

Stark was a tall, sparsely built man, who looked as if he should be the CNO. He sat down behind the desk and immediately offered Boxer a cigar.

"I'll stay with my pipe, sir," Boxer said.

"Feel free to light up. Now to business . . . Nasty stuff this accident the *Sting Ray* became involved in. Sanchez is kicking up all sorts of fucking hell. I had two congressmen call me, four senators and at least a dozen captains of industry . . . All to have me fry your ass . . ." The admiral had a reputation for his salty bluntness. "Even D'Arcy is bothered by you, though not for the same reasons as the others. You don't have a right to make the kind of statement you made on TV."

"There were only two officers on the bridge of the *Sting Ray*," Boxer said, "myself and Cowly. Cowly had the con prior to the accident. The orders he gave to avert it were exactly the same orders I would have given, or — " he paused and looked straight at Stark — "you would have given, if you had the con."

"Maybe so," Stark answered, as he snipped off the end of a cigar and lit up. "But Cowly — "

"Sir," Boxer began, trying to control his growing anger, "Mister Cowly is a fine officer. He will be an excellent officer if he is given the chance."

"Would you trust him in a similar position again?"

"Absolutely," Boxer responded. "Impossible as it may seem, the accident made him a better officer."

"Has it done the same for you?" Stark answered, leaning back in his black leather swivel chair and blowing a cloud of smoke toward the ceiling.

Boxer locked the fingers of his hands together and raised them toward his chin; then lowered them. "It has made me a sadder one," he said in a low voice. "This was the first time I had to write letters to the next of kin . . . . Yes, it has made me a sadder man and a sadder officer."

Stark nodded. "I can understand that," he said.

"Sir, Sanchez should not have allowed his men to drink and smoke pot — "

"Forget about Sanchez," Stark said, suddenly standing up.

"He's not worth a moment more of your thoughts. I didn't ask you here to discuss Sanchez or the accident."

Boxer unlocked the fingers of his hands, while Stark moved to the bar, opened it and said, "I'm a scotch drinker, what are you?"

"The same, sir," Boxer answered.

Stark returned to the desk carrying two shot glasses of scotch. He motioned Boxer to remain seated and handed one of the glasses to him. "To the men of the *Sting Ray*," Stark toasted.

They touched glasses and drank.

Stark sat down again. "The Navy needs an officer for a very special assignment," he said. "We ran several hundred service records through the computer at BuPers and your name came up. We did it several different ways from Sunday and your name came up every time. You know how the computer jockeys are: they had to test their test or some such damn nonsense. Anyway, your name, as I said, kept coming up."

Boxer leaned slightly forward.

"It's a new command," Stark said.

"Another sub, I hope?"

Stark nodded. "But nothing like any other boat afloat."

"As long as it's a sub," Boxer said with a smile.

"You may not be smiling or even want the command after you hear what you will be required to do."

Boxer reached down into his pocket, took out his pipe and tobacco pouch. A few moments later he was smoking.

"The *Shark*—that will be her name—is in the process of being completed at a secret installation. She is twenty-five thousand tons, three hundred and twenty-five feet from stem to stem and has a beam of forty-five feet. She has been designed to cruise at a depth of three thousand feet, at a speed of fifty knots. Her flank speed will be sixty knots."

"I heard rumors about something like her being on the drawing boards but I never thought—"

"She's expected to be operational within six months," Stark said. "She is of course nuclear and uses a highly developed super-high-pressure steam system, HPRESS for short."

"I was wondering how she got her speed," Boxer said.

"The power plant is only part of the answer," Stark said. "Submerged, she looks much like this cigar did before I started to smoke

31

it."

"No sail?" Boxer asked.

Stark nodded. "No sail submerged. But on the surface the *Shark* will look like any other boat only much bigger."

"Now that's been a long time coming!" Boxer exclaimed enthusiastically.

"There's more," Stark said and switching on the intercom, he asked Lieutenant Lowe to bring him "File number SXZ forty-four." Turning off the intercom, he said to Boxer, "I noticed that you've been recently divorced."

"Yes, sir."

"Will that cause any difficulty?" Stark asked, puffing on his cigar. "What I mean is —"

"No difficulty," Boxer answered, feeling a slight twinge of emotion. "Gwen and I are still friends."

"I went through a divorce when I was about your age," Stark said. "Some women just don't understand what kind of a life they'll be getting into when they marry a professional officer. But then I guess some officers don't understand that the woman they want to marry might not be the kind who could hack being an officer's wife. It's not easy for either one."

Boxer agreed.

Changing the subject, Stark said, "This new command, if you take it, will be a difficult one. I'll spell everything out for you after you look at the drawings of the *Shark* and have the opportunity to go over her specifications. . . . By the way, Lieutenant Lowe is more or less our unofficial expert on the *Shark*."

"Oh!" Boxer exclaimed, raising his right eyebrow. He had her pegged for a paper shuffler, a beautiful ornament, a — Boxer suddenly found himself wondering if Stark was sleeping with her? Admiral though Stark was, he was also a man and probably still capable of having sex despite his age.

"Her grandfather served aboard the *Tang* during World War Two," Stark explained, "and her father was a chief aboard the *Nautilus* when it made its historic voyage under the North Pole."

"Runs in the family," Boxer commented with laugh.

"She'd be the first to apply for service aboard a submarine if the Navy would open that branch to women."

Boxer shook his head. "I'm thankful it hasn't. There are enough

32

problems to deal with. . . . We don't have to add to them."

"At least they'd be different from the usual kinds of problems, wouldn't you agree?" Stark asked with a twinkle in his brown eyes.

Boxer was about to answer that *the change wouldn't be worth the risk*, when a soft knock on the door stopped him.

"Maybe someday soon we'll have the opportunity to continue this conversation," Stark said; then looking at the door, he called out, "Come in please."

Lieutenant Lowe entered. She placed a small, cylindrical plastic box on the admiral's desk. "Will there be anything else, sir?"

"Please stay," Stark said, opening the top righthand drawer of his desk. "Commander Boxer might have some questions about the *Shark*." He placed a small control console on the top of the desk. Using a combination of a few buttons, a shade was automatically drawn over the window and the wall on the right side of the room was changed into a projection screen. "This is the part I like best," he said, pulling a small tripod out of the plastic container in front of him. "Would you believe, Commander, a projector complete with film is housed in this little box?" Then without waiting for Boxer to answer, he said, "I was told the camera is even smaller." A moment later an isometric drawing of the *Shark* appeared on the screen and Stark said, "Lieutenant, please feel free to comment and Commander, if you have questions, please don't hesitate to ask them."

The next drawing showed an isometric section of the boat's interior, including something that resembled a double hull. Boxer asked what it was.

"A glass sleeve," Lowe answered. "The outer hull is made of steel; then comes a sleeve of glass and then the inner hull of aluminum."

"A glass sleeve?" Boxer questioned.

"We call it glass because it has all the properties of glass, but it's really a silicon compound. . . . Because of it, the *Shark* will be able to operate at depths of three thousand feet. Perhaps, even more. Like glass, this particular plastic retains whatever spacial configuration it has until subjected to a pressure equal to a depth of twenty-thousand feet. At that pressure it will rupture."

Boxer glanced at Stark.

"You're in for many more surprises, "Stark said. "The *Shark* was

33

designed to be unique and she is."

Drawing followed drawing: some were isometrics, but most were taken from the working plans.

There was too much information for Boxer to digest at one sitting. The *Shark* was a marvel of modern technology, or a combination of technologies.

"Now to her armament," Lowe said, "She is equipped with the following kinds of missiles: surface to surface, surface to air and four ICBMs armed with MIRV nuclear warheads. She also has four torpedo tubes forward and aft. All her torpedoes will be selfguiding. She is also equipped with two six inch guns, should she ever need such conventional fire capability."

Boxer nodded appreciatively. "What about machine guns for — ?"

"There are two radar controlled twenty millimeters for anti-aircraft protection that are located in the sail," Lowe answered with an engaging smile.

"You'll find," Stark said, "the *Shark* has more than she lacks."

"Including the capability to launch two small undersea craft at the boat's maximum operational depth. You would, Commander, be able to use these minisubs for recon missions and — "

"I'm sure the commander would know what to use them for," Stark said.

"It's all right Admiral," Boxer said, "I'm sure Lieutenant Lowe meant no disrespect and was only trying to help. After all, didn't you, yourself, tell me that she probably knows more about the *Shark* than anyone else?"

"Go ahead, Lieutenant," Stark said, putting another drawing on the screen.

Boxer looked at Lowe and winked. From the moment she had begun to explain the drawings, he had been aware of her southern drawl and the herb-like scent of the perfume she was wearing.

"The *Shark*," Lowe explained, looking toward the drawing on the screen, "will enable its skipper to see when the boat is submerged."

"See?" Boxer questioned, raising his eyebrows.

"She will be equipped with a new device that uses the sonar echoes to form an image of her outside surroundings up to fifteen thousand yards on a three hundred and sixty degree azimuth."

Boxer started to stand but stopped himself. "Now that's really something!"

Lowe flashed him a big smile.

"I thought that would grab you by your short hairs," Stark commented with a twinkle in his eyes.

"It most certainly does," Boxer said with a smile.

"Any questions so far, Commander?" Lowe asked.

"How large will be crew be?" Boxer queried.

"Forty men."

"For a boat that size?" Boxer asked incredulously.

"The *Shark* will be as completely automated as modern technology can make her. For example, Commander, the only cook aboard will a baker to make cakes, desserts and ice cream. Everything else will be prepared by the individual crew member using flash frozen foods and a microwave oven. The galley will resemble an automatic dispensing machine. It will be computer controlled, down to the last calorie that a specific individual requires."

"What if there should be a computer malfunction?" Boxer asked. "Hungry men can become angry men, even in our Navy."

"Not to worry," Lowe answered, "there's a manual override."

"That still doesn't account for the *Shark*'s size."

"I'm afraid," Lowe said, "that's the one thing I can not explain."

"Leave it," Stark said and he showed two more drawings; then he pressed several buttons on his control module that activated the lights and raised the shade. "Thank you, Lieutenant," he said to Lowe. "You've been a great help."

Boxer stood up and thanked her too.

Stark waited until Lowe was out of the room before he said, "Sit down Boxer. Now we get to the bottom line of what this is all about and why you're here."

Boxer sat down and relit his pipe.

"The *Shark*," Stark said, "has been designed and engineered for one operation and only one operation, though it can perform several different ones: from firing missiles to hunting and destroying other submarines."

Boxer nodded, "From what you showed me, I'd say she could."

"But that's not her purpose," Stark responded. "Her single most important function will be to carry out covert operations against Russia or any other nation that challenges us in a way that forces

35

us to respond." He paused to take a fresh cigar, trim and light it. "This boat has been on the drawing boards ever since the late seventies and that whole Iranian mess. Well, now she is almost ready to launch and we need a skipper for her and a crew."

Boxer leaned forward.

"As I told you earlier," Stark said, blowing smoke up toward the ceiling, "your name kept coming out of the computer. But before you say anything, let me tell you what will be involved, if you decide to accept the assignment: one, the *Shark* will not be carried on the roster of American Navy vessels; two, you and the men who volunteer to go with you will not be carried on our personnel rosters. To make this more understandable to you, I'll put it this way: the *Shark* and her entire crew will not exist for the U.S. Navy. Are you still interested?"

Boxer's heart was beating very fast and his throat was very dry. But he managed to murmur, "I'd like to hear more, sir."

"Should you be captured by a foreign power while carrying out an assignment, the United States will disavow your existence. But I and the other people involved with the *Shark* and, let me say, there are damn few of them, expect that you would destroy the *Shark,* whether she's on the surface or submerged. Again for the sake of clarity, no member of the *Shark*'s crew is expected to be captured and the *Shark* must never fall into enemy hands."

"Those are damn stiff conditions, sir."

Stark nodded. "There's more . . . No member of the crew will be permitted to tell anyone about his new assignment. He will change from a real person to a kind of phantom. Your time ashore will be spent in civilian clothes . . . In that way the accident with the *Mary-Ann* was fortunate—"

Boxer shook his head.

"Before you say anything,"Stark cautioned,"understand that the entire crew of the *Shark* will be non-people. Their present identities will change. They'll even be issued false social security numbers. Only their immediate families will know who they really are and precious damn little about their assignment. The accident with the *Mary-Ann* makes it possible to put you and any other member of the crew—I assume that if you accept the assignment, you'll take several or all of them to join you—in the necessary state of limbo. From there, it will be easy to move you to the shadow land of the

Shark."

"And what happens to the two men who—"

Stark raised his hands. "I hope you're not asking for a fucking perfect world!"

After a pause, Boxer said, "No, only a just one, at least in this instance."

Stark ignored his comment and said, "There's one more thing you should know."

Boxer nodded. "Go ahead," he said, emptying his pipe into the ashtray.

"From your record," Stark said, "it appears that you'll make flag rank in a few years. But even if you do, you'll never be allowed to leave the special assignment that the —"

"You mean the entire crew will be locked into that shadowed world?"

"For as long as all of you are in the Navy, yes. And even when you leave it . . . But for you that's a long way off, I hope."

"I hope so too," Boxer answered.

"Have you any questions?"

"None. You've explained everything, Admiral."

"Good, I like to think I'm thorough."

"There is one thing."

"Yes, what is it?"

"Given everything the *Shark* is, she's still too big for what she is."

"That information comes under 'the need to know' clause and until you sign on, Commander, you don't have 'the need to know,' isn't that right?"

"Absolutely."

"Take a few days . . . A week . . . One week from today, come back here and give me your answer. If you don't take the assignment, it will not affect your career in the slightest."

"Admiral, what would you do, if you were in my place?" Boxer asked.

Stark leaned back. "I'm not sure I can answer that. To begin with I'm not a submariner. The very thought of being enclosed in a tube underwater makes me go into a cold sweat. Secondly, I've been a paper pusher for so many years now that—" He shook his head. "Any sane man would stay far away from it. But I don't think you're all that sane. If you were completely sane, you'd be in something other than submarines."

"Thank you, sir," Boxer said with a smile.

"It's the best I can do," Stark said. "Remember a week from today. By the way, I spoke to D'Arcy this morning, you don't have to rush back to the hearing today . . . The proceedings up there have been postponed for at least ten days." Stark grinned. "You can do all sorts of things when you're a fucking CNO." Then he extended his hand across the desk.

Boxer stood up and took hold of it.

"Whatever you decide, Jack," Stark said, using Boxer's given name for the first time, "I know will be the right decision for you and for the Navy."

The two men shook hands.

"Do I need someone to escort me out?" Boxer asked.

"Lieutenant Lowe will meet you at the door," Stark said.

"Thanks again, sir," Boxer responded; then he turned and left Stark's office.

Lowe looked up from her computer terminal. "How did the rest of the meeting go, Commander?"

Boxer noticed she had startling blue eyes.

"If you're really interested," he said, in a low voice, "you'll have dinner with me tonight."

"But I thought you had to go back for the inquiry," she said.

"Not immediately . . . At least not tonight . . . Will you join me for dinner?"

"I have sort of a date," she said.

"Break it," Boxer said forcefully.

She looked at him for several moments; then nodded. "I live at twenty two-forty four Fairview Avenue. It's a six story apartment house. Apartment six-D."

"See you about eighteen thirty," Boxer said.

Lowe stood up. "I'll escort you past security," she told him with a nod.

Boxer and Cynthia were sitting across from one another in the Purple Onion, a cocktail lounge across the street from the Watergate Hotel. For the first time since the accident, Boxer felt relaxed. He had taken Cynthia to a small Japanese restaurant and had the pleasure of introducing her to shashimi and sushi, two different ways of preparing raw fish. After dinner, they walked arm and arm across the mall.

"My, my," Cynthia chided, after awhile, "you are a quiet one."

Boxer smiled. "Just thinking."

"About your meeting with the admiral?"

"No," he said, "at least not consciously . . . To tell the truth, I was thinking about how much I've enjoyed the evening." He reached across the table and took hold of her hand.

"Why thank you, Jack," she responded, exaggerating her drawl. "I've enjoyed myself too."

For several moments he said nothing and just looked at her. She was even more attractive in the black dress she was wearing than she had been in uniform.

"You're staring at me," she chided.

"I'm weighing the odds," Boxer answered. He could feel her hand suddenly tighten in his. But he decided the reward would far outweigh the—

"My God, Commander, you do get around!" A woman said, coming toward the table.

Boxer let go of Cynthia's hand. He recognized the voice. It belonged to that gossip columnist, Tracy Kimble. Behind her were two men. One was Byron Hayes, the actor. He had been aboard the *Mary-Ann*. The other man was a stranger.

"Commander Boxer," Kimble said, "You've already met Byron and this is James Hicks. He's something or other in government."

"Lieutenant Cynthia Lowe," Boxer said, introducing Cynthia.

"You Navy people do stay together in or out of uniform, or should I say: in or out of bed?"

"Listen Kimble," Boxer said sharply, "I didn't come to your table; you came to mine. The least—"

"Temper, Commander, temper," Kimble cautioned, waving her forefinger at him.

"Did anyone ever tell you that you're a bitch?"

"Take it easy," Hicks said.

Boxer looked at him. He was in his late twenties or early thirties. Athletically trim. Tan. Good looking, with thin lips and hard restless eyes.

"The lady has an apology coming," Hicks said.

"Why don't you take your boyfriends," Boxer told Kimble, "and —" Boxer saw Hicks hand coming up, grabbed it and forced it down on the table. "I wouldn't, not even for brownie points with Kimble," he said in a low flat voice.

Hicks was bent against the table. He tried to move.

"I'll break it," Boxer said in the same flat voice. He looked up at Kimble. "Tell your would-be hero to —"

"Do what he says," She said in a breathy voice. "Don't be stupid!"

Boxer felt Hicks relax. He eased his hold and then let go of it.

Hicks stepped back. "This one is yours," he said, rubbing his arm.

Boxer gave a snort of disdain.

"Come, let's get out of here," Kimble said to her two companions, "and let the commander give his rooster crow for his lieutenant hen."

Boxer's eyes went to slits. He looked up at her. "You said you were going."

"You don't frighten me," Kimble responded.

"Go!" Boxer ordered.

Kimble finally turned around and walked away. Hayes and Hicks followed her.

Boxer took a deep breath and slowly turned toward Cynthia.

She was sitting very straight. Her eyes were wide with fear. "Would you have broken his arm?" she asked in a whisper.

Boxer shook his head. "Maybe . . . I don't know. Everytime I'm near that woman there's trouble. She was aboard the *Mary-Ann* — "

"I read what she wrote about it," Cynthia said.

"In the gossip column?"

"On the front page with her own byline," Cynthia said. "The accident was the best thing that could have happened to her. She was at the right place at the right time."

"I guess it's true that 'One man's poison is another man's meat,' though in this case the man is a woman and her meat happens to be the deaths of five of my men."

"I'd like to go home," Cynthia said.

Boxer nodded. Kimble and her friends had ruined the night. He wanted another scotch but decided to forego it and take Cynthia home. It was still early enough for him to catch a shuttle flight back to New York. He summoned the waitress and paid the bill.

Outside, Boxer offered to hail a cab.

"It's not that far to where I live," Cynthia said. "I'd much rather walk."

"I guess a walk would be the best thing right now," he answered.

When they came to the first street crossing, Cynthia wrapped her arm around his. "That was a very ugly scene," she said as they reached the other side of the crossing.

"I'm sorry," Boxer replied. "I shouldn't have been as hostile. But—"

"You don't have to apologize or explain to me," Cynthia said.

"Thanks," Boxer said.

Cynthia didn't answer.

"I am sorry about the scene," Boxer said. "But every time that woman says something, it's the wrong thing. I just see red."

"The sparks sure did fly."

"I don't understand why a woman, or a man for that matter, would purposely go out of their way to be obnoxious."

"Can't answer that one," Cynthia said. "But it sure does happen often enough."

It was at least a mile between the Purple Onion and the building where Lowe lived and by the time they reached it Boxer's anger had lost its edge.

On the way up to the sixth floor in the elevator, Boxer reached out and took Cynthia in his arms.

Her face was red from the cold. She closed her eyes and raised her face.

He gently kissed her on the mouth, holding his lips against hers until the elevator stopped and the doors opened.

Hand in hand they walked off.

At the door to the apartment, Cynthia gave her key to Boxer.

He unlocked the door, opened it and stepped back to allow her to enter; then he followed and closed the door behind him. The apartment, he recalled from his visit earlier in the evening, consisted of two rooms and a small kitchenette. On the walls there were several reproductions of famous paintings. He didn't know any of them.

41

Cynthia switched on the lights. She took several steps into the room, turned and faced him. "I'm divorced, Jack. I have a five year old daughter. My exhusband is a psychiatrist of some repute. And—"

"Why are you telling me this?" he asked, interrupting her.

"Because I want you to know I have been around the block a few times myself and I don't want to play games."

Boxer took a deep breath and slowly exhaled. "I'm divorced too; I have a ten year old son."

Cynthia nodded. "I knew that. But I just wanted to hear it from you."

"A test?" Boxer asked, raising his eyebrows.

She shrugged.

Boxer wasn't sure what he should say or do.

"I just wanted everything in the past that really matters to be out in the open," she said.

"I can understand that," Boxer said, taking Cynthia in his arms. This time, when he kissed her, her lips were very warm.

She opened her mouth, giving him her tongue to caress with his. Breathless, she stepped away from him. "I need a few minutes to shower."

"I could use a shower myself," Boxer told her.

"Then we'll do each other's backs," Cynthia said with a laugh.

"I'm for doing that together and a helluva lot more," Boxer answered.

Naked, they faced each other in the shower.

Cynthia's body was even more voluptuous than Boxer had imagined it. Her skin was very white, her breasts, almost hemispherical, with a tracery of blue veins on their sides, splattering of freckles on them and large, dark pink, nipples in their center.

He started to soap her body. Gently he caressed her breasts. His hands moved down her stomach and around to her back.

She came up against him, offering him her lips.

His hands slid over her buttocks and into the crack between them.

Boxer kissed her greedily. He held her tightly to him, enjoying the press of her wet, naked body against his. He opened her mouth with his tongue.

Cynthia played her fingers over his scrotum.

"I think we are clean enough," Boxer said.

"I think so too," Cynthia agreed.

Boxer reached over and shut off the water.

"Dry me and I'll dry you," Cynthia said, throwing a large pink towel to him.

Together they worked on one another's body.

"Easy," Cynthia cautioned, "you'll rub off my skin."

"Sorry, I just got carried away."

Suddenly she stopped, placed the towel around her naked shoulders, knelt down in front of him and lifting his penis, put it into her mouth.

Boxer was too surprised to move. Her lips formed a warm ring around his shaft and her tongue caressed it with a feathery light movements. He reached down and pressed her head to him. "That's great," he said in a low, throaty voice. "Just wonderful!"

Cynthia looked up at him and slowly drew away.

Boxer helped her stand. He couldn't remember the time when a woman did that so spontaneously as she had just done. "That was wonderful. Really — "

Cynthia put her hand up to his lips. "There's no need for you to say anything, Jack."

He nodded and scooping her up into his arms, he carried her into the bedroom.

"Put me down," she said softly, "and I'll fix the bed."

Boxer set her down and helped to take the bedspread off and fold it.

"I'll bring in a bottle of scotch, some ice and a couple of glasses," she said padding out of the bedroom.

Boxer settled down on the bed and closed his eyes. Though he was tired, he was eager to make love to Cynthia. He hadn't been near a woman for a long time and Cynthia was just the kind of woman he needed now. He guessed she understood far more about his reaction to what had happened to the *Sting Ray* than she could show.

"Would you like a drink now?" Cynthia asked, as she reentered the room.

Boxer opened his eyes.

She was setting a tray, complete with a bottle of scotch, two glasses and a small ice bucket, down on an end table. Her naked

43

body was reflected in the mirror on the wall behind the dresser.

"No thank you," he said. "But I do want you." He held out his arms toward her.

She came to him.

Boxer switched off the end table lamp.

"I don't mind if it's on," she said. "There's nothing I'd do in the dark that I wouldn't do with the light on."

Boxer turned the light back on; then easing her head down on the pillow he passionately kissed her, while his right hand moved lightly across her breasts. He kissed the side of her neck and then the nipples of her breasts.

"That feels good," she murmured.

"Tastes good too," he said, lifting his face for a moment and then burying it in the hollow of her stomach.

She ran her finger through his hair.

Boxer gently splayed her naked thighs and caressed the wet lips of her sex. Then he pushed his mouth against them.

Cynthia made a soft purring sound.

Boxer eased himself over her and instantly felt her mouth close around his penis. Avidly he devoured her, while she did the same to him.

"I want you inside of me," Cynthia moaned. "I want you deep inside of me."

Boxer rolled off her and turned around.

"Missionary style this time," she said.

Boxer slipped between her open thighs and he entered her.

"You can't imagine how good that feels," she whispered, as she closed her eyes.

"Oh yes I can!"

She smiled, reached up with her two hands to his face and drew it down to her lips.

Boxer caressed her tongue with his and began to move.

"You taste and smell of me," she told him.

"I like the way you taste and smell," he answered.

"Kiss my nipple," she said.

Boxer bent his head to the nipple on her right breast; this time he sucked it and then slowly rolled it between his teeth.

Cynthia reached down and gently moved her hand over his scrotum.

Boxer quickened his movements.

"Oh yes," she breathed. "Yes, faster . . . Go faster!"

Boxer felt as if he were a jack-hammer. His own passion boiled in his groin, while her body tensed under his.

"I'm almost there!" she exclaimed in a whisper. "I'm almost there . . ." She raised her naked thighs and clamped them around Boxer's back.

He drove into her. He felt the rapid contractions in her body.

She grabbed hold of his shoulders and with a tremendous shudder, cried out, "So good . . . Oh so good!"

Boxer's world narrowed down to the intense feeling that for a moment made it seem as if he glimpsed some great truth; then it was gone, washed away by a blaze of reds and oranges that flung themselves across the inner surface of his closed eyelids . . . The bright reds and oranges changed to shades of blue . . . Then the color vanished altogether.

He opened his eyes and looked at Cynthia, only to find that she was looking at him.

"Now do you want a drink?" she asked.

He knew she did and nodded.

Cynthia left the bed, fixed two scotches on the rocks, returned and handed one glass to Boxer. "A toast, let's toast something."

"Go ahead you make it," Boxer said.

She hesitated.

"Go on," Boxer said. "The toast is yours."

"You won't laugh?" She asked with a twinkle in her eyes.

"I won't laugh, I promise."

To his complete surprise, she put her free hand over his penis and lifting her glass, she said, "To the pleasure it has given me tonight."

"I'll drink to that," Boxer said, touching his glass to hers. He did drink, but he purposefully didn't finish the scotch. "Now it's my turn to toast," he said.

Cynthia nodded.

He reached over to where she was, put his hand between her thighs and his forefinger into her sex. Then with a smile, Boxer said, "One good toast deserves another . . . To a lovely cunt, if there ever was one!"

She smiled broadly, touched his glass with her and said, "Thank you, I'll drink to that!"

Neither of them had a second drink. Cynthia cuddled up alongside Boxer. He switched off the lamp and for a time he caressed her breasts; then slowly he drifted into a deep and restful sleep . . .

The next morning Boxer awoke slowly, coming—it seemed to him—from some gray misty place. He opened his eyes and for several moments he didn't know where he was, or how he had gotten there. But as soon as he became aware of the woman next to him, he remembered, smiled and reaching toward Cynthia's bare shoulder, he caressed it gently.

Waking, she said, "I was having such a nice dream." And moved closer to him. "What about you, did you have a nice dream too?"

"Not that I remember . . . Something about mist and rain . . . I guess it had something to do with the *Sting Ray*."

Facing him, she rolled on her side and propping up her head with her hand, she asked, "What do you think the board of inquiry will recommend?"

It was the first time she mentioned the *Sting Ray* to Boxer. But because of his conversation with Stark, he decided to make it the last. "Please, I don't want to talk about it . . . They'll call it the way—"

"It's all right," she quickly told him. "You don't have to talk about it."

He ran his hand over her face. "Thanks."

"There's not much time left before I have to get up," she said, glancing toward the dresser where a digital clock displayed the time with green numbers.

"How much time do we need?" Boxer asked with a smile.

"Ten minutes . . . maybe less," she answered and taking hold of his hand, she guided it to her sex.

"Lady, what has been going on in your head?"

"For starters, let me show you," Cynthia answered straddling him.

Boxer reached up and brought her face down to hers. "You're in the driver's seat."

She smiled, put her lips to his and opened her mouth.

They moved slowly; then faster and faster until they climaxed simultaneously.

Cynthia glanced over her bare shoulder at the clock. "That took seven minutes and thirty-nine seconds," she said.

"Is that good or bad?"

"I'll tell you over breakfast," Cynthia said, kissing Boxer lightly on the nose. Naked, she left the bed and padded into the bathroom.

A few minutes later it was Boxer's turn to go into the bathroom. "Have you anything resembling a razor?" he asked.

"In the medicine cabinet you'll find one of those plastic jobs and a tube of cream," she answered. "There's a fresh toothbrush there also."

"All the comforts of home," Boxer commented.

"Just some," Cynthia said.

By the time Boxer shaved, showered and brushed his teeth, he could smell the fresh coffee and frying bacon. It had been a long time since he sat down to breakfast in a kitchen opposite a woman. Usually the morning after was in some motel, or hotel room, or a coffee shop.

"Just like real people," Boxer said, coming to the table dressed.

Cynthia smiled and said, "I don't usually bother to fix all this. But for a guest, I thought it would be nice."

"It's very nice," Boxer responded, taking her hand for a moment.

"Are you going back to New York?" she asked, as she speared a piece of bacon with a fork.

Boxer nodded. "But I'll be back here in a week."

"To see the admiral?"

Boxer nodded again. "Maybe we could spend some time together . . . a couple of days?"

"I'd like that."

"Good; then I'll see you in a week," Boxer said with a broad smile.

When they finished eating breakfast, Boxer collected the dishes and put them in the dishwasher, while Cynthia went into the bedroom to dress. Through the open door he could hear her humming. "Do you sing too?" he called out.

"I did once," she answered.

He went to the doorway of the bedroom. She was wearing a thin, white bra that increased the thrust of her breasts and sheer briefs

47

that separated the lips of her vagina and accentuated each cheek of her buttocks. She really did have a beautiful body . . .

"Why are you staring at me?" she asked.

"To compensate for the ticking of the clock," he answered.

"I don't understand."

"Remember the old line that goes: 'Honey, if you have the time, I have the place?' . . . Well, we have the place but according to that clock not the time."

"Sad but true," Cynthia answered, putting her arms around him. "But there'll other times."

Boxer ran his hands over her back. "I'll be back in a week at the latest and, if I can, earlier." He kissed her passionately on the lips; then letting go of her, he retreated out of the doorway.

"I'll be ready in a few minutes," Cynthia said.

Boxer walked to the window and looked up toward the sky. It was clear and though it was still too early for the sun to have risen, it was too light for him to see any stars. He turned away and began looking at one of the paintings: a seascape done, judging from the clothes the people in it were wearing, early in the century, or the very end of the previous one.

"The newspaper is probably here by now," Cynthia called out from the bedroom.

Boxer went to the door, unlocked it and cracking it a bit, he bent down and picked up the paper. A few moments later, he was settled in an easy chair and began to scan the newspaper, which to his surprise was the *Washington Globe*. He would have thought Cynthia to be a *Times* reader, even though she had told him that she read the *Globe*.

"Anything interesting?" Cynthia asked, as she went from the bedroom to the bathroom.

Boxer was about to answer with a definitive no, when he read: SUB DISASTER CAPTAIN FROLICS. "That bitch!" he exclaimed, jumping to his feet. "That goddamn bitch! Will you listen to this."

Cynthia came out of the bathroom.

"That Kimble woman has been at it," Boxer said and he began to read, "Commander Boxer, captain of the ill-fated submarine *Sting Ray* was in our town last night for a pleasure cruise with an attractive lieutenant. Don't worry folks, the bad captain isn't gay. The lieutenant is every inch a woman, at least from the outside and from the way the rude captain was holding her hands when I first saw them in the Purple Onion, I'd have to say, he was very much aware of her womanly attributes . . ."

"That I don't think much of this man hardly states my opinion of him. But last night he really did hit rock bottom. Not only did he insult me for asking why the Navy has permitted him to go frolicking when he should have been in New York—"

"Can you believe this? . . . Can you really believe this? The shit is really going to hit the fan when the CNO starts getting phone calls this morning."

"Don't worry about it," Cynthia said. "He can handle them."

"She says further on, 'I hope one of our elected representatives will ask for an investigation of Commander Boxer's presence here in Washington, when the bodies of the men who died because of his ineptness have not yet been released to their next of kin. Something smells here and that something has to be influence. Who does this man know that we should also know? Perhaps if we knew, the deaths of five brave men would have some meaning. But as things stand now, they died for nothing. They died because their captain, the man they trusted, failed them.' As he read the last few words, Boxer's voice trailed off. Slowly, he lowered the newspaper. His vision was blurred and his throat ached.

Cynthia took the newspaper from him.

Boxer turned away from her and walked to the window. "Those were my men," he managed to say. "What the hell can she know about my feelings? . . . Goddamn it, one of them was a good friend." He shook his head. "I don't understand why she's doing it." He used his handkerchief to clear his eyes. "Before the accident, I didn't know Tracy Kimble existed. But now—" He faced Cynthia. "I have the awful feeling she's trying to destroy me."

"Maybe," Cynthia answered.

"I have no way of protecting myself," Boxer said, raising his hands, then dropping them to his sides . . . "At least, she had the decency not to use your name."

Cynthia put her arms around him. "There's nothing I can say to make you feel better . . . But anyone who knows you knows that you're not the man she's writing about."

He hugged her. "Thanks."

"If you should see her again," Cynthia said, "try not to get your back up . . . Maybe, if you don't, she'll find you boring and leave you alone."

Boxer shook his head. "Not until the inquiry is over and if its recommendations go against me, she'll be at me like a vulture."

"That can't happen!" Cynthia exclaimed, momentarily holding him tighter. "Could it really go that way?"

Boxer nodded and said, "We had better leave, if you're going to get to the office on time."

She stepped away from him. "What are you going to do?"

"Take a shuttle flight back," Boxer answered. "I have the rest of the day to myself . . . I was thinking of going to see my folks. I haven't seen them yet, though I spoke to them on the telephone several times . . . And if I can, I'd like to see my son."

"Will you phone me?" Cynthia asked, going to the closet for her coat.

"Yes. Tonight if you like," he answered, helping her with her coat.

"I'd like," she said.

They left the apartment.

Boxer took a moment to lock it and gave the key back to Cynthia. In the elevator, he kissed her gently on the lips.

She touched his face. "Try not to be too upset about the article."

"I'll try," he said.

A few moments later they were in the street.

"I get a bus at the corner," Cynthia told him.

"I'll wait with you until one comes," Boxer said, "then I'll hop a cab to the airport."

Cynthia linked her arm with his. "Are you all right?"

"I'm okay . . . It's just that I don't understand why Kimble wants my scalp."

"Maybe her friend, Sanchez does?" Cynthia suggested.

"I never thought of —"

"My bus is coming!" she exclaimed.

Boxer turned her toward him. "Thanks," he said, "thanks for — for being you." And he kissed her hard on the lips.

The bus pulled up, stopped with an explosion of escaping air and opened its doors.

Cynthia boarded it. "Call," she said, glancing at Boxer over her shoulder.

"Yes. Yes, I'll call . . . This evening," Boxer replied. He waited until the doors closed and the bus swung away from the curb before he started to walk away. The prospect of returning to the inquiry didn't sit well with him. Even if he accepted Stark's offer, he didn't want that Kimble woman to write anything more about him; it hurt too much. Suddenly aware of the wind, Boxer pulled up his collar and began to look for a cab.

4

Captain First Class Igor Borodine, naval attache, was seated in front of the ambassador's large ornately carved desk. He had stopped by the embassy to say goodby for the last time to his colleagues and friends before he left for his new assignment.

"So it's back to your boats, eh Borodine?" the ambassador said with a broad smile on his jowly face. "You know, I could have kept you here for at least another year . . . Your lovely wife, Galena, would have liked that now, wouldn't she?"

Borodine flushed. He'd warned Galena she was too loud, too often in her praises of the United States. "I don't think—" he started to say.

The ambassador held up his thick hand. "The KGB is very effective . . . But what she says is true. If our people had all the material things the people here have, then our country would truly be a paradise." He smiled broadly again. "She was only voicing the obvious."

"There's too much here," Borodine replied. "Too much food, too many automobiles." He shook his head.

The ambassador gave no sign that he either agreed or disagreed. "Are you making any stops on the way home?" he asked, reaching into a humidor for two Cuban cigars and offered one to Borodine.

Accepting the cigar, Borodine said, "London and Paris . . . I have a month's vacation coming to me and Galena has always wanted to see those cities . . . It will be a long time before she has the opportunity to visit them again."

"Have you any idea what your new assignment will be?" the ambassador asked.

"None," Borodine answered, lighting the cigar and blowing

52

smoke toward the ceiling. "Just the usual orders."

"I made a few discreet inquiries."

Borodine leaned slightly forward. He was a dark complexioned man of forty years. Average height, with strong Tartar features. He was considered by his superiors to be one of the country's ablest officers.

"Just whispers of you being assigned to the Murmansk or Vladivostok," the ambassador said through a curtain of cigar smoke. "Would that please you?"

Borodine nodded vigorously. "Very, very much," he replied.

"So, the more danger there is, the happier you are, eh?"

Borodine smiled sheepishly. "It's not the danger, it's the challenge . . . There's so much we don't know about navigating under the polar seas. We must be able to do it as efficiently as we navigate the other oceans of the world."

"You don't have to convince me," ambassador said. "I'm crazy but not crazy enough to want to do that . . . No, I'll stay on the surface, thank you, anytime."

Borodine tried to think of something witty to say, but couldn't.

"Have you been reading about this accident between the submarine *Sting Ray* and the *Mary-Ann*?" the ambassador asked.

Borodine nodded. "Yes."

"What do you think — "

"According to the newspaper accounts, the submarine's captain did everything possible to avoid the crash."

"Is that what you think?"

Borodine nodded. He had no intentions of speaking ill of the American officer. Secretly — he hadn't even spoken to Galena about it — he admired the man, especially after hearing him on the TV the previous night. An officer who was so devoted to his men that he was willing to risk his career, had to be among the best in the American Navy, if not the best. Besides, though they were light years apart politically, they were still submariners. And as far as he was concerned, unless they were actual adversaries, that was a very special bond.

"Something appears to be working against him," the ambassador said. "The media isn't treating him too kindly, especially — "

"The media won't decide the outcome of the inquiry," Borodine said. "Crazy as the Americans are over their 'freedom of the press', they won't let it destroy the career of an excellent officer."

"Listen to this," the ambassador said, picking up a newspaper clipping. "It was written by a Miss Tracy Kimble, a reporter for the *Washington Globe*. She was aboard the *Mary-Ann* at the time of the accident . . ." And he proceeded to read the article in the *Globe*.

Borodine listened intently. He had, as he said, read the newspaper accounts of the accident. He had even read naval intelligence's report, though he hadn't mentioned that to the comrade ambassador. But, because he and Galena were busy with last minute packing, he hadn't even seen a newspaper that morning.

The ambassador put the clipping down. "The question, Captain, is simply this: what was Commander Boxer doing here given the situation he is in?"

Borodine removed the cigar from between his lips. "The inquiry would take precedence over everything else; unless — "

"He was summoned here by someone who can overrule the authority of the inquiry."

"The president can do that, of course," Borodine said.

"And who else?" the ambassador pressed.

"Any of the joint chiefs of staff . . . And the chief of naval operations, Admiral Stark."

The ambassador nodded. "Then it is clear that he was not here just to 'frolic', as the writer of this article would have her readers believe."

"That hardly would be possible."

The ambassador relit his cigar and leaned back in his swivel chair. "Then you would agree with me that Commander Boxer requires watching and more investigation."

"Certainly, under the circumstances."

"Does naval intelligence have a file on him?"

Borodine nodded. He knew the KGB kept an active dossier on every American officer and the ambassador could easily obtain the information he wanted on the commander from it. He almost pursed his lips, as was his habit, when he was confronted by something he didn't understand.

"Good, I'll get it from your replacement," the ambassador said, blowing smoke off to the side. "Well, you needn't bother yourself about this matter any more . . . You'll be off among the ice floes soon and your problems will be very different from those you dealt with in Washington."

"Yes and I'm sure there will be times when I'll say to myself, 'Idiot, you could have had another year in Washington if the comrade ambassador wasn't so anxious to get rid of you.' "

The ambassador laughed so heartily that his jowly face turned red. "I doubt that you will ever say that to yourself or anyone else."

"Probably not," Borodine admitted. "It was an experience to be here. But being at sea is where a seaman belongs."

The ambassador stood up and offering his hand across the table, he said, "You're a credit to the Navy and to our diplomatic corps here."

Borodine stood up and shook the ambassador's hand. "Thank you, comrade Ambassador."

"When does your flight leave?" the ambassador asked.

"Not until nine this evening."

"Then you have a whole day to relax and enjoy yourself."

"There's still some last minute things to be done."

"Yes, yes . . . There always is, when one is changing stations. So many things to bring home, eh? Things that our relatives and friends can't buy, even in Moscow."

Borodine felt his cheeks burn. "Records," he said. "Recordings of classical music."

The ambassador came around to the front of the desk. "Come comrade Captain, I will walk you to the door." And as he put his chubby hand on Borodine's shoulder, he said, "I hope our paths cross again Igor . . . I really hope they do."

Borodine was so completely surprised at hearing his given name that his step faltered. It was the first time that the ambassador addressed him by it. "I would like that too," he managed to say after what he thought was a long pause.

They reached the door and the ambassador opened it. The two men embraced and kissed one another on the cheek.

"Take care of yourself and your lovely wife," the ambassador said. "And very good luck be with you all of the time."

"Thank you —" Borodine was tempted to use the man's given name but decided not to. "Thank you very much, comrade Ambassador."

A moment later Borodine was out of the doorway and on his

way down the hallway to say goodby to a friend in the code room. He was pleased with the way the ambassador treated him. The man was not known for his friendliness. Indeed, his reputation for being aloof and testy provided the embassy staff with many anecdotes: some humorous and several, if true, showed the man's savagery. Borodine approached Marine Sergeant Andrei Dimitrov, the security guard on duty at the door to the code room.

"Captain First Class Igor Borodine," he said, identifying himself and showing his plastic badge, "here to see comrade Major Alexander Petrovich." And he started to reach for the sign-in book.

The guard stood up. "Sorry comrade Captain," the man said, "but you no longer have code room security clearance."

Borodine looked at the man with disbelief. He was too stunned to respond immediately. Finally, he asked, "By whose authority?"

"The order came this morning straight from the comrade ambassador's office."

Borodine's heart began to race. His cheeks flushed. He was very angry.

"I'll call the comrade major," the guard said. "I'm sure he'll come out to see you."

"Thank you," Borodine answered. "I'd appreciate that."

The guard picked up the phone, pressed several buttons and speaking directly to Petrovich, he explained the situation." Yes, comrade major," he answered, "I'll tell him." He put the phone down. "The comrade major said he'll be out in a few minutes and asks you to wait for him in the staff lounge."

Borodine nodded. "Thank you," he said and turning away, he went directly to the staff lounge.

Borodine was standing at the window, looking out on the street, when Petrovich came up behind him and putting a hand on his shoulder, he said, "Igor, I'm sorry about the security—"

Borodine turned. "I know you had nothing to do with it," he said.

"We can't talk here," Petrovich whispered. He was slightly shorter than Borodine. A solidly built, fair complexioned man with blond hair, a strong jaw and a bull's neck. He had come up through the ranks, after having joined the Naval Marines at the age of eighteen. "Too many ears," he added, still whispering.

"Have you enough time to go outside?" Borodine asked.

Petrovich nodded.

The two men left the lounge, walked down the hallway to the elevator and rode it down to the first floor without speaking to each other.

Only when they had reached the street did Borodine ask, "Which way, up or down?"

"Down," Petrovich answered. "We'll see more of the stores."

They crossed to the other side of the street.

"You're angry about the security order," Petrovich said.

"Wouldn't you be, if it happened to you?"

"Yes," Petrovich answered. "But that wouldn't be reasonable either . . . By withdrawing your clearance the comrade ambassador was only showing you—at least so he thinks—his power. He doesn't understand that what he's really showing you and everyone else in the embassy is that he is basically a very small man."

Borodine glanced at his friend, smiled and said, "I guess you're right."

"I know I am. And you should know it too."

"You can't imagine how friendly he was when I went to say goodby to him. He even said that he hoped our paths would cross again. He said I was a credit to the service and to the embassy."

"And he meant every word of it," Petrovich said. "I saw the fitness report he gave you . . . You were rated excellent in everything."

"I had no idea—"

"Of course you didn't. You'd only be told if any of the ratings had been unsatisfactory. You understand, you must never indicate you know any of this?"

"I know that."

"Not even to your wife."

"Not even to her," Borodine answered.

They paused in front of a large bookstore and looked at a Christmas window display.

"It must have cost thousands of dollars to do," Petrovich commented, "and all of it to celebrate a fairy tale and a stupid one at that."

Borodine uttered a wordless sound, which he hoped his friend would take as his agreement. Within the last few years, especially during his stay in the United States, he had come to be of two minds about religious belief: because of his training, he couldn't believe but he saw no reason why other people shouldn't. And he had to admit he liked the ritual of the church.

"There's something else," Petrovich said, as they turned away from the window.

Borodine remained silent, waiting for his friend to speak.

"Your new assignment will be a temporary one," Petrovich said.

"Oh!" Borodine exclaimed with surprise, coming to a momentary halt.

"Continue to walk, please," Petrovich said.

His voice almost a whisper, Borodine asked, "How do you know that?"

Petrovich ignored the question. "You'll be reassigned within eighteen months, or two years. When it happens, remember you first heard it from Petrovich."

Borodine suddenly had many questions, but he knew that his friend, even if he could, would not answer any of them. The subject was closed.

The two men walked toward the White House. The tall Christmas tree was already in place and fully decorated.

"If it does nothing else," Borodine commented, "the holiday season puts most people here in a better frame of mind."

"That's because they enjoy being children again and believe in fairy tales."

"You're probably right," Borodine admitted. "But aren't there times when you've wanted to be a child again, or if not a child, then perhaps a young man?"

"Only when I look at the young women, especially during the summer when they wear so little clothing, and let my imagination wander."

The two men looked at one another and laughed.

"I will miss you, Igor," Petrovich said.

"And I will miss you, Alexsa," Borodine responded, using the diminutive form of his friend's name to show his affection for him. Then he added, "In the service a man has many acquaintances but makes very few friends; that's especially so when he starts going up

58

in rank."

Petrovich agreed and said, "Friendship or not, I had better be getting back to the embassy . . . I'll say goodby to you here."

"I'll walk you back," Borodine offered.

"Not necessary."

Borodine nodded and embraced his friend. "I'll write and tell you where I'm stationed; then when you come home on leave, you can come to see us. My house will always be open to you."

"Since I haven't a wife or a house of my own, I can't offer the same hospitality. But if I did have a wife and a house, you know that, as the expression goes, 'mia casa es sua casa.' "

They separated.

"Good sailing," Petrovich said.

"Thanks," Borodine answered. "And very good luck to you."

They turned away from each other and went their separate ways.

Boxer lunched with his parents. He sat at a small, round, white table in front of a sliding glass door that looked out on a wooden deck and a yard. At the far end, there were two tall lombardy poplars and a red Japanese maple. The sun streamed into the kitchen, brightening and warming everything in the room.

His mother, a petite sixty-two year old woman with green eyes and finely chiseled features, prepared an omelet filled with ham and cheese, which he ate with gusto.

Neither one of his parents mentioned the accident, or the inquiry. But now and then his father, a man of middle height, with slate gray eyes, looked as if he were about to speak, but changed his mind. Sooner or later the two subjects would have to come up, but Boxer decided they could wait until lunch was finished. In the meantime, they spoke of other things.

Over coffee, Boxer said, "When I divorced Gwen, you told me I was making a mistake." He was looking at his father as he spoke.

"I still think it was a mistake," he said.

"Maybe, maybe not . . . But if it was a mistake, it was one all of us could live with."

"Have you seen her yet?" his father asked. "Have you seen your son?"

"I'll see them tonight," Boxer answered. He poured another cup

59

of coffee for himself. His parents loved Gwen, especially his father, who thought of her more as his daughter than daughter-in-law. "I couldn't get away from the boat and yesterday and today I had to be in Washington . . . The one time I wanted to see her, she was busy."

"I wouldn't give a damn about it," his father said, "if I didn't know that you still love her and there's John — "

"Dad!" Boxer exclaimed, gently putting his hand on his father's arm.

"Okay . . . Okay, I'll keep my mouth shut," he said.

Boxer took a sip of coffee and looked at his father over the rim of the cup. There was more than just a blood bond between them. They were friends. Theirs was a unique relationship, he had learned over the years that very few sons and fathers ever have the joy of experiencing. Boxer set the cup down on the saucer and fished a pipe out of his pocket. "There's a possibility," he said, filling the pipe's bowl with tobacco, "that the inquiry might not go well."

His mother uttered a gasp and her right hand went to her breasts.

"Was that why you wre in Washington?" His father asked.

Boxer lit up and holding the stem between his teeth, he sid, "no, there was some other business I had to take care of . . . But I want you to know that there's a possibility that . . . that the board might recommend I be censured." Even as he spoke, he realized that without having consciously thought about Stark's offer to any great extent, he had already made the decision to accept it.

"What do you mean, you'll 'be censured?' " his father asked, his brow suddenly furrowing.

Boxer hesitated.

"Those two men on the *Mary-Ann* are responsible for what happened," his mother said in a low, tight voice.

Boxer rested the palms of his hands on the edge of the table. "Mister Sanchez is a very powerful man . . . He has many friends in Washington . . ." he let his voice trail off.

"If you are censured, aren't you going to try and fight it?" his father asked. "I sure as hell would." His father's face was red with anger. "I would fight the bastards!"

Boxer felt that he was getting in deeper than he wanted to. But he wanted to prepare his parents for the eventuality of it happening.

His guess was that as soon as he told Stark that he accepted the assignment, the board would issue its recommendation that he be censured; then whatever Stark wanted him to do, he'd do. "If I am censured," he said quietly, "I want the two of you to know that —"

"I have some money," his father offered. "for a good lawyer to handle your appeal . . . Can't you ask for an appeal, or a court-martial?"

Boxer shook his head. "The cards would have already been stacked against me."

"Is that what you were told in Washington?" his mother asked.

Boxer saw his way out and nodded. "Something like that."

"And what will happen to your career?" his father asked.

"I started off by saying that we could live with my divorce," Boxer answered, "but this is going to be a lot harder to live with for the two of you and for me and maybe even for Gwen and John."

"But you're innocent!" his mother suddenly cried out. "Why should you be branded guilty when you're innocent?" Tears streamed down her cheeks.

Boxer reached across the table and took hold of his mother's hand. "We're going to have to survive it," he said gently. "We don't have any other choice, Mom."

"But all the years you put in!" she sobbed. "What will happen to them? . . . You're too young to retire . . . You'll lose everything!"

He looked at his father.

His father misunderstood. "Maybe I could do something to help you," he said. "I still have friends at the *Times*."

"It wouldn't do any good," Boxer answered. With his free hand he took hold of his father's hand. "As long as the two of you know I'm innocent, I'll be able to deal with anything else that comes along."

"We'll be all right," his father said.

"Ma?" Boxer questioned.

She nodded and, using a paper napkin, wiped the tears from her eyes.

"I'll have to be going," Boxer said. "I want to shower and change my clothing before I meet Gwen and John."

"You have clothing here," his mother said.

Boxer nodded. "There are a few things that I must do at the base," he said.

61

"When will we see you again?" his father asked.

"I'll take the two of you to dinner on Thursday night," Boxer said, getting to his feet. "Okay?"

"That'll be fine," his mother answered.

"Fine with me too," his father said.

The three of them left the table and walked to the front door. Boxer hugged and kissed his mother.

"How will you get back to the base?" his mother asked.

"I'll take the ferry from Manhattan," he answered. "There's a bus that runs from the ferry terminal to the base," he answered.

His mother nodded, stepped back and bit her lower lip.

"You give Gwen and John a kiss for me," his father said, as he helped him into his coat.

"I will," Boxer said, hugging his father. "You take care of Mom and yourself. You look very tired."

They held on to one another for a few moments.

"I meant what I said about the money," his father said in a choked whisper.

Boxer shook his head. "The money wouldn't help, Dad," he said. "Use it for you and Mom." He separated from his father and opened the door. "I'll call you and set something up for Thursday night." Then he hurried down the steps, turned, stopped and said, "Go inside . . . It's too cold to be standing in an open doorway . . . Go on, Dad, take Mom inside."

The door slowly closed; then he saw them looking at him from the living room window. He waved and feeling miserable about the pain he had just caused them, he turned and walked rapidly down the deserted street.

By nightfall the weather changed: the temperature dropped and it started to snow. Just before Boxer left the base to visit John and Gwen, he phoned Cynthia.

He told her, "I should be back in Washington within a week."

"For how long?" she asked.

"Don't know," Boxer answered. "But we should have a few days together."

"I'd like that," Cynthia said. "I'd like that very much."

Boxer said goodby to her and hurried to the bus that would take him to the ferry terminal.

The ferry trip back to Manhattan took fifty minutes, instead of the usual twenty-seven. And the subway uptown stopped several times because the doors didn't close properly.

Earlier in the day, when he had spoken to Gwen, she had told him she'd prepare dinner and she had asked him to please be on time. Dinner had been set for seven-thirty. It was already eight-fifteen and he was just entering the lobby of the apartment house where Gwen and John lived.

The uniformed doorman asked Boxer for his name and whom he was going to visit.

"You may go up, sir," the doorman said, after speaking with either Gwen or John on the phone. "It's apartment twenty-four C."

Boxer nodded and a short while later, he was pushing the apartment's buzzer.

The door opened and John flung himself into Boxer's arms. "I thought you weren't going to come," the boy said. "I thought maybe the snow and all would stop you."

Boxer eased his son down. "The snow and all just made me late," he explained.

John took hold of his father's hand and pulled him across the threshold.

"Hey," Boxer laughed, "take it easy . . . You're strong . . . Let me take a good look at you." John was taller than he remembered and his features were more Gwen's than his. "You look great, just great."

"Take your father's coat," Gwen said, from the doorway between the dining and the living room.

Boxer looked at her.

She was wearing a pale blue sweater and dark blue slacks. A dark blue headband held her long blonde hair in place. He still found her beautiful.

"Do I pass inspection?" she asked.

"Always did," Boxer answered, handing his hat and coat to his son.

She started for the kitchen. "Ten more minutes," she said, "and we would have started without you . . . John has school tomorrow morning and I have a nine o'clock appointment at the studio."

Boxer walked into the dining room. The table, complete with two lit candles, was set for three. Aware of the savory odors coming from the kitchen, he asked, "What are we having for dinner?"

"A dinner Italiano," Gwen answered.

Boxer nodded appreciatively. Gwen was not only an excellent cook, she was excellent at everything she did. If she couldn't do something with facility, she didn't do it. She even made love that way. He shook himself free of that thought and went to the sliding door that overlooked the terrace. Snow had already blanketed the concrete floor and none of the nearby buildings were visible, although the lights from their windows created weird looking patches of yellow that appeared to be suspended in the darkness.

John came alongside of him. "I'm sorry, Dad," he said.

Boxer put his arm around his son's shoulders. "Thanks," he responded softly.

"All right you men," Gwen called, "to the table . . . John did you wash your hands?"

"Before Dad came," the boy answered.

"Jack you sit at the head of the table," Gwen said, coming into the dining room with a large pan filled with sizzling lasagna. "John sit on your father's right."

"Bossy, isn't she?" Boxer said, winking broadly at his son.

"That wasn't funny!" Gwen exclaimed, with an angry frown quickly creasing her forehead.

Boxer accepted the rebuke without comment. But he had the distinct feeling Gwen was more touchy than usual.

"Are you going to spend the night here?" John asked. "There's an extra bed in my room."

It was the wrong question at the wrong time. "I have a lot of paper work to do back on the boat," Boxer said, fielding the question with a lie.

Gwen returned from the kitchen a second time with a large platter of broccoli. "Now for the wine," she said and went to the refrigerator for the bottle. "I hope you like it," she said, handing the bottle and opener to Boxer. "Red wine usually goes with lasagna, but I prefer a white."

"It'll be fine," Boxer answered, pouring wine into Gwen's glass; then into his own and finally a bit into John's glass. "What shall we toast to?" he asked.

"You make the toast, Dad," John said.

Boxer glanced at Gwen.

She nodded.

"To the crew of the *Sting Ray*, may they always have good sailing!"

The three of them drank.

"Mom and Dad send their love," Boxer said, cutting a piece of the lasagna for Gwen. "There's sausage in it!"

"I remembered that's the way you like it," Gwen responded.

Boxer nodded, cut a portion of the lasagna for John and then for himself. "This is the second time today I've had something to eat that I really like. Mom made one of her special omelets. Stuffed with all sorts of goodies."

"Don't you get the food you like aboard the boat?" John asked.

"Yes, but it's nothing like a home cooked meal," Boxer answered.

Gwen finished her wine and asked for more.

Boxer asked them what they were planning to do for Christmas.

"That's something I wanted to talk to you about," Gwen answered. "But it can wait until later."

Boxer understood that was her way of telling him that she didn't want John to hear the conversation. He turned to his son and asked, "How's school coming along?" John was an excellent student.

Hesitantly, the boy answered, "Okay, I guess."

"Why the 'I guess?' "

John cast his eyes down at his plate.

"Go on," Gwen said, "tell him."

"Mom you said you wouldn't—"

"If anything is wrong," Boxer said, "I want to know about it."

"It's because of that woman—the reporter who was aboard the *Mary-Ann*," Gwen said. "What's her name?"

"Kimble . . . Tracy Kimble," Boxer said tightly. "I didn't know she was being picked up by the New York papers."

"Only since she started to write about the accident," Gwen said. "She has even been on some of the morning talk shows. Did you know the woman in the biblical sense?"

Boxer shook his head. "The first night I saw her was the night of the accident."

"She hates you, or so it would seem from the way she writes about you."

"I have that effect on some women," he said. Then he turned to John and asked, "Now you tell me what has been happening at school?

"Must I?"

"I want to help you, if I can," Boxer answered.

"Some of the kids —"

"Go on, son," Boxer said.

"Some of the kids said you were drunk and that's why those men got killed."

Boxer shook his head. Before the past few minutes, he hadn't realized how much John had been affected by the accident and how much more he would be affected by what would happen in the next few days. "First," Boxer said, "let me tell you that I wasn't drunk; secondly, one of my best friends was killed in that crash."

"Dad, I didn't believe —"

Boxer held up his hand. "John, I know you didn't . . . But listen to me . . . Listen very carefully to what I say . . ." Boxer paused to collect his thoughts. He had to find the right words to prepare his son for what might happen in the next few days. "Sometimes things happen and we don't understand why they happen. But we have to accept whatever does happen. We may not like it, we may even hate it, but we have to accept it. . . ."

John nodded.

"Are you trying to tell him that you may be found guilty?" Gwen asked.

"The board isn't a court-martial," Boxer answered. "It can only make recommendations."

"What kind of recommendations?" Gwen wanted to know.

"I can be censured, or they can recommend that I stand trial for dereliction of duty . . . But I don't think they'll go that far." It pained him to see the expression of disbelief come into Gwen's face.

"But your career . . . Your whole life has been the Navy!"

He nodded.

"I don't understand," she said. "Your world is about to come crashing down and you're calmly sitting there, talking about it as if it's some trivial matter."

66

"I assure you," he said softly, "It's not at all trivial. But becoming hysterical about it, won't change it."

"But what are you going to do, if you're censured?" Gwen asked. "That'd mean the end of your career."

Boxer took another sip of wine before he said, "I'll make do . . . That'll be all I'll be able to do."

"That's not much of an answer," Gwen said derisively.

Boxer shrugged uncomfortably. He resented having to be on the defensive, though he realized that it probably would have to be his position for some time to come.

"It's not like you to roll over belly up," Gwen said. She shook her head. "Something isn't right . . . Something—"

"Leave it alone, Gwen!" Boxer snapped. "It's the Navy. You never wanted to understand it in the past and now isn't the best time to try. Whatever happens," he said, softening his tone, "I'll make do."

For several moments, no one spoke. But John broke the silence by asking, "Dad, don't you like Mom anymore?"

Boxer looked at his son; then at Gwen, who was having trouble lifting her glass of wine because her hand was trembling. "I love the two of you," he said, moving his eyes back to the boy.

"Dad loves you," Gwen commented. "He loves you very much."

Boxer reached over and tousled his son's hair. "After dinner, how about watching TV with me."

"Mom, can I do that?" John asked.

"Have you finished your homework?"

"I did it this afternoon, as soon as I came home from school."

"Only until ten o'clock," Gwen said.

"Please, Mom, 'till ten-thirty?"

"Ten . . . You have to get up early for school tomorrow . . . Now who wants ice cream? . . . I have vanilla, strawberry and rum raisin . . . I also have expresso for us, Jack, with anisette."

"Fine," Boxer answered. "And I'll have some of that rum raisin ice cream."

"Coming up!" Gwen exclaimed cheerfully, as she left the table.

By ten thirty, John was asleep and Boxer was sitting in the living room, watching the end of a news program. That there was nothing about him or the *Sting Ray*, pleased him and he was about to go to the wooden bar cart to pour himself a shot glass of scotch, when Gwen came into the room.

"We have to talk," she said, settling into an easy chair opposite Boxer.

"Okay," he answered, "we'll talk . . . But first I want to get a scotch . . . Do you want one?"

Gwen shook her head.

"I'm listening," Boxer said, settling down in the chair he'd previously occupied.

"I'm going away with someone for Christmas," she said, folding her hands on her lap.

"Oh!" Boxer downed half his drink.

"I'm going to take John with us," she said. "I'm only telling you this because you asked if John was here when you called a few nights ago."

Boxer nodded. "I'm listening," he said.

"Jack, I want to live with him."

"Does he have a name?" Boxer asked tightly.

"Paul . . . I want John to get to know him. And I want you to understand . . . I want to try to have a relationship with Paul. If it works out, I'll marry him."

Boxer finished his drink and went for another. He understood why Gwen appeared to be edgy. "I can't stop you, can I?" he said, coming back from the bar cart again. Only this time he didn't sit down. "You're old enough to make your own mistakes, right?"

Gwen stood up. "I don't ask you about the women you sleep with," she said. "I don't ask—"

"I haven't asked you about any of the men you've fucked. I haven't even asked you about Paul . . . You decided to tell me about him without me asking."

"Because of John," she said moving to the far side of the room. "I told you because of John."

"Thanks . . . Thanks loads . . . It makes me feel real good to know that my son will soon know his mother is fucking a strange man."

"He doesn't know—"

"Maybe he doesn't now," Boxer said. "But he'll sure as hell know all about it as soon as he realizes you and your Paul are in bed together."

"You're impossible!"

"I guess I am," Boxer said. He put the empty shot glass down on the table. "I had better be going . . . Thanks for a wonderful dinner and the great news about you and Paul." He started for the hall closet, where John had put his coat and hat.

Gwen went after him. "Can't you believe that I might be in love with him?" she asked, raising her voice.

"No."

"Why not, damn you? Why the hell not?"

"Because if you did love him, you'd marry him now . . . You wouldn't have to play at being married to find out if it would work."

"I don't want to make the same mistake twice," Gwen answered.

Boxer put on his coat and hat and went to the door.

"And this is the way you want to leave it?" Gwen asked.

"No," he said. "No . . . I want you to know that I love you and — "

"Jack, I've got to do something with the rest of my life . . . I know you love me and I know that in bed we're great but what else do we have?"

"John for starters and a few more things," Boxer answered. "But you — ah what the hell is the use!" He opened the door and stalked out of the apartment, slamming the door behind him. He was angry and hurt. He had tried to stop loving her, but he couldn't. Maybe this time he could. . . .

5

When the board of inquiry resumed hearing additional testimony from the crews of the *Sting Ray* and the *Mary-Ann*, Admiral D'Arcy went out of his way several times to point out to the other members of the board that of the two officers on the bridge of the *Sting Ray* at the time of the accident, Boxer was the senior and therefore the more experienced. "The question," D'Arcy said, "at the end of the day, "is whether or not Commander Boxer perceived the danger from the *Mary-Ann* soon enough to take the necessary evasive maneuvers to avoid having the *Sting Ray* collide with the *Mary-Ann*?"

D'Arcy, not too subtly, had turned the accident around: now the *Sting Ray* had collided with the *Mary-Ann* . . . Boxer was furious, but there was nothing he could do. At the end of the day's hearings, he was exhausted and too depressed to do anything else but return to his quarters aboard the *Sting Ray* and brood about the events of the day and his argument the night before with Gwen.

At ten o'clock, Harris and Cowly came by.

"How about finishing this day with a few drinks at the Wardroom," Harris suggested.

Boxer waved the suggestion aside. "I'd really be lousy company," he said.

"That's just it, sir," Cowly offered, "all of us would be lousy company . . . You know the old saying, 'Misery loves company.' "

Boxer managed a smile.

"Com'on," Harris urged. "I bet you didn't bother eating dinner."

"Wasn't hungry," Boxer answered.

"We could have something in the Wardroom . . . A couple of burgers . . . Come on, Captain!"

"Okay . . . Okay . . . I'll go," Boxer answered.

A few minutes later the three of them left the *Sting Ray* and walked out of the front gate. Despite the fact that their breath steamed in the cold air, the night was clear. They walked quickly and without speaking to one another.

When they reached the Wardroom, Boxer found several members of the *Sting Ray*'s crew there. They greeted him warmly; then he, Harris and Cowly slid into an empty booth. When the waitress came to the table, each of them ordered a beer and a hamburger deluxe.

"Put lots of pickles on mine," Cowly said.

"Mine too," Boxer added. He was glad now that Harris and Cowly had come for him. He wasn't feeling nearly as down as he had.

They spoke about Christmas and Harris said, "I think I'm going to go home and take the wife down to Florida for a few days. Soak up some sun and just do nothing."

Cowly said he wanted to get in a few days of skiing and might even fly out to Colorado to do it.

"I'm not sure what I'm going to do," Boxer said truthfully. He wasn't at all sure he'd be able to take the time off. Stark might want him to begin his new assignment immediately. "But if I get the time off, I'm sure I'll think of something."

The waitress returned with their beers. "The hamburgers will be ready in a couple of minutes," she assured them.

"Not to rush," Harris said. "We're slow drinkers."

When she was gone, Cowly suggested to Boxer that he try skiing. "It's really great skipper, especially that time called 'apres skiing'— you know when all the guys and the women get together and—"

"And I almost believed you were really into skiing," Harris said. "And now I find out that skiing is just a means to an end; it's a way to get you into what you really want to get into: some lovely looking woman's warm and juicy cunt."

"That's only part of it," Cowly admitted with a wry smile. "The other part is the skiing."

"Do you believe that, skipper?" Harris asked.

"Sure, the way I believe in Santa Claus," Boxer answered.

"Three hamburgers," the waitress announced, returning to the table. "Two with lots of pickles." She set the three plates down on

71

the table. "Anymore brews?"

"Another round," Boxer said.

The waitress flashed him a big smile and left.

"Now there's something you might try," Harris said to Cowly. "She looks like she might be willing to give you what you want and you wouldn't have to go flying off to Colorado to get it . . . You'd sure be saving a hell of a lot of money."

"I've already thought about asking her when she gets finished working," he said.

Boxer nodded and lifted his burger, bit into it. Harris and Cowly did the same.

"Now why can't we get Cook to make his burgers this way aboard the *Sting Ray*?" Harris asked.

"Or the fries?" Cowly questioned.

Boxer shrugged. "Maybe it's a matter of love," he answered and took another bite of his burger. Suddenly he realized he was looking at a TV screen and Sanchez was on it. He was being interviewed by Robb Downs, host of the late night talk show, People In The News.

Boxer put his burger down on the plate. He had difficulty swallowing what was in his mouth. He managed to do it and then he took a long drink of beer. "Listen, you guys," he said, "stay here. I want to catch a few minutes of TV."

Harris turned and looked at the screen and nodded.

"I'll be back," Boxer said, leaving the booth. He went up to the bar and stood close to the TV.

"And now ladies and gentlemen, we have with us Senor Julio Sanchez, the owner of the yacht *Mary-Ann*. Senor Sanchez is reputed to one of the world's richest men with holdings in oil, steel and electronics. His yacht, the *Mary-Ann* was involved in a collision with the American submarine *Sting Ray*. That accident caused the death of five members of the *Sting Ray*'s crew. A board of inquiry is presently investigating the circumstances of that unfortunate accident. Senor Sanchez will be at the investigation tomorrow morning . . . Senor Sanchez, can you tell us what you'll be saying to the board of inquiry about the accident?"

Sanchez moved slightly forward and said, "Because I am a foreign national I cannot be made to testify but in the spirit of justice I don't see that I have any choice. No officer, not even one in your

Navy, has the right to board a foreign ship and seize another country's seamen. If I remember my history correctly, your war of eighteen twelve was fought to secure for your country's ships the right to sail in any part of the world without fear of search or seizure." Then with a totally ingratiating smile, he added, "I feel very much like a mouse who believes in justice enough to tweak the nose of the tiger to get it."

"And what to your way of thinking would be justice?" Downs asked.

"I'll leave that to the officers who sit on the board," he answered with a toothy smile. "I'm sure they know your country's history as well as I do."

"Was the captain of the *Sting Ray* responsible for the accident?" Downs asked.

"Again I do not think that my opinion is important . . . five American seamen are dead . . . If there's any culpability for that tragedy, then the members of the board of inquiry will be judicious enough to place it where it belongs, even if it rests with Commander Jack Boxer."

"Thank you Senor Julio Sanchez for coming here tonight," Downs said.

"My pleasure," Sanchez replied.

The camera cut away from the interviewer and a commercial filled the screen.

Boxer stood very still. He held the edge of the bar so tightly his knuckles turned white.

"Com' on skipper," one of the crewmen from the *Sting Ray* said, "Mister Harris and Mister Cowly are waiting for you."

Boxer looked at him and nodded. "Thanks, Mahony." He let go of the bar.

Suddenly a man at the bar said to his companion, "That Captain Boxer is a joker . . . The guy should get the fuckin' book thrown at him . . . I mean, he's responsible—"

"Mister," Mahony said, "better button your lip or—"

"Who the fuck do you think you're talking to?" the man, growled. He got off the stool.

"It's all right," Boxer said, looking at the man. "Let me buy you a drink."

A semicircle of men quickly formed around Boxer, Mahony, the man and his companion.

"What the hell is it your business?" the man responded. "Nobody tells me to button my lip . . . Nobody!"

Boxer's blood began to race. "What about someone telling you to sit down, do you think you'd be smart enough to do it?"

"What the fuck —"

"Sit down," Boxer ordered, his voice flat with anger. "Sit down before —"

The man threw a punch.

Boxer blocked the blow. He crouched and delivered a driving right to the man's stomach followed by a savage left hook to his jaw. The man dropped to the floor. "Take your friend outside," Boxer said to the man's companion. "The fresh air will make him feel better."

Several of the men from the *Sting Ray* slapped Boxer on the back. "Didn't know you could fight like that," Mahony said. "Man, you moved like a damn cat!"

"Okay guys," Boxer told them, "all this flattery will get you one drink on me . . . One drink, Mike, for each of my men . . . Now let me get back to the booth and finish my burger!"

Boxer sat down. He was exhausted. He hadn't brawled like that since he was a junior officer.

The waitress came back to the table. "Mike says you three guys have a drink on the house comin'," she said.

"Chivas," Harris told her.

"Old Turkey, Bourbon," Cowly said.

"Vodka," Boxer ordered. "Make it a hundred proof on the rocks."

When she left the table, Cowly asked, "What do you guys think about her tits? I mean are they real or padded?"

"Padded," Harris said. "They stand out too straight to be real."

"What do you think skipper?" Cowly asked.

"About what?" Boxer asked. Involved with his own thoughts, he hadn't been listening to the conversation. He had almost reached the conclusion the pressure was too much for him. He couldn't play act as well as he thought he could. It didn't seem quite as difficult to do when Stark had told him about it. And the really hard part was yet to come!

"The waitress's tits . . . Do you think they're real, or padded?

74

Harris thinks they're padded. I think they're all hers."

Boxer shook his head. "I'm sorry . . . I told you before we went out that I'd probably be lousy company."

"Anyway you were true to your word," Harris commented with a straight face.

Boxer smiled. "Listen. I don't feel like a vodka. I'm going back to the boat. You guys stay here and finish your drinks."

"We'll go —" Harris began.

"I'm okay," Boxer said. "I just have some heavy thinking to do and I can't do it with the two of you trying to decide whether the waitress's boobs are padded." He stood up, put on his coat and hat and dropped a ten dollar bill on the table. "That should cover the burger and the two brews, with something left over for the waitress."

"Sure will," Cowly said.

Boxer exchanged goodnights with them, walked quickly to the door and stepped into the cold, clear night.

As soon as Boxer cleared the room, Harris was on his feet.

"What's up?" Cowly asked.

"I'm not going to let him go back alone," Harris answered. "He just might never make it back to the boat." He went to the table where Mahony and some of the other men from the *Sting Ray* were drinking. "The skipper needs an escort to shadow him until he passes through the base's front gate."

"How many do you need?" Mahony asked.

"Two . . . three would be better."

The four men at the table stood up.

"Thanks," Harris said. "Just tail him . . . If he sees you, he'll probably think you're going back to the base."

"Might as well," one of the other men commented. "I'm tired and it's late."

The other men agreed. They put on their coats and hats.

"Don't worry about your tab," Harris told them. "Mister Cowly and I will pick it up."

The men thanked him and left.

Harris returned to the table. "We'll split their check," he said.

Cowly nodded.

"As the old saying goes, 'An ounce of protection is worth a pound of cure.' The skipper doesn't need any more bruises, he has been hurt enough."

"What do you think will happen to him?" Cowly asked.

"I don't know . . . But it doesn't seem to be good . . . D'Arcy did a real number on him today."

"Maybe it'll go better tomorrow," Cowly offered.

"I doubt it . . . It will probably be worse," Harris said.

"The waitress is coming back with our drinks," Cowly announced.

"Good, I could use one."

"To get back to the subject of her tits, I'm going to ask her," Cowly said.

"You do that!" Harris laughed.

"I will . . . I most certainly will."

The following morning came cold, windy and gray with the promise of snow.

Boxer walked quickly to the base headquarters where the inquiry was being held. He had spent a restless night thinking about the inquiry and Gwen. And he had come to a decision about each. As far as the inquiry went, he couldn't afford to care whatever Sanchez, or Kimble, or for that matter whatever anyone else said about his culpability. Because of his new assignment, he couldn't let it matter. And as for Gwen? Well, he overreacted. She had a right to sleep with whomever she pleased. After all, he did and never thought twice about it. . . .

Feeling better about the inquiry since it began, Boxer walked resolutely up the steps and a short while later sat down in his assigned seat and waited for the proceedings to begin.

Admiral D'Arcy asked Cowly to repeat his previous testimony; then he asked Boxer to do the same.

Harris was called back by one of the board's members and asked, "Would you tell the board, Commander, the number and sequence of commands that you heard being transmitted from the bridge to the engine room immediately prior to the crash?"

"If I remember correctly," Harris said, "the first command was full speed ahead on starboard engines one and two and half speed reverse on port engines one and two; then after a lapse of perhaps a forty-five seconds to a minute, full speed was ordered."

"And who gave those commands?"

"Lieutenant Cowly, sir."

"Then as the tapes indicate, the first order given by Commander Boxer is to rig for a crash."

"Yes, sir."

Harris was excused and the helmsman was questioned again.

"Chief," Admiral D'Arcy asked, "who gave you the last order before the crash and what was that order?"

"Mister Cowly told me to hold the *Sting Ray* steady at three hundred degrees, sir."

"Then what happened?"

"Mister Cowly ordered 'full speed ahead' and then he shouted, 'she's going to ram us!' "

"And up until that moment Commander Boxer did and said nothing?"

"Yes, sir."

Boxer wondered why the board was going through all of this, when everything was on tape?

Admiral D'Arcy called Luis Revera to give testimony.

Surprised, Boxer turned to look at Revera. With him was Diaz. The two of them looked like prosperous businessmen. Boxer hadn't seen either of them since the night of the crash.

Through an interpreter, Revera said, "There's nothing to tell. The submarine cut in front of the *Mary-Ann* . . . There was no time to change course."

When Juan Diaz was called to give testimony, he repeated the same lie.

But the highlight of the day came when Sanchez appeared before the board and repeated essentially what he had said the previous night on the Robb Downs show. But instead of referring to himself as the "mouse who tweaked the tiger's nose," he said, "I came here to seek justice, to have my countrymen vindicated and I am sure, gentlemen, that my testimony here today will not have been in vain."

For several moments the room was very quiet, then Admiral D'Arcy said, "On behalf of my country and this board, I thank you for volunteering to come here and testify."

Sanchez nodded respectfully, turned and walked toward the door of the room.

"This board of inquiry will adjourn to consider its recommendations," D'Arcy announced. "Commander Boxer, you will hold yourself in readiness to appear before this board when it reconvenes."

"Yes, sir," Boxer answered.

D'Arcy rapped three times with the gavel and said, "This board of inquiry stands adjourned until further notice."

Boxer uttered a sigh of relief . . . It was over; he'd probably be censured. The board might even recommend a reduction in rank. He'd become the phantom the CNO wanted . . .

He left the room with Harris and Cowly at his side. The other officers and crewmen from the *Sting Ray* brought up the rear. Boxer found himself wondering how many of them would be aboard the *Shark* with him?

6

"All right," Admiral Stark said, after handing Boxer a cigar, "let's get certain things out of the way first; then we can get on with the real business . . . The board of inquiry will recommend that you be censured."

"I thought they would," Boxer said, lighting up.

"And that you be reduced in rank."

Boxer nodded. "I figured that might be a possibility."

"The Navy, of course, will let both recommendations hang. But in the meantime, you will resign, or to be more precise, you will put your papers in, so that they'll be on file, should anyone ever want to see them. By the way, every man from the *Sting Ray* who goes with you to the *Shark* will also have to go through the charade of resigning. The Navy will accept your resignation. Soon afterward you will apply for and be hired by the Thomas W. Williams Company, owner of the newly commissioned super tanker *Tecumseh* — you know who Tecumseh was?"

"An Indian chief," Boxer answered.

Stark smiled, leaned forward and pointing his as yet unlit cigar at Boxer, he said, "On the company books you'll be the captain of the *Tecumseh*."

"There's another company involved, isn't there?" Boxer asked.

Stark took time to light his cigar before he answered. "The Williams Company is a ghost company," he explained. "It doesn't even exist in the phone book . . . Most of your missions will be closely coordinated with the real owners of the *Tecumseh*."

"Will that be our cover?" Boxer asked.

"Yes and the cover for the *Shark* too," Stark said. "The *Tecumseh* is large enough to hold the *Shark* inside of her and still have room for a masking cargo of oil."

Boxer raised his eyebrows.

"The *Shark* will come in under the *Tecumseh* and because you will now be able to see outside, you'll be able to bring her inside with no trouble at all. Believe it or not, the idea comes from an old James Bond film."

Boxer shook his head. "Has any one done it . . . I mean bring a boat into the *Tecumseh*?"

"You'll be the first. Your boat will have the eyes, remember?"

"Our engineers think it can be done with the two vessels underway, or at the very least with the *Tecumseh* moving at about fifteen knots, which by the way is her cruising speed. She's been designed to appear to burn the usual bunker number two oil. But in reality she's driven by a highly advanced version of the W-sixteen nuclear power system."

This time Boxer did let out a low whistle. "That's the power plant for the big carriers."

"And the *Tecumseh*," Stark said. "Of course there'll be a regular crew aboard. But they'll be company men. But in any crisis situation, you will have the final say."

"What about my fighting team?" Boxer asked, flicking ash from the end of the cigar into an ashtray on Stark's desk.

"It'll be comprised of volunteers from all of the services," Stark explained. "In a month or so we hope to have you meet the team's senior officer. He will, of course, be responsible to you."

Boxer nodded.

"There's one more thing that you should know about," Stark said, "everything else you'll learn in the next few months. By the way your orders have been cut reassigning you to BuPers, where until you resign, you'll be Admiral Quinn's aide. He won't ask you to do anything. But you must be carried somewhere and it will give you a good reason to take several long trips, for the admiral of course, which will enable you to familiarize yourself with the *Shark*."

"Does Admiral Quinn know about this project?"

"No and he won't. He has no need to know. What he will know is what everyone else will know."

"He has a reputation for being—"

"A tough old sea dog, yes. That is why you'll be assigned to him.

He won't like it and most assuredly won't like you, especially when he's told not to assign any work to you."

"You're really not making it easy for me, are you?"

Stark shook his head. "After the holidays I want you to recruit those men you want from the *Sting Ray*. Tell them as much as they need to know in order to make an intelligent decision. I want a full crew assembled within three months, which is when the *Shark* should be ready for her first sea trials."

"Yes, sir," Boxer answered.

"The last thing I want to tell you today has to do with you and your assault team." He reached down, opened the side drawer of the desk and took out what seemed to be a scuba mask. "This device will enable your men to fight under water at depths of five hundred feet. How does that grab you?"

"I'm not at all sure," Boxer said. "I never thought we'd be called upon to do that."

"That and more," Stark responded. "This device extracts individual atoms of oxygen dissolved in the water. Your men will not have to wear air tanks. All they'll need is this small mask."

"What about the pressure at five hundred feet?" Boxer asked.

"I'm told by our scientists that the human body can function at that depth but will need time to depressurize upon reentering the *Shark*. Depressurization chambers have been built into her."

Boxer put the unlit cigar stub into the ashtray. "I'm going to want to try the mask out before I give it to my men," Boxer said.

"You'll have your opportunity. Probably within the next two or three weeks. There is one other item I want to mention to you."

Boxer couldn't resist and he said, "Now you're going to tell me that my men are going to be issued wings for short distance flights."

"Nothing like that, though it's a good idea, Captain," Stark said with a smile.

"Captain?" Boxer repeated.

"Of course that's not for public consumption. But that will be your new rank as of the first of the year and you will draw the pay that goes with the rank."

"Thank you, sir," Boxer said, thinking how very much the promotion would mean to his parents and son. Perhaps even to Gwen?

"You'll need the authority," Stark said. "All right, now you have

81

the picture of what will happen. Take the next few days off. Make it all of Christmas. D'Arcy says he'll reconvene the board on January second. After that you report here and from here you'll go to Quinn. Any questions, Captain?"

"Too many." Boxer replied. "But I'm sure they'll all be answered in time."

Stark stood up, extended his hand across the desk. "I'm goddamn glad you decided to come aboard."

Boxer got to his feet and shook Stark's hand. "I don't think I had much choice," he said with a smile.

"Given what you are and who you are, I don't see that you had any choice," Stark answered. "We are, I like to think, what we do."

Boxer agreed with a nod.

"You don't need me to walk you to the door," Stark said.

"No sir."

"See you after Christmas," Stark said.

Boxer turned and walked to the door, just before he opened it, Stark called out, "Don't look so damn pleased. You're supposed to be up shit creek without a fucking paddle. Look miserable, absolutely miserable!"

"Yes sir," Boxer answered. "But it's damn hard to look miserable when you've just been promoted to captain!"

"Miserable!" Stark shouted. "Miserable!"

Two days before Christmas Boxer went to see Gwen and John and give them their presents. He bought John a voice actuated typewriter, several video games and two books: one about the Vikings and the other was a novel about a dog named Dimitri.

John was thrilled and immediately asked if he could open them.

"It's okay with me," Boxer answered. "But you better ask you mother?"

"It's all right," Gwen said.

Before John started to unwrap his gifts, he went to the tree, picked up two boxes and handed them to Boxer. "For you, Dad," he said.

Boxer hugged his son. "I'll open them while you open yours," he said.

"There are presents for your mother and father," Gwen said.

"I'm sure they have something for you and John," he answered, unwrapping his gifts. "Hey, this is great!" he exclaimed, discovering a new chess set in the first box. "It's just wonderful!" He held up the knight and examined the carved figure. It was dressed in armor, complete with sword and spear.

"John saved for that for two whole years," Gwen told him.

Boxer felt a sudden tightness in his throat, cleared it and said, "He's a terrific boy. You're really doing a great job bringing him up."

Gwen nodded.

"Now let's see what this second box is all about," Boxer said, taking the wrapping off it. "A pipe!" he exclaimed. "A free form pipe." He hefted it. "It's light."

"You told me," John said, looking up from his typewriter, "that you like a light pipe."

"So I did," Boxer said, putting down his gift. He crossed the room, swept John up into his arms and hugged him fiercely to him. "Thanks son," he said. "Thanks!" Then he kissed him and putting the boy down, he looked at Gwen and said, "I have something for you." He recrossed the room, reached into his breast pocket, took out a thin square box and handed it to her.

She hesitated.

"Go on, take it," Boxer said.

"We don't exchange Christmas presents, remember?"

"This is only half a Christmas present," Boxer said with a laugh. "The other half is just a gift . . . a way of saying I'm sorry for—"

"No need to say it Jack," she said.

Boxer nodded. "Go ahead and open it," he said.

It took Gwen a few moments to unwrap the box and open it. "My God, Jack, pearls . . . A double string of matched pearls!" She held them in her hand. "They're exquisite!"

"Let me put them on," Jack said.

Gwen gave the pearls to him and turned around.

"There," Boxer said, closing the catch. "It's done!" His hands lingered on the back of her shoulders.

She reached up, drew them over her breasts and leaning back against him, she said, "I'm sorry I gave you such a hard time."

Boxer nuzzled her hair. "I love you, Gwen."

"There are times, believe me, that I wish you didn't."

"Now?"

"No not now," she answered. "But we can't stay like this much longer," and she started to move away from him.

Boxer let her go.

"I have some of last night's leftovers I could heat up for supper," Gwen said.

"Suppose we go out to a Chinese restaurant," Boxer suggested.

"Could we really?" John asked, leaving his gifts and going to where his mother was standing. "Mom, could we go?"

Gwen smiled. "Sure . . . Why not!"

"I think it's time you learned to eat with chopsticks," Boxer said, putting his arm around John's shoulders, as they left the apartment.

"I already know how to do that," the boy answered.

"Who taught you?"

"Mom," John answered proudly. "Mom taught me!"

Boxer put his free arm around Gwen's waist and gently squeezed her hip. "You know," he said, "it's been a while since I've felt so good . . . So very, very good!"

"Me too," John said. "What about you, Mom?"

"Me too," Gwen answered, purposely making her voice squeaky.

Laughing the three of them stepped into the elevator. . . .

Boxer spent Christmas eve and Christmas day with his parents. He bought each of them a Rolex watch. While he was with them, he walked a narrow line between the holiday spirit and the way he thought he should act, given the circumstances in which he was supposed to be.

For the remainder of the holidays, he was back in Washington. He saw Cynthia three times and spent the night with her twice. She was good company in and out of bed. Boxer liked her very much, but he wasn't in love with her. And he knew, sooner or later, he'd have to tell her that. The time came sooner than he had thought it would. It was Wednesday night, they had just finished having a wild, delicious session of sexual pleasure and were lying naked in each other's arms, when Cynthia said, "I think we should make this something more permanent. What do you think?"

He hadn't thought of their relationship going that way.

"I was thinking of asking you to come home with me for New Year's," she said.

"You mean like home in Virginia?" Boxer asked, disentangling himself from her and propping his head against the bed's headboard.

"Yes. I'd like you to meet my daughter and my parents."

"It won't work, Cynthia," he said quietly. "Not the way things are."

"You mean what will happen to you?" she asked.

"Something like that," Boxer answered. He had an out and he was going to use it. "I'm not going to walk away from the inquiry without—"

"That doesn't matter to me, Jack," she said. "What the inquiry does or doesn't do, doesn't matter. If you have to leave the Navy, it'll be tough for a while. But you'll make out. I know you will."

"Thanks for the vote of confidence," he said, gently squeezing her bare breast.

"Did the admiral give you any indication of what was going to happen?" she asked.

Boxer shook his head.

"For a while, I thought you'd be given command of the *Shark*," she said.

"Just because he briefed me?"

"I was almost sure," she told him. "But I guess the inquiry got in the way. I don't even know if the *Shark* exists anywhere, except on the spec sheets and in the drawings you've seen. It would be real weird if I knew so much about something that doesn't exist."

Boxer was at a loss for an answer. He was certain that Cynthia was one of the few people who had the need to know about the *Shark*. But if she didn't know that it really did exist, then the security surrounding its building was extremely tight.

"Getting back to us," Cynthia said, "you'd have a home here and all the comforts that go with it."

Boxer knew she meant sex.

"A woman can't give a man much more than I'm willing to give you. If you can think of something, tell me."

Aware that her voice had become more intense, Boxer didn't want to continue the conversation.

"The trouble is, Jack" she said in a low throaty voice, "is that I'm

85

falling in love with you."

He stroked her head.

"No answer?" she asked.

"I told you the first night we spent together," he said. "I'm still in love with my ex-wife."

"I didn't forget that," Cynthia answered. "But —" She cleared her throat. "I thought that we might have something more going than just fucking." Then she said, "I know I'm a good lay . . . God, I've been told that I was often enough. But I'm good for something else too. I could make a good wife to the man I loved."

"I don't doubt that," Boxer told her.

"But you don't love me! I'm just the woman you go to to get your rocks off," she said, suddenly sitting up.

He put his hand on her bare arm but she shook it off.

She left the bed and padded into the bathroom.

He could hear the toilet being flushed and the water running in the sink. He waited until she returned; then he said, "I think I better go."

"Where will you go? It's two o'clock in the morning. Besides," she added bitterly, "you've already had what you wanted." She climbed back into bed but stayed away from Boxer. "Go to sleep," she said, pulling the blanket over her head.

"Listen," Boxer said, turning his head toward her. "It's not you; it's me. I'm the guy with the hangup . . . I like you, Cynthia, I really do."

"I don't want to talk about it," she said, her voice muffled by the blanket.

Boxer ignored what she said. "Would it have been better if I had lied? Would you have wanted me to move in with you for my convenience and not because I was thinking of marrying you?"

Cynthia uttered a ragged sigh.

Boxer caressed her bare shoulder. "I want to be honest with you. I don't want to hurt you."

Suddenly she turned toward him. "I . . . I'm more than just tits and cunt . . . Much more!" Sobbing, she buried her face in his chest.

Boxer put his arms around her and held her very tight.

After a while, she said, "I've lost you, haven't I?"

"Only if you want to," Boxer answered softly. "We can still be

86

very good friends." He paused to carefully consider what he was going to say before he said, "Whether you still want to go to bed with me again — well, you have to decide that for yourself."

"Do you?"

"Yes . . . I like being with you in and out of bed. But if having sex with me is going to cause you problems, I'd rather we just remain friends."

"I'd be spiting myself, if I said I didn't want you inside of me."

Boxer kissed her gently on the forehead. He was sorry that he couldn't love her the way she wanted him to. He knew all too well the heartache of that situation. He had been and still was there with Gwen. . . .

On the day before New Year's, Boxer was awakened by the ringing of the phone.

Cynthia answered it; then handing it to him, she whispered, "Someone from the Navy."

"Commander Boxer here," Boxer said, pushing himself up against the headboard.

"Go ahead, Admiral," the voice on the other end said.

"This is Stark . . . Be at my office by oh eight hundred this morning," he said. "You and Major Thomas Redfern are going to do some swimming off the island of Bimini."

"Yes, sir."

"You'll be back some time tonight."

"I didn't have any special plans," Boxer answered.

"It's oh six-fifteen now," Stark said.

"I'll be there," Boxer responded.

The line went dead.

Boxer hung up and said, "I have to go to the Department . . . I'll be back late . . . Maybe too late to do any celebrating . . . Can you find a party to go to?"

Cynthia nodded. "Do you know why you were called?"

"Maybe it has something to do with the inquiry," he answered, from inside the bathroom. He shaved and showered and in a half hour he was fully dressed and on his way out of the door.

"Good luck!" Cynthia said from behind the door.

Boxer stopped, turned, took hold of her under the chin and

kissed her on the kips. "See you," he said and hurried away.

An hour after Boxer met Major Thomas Redfern, the two of them were on their way by jet to the attack carrier, *Stephen Decatur*, located ten miles off the southeast corner of Bimini.

Redfern was a tall rangy man, with a craggy face, black eyes and straight black hair. He spoke with a slow western twang and had a wry sense of humor, which Boxer discovered, when he said to Stark, "Admiral, I can't rightly say that I mind being called at oh six hundred in the mornin', but Sue-Ann does, especially if we're doin' what married folks . . . She is screaming mad at you. But she don't know it's you, so you're safe."

Stark looked confused.

"It's okay, Admiral, I said you were safe," Redfern said with an absolutely straight face. After that Boxer knew that he and Redfern would get along fine. . . .

The flight lasted an hour and during that time, Boxer and Redfern exchanged information about themselves.

Redfern was a full blooded Apache, whose great-great-great-grandfather was Geronimo. He was married fifteen years to his wife. He had a son graduating from high school and a daughter in her freshman year.

Boxer told him about John and Gwen and about his parents.

"I tell ya," Redfern said, "when the admiral told me what you're doin', I said that man has more guts than I have . . . I couldn't take the kind of rap you're takin'."

"Not much choice, if I want this assignment," Boxer answered.

"Know what you mean," Redfern said. "I had to resign from the Corps . . . Sure as hell wasn't easy for me to do that." Then he pulled out a leather pouch of chewing tobacco, pulled off a piece and handing the pouch to Boxer, he said, "Have a chaw . . . Nothin' like it to calm the jumps."

"You've got them too?" Boxer asked. He had been feeling jumpy himself about the dive.

Redfern nodded.

Boxer took a piece of the tobacco, stuffed it in his mouth and began to chew. He had chewed tobacco before but he couldn't remember when.

The plane made a perfect landing on the carrier's deck. Minutes later they were changing into wet suits for the dive.

"You go down easy," Lieutenant Jenkins, the diving officer, said. "There are frogmen at fifty foot intervals, all the way down to the bottom . . . On the bottom there's a deep diving rescue craft . . . You board it through its bottom hatch. Once you're inside, the operators will blow the water and start your decompression . . . Your ETA back here on deck is six hours from the time you enter the water . . . Any questions?"

Boxer shook his head.

"What about sharks?" Redfern asked.

"The frogmen will take care of any that become a problem," Jenkins said. "You just keep going down."

"If these gismos are supposed to allow a man to function at five hundred feet, maybe we should do some functioning down there beside just going down and climbing into the salvage craft," Boxer said.

Redfern agreed.

"I was told this was only to be a deep dive test," Jenkins said.

Boxer guessed that he hadn't been told anything about who was going to use the masks. "Okay," Boxer said, looking at Redfern, "deep dive test only . . . Okay?"

"Sure . . . Sure," Redfern answered. "We'll dive deep."

"Don't put these masks on until you're under water," Jenkins told them. "You clear them the same way you'd clear an ordinary scuba mask. The main thing you have to worry about is the rapture of the deep. If you begin to feel the slightest bit strange, signal one of the frogmen. If either of you see the other acting strange, stop the dive, signal a frogman and have him bring the man either up or down, depending how deep you are at the time. The frogmen have additional scuba breathing apparatus for you, should you need it."

At 1100 hours Boxer, Redfern and two sailors were lowered away from the deck of the carrier in a whaleboat. Ten minutes later they were over the dive area. One of the sailors was in radio communication with the dive officer. "Lieutenant Jenkins," he said, "says you can begin your dive whenever you're ready."

Boxer and Redfern put on a belt with sixty pound of lead weights attached to it and positioned themselves on the boat's gunwale for a backward flip.

"Now!" Boxer said, and flipped backward into the clear warm water. He went straight down, arched up, put the diving mask over his face and blew it clear. He looked toward the surface. The light was mottled. Almost directly above him was the gray shape of the whaleboat, a distance away was the huge dark mass of the *Decatur*'s hull.

Redfern came alongside and signaled he was going down.

Boxer nodded and arched over. With his hands flat against his sides, he moved his legs to propel himself down. He breathed normally and quickly discovered that he wasn't leaving a trail of bubbles behind him.

Boxer and Redfern descended together. They passed the first frogman at the fifty foot level and waved to him. He was hanging on to a line which made him look like some huge undersea flower attached to a very thin stalk.

At seventy-five feet, the light was diffuse. Boxer could still see it was bright at the surface. But where he and Redfern was it was blue; something like a summer sky before the clouds turn black and the thunderstorm comes.

They paused at the hundred foot level, made their way to the frogman and clung to the line for a couple of minutes.

When they resumed their dive, Boxer led the way. The water was significantly cooler than it had been. Now and then, in the murky distance, he could make out the almost black, streamlined shape of a shark.

At the two hundred foot level, Boxer slowed his downward movement and signaled Redfern to switch on the high intensity light each of them wore on their heads. Suddenly, two white cones pierced the dark water, becoming less intense some distance from them and completely disappearing farther on; it was as if the sea absorbed the light into itself.

Boxer had scubaed many times before, but always around the thirty to fifty foot depth. Always for pleasure off the coast of some tropical island, like Bimini. He and Gwen did some scuba diving off St. John, when they spent a vacation at Caneel Bay, the second year after they had been married. Those first few years together, he told himself, were good. Very good!

Suddenly Boxer realized that Redfern was signaling to him, pointing to the right. Boxer looked. Two huge blue sharks were caught in the merging cones of both their lights.

Redfern tapped Boxer on the arm and by making an ever decreasing circular motion with his right hand, he indicated the sharks were coming closer and closer.

Boxer looked at the depth gauge on his wrist. They were at two hundred and seventy-five feet: between the frogman at two hundred and fifty feet and three hundred feet. He couldn't tell if either one of them had spotted the sharks.

Redfern indicated the sharks had tightened their circles.

Boxer pointed to the knife strapped to his right leg.

Redfern nodded.

The two arched over and began to descend again.

Boxer was sorry he didn't insist on carrying a bang stick, or at least a high powered spear gun. The sharks worried him. He paused to look at them. They were still out there, following him and Redfern down.

At three hundred feet the water around them was dark blue. The cone of light from their high intensity lamps was squeezed even closer to them.

Boxer looked for the frogman but couldn't see him. The line from the buoy on the surface to the anchor on the bottom probably had been bowed by the currents. He turned to Redfern and signaled he was going to continue the dive.

Redfern nodded. He pointed to his knife and then to the left, indicating he was going to swim in that direction.

Boxer shook his head and pointed down.

Redfern waved goodby and began to slowly swim away.

Boxer realized what was happening. Something had gone wrong with Redfern's face mask. He wasn't getting enough oxygen. He was suffering from rapture of the deep. Boxer swam after him and grabbed hold of his leg.

Redfern pulled free and beat his chest with his fists. Then suddenly, he reached down, pulled his knife out of its rubber sheath and came at Boxer.

Boxer whirled away, dove down a few feet and tried to come up behind Redfern.

But Redfern turned and thrust the knife at him.

Boxer slid off to the right and caught a glimpse of the two sharks. They had moved closer. He pointed to them, hoping to divert Redfern, long enough to get the knife away from him.

Redfern slashed at him and missed.

Boxer grabbed hold of his wrist and bent it over his upraised knee.

Redfern struggled to free himself.

Boxer snapped his wrist.

Redfern winced with pain and released the knife. It dropped slowly into the gloom. With his good hand, he tried to rip off Boxer's face mask.

Boxer pushed away and arched back. He dove down a few feet and came up behind Redfern. He was breathing hard. He could feel the beads of sweat skid down his back.

Redfern seemed to be confused. He was thrashing violently, stabbing at phantoms with his broken wrist.

Boxer looked for the sharks. There were four now. And one of them had already assumed the attack position: its back was arched and its dorsal fins were pointing straight down. The shark suddenly stopped circling and swam straight for Redfern.

Using his arms and feet to plow through the water, Boxer placed himself between Redfern and the shark. The cone of light illuminated the shark.

The fish veered away.

Boxer was about to turn toward Redfern, when Redfern struck him on the back. The blow sent Boxer forward. Before he could recover, Redfern had come down on him, circling him with his legs and locking his neck firmly in the crook of his arm.

Boxer tried to free himself, but the more he struggled the tighter Redfern's hold became. Boxer was having difficulty breathing. He had to free himself, or Redfern would strangle him. He grabbed hold of Redfern's arm and tried to pry it open. He couldn't. Boxer reached down, took hold of his knife, brought it up and stabbed Redfern twice in the arm that held his neck.

Redfern released him.

Boxer swam some distance away from him. His back, neck and sides ached.

A shark came hurtling at them!

Boxer didn't have time to move and Redfern was looking at the blood coming out of his two wounds.

Suddenly there was a muffled explosion and the shark reared up and then began to drop, leaving a trail of blood in the water.

Boxer signaled the frogman that Redfern was in trouble. The two of them swam toward Redfern. To divert him, Boxer swam in front of him, while the frogman got behind him.

Another frogman swam into the cone of light.

Between the three of them they managed to put a regular scuba mask onto Redfern's face and got him to breathe a combination of oxygen and helium.

One of the frogmen signaled he was going up.

Boxer pointed to Redfern and to himself; then he pointed down.

The frogmen indicated they still had two hundred feet to go before they reached the diving craft.

Boxer nodded and signaled the frogmen to accompany him and Redfern down. Despite the near disaster, Boxer wanted to finish the dive.

Boxer sat on a chair next to Redfern's bed in the *Decatur*'s sickbay. The man looked pale and washed out. His broken wrist had been set and the two stab wounds had been bandaged.

"All the comforts of home," Redfern said, with a rueful smile. "But Sue-Ann is sure goin' to raise almighty hell 'bout missin' her New Year's party."

"Have you spoken to her?" Boxer asked.

Redfern nodded. "Ship's cap'n got me a radio phone hook up," he said. "But I couldn't tell anythin' much that'd calm her."

Boxer nodded. Gwen's reaction would have been the same if he still had been married to her.

"Listen," Redfern said, "I'd be much obliged if you dropped in on Sue-Ann tonight and just tell her I'm sorry as hell 'bout missin' her shindig. You'll have yourself a real good time. I didn't tell you this before, but her daddy is Senator Ross. Big Sam Ross from New Mexico."

Boxer gave a long, low whistle.

"I figured you'd know the name. Didn't tell you before, 'cause I didn't want you think I was pitchin' for points. Now will you go? There's goin' to be all sorts of government and society people there."

"Okay, I'll drop by," Boxer said.

"Man, I'm all tuckered out."

"You get some sleep," Boxer said, "and I'll be on my way." He started to stand.

"Sit a bit longer . . . I got somethin' to say to you."

Boxer sat down.

"The doc tol' me, you and the frogmen saved my life . . . if it weren't for you, the sharks—"

"Come on," Boxer exclaimed, "I didn't do anything you wouldn't have done for me."

Redfern shook his head. "Don't know that . . . You were tried an' not found wantin' . . . I don't ever remember sayin' this to any man, but you're about the best there is." He took hold of Boxer's hand with his good one. "A hundred an' fifty years ago, we'd have become blood brothers," he said with emotion. "But we don't have to mingle our blood to be brothers."

Boxer shook his head. "I always wanted a brother," he said, trying hard to keep the emotion he felt out of his voice.

"You don't have to want one any more," Redfern told him, as he let go of his hand.

"Thank you," Boxer said.

"Now you go back to shore an' have yourself a ball," Redfern said. "Remember now, visit Sue-Ann an' tell her I'll be home tomorrow, or the day after."

"Sure," Boxer answered, getting to his feet.

Redfern closed his eyes. "I'm tired . . . very tired."

"See you soon," Boxer said, standing.

"Sure," Redfern answered.

As Boxer walked out of the sickbay, he stopped one of the doctors on duty. "Doc, how's Major Redfern doing?"

"He'll be fine in a day or two," the doctor answered. "Right now he's not feeling too good . . . Probably very tired."

Boxer nodded.

"After he gets a good night's sleep," the doctor said, "he'll feel much better."

"Thanks, doc," Boxer said with a smile and hurried up to the main deck, where there was a small, twin engine jet waiting to fly him back to Washington. He had already spoken to Cynthia by radio telephone and again had told her to go to the party without him. He didn't feel much like partying, even though it was New

94

Year's Eve. All he intended to do was pay a visit to Redfern's wife: tell her Redfern was okay and then go back either to Cynthia's apartment, or his hotel room and sack out. Like Redfern said, Boxer repeated to himself, "I'm just plumb tuckered out . . ." He smiled and hurried out on to the flight deck.

By ten o'clock, Boxer arrived at Redfern's home, which was located in the Chevy Chase district of Maryland. The house was at the end of a cul-de-sac. It was a large two story structure with broad well manicured lawns all around it, that were appropriately decorated for the holidays.

The New Year's Eve party was in full swing. No one stopped him from entering the foyer. There were people everywhere. The men were dressed in tuxes and the women in evening gowns. Still in uniform, Boxer immediately felt out of place. He wanted to meet Sue-Ann, assure her that Thomas was all right and get out of there, as quickly as possible.

A servant carrying a tray of canapes was nearby. Boxer went up to her and said, "Would you please tell Mrs. Redfern that Commander Boxer would like to speak with her."

The woman gave him a questioning look.

"Now please," Boxer said. "I'll wait right here."

The woman nodded and went off.

Boxer used the time to look around. Never had he been in so large a house. On one side the foyer opened into an enormous dining room and on the other into a living room of equal size. A curved staircase led to the upper floor. It had a certain elegance about it that was usually associated with the South before the civil war.

"Commander, I was told you wanted to speak to me," Mrs. Redfern said, coming out of a nearby group of people. She was a dark haired woman, with an athletic body and a childish pout on her face. Like her husband she spoke with a decided western drawl.

"Tom asked me to stop by and—"

"He's just about ruined my party," she pouted.

"I'm sure he didn't have that intention," Boxer answered, wondering if Gwen's reaction would have been the same if she were in the same situation as Sue-Ann.

"I suppose you can't tell me why he couldn't be here?"

Boxer shook his head.

"I can't imagine what could be so important that it would keep him away from here," she said.

"Believe me Mrs. Redfern—"

She shook her head. "I know what you're going to say and no matter what you say, it won't stop me from being annoyed at Thomas . . . I have been planning this party for months."

Boxer remained silent.

"I'm sorry," she said. "I'm not in the least bit angry with you. Come in and have a drink. There's plenty of food. Please, join us."

Boxer hesitated. He was very tired and really didn't feel like partying, even though it was New Year's Eve.

"Please?"

"Just for a short while," Boxer answered.

"You just go in and have a good time," she said, taking his coat and hat. "I'll have these put in the coat room."

"Thank you Mrs. Redfern."

"Call me Sue-Ann . . . Everyone does."

"Fine, if you'll drop the commander and call me Jack."

"Jack it will be from now on," Sue-Ann said with a smile. "Now go and enjoy!"

Boxer walked into the dining room, saw the bar next to the French doors and headed straight for it.

"Scotch neat," he told the barkeep. He drank it quickly and asked for another. The incongruity of where he was and where he had been earlier in the afternoon was almost palpable and made him feel more the stranger than he ordinarily would have.

"Why the frown, Commander?"

Boxer half recognized the voice. He made a half turn to the right and found himself looking at Tracy Kimble. She wore a black, off the shoulder evening gown that revealed the tanned top of her right breast. From the way the gown clung to her, Boxer guessed she wasn't wearing much under it, or nothing at all.

"Do you like what you see?" she asked.

"The body, yes."

"But not the woman whose body it happens to be?"

"I'm not Christ," Boxer said. "I can't forgive the person who put a knife in my back."

"Even for tonight?"

"If you tell me why you did it?" Boxer answered.

"Let me get a drink," she said. "And I'll tell you." And she asked the barkeep for a "a very dry martini, with an onion."

Boxer looked at her: she was indeed a very attractive woman.

With the martini in her hand, Tracy turned to Boxer and said, "I was at the right place and the right time . . . I have been doing the gossip column for a few years and needed something to get me away from it. The accident was the perfect vehicle and you, Commander, provided me with someone to go after."

Boxer could feel his face flush.

"Now you're angry," she chided. "You asked me to tell you why I went after you and now that you know, you're angry."

"Five men died and one of them was a very good friend of mine," he said tightly.

"I'm not responsible for that," she answered. "And I'm truly sorry about the deaths of those men. Believe me, I am."

"Oddly enough," Boxer said, after a few moment's pause, during which he realized that she was being honest with him, "I do believe you."

"Truce then for tonight?" she asked.

"Truce," Boxer said, lifting his glass to touch hers.

"Now, tell me how come you're here?" she asked.

"Major Redfern asked me to stop by. He was unable to return home for the party."

"Then you were with him?" Tracy asked.

"I can only tell you that I saw him," Boxer answered.

"Before you ask," she said, "I know Sue-Ann from childhood. At college, we were sorority sisters and I was her maid of honor at her wedding. My father—well, there has been a long family relationship even before I was born. Telling you all of this has made me hungry and I happen to know they serve very fine food here," she said with a mischievous smile.

The mention of food made Boxer realize he too was hungry. Except for coffee and the two doughnuts he had after the dive, he hadn't eaten anything since breakfast. "You lead the way," he said, "but only if you promise not to write about what I eat or my table manners?"

"We have a truce, remember?"

"Sorry!" Boxer exclaimed, throwing up his hands.

"You're not and I don't blame you. But tonight we're just two people at a New Year's Eve party," she said.

Boxer liked what she said and the way she said it. He took her hand. "Thanks for coming over to me," he said. "I was feeling very much out of place."

"Was that why you were frowning?" she asked.

He didn't want to lie to her and he couldn't really tell her the truth. "I think," he explained choosing a line between the two extremes, "I was thinking about something profound and whenever I do that, I frown."

"Many people do that," she said.

Boxer didn't answer.

A short time later they were seated at a small table enjoying barbecued baby ribs and Texas style chile. Neither one of them mentioned the accident, or anything connected with it. Boxer didn't talk much, other than to tell her he was born and raised in Brooklyn and even as a boy, he had wanted to make the Navy his career.

Tracy did most of the talking.

Boxer discovered she came from a very wealthy family, which he had already guessed. She had a brother Luke, who was two years older than she and who was a professor of archaeology at Washington University. Her parents were divorced when she was ten years old and her father married a much younger woman.

"There are children from the marriage," Tracy said, "and I love them very much."

"As much as you love Luke?" Boxer asked.

"Don't be a smart ass," she replied. "The role doesn't fit you. Do you want to dance?"

"If you're willing to dance with a very tired man."

She looked hard at him. "You are tired, aren't you?"

Boxer nodded. "It has been a hard day."

"Okay, we'll skip the dancing. What would you like to do?"

"That's a leading question," Boxer said.

"Answer it."

Boxer's heart began to race. He took a deep breath. "Sleep quietly next to you with my head on your breasts."

She flushed.

"You asked," Boxer said.

98

She nodded. "So I did."

"I better go," Boxer told her. "I'm bushed."

"I'll go with you," she said. "I'm staying at a place just down the road. You didn't drive here from Washington, did you?"

Boxer shook his head. "I took a cab."

"Here are the keys to my car," she said. "It's an eggshell blue Jag. It's parked on the right side of the driveway as you come in. I'll be with you in a few minutes. I want to say good night to Sue-Ann."

"It's not even midnight yet. Won't she mind you leaving?"

"No . . . She'll ask me why and I'll tell her I'm going to go to bed with you."

"Are you really going to tell her that?" Boxer asked raising his eyebrows.

"Are you ashamed —"

"Not in the least," he said with a broad grin. "Not in the least!"

"Well, neither am I. See you in a few minutes."

Boxer watched her walk away from the table. In a few minutes he'd know whether she was wearing anything under that gown."

"And what did Sue-Ann say to you," Boxer asked, when Tracy joined him in the Jag.

"First things first," she answered. "You fit enough to drive, or do you want me to?"

"You drive," he answered, handing her the keys and sliding out from behind the wheel.

It took Tracy a couple of minutes to get behind the wheel and readjust the seat for her comfort. "Okay, we're off!" She switched on the ignition, put the lights on, released the hand brake and put the car in drive.

Boxer leaned back and closed his eyes. "You still haven't told me —"

"Sue-Ann just nodded and said, 'have a good time honey.' But I neglected to tell her how tired you are and what I'm really doing is helping a fellow human being and that the only 'good time' I'll have is watching a late night TV show, or reading the novel I brought along with me."

"You just didn't want to disillusion her."

"That's absolutely right. A woman has her reputation to protect,

...en if it's a slightly unsavory one."

Boxer opened one eye and looked at her. She was concentrating on the road, which was narrow and twisting. But he was positive she sensed what he was doing. He closed his eyes, waiting for her to say something else.

She didn't.

Boxer wasn't sure how to read what was happening. He was physically attracted to her. But no more than he might be to any attractive looking woman. He really didn't have strong feelings about going to bed with her, other than it would be nice to rest his head on her breasts. He knew what he wanted but he couldn't begin to guess what she wanted from him. There were other men at the party who would have been only too happy to go to bed with her. He was puzzled why she had chosen him . . .

"We're here," Tracy announced.

Boxer opened his eyes, just as they turned into a tree lined driveway. The place was an inn.

"Used to be a mill," Tracy explained. "The race is still there and in the summer, when the creek isn't frozen, the water wheel actually turns the mill stones. The owners grind their own flour and sell it."

Boxer made wordless sounds of appreciation. In a million years, he wouldn't have thought she'd be the kind of person to have any feeling for something like a restored mill.

"Let's go," Tracy said, already out of the door on her side.

Hand in hand they walked up to the front door. Tracy had a key and unlocked it.

The foyer was small. No one was there.

"My room is in the rear," Tracy said. "I have a lovely view of a large open field."

Boxer followed her.

"I always have the same room when I come here," she explained, opening the door and switching on the light.

The room was large; furnished in early American that included a stone fireplace in which there were the glowing red embers of a fire.

"I'll put some wood on the fire," she said, mindless of the fact that she was wearing a mink coat and an evening gown.

Boxer offered to do it.

"You just relax," she told him. "That's why you're here, isn't it?"

100

"That's why I'm here," he said with a nod. He took off his hat, coat and jacket and put them down on the chair.

"The bathroom is through that door in the corner," she said, laying wood on the brass andirons. "There are plenty of towels and the water is always hot."

Boxer went into the bathroom, stripped, showered and returned to the bedroom with a towel wrapped around his waist. The only light in the room came from the fireplace. He glanced at the bed: she had turned it down.

"I'll be out soon," she said, going toward the bathroom. "If you want a drink there are bottles of scotch and rye, glasses and ice on the desk."

Boxer helped himself to two fingers of scotch on the rocks. He moved to the bed, sat down and drank some of the scotch. The fire was going good and the room was pleasantly warm. He was seeing a side of Tracy that was very different from the one he encountered aboard the *Mary-Ann*, or for that matter, anywhere else. He finished his drink, put the glass down on the end table and pulled the blanket over him. He lay with his hands under his head and looked up at the underside of the canopy, where the wavering light from the fireplace made the shadows dance. He closed his eyes. His muscles ached more than before. The effort it had taken to subdue Redfern had been enormous, especially under two hundred and seventy five feet of water. He would recommend that the masks be equipped with radios to allow communication between individual divers. Hand signals weren't good enough and could easily be misunderstood. . . .

Boxer suddenly became aware of another body's warmth and the delicate scent of tea roses.

"You asleep?" Tracy asked.

"Almost."

"Still want to rest your head on my breasts?"

Boxer moved closer to her, moved a bit lower and pressed his face against her warm breasts. "Feels good," he said.

She ran her fingers through his hair. "Go to sleep," she told him.

Boxer gently caressed her back.

She put her thigh over his.

He could feel its warm inside surface against him and tufted kinkiness of her love mound rested against the head of his flaccid nis.

"Did you ever think you'd wind up in bed with me?" Tracy asked.

"No . . . But I did wonder what you'd be like in bed," he admitted.

"Really? . . . When?"

"Can't remember," Boxer said, moving his hand over the graceful curve of her buttock and imagining how he'd sculpt it, if he had the talent to do it.

"I like that," she said in a softer voice.

"When you gave your testimony to the board," Boxer said. "I'm sure that's when I thought about it." He trailed his fingers in the crack between the cheeks of her rump; then along the moist furrow between the lips of her vagina and then back up again to that small indentation at the base of her spine.

"I thought you wanted to sleep," she chided.

"I do," Boxer answered. "But first I have to unwind."

"And you think you're going to do that by winding me up?"

"Is that what I'm doing?" Boxer mumbled, still pretending to be half asleep.

She took hold of his penis and rubbed it gently over her love mound. "This should wake you and it up," she said. "My . . . My . . . How quickly you've become hard . . . Now since one part of you is very much awake, what about the rest of you, Jack?"

He raised his head from her breasts and brought his lips down on hers.

She opened her mouth and gave him her tongue.

His hand moved over her breasts and down her stomach.

"Kiss my breasts," she said, pressing his head down to them.

Boxer teased her nipple with his tongue and gently scored it with his teeth.

"Suck it!" she exclaimed. "Suck it hard . . . That's it . . . That's the way."

Boxer caressed the lips of her vagina and each time he touched her clit, she trembled and uttered a low moan . . . Her hand moved over his scrotum, along his penis and over its head. Her touch was light and tantalizing.

"You keep diddling me,' she said, "I'm going to come."

"I won't hold it against you," Boxer answered, kissing the hollow of her flat stomach. He guessed she kept in shape by going to a

102

gym or jogging. Maybe both. He found it strange that he could b.
making love to her and thinking about how she kept in shape. But
he knew he wasn't making love, he was having sex.

"Soixante-neuf?" she asked, in almost a whisper.

"Remember, I'm here for a rest cure," Boxer answered.

"You want to stop?"

"I didn't say that . . . I only said —"

Before he could finish, she sat up, turned around and straddling
him, put his penis in her mouth.

Boxer arched up, pushing more of his penis into her mouth,
while bringing her vagina against his lips. She was very wet and
smelled somewhat spicy.

Tracy pressed her bottom down on him.

He worked his tongue over her clit and long the inner edges of
the vagina.

She was licking his scrotum.

"That feels good," he told her.

"Play with my ass," she said.

Boxer used her own juices to lubricate his finger and pushed it
into her anus.

Her body trembled with pleasure.

"Move it in and out," she gasped.

He hesitated.

"Do it! . . . That way . . . Yes . . . Yes . . ." Suddenly she jerked
away from him and turning around, she said, "Let me ride you."

"Ride," Boxer answered.

She inserted his penis into her and leaned back, bracing herself
on her hands. "I want you deep in me," she said.

Boxer reached up and put his hands over her breasts. He was
aware that their shadows were on the wall opposite the bed and on
the canopy.

"I'm going to play with your balls," she said, moving slightly forward and putting one hand under her. "How does that feel?"

"Tell me how this feels first," Boxer answered, bringing her
breasts down to his mouth and sucking on one nipple and then the
other. "Or this," he added bringing his hand around her buttock
and teasing her anus with his finger.

She began to move.

Boxer thrust deep into her.

God, I love fucking!" she exclaimed.

...er used his free hand to stroke her clit.

Tracy eased her self down and let her nipples touch Boxer's chest. "I'm ready to explode," she said in a breathy voice.

"I'm not too far from there myself," Boxer answered.

She quickened her pace. "Your prick . . . My cunt . . ."

Boxer grabbed hold of her at the hips and in a moment, he had rolled her under him.

"Fuck me, Jack . . . Fuck, me!"

He quickened his pace.

She arched her body and threw her naked thighs around his flanks. "From the moment I saw you," she gasped, "I wanted you to fuck me."

Boxer moved his hand under her and pushed his forefinger into her anus.

She uttered a low cry of pleasure.

The fluttering contractions of her vagina along his penis felt like the movements of hundreds of pairs of lips.

"Fucking," she cried. "Fucking . . . Fucked!" Her body tensed and then began to tremble. "I'm coming . . . I'm coming." She threw her arms around his neck and forced his head down to her breasts.

Boxer's fluid gushed from him, giving him an exquisite sensation that began at his toes and roared its way up into his groin. Satisfied, he stretched out and rested his head on Tracy's warm breasts. The nipple of the right one was very close to his mouth. He moved it closer and his tongue to it.

"Now the two of us can sleep," Tracy said.

Boxer didn't answer. He closed his eyes and let sleep come. It came quickly. . . .

7

"Commander Jack Boxer," Admiral D'Arcy said, "please stand and hear the recommendations of this board of inquiry."

Boxer stood up. The room was filled with people, including the crew of the *Sting Ray*, media people and Tracy, whom he hadn't seen after she had driven him back to Washington on New Year's day.

"This board will recommend that in the light of the testimony given to its members that you be held responsible for the crash between the attack submarine *Sting Ray* and the yacht, the *Mary-Ann* on the night of—"

Boxer tuned out the rest of what D'Arcy was saying. He wasn't interested. From this moment, his life would be entirely different . . . It was almost as if D'Arcy was reciting an incantation whose purpose was to phantomize him.

"We will also recommend you be reduced in rank and be tried by a court-martial for dereliction of duty."

An excited whisper ran through the room.

Boxer showed no emotion, even though he didn't expect the board to recommend he be court-martialed. But after a few moments thinking about it, he realized Stark probably had something to do with it.

"The finding of this board and its recommendations will be passed to the proper command . . . This board is now permanently adjourned."

Though his inclination was to hurry out, Boxer stood very still for several minutes. He had to give the impression that he was a wrecked man.

He walked very slowly. The members of his crew followed him.

As soon as he was in the hallway, he was besieged by the TV reporters. Scowling, he pushed through them; made his way outside and hurried to the *Sting Ray*.

At intervals, throughout the day, the members of the crew sought him out. Some said, "It was a bum rap, Skipper." Others assured him of their support, respect and loyalty. He was deeply touched by their concern for him. He decided to call them together the next morning and offer them the opportunity to serve with him aboard the *Shark*.

Late in the afternoon he received four phone calls. The first was from his father and mother. They had heard the board's findings and recommendations on a TV news program.

"Are you all right?" his mother asked.

Boxer assured her that he was.

"If there is a court-martial," his father said, "I want you to have a civilian lawyer there."

To end the discussion, Boxer agreed to have a lawyer there and let his father pay for him.

Gwen called. She was very solicitous about his emotional and psychological state. "I know you keep everything bottled up inside of you," she said. "But this is something different. In a way this is a life and death matter. That's something you never had to face before. Jack, your whole life is at stake."

As he listened to her, Boxer wondered what she would say if he told her about his dive with Redfern?

"That was part of the trouble with our marriage," she told him. "You never communicated with me. You never let me know what was going inside of you. I didn't really know you."

"Nothing went on inside of me that was worth talking about," Boxer answered.

"That can't be so," Gwen protested. "It can't be so . . . You had to have —"

"Gwen, I don't want to talk about it, at least not now."

"I'm sorry. But promise me that if things get too difficult for you, you'll seek professional help?"

"Okay, I promise," Boxer said, smiling broadly.

"You're just not saying that to make me feel good?"

"Absolutely not," he answered.

The rest of the conversation was about John's reaction to the findings of the board. Gwen was afraid that the children in school would make life more difficult for John than they previously had.

"I don't know what to tell him," Gwen said.

"Tell him that he must continue to believe in his father," Boxer said, knowing that he was asking the boy to do something that was impossible. But he had no other answer.

When the conversation finally came to an end, Boxer was almost happy to put the phone down.

Twenty minutes later Tracy called. "Are you free tonight?" she asked.

"I don't have any special plans," Boxer answered.

"I think you need some tender loving care," she said.

"Oh?"

"A quiet dinner and—"

"Fucking afterwards," Boxer said.

"You don't have anything against fucking after eating?"

"Absolutely nothing."

"Good," Tracy answered.

"Where shall I meet you?" Boxer asked.

"I'll make a reservation in my name at the Casa Venito, it's on Fifty-Second Street, between Park and Madison Avenues. Say around eight-thirty."

"I'll be there," Boxer said.

"Good," Tracy answered and hung up.

Boxer filled the pipe that John had given him for Christmas, lit it and leaned back. That Tracy used obscenities during sex fascinated him. Few women did. But saying the words most certainly heightened her excitement. It was one thing when Cynthia tasted his prick—that was both humorous and charmingly erotic. But it was something else when Tracy shouted out, "Fuck . . . Fucking . . . Fucked . . ." He found himself wondering just how much Tracy really enjoyed sex?

His thoughts were interrupted by a call from Cynthia. She never mentioned the board's findings. She asked him when he was coming to Washington again.

"I don't know," Boxer lied. "But when I do I'll see you." He hadn't seen her since the day before New Year's. After Tracy dropped him off, he didn't return to the apartment. Instead, he went to his hotel room, packed his bag and took a flight back to

New York.

"I really want to see you," she said. "I'm sorry—"

"There isn't any reason for you to be sorry," Boxer told her. "When we're together we'll talk about it."

They spoke for a few more minutes; then Boxer was interrupted by one of the crewmen and told he was wanted in the commo room.

"I've got to go," he told Cynthia.

"I hope to see you soon," she answered.

They said goodby to each other and Boxer hung up. A few minutes later, he went into the commo room and asked the officer on duty why he was called.

The officer handed him a coded message that said, "To be handed to Commander Jack Boxer, captain of the submarine *Sting Ray*: for his eyes only."

Boxer returned to his quarters and quickly deciphered the message. It was from Stark, telling him to report to Admiral Quinn on January 5th and to have a roster of men willing to serve aboard the *Shark* by that date. Stark also said that, "under no circumstances are you ever to call me. I will contact you and tell you what I want done." At the end of the message, he wished him luck with Quinn.

Boxer ran the message through a shredding machine and for the next few hours he read reports about the repairs that were still going on aboard the *Sting Ray* before she could be put in dry dock for the major work.

The Casa Venito was a small, dimly lit restaurant that had red-checkered tablecloths on the tables, a candle in an old wine bottle whose sides were coated with wax, sawdust on the floor and the day's menu written on a blackboard.

Tracy was already there when Boxer arrived. She was dressed in a black, slinky cocktail dress. Her hair was pushed up into a bun.

"This is a very in place," she told him, after he had given the waiter his order for a scotch on the rocks.

Boxer shrugged. "Seems like just another mom an' pop Italian restaurant. When I was growing up in Brooklyn, there were lots of them around."

"I didn't know you grew up in Brooklyn," she said.

"We never got around to talking much about anything," he said, pointedly.

"Touche!" she responded with a smile. "But then think of what we might have discussed, if you weren't so tired."

"Is it now my turn to answer touche?"

"Suit yourself!"

"In that case I'll have to ask what made you so solicitous about me, especially since—"

"Don't be a spoilsport," Tracy said. "I know you've been hurt. But I do have something to celebrate. In fact this dinner is my treat to you."

"You were taken off the gossip column," Boxer said, marveling at the woman's lack of feelings.

"Yes . . . I now am a regular reporter . . . Isn't that super?"

"Super," Boxer repeated without enthusiasm.

"I wanted to share my good fortune with you," she said." After all, in a way, you made it happen."

The waiter came with Boxer's drink. "Better bring another one of these," Boxer said. "I'm sure I'm going to need it." He drank it before the waiter left the table.

Tracy took hold of his hand. "Don't drink too much," she said in a low voice. "Really, I want to fuck you later."

"That's a helluva way to atone for your sins."

"There is no better way that I can think of," she said with a smile. "Com'on, Jack, let's enjoy ourselves."

"Okay," Boxer answered, "we'll enjoy ourselves. I can sure use some enjoyment today."

Tracy squeezed his hand.

The waiter returned with the second scotch and asked Boxer if he would like to see a wine list before he ordered.

"She would," Boxer said.

The waiter raised his bushy eyebrows.

"She's paying," Boxer said with a grin.

Tracy didn't miss a beat. She ordered a Bardolino for the red and a Verdicchio for the white, explaining, "I always like to have both a red and white at dinner."

Boxer grinner. "Me too."

"And would madam care to order?" the waiter asked. He pointed to the blackboard.

"Antipasto for two," Boxer said.

"Yes," Tracy said.

"Seafood d'Casa Venito," Boxer told him. "But first clams in white sauce."

The waiter looked at Tracy.

"I'll have the veal spendini," she said, "with a small order of risotto."

"Very good madam," the waiter answered and left.

"You didn't have to act like Peck's Bad Boy," she chided.

"Pecker's—" He stopped. Across the small room, Gwen and a man were being led to the table by the maitre d'.

"What's wrong?" Tracy asked. "You just went pale."

"Nothing."

She glanced over her shoulder. "Do you know those people?"

"The woman," Boxer answered.

"Someone you've slept with?" Tracy asked.

"Someone I was married to," Boxer answered.

Tracy looked at Gwen and her escort. "She has seen you too," she said matter of factly. "Are you going to go over to her, or better still are we going to go over to them?"

"Yes," Boxer said, "we are."

Tracy linked her arm with his. "You never mentioned you'd been married," she whispered as they crossed the room.

"It was just another subject that we didn't have time to talk about," he answered.

Tracy smiled up at him. "Then we'll just have to make time to talk about all those subjects, won't we?"

"Not if you're intent on fucking all the time."

She squeezed his arm. "The way you say that gives me goose bumps."

"Hello, Gwen," Boxer said, moving his eyes from her to her escort. The man was tall, thin and had wispy blond hair.

She seemed unable to speak.

"I'm Jack Boxer," Boxer said, extending his hand toward the man.

Gwen found her voice. "Doctor Paul Harrid."

Boxer shook his hand.

"I've heard so much about you," Harrid said.

Boxer nodded. "I hope it wasn't all bad." And turning to Tracy, he said, "Ms. Tracy Kimble."

110

"I'm so glad to meet you Mrs. Boxer," Tracy responded.

"Are you—" Gwen started to ask.

"Yes," Tracy responded. "I'm the gal who's been tearing into the commander."

Gwen looked at Boxer. "In a million years I wouldn't have guessed I'd be seeing you tonight."

"We're out celebrating my new job," Tracy said.

"And the end of Jack's career," Gwen answered with a smile. "I can see the relationship and the reason for the celebration."

Boxer glanced at his table. The waiter had brought the wine and was waiting for them to sample it. "It's been nice to see you, Gwen," he said. "I'll be in touch. Give John a hug for me."

"Yes," Gwen answered flatly.

"A pleasure," Boxer said to Harrid.

"A pleasure," the man repeated.

"Oh yes, a pleasure," Tracy said, looking straight at Gwen and forcing her to repeat the 'pleasure' again.

Boxer smiled, turned, and with Tracy on his arm, made his way back across the room.

"I bet you ten dollars," Tracy said, as they sat down, "that they don't stay."

Boxer looked at Gwen and Harrid; they were engaged in earnest conversation.

"Her line is," Tracy said, "that she can't stay here with my ex-husband looking at me, or maybe she'll say I can't stay and look at that woman. What she really means is that she can't have you looking at her, knowing she's fucking the doctor, or that she knows you're fucking me."

"You're probably right," Boxer said. In some strange way, it made him feel good to put Gwen off balance.

Tracy stole at look at them. "I'll tell you something else," she said, "I'd say the good doctor is going to fold. He'll give in because he doesn't want to miss the goodies later. If she's pissed at him, he won't be in her bed tonight."

Boxer shook his head.

"Believe me," Tracy told him. "I know from experience what role she's playing."

"Bitch."

"Absolutely," Gwen answered. "Bitch. And let me tell you this:

111

very few men stand up to it. Somewhere around puberty a girl learns that she's got something between her legs that a boy wants. From that moment on, it becomes many things to her and one of those things is a weapon to use against the boy."

"Kimble's battle of the sexes," Boxer commented.

"Right!"

The waiter returned to the table and poured some of the white wine for Tracy to taste.

She nodded approvingly and said, "Jack, you do the red."

"I don't have much of a tongue."

"I wouldn't say that," she responded with a smile.

Boxer could feel the color rise in his cheeks. He nodded to the waiter, who poured a bit of the red wine into a glass. Boxer sipped it. "Fine . . . Full bodied."

"Would you like the antipasto now?"

"That would be fine," Tracy said.

"They're still here," Boxer commented.

"I don't want to be too obvious," Tracy said with a smile. "Tell me what they're doing?"

"Still talking."

Tracy snorted with disdain. "If I were in her shoes, I'd get up and walk out. But she's too much of a lady to do that."

Boxer smiled.

"If the smile is supposed to mean that I'm not," Tracy said, "I'd have to agree with you in part . . . I'm a lady where it matters . . . Where it doesn't matter, well — I don't give a fuck what I'm called."

"The doctor has just summoned the waiter . . . They're leaving!"

"It took a while," Tracy said smugly. "But she won. They'll stop here on the way out and one of them will make some excuse to explain their departure."

Boxer knew Tracy was right.

Redfern was signaling to him, making circles in the black water . . . .

"Sharks, Tom. Sharks!" Boxer called out. He watched Redfern go for his knife. "No, don't . . . Must keep going down." The water was black except where a yellow circle touched the bodies of the sharks. "Tom?"

Suddenly Boxer began to gasp. "Can't breathe . . . Can't breathe . . . Must get free . . . Knife . . . Use knife . . . Tom . . . Tom . . . Tom. . . ."

Suddenly Boxer was awake. Soaked with sweat and trembling, he bolted up.

"It's all right. It's all right, Jack . . . You were dreaming."

"Huh? Dreaming?" He was disoriented.

"Having a nightmare would be more accurate," Tracy said, "Something about someone named Tom and sharks." She sat up and wrapped part of the blanket around his trembling body.

Boxer took several deep breaths. He remembered Tracy and that they were in her hotel room. He even recalled having met Gwen and Harrid earlier that night.

"Are you okay?" Tracy asked.

"I'm fine," he said, taking hold of her hand. He was worried he'd unwittingly revealed something he shouldn't have. But he didn't know how to find out what he'd said without arousing Tracy's professional curiosity. "I haven't had a nightmare like that for years," he admitted. "It was a beaut."

"So was the case of the shakes that followed it," she commented.

"You've just been witness to one of Commander Jack Boxer's weaker moments," he said with a force laugh.

"Seems as if you were fighting sharks."

"I did some scuba diving a few years back," he said. "I guess sharks were my chief fear. But I never fought any."

Tracy reached to the end table, slipped a cigarette out of a pack and lit it. "Tom couldn't be Thomas Redfern?"

Boxer knew he was better at telling half truths than complete lies. "Listen," he said, "I'm going to tell you something that you can't write about."

"You were with Tom, right?"

"For everyone's good you must not write anything about this," Boxer said.

"Cross my heart and hope to die," Tracy said, making the sign of the cross over her bare breasts.

"I'm not joking!"

"I promise not to write anything about it," she said.

"Tom and I tested a new device off Bimini," he said. "An underwater camera and there was some trouble with sharks."

113

"That's why he couldn't be at the New Year's Eve party?"

Boxer nodded. "He was hurt."

"Oh my God, he was bitten by a shark?"

"Nothing like that," Boxer said.

"Did you tell Sue-Ann—"

"No . . . But by now Tom is home and she knows . . . But she won't know how it happened and you're never to tell her. Understand?"

"What happened?"

"I told you as much as I'm going to," Boxer said. "I can't tell you anymore . . . You just have to be satisfied with what you know."

Tracy nodded and tamped out her cigarette.

"Let's go to sleep," Boxer said, "I have to be back to the boat early."

The two of them slid down and Boxer put his hand on Tracy's breasts.

"What I don't understand," she said, "is why you and Tom were chosen to make the tests? . . . After all, your standing with the Navy isn't the very best at this moment . . . And Tom is a Marine."

"Let it alone," Boxer said.

"Okay . . . Okay," she answered, snuggling up to him. "I'll let it alone."

But Boxer knew she wouldn't. She'd ask him more questions and when the opportunity came along, she'd question Tom. For security reasons, he'd have to tell Stark what happened.

"I didn't realize it before," she said, "but you're a very mysterious man."

"You've got to be joking! I'm the least mysterious man I know."

"And being mysterious somehow makes you all the more sexy," she said, taking hold of his penis and caressing it.

"You're going to have to tell me what doesn't turn you on," he answered, inserting his hand in her crotch.

"Are you complaining?"

"Not yet," Boxer said.

She rolled on to her stomach. "Let's go Greek this time."

"Why not," Boxer answered, mounting her. "We've done it every other way."

Boxer returned to the *Sting Ray* at 0900 hours the following day and found orders relieving him of command of the *Sting Ray*. As of 1400 that day, he was to turn his command over to Commander Steven L. Bush, the third, and report to Admiral Quinn at BuPers the next day.

At 1100, Boxer called the crew into the boat's lounge area. "Smoke if you want," he said. "By now all of you know that the next few hours will be my last on the *Sting Ray* and that a new skipper is taking over. I expect you to give him the same cooperation and high performance that you have given me. It's been a pleasure and a privilege to serve with you."

"For us too," one of the men called out.

The entire crew repeated those words.

Boxer held up his hands. When the men finally quieted down, he said, "I said what I was expected to say. Now I'm going to tell you something else. Something which each of you will have to think about and make up your minds about. Whatever I tell you must be treated as top secret; that means you can't discuss it with your friends here in the base, your wives, sweethearts or anyone else who isn't a member of the crew. Should any word about what I'm about to tell you leak out, the source will be traced by our intelligence people and by other federal investigators and once the man is ID, he will be brought up on charges for breaching security."

"That tight skipper?" one of the men asked.

Boxer nodded. "Any man here who wants to be excused is free to go."

None of them moved.

"Okay here goes. First, whatever you think happened at the board of inquiry didn't."

The men looked questioningly at one another.

"My assignment to BuPers is a cover. The recommendations of the board are part of that cover. I have been given command of an entirely new kind of submarine. The assignment is a voluntary one on my part and for anyone who decides to join me . . ." For the next hour he explained what would happen to the men who decided to volunteer. Finally, he said, "Once you become a member of the *Shark's* crew you will never again be permitted to serve on any other type boat. If you are career men, your career will be in that phantom service."

The men were silent; then one man asked, "What do we tell our people, our friends?"

"All of you will be hired by the Williams Company to crew the super-tanker *Tecumseh*."

"Why that ship?"

"I can't tell you that now," Boxer answered.

"Will we still be in the Navy?" Mahony, the helmsman, asked.

"Yes. But no one will know it."

"What happens if we're killed or injured?" another crew member asked. "I mean who pays the insurance?"

"The government," Boxer answered. "If you're injured, you'll be sent to a Navy hospital."

The men discussed amongst themselves.

"I have to have a roster of men by tomorrow for the CNO," Boxer said. "I know that doesn't give you much time to make up your minds. But there's nothing I can do about that."

"I'll go skipper," Harris said.

"You know that you'll probably be giving up a command of your own if you do?

"But if I didn't go, I'd always wonder what I missed," Harris said.

"Count me in," Cowly called out.

Boxer nodded.

"I'm with you, Skipper," Mahony said.

Several men from the engine room agreed to volunteer.

"Skipper," said one of the men, "I don't think I could do it."

"I understand," Boxer said. "Are there any other men who do not want to volunteer?"

Some of the men hesitated but eventually fifteen of them raised their hands.

"You men are excused," Boxer said. He waited until they cleared the room; then he asked Harris to get the names and serial numbers of the rest of the men.

"Skipper," Mahony asked, "just how will we be transferred from the *Sting Ray* to your command?"

"Don't know," Boxer said. "But be assured the Navy will find a way."

"Skipper," one of the men asked, "suppose a man changes his mind between now and tomorrow morning?"

"Good question," Boxer said. "Okay men, I want you to listen very carefully to this: any man who changes his mind between now and tomorrow morning has the right to do so. All he has to do is come to me and say that he's sorry to see me go. That's just in case someone else is nearby or I'm with someone. Remember, just say, 'I'm sorry to see you go.' "

After a few minutes, Harris handed Boxer the list of men. "We've got every man in the room," he said, "a total of a hundred and twenty five men, including the cooks and bakers."

Boxer nodded approvingly. He was truly gratified by the showing. "All right men, back to work. The new skipper comes aboard at 1400 and we want to be ready for him."

"Does he know that he's going to lose his crew?" Cowly asked.

Boxer shook his head. "He'll be better off with new men than with old dogs like you."

The men laughed.

"Remember what I said when I began to speak to you: I expect you to give your new skipper the same high performance that you gave me. That's it for now!"

Harris called the men to attention and Boxer dismissed them.

For the next few hours, Boxer busied himself with the paper work involved in turning over the *Sting Ray* to the new skipper. It was routine and boring. A good part of the time his thoughts were elsewhere: either on his meeting with Gwen the previous night, or what his life would be like from now on. . . .

Obviously Gwen had been very disturbed by the meeting—and as Tracy had predicted—she and the doctor had stopped at the table on the way out to say that the doctor had an "emergency." She hadn't said it; the doctor had and not too convincingly either. Boxer expected her to be very angry at him the next time he spoke to her on the phone, or saw her.

And as for Tracy, she was a good fuck. She didn't want to be anything else to him and he had no desire to be anything else to her. They weren't even lovers: they were sex partners. It was an uncomplicated relationship, unlike the one he had with Cynthia, where she was in love with him and he had a genuine affection for her. But he was still in love with Gwen. . . .

Whenever Boxer tried to grapple with the future, he found himself in the peculiar position of not really knowing what kind of

117

covert operations the *Shark* would be used for. Equipped as she was, she could be used for almost anything from putting a strike force ashore to hunting and destroying any vessel afloat, including any other submarine. The possibilities were mind boggling! But more important than anything else, as far as Boxer was concerned, was the fact that no matter what kind of mission the *Shark* would be sent on, it would never be routine; it would always be dangerous! And those two elements excited him in a very special way. . . .

By 1400, the *Sting Ray*'s crew was standing at attention on the afterdeck as Boxer turned over his command to Bush, who was a handsome, narrow shouldered man with light green eyes and a fair complexion.

Because it was bitterly cold, Boxer wanted to have the men dismissed as soon as possible. He hurried through the formal part of the procedure and when it was over he suggested, "the men be permitted to go below."

Bush nodded and said, "This crew is now mine, Commander, and I will send them below when I am ready to."

Boxer said nothing nor gave any indication he heard Bush. He moved a step forward and said, "Crew dismissed!" Then he turned to Bush and said, "Your move, Commander."

Bush's face turned very red.

"Shall we go below," Boxer said. "I'm sure you want to speak to the men."

"I was warned about you," Bush said through his teeth.

"Then I take it, the warning wasn't wasted," Boxer asked, starting for the door in the sail.

"I will of course report your actions to SUBATCOM," Bush said, following him into the boat.

"Of course," Boxer answered. "It never crossed my mind that you wouldn't."

A few minutes later, the crew was assembled in the lounge room to listen to their new captain.

Boxer stood in the back of the room. Now and then a man would turn and nod, or wink but he pretended not to notice any of them.

"My name is Steven Bush, the third," Bush began. "My family has been Navy since the Revolutionary War. There was a Bush

118

on *Old Ironsides* during the War of Eighteen Twelve and there was a Bush in every major American naval engagement since . . ." He paused to let the men digest what they had just heard.

"Can't say the same for my family," one of the younger members of the crew said. "But I reckon that from the time they got here, 'bout the time of the Revolutionary War, there's been one of our men folks in some jail or t'other, 'cept me. I'm Navy all the way!"

The men laughed and Boxer couldn't help smiling.

Bush remained expressionless. When the laughter subsided, he continued. "I was born and raised with the Navy. I know its ways. I know what it expects of me and I know what I expect of you. And that brings me to the main point I want to make with you men. The *Sting Ray*, as it was, is not the kind of boat I would tolerate. The accident that occurred was due to human error, not to mechanical failure. From this moment on, my effort, the efforts of all my officers and the efforts of this crew will be bent toward erasing any vestige of the poor performance that resulted in the accident and the death of five members of the crew. Under my command the *Sting Ray* will become the most efficient submarine in the service."

Boxer was furious. Bush had no right to impugn the performance of the crew.

"Beggin' your pardon, sir," Mahony said, "I was on the bridge the night of the crash. The *Mary-Ann* rammed us; we didn't go chasing after her."

"Mister Harris, dismiss the men!" Bush ordered. "Then pass the word, I want to see all officers in the wardroom at seventeen hundred."

Harris called the men to attention as Bush left the room; then he dismissed them.

It took Boxer another hour and a half to sign over everything aboard the *Sting Ray* to Bush. They worked at the small desk in the captain's quarters. Neither man spoke to the other, unless it was connected to what they were doing.

When they finished, Bush said, "I would like you to accompany me to the damaged area and explain what repairs have been made, the repairs in progress and what will be done when the *Sting Ray* is put in dry dock."

"All that information is contained in the damage control and the daily repair reports."

"It's my way of making sure those reports haven't been falsified by the repair crews."

"Commander," Boxer said, "I have been with these men —"

"The answer is either yes or no. I don't want or need an explanation."

"Then the answer will be no, without an explanation and you can put that in your report to SUBATCOM."

"And that's your final word?" Bush asked.

"No. My final word is that you're a horse's ass, even though, or maybe because, you're Steven Bush, the third."

"But I'm not the officer who rammed my boat into another ship and caused the death of five of my men," Bush answered, his face red with anger." Remember that, Boxer, when you call me or any other officer a 'horse's ass.' "

Boxer balled his fists. He could deck the bastard but that wouldn't solve anything. He was going to have to learn how to put up with insults of every kind. Slowly, he relaxed; said nothing more and turning, he left Bush sitting at the desk.

Boxer left word with Harris that he'd either be in the BOQ, or at the Wardroom, if any of the men wanted to speak to him. He put his bags in his room at the BOQ; then he went directly to the Wardroom, sat down on a stool and ordered a double scotch, neat.

Boxer drank it swiftly. Putting up with someone like Bush wasn't going to be easy for him, no matter how many times, he told himself, he had to do it. He shook his head and looked toward the telephone. There was no real reason for him to stay on the base at night. If any man had changed his mind, he would see him in the morning, just before he left for Washington. He needed to be away from the base, away from the crew of the *Sting Ray*. He needed what Tracy had euphemistically called, 'tender loving care,' which was her way of saying, 'fucking.'

Boxer took a deep breath. Tracy had gone, or would soon be going back to Washington. Gwen was out of the question. He looked back at his empty shot glass. He'd solve nothing by having a few more doubles. Though it was difficult for him to admit it, he was far more thin-skinned than he had thought. Far more sensitive, to what other people thought and said about him than he would have believed. He looked at the phone again and decided it would be a good night to spend with his folks. It would be awhile before he saw them again. And maybe later, he'd phone Gwen and John. Maybe Gwen would speak to him.

Early the following morning, Boxer returned to the base. It was very cold and the wind was still blowing strongly from the northwest.

He had a good visit with his parents and he had phoned Gwen. She did not speak to him but he had a long conversation with John. He could tell from what the boy said and the tone of his voice that he was upset and confused by what had happened. But there was nothing he could do to help him. Nothing. . . .

Boxer went straight to the *Sting Ray* to see the men. Two of them came up to him and said they were sorry to see him go. Boxer crossed their names off the list.

By 1100, he was seated next to the window on the shuttle flight to Washington, out of La Guardia. On the way down, the weather worsened and before the plane landed, the captain informed the passengers that snow had already begun to fall in the capital.

The flight, usually 55 minutes, lasted two and a half hours. They made a hard landing and slid a long distance before coming to a halt. From what Boxer could see through the curtain of snow, they were almost at concrete barriers at the far end of the field; another few feet and they would have crashed into one of them. It took another thirty minutes to move the plane over the ice covered runway to the terminal, where they finally deplaned.

Boxer found an empty cab and went straight to BuPers and reported to Admiral Quinn, who kept him waiting for the rest of the afternoon before seeing him.

Quinn's office was decorated with memorabilia of his career, including several glass-cased scale models of the ships he'd commanded. There was a plush blue carpet on the floor and a large photograph of the president on the wall directly behind his very large, teakwood desk.

Boxer formally reported in and submitted his orders to the admiral.

Quinn nodded, pushed himself back into his leather swivel chair and said, "I didn't want you, Commander. I don't know why you're here. But as far as I'm concerned, you don't deserve to wear that uniform, let alone hold the rank you do."

Boxer looked straight ahead. His heart beat very fast.

"I was ordered not to assign any work to you. I was also told that from time to time you would not report to this office but I was to count you present for duty."

"That was my understanding too," Boxer said, unable to keep silent.

"It was hinted that you have very special friends in very high places. Well, Commander I don't give one good goddamn about them, I want you here on time every morning when you're not somewhere else. Do you understand that?"

Boxer suddenly realized how humorous the situation was and smiled.

"I don't see anything particularly funny about what I said," Quinn suddenly roared.

Boxer decided to play with him a bit, if for no other reason than to relieve his own tension. "Sir, I naturally would be here, when I'm not somewhere else. But when I am somewhere else I couldn't possibly be here and when I am here, I will be here at the required time. But if I am somewhere else, I will be there at whatever time I'm told to be or choose, and that time, sir, may or may not be the same time that I'm required to be here."

Quinn became flushed. He stood up and glaring at Boxer, he said angrily, "I would have thought you to be more of an officer than a clown, but I see that I was wrong."

"Sir, I am very much an officer," Boxer responded. "But as you do not want me here, I do not want to be here. But since I am here and your jurisdiction over me consists only in telling me to be here on time when I am here; then it seems to me that I am not the clown."

"By the living God," Quinn thundered, "I certainly will bring you up on charges for insubordination and insulting a superior officer!"

Boxer shook his head. "Sir, it was you who drew the conclusion that you are a clown from what I said. I never said you were a clown."

"Get out," Quinn roared. "Get out!"

Boxer nodded, put his cap on and executing a very military about face, he walked slowly to the door. When he was on the other side of it, he hurried to the men's room and laughed until he hurt. No doubt Stark would know about the interview, if he already didn't. This was the first time in his entire career he had ever dared to speak to a superior as he had spoken to Quinn and it felt good. Very good indeed to be in a position to let some of the hot air out of the admiral.

Boxer looked at himself in the mirror. Though he couldn't see any evidence of it, he was changing. If he wasn't, he'd have never spoken to Quinn the way he had. The only reason he could do it was that he no longer had to concern himself with what Quinn, Bush, or anyone else in the regular navy did or didn't think of him. He was responsible only to Stark. In a manner of speaking, he was freer than he ever had been in the past twenty five years.

He took time to wash his face and comb his hair. He left the men's room, found a phone booth, called Cynthia and asked her if she wanted to have dinner with him.

"Yes," she said. "But the weather is real bad. Maybe you'd like to have dinner here. I have a couple of steaks in the freezer and a can of soup in the closet. I wouldn't mind preparing them."

"Fine," he said. "I'll be over 'bout seven. Anything you want me to bring?"

"Some cake, if you happen to pass a bakery," she said.

"I'll make it my business to pass one," he answered. "See you!"

"See you," Cynthia repeated.

Boxer hung up, knowing he'd spend the night with her.

8

The next morning Boxer was assigned a cubicle and left to his own devices. The hours passed slowly. Several times he left his desk and walked around. None of the officers would speak to him. From the looks they gave him, they obviously had been told who he was and warned not to speak with him, lest they catch whatever he had. He was BuPers own pariah!

Impatiently, he waited for the end of the day when he could leave the office and resume something like a 'normal' life. The second afternoon he phoned Redfern, but was told by Sue-Ann that her husband had gone away for a few days.

She then proceeded to tell him what a wonderful woman Tracy was. "She only needs the right man to make her settle down," Sue-Ann said.

"I assure you," Boxer said smiling, "I am well aware of her womanly qualities."

"Commander, I think you're referring to her physical self, while I'm talking about the inner woman, the real Tracy."

The conversation continued in the same manner for several minutes until Sue-Ann said, "If I tell you something in strictest confidence, you'll never tell Tracy I told it to you?"

"Never."

"Promise me."

"Promise," Boxer answered, having difficulty now controlling his laughter.

"She told me," Sue-Ann said, her voice suddenly taking on a conspiratorial tone, "that she could become interested in you."

"Really? I find that hard to believe," Boxer answered. "I really do."

Sue-Ann went through great verbal pains to assure him that she was giving him the gospel, according to saint Tracy.

Afraid that he would explode into laughter, Boxer ended the conversation by telling her his other phone was ringing.

"I don't hear it," she said innocently.

"It has a flashing light and it's flashing now. Tell Tom I called and thank you for a lovely conversation," Boxer said, putting the phone back in its cradle. Then he leaned back and laughed so loudly that two of the officers in cubicles adjacent to his came to the door and looking in, asked if he was all right.

"I'm fine," he assured each of them.

Eventually, he stopped laughing and went off to the commissary for his afternoon break, which as far as anyone was concerned, could have begun with lunch and lasted until quitting time.

He sat down with his coffee and apple pie at a table next to a window overlooking a piece of garden laid bare by the winter. But the sun was shining, though it was cold enough for the window to be coated with a film of mist. What really made the conversation with Sue-Ann so funny was that he had arranged to spend the weekend with Tracy.

Suddenly he found himself looking at a black man, one of the civilian employees.

"Mind if I sit here?" the man asked.

"Suit yourself," Boxer answered, though he couldn't understand why the man chose to sit at a table already occupied when there were so many empty ones available.

"Ronald Courtney," the man said, offering his hand to Boxer. "My friends call me Ron."

"Jack Boxer," Boxer responded, shaking the man's hand.

Courtney smiled, sipped his coffee and in a low voice said, "Have you the crew list for the *Shark*?"

Boxer gagged on the piece of pie he was swallowing. "Went down the wrong pipe," he said, taking a drink of coffee.

Courtney nodded, waited until Boxer had stopped coughing and repeated the question.

"Yes," Boxer said.

"Good, the admiral will be pleased. I will be your contact man," Courtney said. "I have a special number for you to call if you should find it necessary to speak to the admiral."

"How long am I going to stay here?" Boxer asked.

"Not long. In fact, tomorrow morning you're going to fly to St. Louis. You'll be met at the airport by Major Redfern and two other men. The four of you will drive to where the *Shark* is now being fitted for sea."

"What about Quinn?" Boxer question.

"Nothing about Quinn," Courtney said. "He'll receive a phone call in the morning from the admiral."

"How long will I be away?"

"A week. Maybe less."

Boxer told him about his conversation with Tracy. "She's a smart woman," he said. "She's very friendly with the Redferns and just might put a few things together."

"I'll pass it along to my superiors and to the admiral," Courtney answered. "But if I were you, I'd be very, very careful what I say to her or any other woman with whom I happen to be in bed."

"I'll remember that," Boxer said, not wanting to explain to Courtney that Tracy wouldn't have picked up on anything, if she hadn't been a good friend of Sue-Ann Redfern.

"I'm going into the men's room," Courtney said. "But first I'm going to buy a newspaper. You do the same. Put your list in page six. I'll put my information to you in the same page. We'll switch papers at the sink. You should be getting a phone call about your travel plans at sixteen hundred hours. Don't worry about anyone listening to your conversations. You phone is a special one. The calls you receive from certain numbers and make to those numbers are scrambled." Courtney stood up, nodded, picked up his empty coffee mug and left the table.

Boxer waited until Courtney reached the door; then he followed.

As soon as Boxer deplaned in St. Louis, a man came up to him and said, "This way, please, Commander."

"My bag—"

"It will be taken care of," the man said. "Please follow me."

Boxer nodded and in a matter of minutes they were in the snow covered parking area.

"That car there, Commander," the man said, pointing to a black limousine.

The rear door swung open and Redfern stuck his head out. "Com'on Jack, shake your butt!" he called.

Boxer settled himself in the rear seat. Redfern sat between him and another man and a second man was seated on the jump seat. Both men were bearded.

"Richard Pierce," Redfern said, gesturing toward the man next to him, "Chief engineer for the *Shark*."

Boxer introduced himself and shook Pierce's hand.

"That's Nathan Monty," Redfern said, pointing to the man on the jump seat. "Chief electronics engineer for the project."

Boxer shook his hand.

"These two gentlemen will be with us for a while," Redfern said.

Boxer nodded. From experience, he knew that usually meant they'd be along for the sea trials.

"Well," Redfern said, "aren't you going to ask how my wrist is doing?"

The moment Boxer entered the car, he noticed that Redfern's right hand was in a cast. "I figured you'd get around to telling me sooner or later," Boxer said.

"For christsakes, I'd have thought you'd have been just a bit more interested, since you're the one who broke it." Then talking to Pierce and Monty, he said, "Never, never hand wrestle with him. He has a crusher for a hand." He looked at Boxer again. "The doc says it'll be fine in a month or so."

Boxer was going to ask him about the knife wounds but since they weren't visible, he decided not to.

They drove into St. Louis, rolled into an underground garage and changed from the limousine to a four door, gray Chrysler sedan. Monty took the wheel and Pierce sat next to him.

"We have a two hour drive," Redfern said.

Boxer shrugged. "I don't have anywhere else to go."

Monty turned on the radio and tuned to a station playing country music.

Pierce turned half around. "She'll be ready for sea trials in about ninety days."

"What more has to be done on her?" Boxer asked.

"The electronic gear has to be made operational and the reactor has to be brought on line."

"But the really big job is to bring her down river and out into the

127

Gulf of Mexico without the Ruskies knowing about it," Pierce said.

"How much do we think they know?" Redfern asked.

"No idea," Pierce answered.

"Even if someone knew the answer to that question, we wouldn't be told," Monty said. "We don't have any need to know."

The four men laughed.

"Speaking about the need to know," Redfern said, "my wife wants to know—"

"About Tracy and me?"

"Absolutely," Redfern said. "She's into matchmaking in a big way. She'd consider it a real coup if she was responsible for putting the two of you together. She even said she'd make the wedding."

"And when did she tell you all this?"

"About two minutes after you hung up," Redfern said.

"She didn't waste any time," Boxer laughed.

"I called her and she immediately told me she had just finished speaking to you and you were to use her words 'impossible to get any information from' and 'worse' than I am. That of course was supposed to be the supreme insult."

"I'm supremely insulted," Boxer laughed, aware they were driving north along the Mississippi River. Now and then they'd pass a string of barges moving downstream pushed by a large flat bowed tug.

They drove through a few river towns but most of what they saw was snow covered farm land.

After awhile, Boxer closed his eyes and listening to the country music allowed himself to doze. Suddenly, he sensed the car slowing and opened his eyes.

Directly in front of the them was a large iron gate, a kiosk on each side with M-20s pointed at them.

He couldn't see them. But he was certain they could see everyone in the car.

"Identify yourselves," a voice said over a loudspeaker.

Pierce opened the glove compartment and took out a small radio. He gave his name and ID number; then he handed the device to Monty, who did the same and passed it back to Redfern. Finally, Boxer gave his name, rank and serial number.

"Cleared," the voice announced over the loudspeaker.

The gate opened and Monty drove through.

"How do they ID with that?" Boxer asked.

"Voicegrams," Pierce said. "If you're wondering how they got yours, don't. They probably have had it for months, if not a couple of years. But it would be almost impossible for someone to come through that gate without being ID."

Suddenly Boxer realized they were driving under a huge roof and asked, "What's that all about?"

"Protection from Ruskie satellites. They can't photograph what's going on underneath. There's special material between the surface and the roof that absorbs all the infra red and ultra violet frequencies that are produced under it. The pictures the Ruskies get is just more farm land,"

Monty slowed down and stopped alongside a very large barge. "We're here," he said, shifting into park, stepping on the brake and turning off the ignition.

A door in the side of the barge opened. Three men wearing hard hats trooped out and headed for a nearby pickup truck.

"The *Shark* is on the other side of the barges," Pierce said, "between two sets of barges."

The four of them left the car and walked toward the door in the side of the barge.

Suddenly Boxer was excited. His heart was beating very fast. Quickening his pace, he stepped out in front of the others. He opened the door and stepped through it. The interior of the barge was brilliantly illuminated with high intensity fluorescent lighting. The noise was almost deafening. Workmen were everywhere.

And in front of him was a huge convex wall of steel that formed one side of the *Shark*. He stopped and looked toward one end and then the other. Her bow was pointed downstream. She was enormous.

"My God," Boxer exclaimed, "she's big!"

"She'll seem even bigger with the sail up," Pierce said. "But we don't elevate it unless we know there aren't any Ruskie spy satellites around. We're notified when they're overhead. But I assure you the sail goes into its surface position just as easily as a baby sucks its thumb."

"Let's go aboard," Monty said. "You have to absorb an enormous amount of information about her in the next few days."

Boxer was the first one up the gangplank leading from the barge to the deck of the *Shark*. "Is she afloat?" he asked.

"Yes," Pierce said. "A special channel was dredged out for her and it's kept open. Once she begins her trip down river, she'll have enough water under her. But she won't be going down under her own power. The barges and the *Shark* will go down river just like any other bulk cargo."

Boxer nodded. That would be done for security reasons.

"By the way," Pierce said, "you can take notes while you're here. But you must surrender them when you leave the construction site."

"You mean we're goin' to live out here?" Redfern asked.

"There are quarters a few hundred yards from where we are. You'll be staying there for the next few days and every time you come here."

"Ah jest can't get away from livin' in the boonies," Redfern commented. "Ah jest can't!"

Boxer rolled his eyes. "Your house isn't exactly the boonies," he said.

"It is if you sleep outside in a pup tent," Redfern said with a straight face.

Boxer punched him on the shoulder. "Com'on let's get to this boat."

Redfern grinned. "This is some mother of a boat . . . Some mother of a boat!"

"The best way for you Jack — I hope you don't mind me calling you Jack," Pierce said.

"That's my name," Boxer answered.

Pierce nodded. "I'll walk you through the *Shark* for the next few days and explain everything about her that's different from the ordinary sub; then Monty will do the same on the electronic gear. This should take us into the middle of next week. By that time the two of you will have had enough. When you come back we'll go through it again. By the fourth time, you men will be telling me what I have been telling you."

"That sounds okay with me," Boxer said, looking at Redfern. "What about you Tom?"

"Okay with me too," Redfern answered.

The next six days passed swiftly. Both Pierce and Monty were hard taskmasters. But Boxer and Redfern were beginning to get a good picture of how unique the *Shark* was.

As Boxer was told during that first briefing in Stark's office, he was in for more surprises than he could possibly imagine existed. Her size alone made it possible to give more working space, have more equipment and be more versatile.

"The reason why a much smaller crew is needed," Monty explained as they were standing in the large control room, "is that everything is controlled electronically. The skipper doesn't need a diving officer, for example, because he dials in the depth he wants and the EPC, the electronic plane control does the rest. In the event that the primary system fails there are two back up systems. Should they all fail, control of the diving planes immediately shifts to manual. The same situation exists for setting the speed. But he does need his engineering officers and crew—more to take care of any emergency situation than run the power plant. As you can see, your navigation isaccomplished by a much more accurate NAVCLOCK. Here you have an actual GRID DISPLAY TABLE, or GDT, which displays a map of your precise location and if you press that button there, you'll get a three dimensional reading of the ocean around you and everything in it worth knowing about for a distance of five thousand yards on a three hundred and sixty degree azimuth. That's for the CIC to use in any action. The skipper has his own GDT but his range is limited to two thousand yards. This next device regulates the flow of air. It too has three back-up systems. . . ."

Boxer and Redfern made copious notes, which they studied at night and asked questions about the following morning. It was imperative that Boxer learn everything he was being taught and he worked hard at it, even to the point of drawing from memory, diagrams of the control panels at any of the control stations aboard the boat. He worked late into the night and rose early in the morning to review the previous day's work.

Pierce and Monty and the engineers who worked for them had thought of everything that a skipper of a submarine might need to make his mission easier. But the most important device was the UNDER WATER IMAGE SCREEN, or UWIS, that made it possible to see underwater in all directions.

"The difference between the three-d presentation you get on the GDT and on UWIS is the UWIS projects an actual image, a picture put together by a computer and optically transmitted to your viewing screens, whereas the GDT gives the viewer a dimensional view of the return echoes translated into specific line patterns and shapes to give the illusion of dimension. When both devices are used together, the skipper has two very powerful instruments that enable him to see where he is and what's around him. You also have an improved AIRCRAFT TARGET INDICATOR, or ATI, which enables the radar officer to track as many as fifty targets simultaneously, determine which are aircraft and which are missiles and use the same radar to direct counter fire from the *Shark*."

Boxer gave a long, low whistle.

"Naturally you have three identical systems," Monty said.

Boxer nodded to Redfern and said, "Naturally."

Redfern repeated the word and the three of them laughed.

By the fifth day, Boxer decided that it was important to have Harris, Cowly and all of the radar and sonar officers go through the same kind of orientation program that he and Redfern were experiencing.

He made the suggestion to Pierce and Monty, at the end of the day as they walked back to their living quarters.

They agreed with him and Monty said, "I think all of the officers should go through the program, if that's what you want to call it. I also think that each of the officers should know enough about another officer's specialty that he can take over in an emergency. This boat is so automatic that the officers should have no difficulty learning two, possibly even three specialties."

"Good idea," Boxer said. "I'll make it SOP for the entire crew."

"Do you think Stark will agree to having the officers come here?" Redfern asked.

"It's worth a try," Boxer answered. "All he can do is deny the request."

"My gut reaction is that he'll go for it."

"Mine too," Boxer answered.

Before Boxer went to sleep, he thought about the *Shark*. Big and complex as she was she still was nothing more than a steel

132

envelope filled with a collection of electronic and mechanical devices. She'd only become something more when she's in her element. Then she'd take on a distinct personality, almost the way a human being did the moment it was born. She'd handle differently from any other boat. She'd develop quirks — a behavior pattern all her own, which he and the rest of the crew would laugh at, tolerate or hate. He more than anyone else would pamper her and in return expect her to do more than Pierce and Monty ever dreamed she could. . . .

Boxer put his hands behind his head. His relationship to her would be in no small way like a lover to his beloved. He'd know every inch of her body and what response he could expect by manipulating any part of her. That special, almost profane, understanding he'd come to have about her had to take place, or he'd never really control her.

He imagined that every captain, since the time men took to going to sea in ships, came to feeling that way about the inanimate object under his feet. Masters of the sailing vessels knew it and developed a special vocabulary to describe how well their ships sailed in all sorts of weather. Any skipper today, worthy of being called captain, had to know what his ship would or would not do.

"That's why," Boxer mumbled, turning on his side to go to sleep, "her sea trials have to be harder than any ordinary boat would be put through. That's why I'm going to take her into the Arctic, where she and I'll be tested." He smiled and slipped quickly into a deep and restful sleep.

The next morning Boxer and Redfern left the construction site in two different cars. Redfern was driven to a nearby town where he boarded a train for Chicago, while Boxer returned to the airport in St. Louis and was back in Washington before noon.

He went directly to his hotel and using the special number given to him, he phoned Stark.

A woman answered. "Your ID please?"

He gave her his serial number.

"Please place your call from the public phone booth located directly across from the National Gallery," she said.

133

The line went dead.

A few minutes later, Boxer dialed Stark's number again.

The woman came on the line again and asked for his ID again

Boxer repeated his serial number. Two or three seconds passed then Boxer heard a click and the admiral said, "Boxer, it fucking well better be important."

Boxer didn't waste words. "I want my section officers to be given the same orientation that Redfern and I are getting."

"Just like that?"

"Yes."

"How can I explain pulling all the officers at the same time?" Stark asked.

"That's not my problem, Admiral."

After several moments of silence, Stark asked, "Anything else?"

"Nothing."

"I have something else to say to you," Stark told him.

Boxer waited.

"Quinn is after your ass," Stark said.

"I thought he would be."

"That's all you have to say?"

"Yes, sir,"

Stark chuckled. "I didn't realize it when I first interviewed you, but you're an insolent bastard."

"Yes, sir," Boxer answered.

"Go easy with Quinn," Stark said.

"Can't. He thinks I'm a disgrace to the service. For that reason alone, he wants my balls."

"Okay, play it the way you have to. In three months at the most you'll be out of there."

Boxer was pleased by that news.

"Now don't call me again unless it's an emergency," Stark said gruffly.

"Will my officers—"

"You asked for them, didn't you," Stark answered and hung up.

Boxer put the phone down. If he had asked for his whole damn crew, he'd have gotten them.

That same afternoon, Boxer reported back to BuPers and as soon as he sat down at his desk, he received a phone call from Quinn's aide, telling him to report immediately to the admiral's office.

Boxer took his time and a half hour later, he was standing in front of Quinn's desk.

The admiral was bristling. "I want to know," he said, "where you've been for these past seven days."

Boxer shook his head. "Sir, I'm sure you were told—"

"I don't care what I was told," he said sharply. "I want an explanation."

"I can't give you one," Boxer answered.

"Can't or won't?"

"The choice is yours, sir," Boxer said.

"I don't know what you're doing and I certainly don't know why. But I assure you, mister, I will find out and when I do—"

"Sir, if I were you, I wouldn't bother yourself. You'll only be wasting your time."

Quinn slammed his fist down on the desk. "I'm going to be the one, mister, who breaks you, by Christ I will!"

"May I go now?" Boxer asked calmly.

Quinn glared at him for several moments; then he snarled, "Dismissed!"

Boxer did a smart about face, left the office and went straight to the cafeteria for a sandwich and a cup of coffee. It was perverse, but he actually enjoyed the session with Quinn. It certainly would give him something to tell Redfern about.

Having thought about Redfern, Boxer wondered how he was faring with his superiors. He had never thought to ask him what his cover would be once he resigned from the Corps.

Boxer picked up a ham and cheese sandwich and a cup of coffee and went to the same table he had occupied before. The sun poured in through the window but it was still cold enough outside to steam the glass.

For Boxer, the next few days weren't quite as bad as the first few. He busied himself recalling what Pierce and Monty had taught him about the *Shark*. Whenever he'd put something down on paper, he was careful to shred the paper as soon as he was finished with it. He was surprised at the amount of information he had retained.

At night he saw either Cynthia or Tracy. Twice he dated a third woman named Monique Gide, who was a member of the French embassy staff and whom he had met on the subway.

He saw Courtney several times, usually in the cafeteria, or leaving the building at the end of the day. They shared the same table and once went for a beer together. Neither one ever spoke about the secret they shared.

The following Wednesday he was back on the *Shark* with Redfern. This time the session lasted until Saturday morning and just before he was about to get into the car, for the return drive to St. Louis—Redfern was already gone—Pierce said to him, "Several officers were here from Monday until an hour before you arrived. They're coming back later today."

Boxer was pleased Stark had acted so quickly on his request. He nodded and asked, "How are they doing?"

Pierce nodded. "Very good. Almost as good as you and Tom."

The compliment brought color to Boxer's cheeks.

"Nothing to be ashamed of," Pierce said. "You and Tom and the rest of the officers who'll man the *Shark* are being rated by myself and Monty. Your boss in Washington wants to know how you are doing and so do certain other individuals. After all Jack, the *Shark* is just too expensive to turn over to a skipper and a crew who don't measure up to her."

"I understand," Boxer answered with a nod. Then he shook Pierce's hand and, slipping into the car, he said, "Tell Monty, I'll see him in a few days."

Pierce laughed. "He's so busy running tests he won't realize you're gone until sometime tonight or tomorrow."

They both laughed.

Boxer closed the door, leaned back and told the driver to go.

Another week passed and Boxer spent the better part of it on the *Shark*. This time Tom wasn't with him. But when he returned to Washington he found a message waiting for him in his hotel room to phone Mrs. Redfern.

His first thought was that Tom had been in an accident. But

then he realized if that had been the case, Courtney, or someone from his office would have either notified him in person or phoned.

When Sue-Ann came on the line, Boxer knew from the tone of her voice that it was nothing serious.

"I know this is late to ask you," she said. "But I'm having a few people over for dinner tonight and I'd be much obliged if you'd come. Tom would have called you," she raced on, "but he won't be home for another few hours yet and doesn't even know about it. The dinner is for some of Daddy's friends and it's going to be so dull without you. It was Daddy's suggestion that I call you. He said, 'have that friend of Tom's over with a lady friend so you and Tom don't fall asleep at the table. Will you come?"

Laughing, Boxer answered, "I'll be there."

"You're a sweet man!"

"What time?"

"Eight o'clock will be just fine," she answered. "I guess I should tell you Tracy is down for the weekend."

"Thanks," Boxer said. "You've saved me the trouble of asking her."

Sue-Ann giggled. "See you, sweet man," she said and hung up.

Boxer smiled. He had been called many different things by the various women he had known but none had ever called him that. Surely not Gwen, who often claimed he was a hard man. And not Cynthia, she had, on more than one occasion, told him he was a "gentle and considerate lover." And as for Tracy, the last kind of man she would want would be a sweet one.

The phone rang again.

Picking it up, he said, "Boxer here."

"Tracy here," she mimicked.

"I was going to call you but I've just been told by Sue-Ann that we'll be seeing one another tonight."

"That's what I'm calling you about," she said. "I'm driving out to the Redferns and I'm going to stay at the Inn. You want to go out with me?"

"Why don't we spend the weekend together?"

"I was going to suggest that," she said with a sexy laugh.

"Good; then we're in sync."

"In what?"

"Never mind. I'll show you when we're in bed," he said.

She laughed again.

"Sue-Ann said to come around eight," Boxer said.

"If we arrive at the Inn early, you don't have to wait until eight to come," Tracy said.

"Don't you ever think of anything else or talk about anything else?"

"Sure. But seldom when I'm talking to you," she answered.

"Well, there's no false modesty about you. I'll say that for you."

"Pick you up at six," she said.

"Okay," Boxer answered and put the phone down. After speaking with any other woman, he'd wait until she'd hang up; then he would. But not with Tracy. He was sure she didn't give a damn whether he hung up or not, as long as she had the opportunity to say whatever she had called to say.

Boxer finally took off his jacket, loosened his tie and opened his collar button. He took the pipe John had given him for Christmas, filled it with tobacco, lit it and after it was drawing to his satisfaction, he sat down in the one easy chair in the room and turned on the TV to see the late afternoon news.

There was the usual coverage of fires, a train wreck in West Virginia, a very sad story about the continuing drought in central India and then a story with a Paris dateline, reported by Jacques Bolonge, of station PNG, Paris. Speaking in English, M. Bolonge said, "I have just come back from the Soviet Union, where for the first time I had the privilege of meeting some of their submarine commanders, who, according to leading western naval analysts, are as well trained as any in the west, perhaps even better. Among this elite group of officers, I was introduced to one in particular, whose name I cannot tell you. But let me assure you that he is dedicated to his country, to his service, and to his formidable assignment, which is to make a thorough study of Arctic marine life. . . ."

Boxer leaned so far forward, he was almost at the edge of the chair.

". . . Russia, I was told," Bolonge said, "plans to use more of their submarine fleet to examine the marine life in all of the world's oceans, with the hope of finding solutions to many of the ecological problems resulting from world-wide abuse of the seas by man."

The camera cut to a commercial.

Boxer went to the dresser, found a packet of hotel stationery in the top drawer and wrote down the French reporter's name and the call letters of the Paris station where the program originated. The next time he saw Courtney, he'd ask him if his people could come up with more information about the Russian Arctic program and if possible the name of the captain Bolonge had interviewed.

9

Tracy drove and Boxer sat beside her. The drive from Washington was pleasant. Tracy had the radio tuned to a station playing classical music.

Boxer was aware that the music matched his own feelings of contentment. Tracy, too, seemed to be under the influence of the music.

When they reached the Redfern's house, Boxer said, "Sue-Ann told me this was going to be a small party. There are at least twenty cars parked outside and half of those are chauffeur driven limos."

"Your idea of small and her idea of small is most certainly different," Tracy answered. "You probably thought there'd be six other people here besides the two of us and the Redferns,"

Boxer didn't answer. But that was his idea.

"Believe me when Sue-Ann really gives a dinner party you'd see fifty, maybe sixty cars out here."

"I'm impressed," Boxer said.

Tracy parked close to the house, switched off the lights and turned off the ignition. Then turning to Boxer, she said, "Hold me!"

He started to embrace her.

"No, not that way," she said and reaching down she hiked up her lam5e evening gown. "Hold my cunt!"

Boxer put his hand between her warm thighs. His fingers moved the flimsy crotch of her panties aside. Her labia were wet.

She closed her eyes and began to move against his hand.

Boxer wondered if she'd been thinking about doing this all the way out from Washington.

She was making soft moaning sounds now. Her breathing was fast. "I'm almost there," she said in a tight voice.

Boxer teased the opening of her vagina.

"Oh how I'd like your tongue there!"

"Later," he answered. "Later!"

Tracy's body tensed; then began to violently shake. She clamped her thighs together; then flung them open, only to shut them again. "That was good," she said, leaning her head back against the side of the door.

Boxer removed his hand from her vagina.

"There are tissues in the glove compartment," she sighed.

Boxer dried his hand.

"Are you okay," she asked, putting her hand over the front of his pants.

"If you don't stop that," he said, "I won't be."

"I owe you," she told him, as she adjusted her gown and then lit a cigarette. "I need a couple of minutes; then we can go in."

"Take all the time you want," Boxer answered. He needed some time too to "chill out," as some of the younger members of his crew might have said, had they found themselves in a similar situation.

Tracy took two rapid drags on the cigarette and stubbed it out. "I'm ready," she announced.

"Okay let's go," Boxer said. He left the car, went around to her side and opening the door, he offered her his arm.

"Aren't you the gallant one!" she commented.

"Sometimes," he answered. He would have preferred to say something more cutting. He did not appreciate being used to sexually satisfy her. If she needed to have an orgasm that badly, she should have masturbated.

A butler greeted them at the door and took their coats. "If you will please go into the living room," the man said, "Major Redfern and Mrs. Redfern will greet you."

Tracy took hold of Boxer's hand and as they walked toward the living room, she asked in a whisper, "Are you sulking?"

"I really don't like being used," he answered.

She smiled at him. "Don't think of yourself as having been 'used', but rather as having been a good Samaritan. You probably earned two, maybe even four Brownie points for heaven for your act of kindness. After all, not too many men would finger fuck me, even if I asked and said 'please.' "

Boxer stopped and looked at her. "You're weird," he said. "Real weird."

"Yes, I know. That's one of my most valuable assets," she answered with a smile. "Now let's go into the living room and have a good time."

The moment Sue-Ann saw Boxer and Tracy, she detached herself from the group she was with and hurried toward them. She greeted Tracy with a hug and kiss, did the same to Boxer and said, "You know Tracy, this is a really very sweet man."

Without the slightest hesitation, Tracy said, "Oh he does taste as sweet as he is."

Boxer flushed.

"You're really impossible!" Sue-Ann exclaimed. "Absolutely impossible."

"Where's Tom?" Boxer asked, hoping to change the direction of the conversation.

"He's over by the bar talking to Dad and Admiral Stark," she answered matter of factly. "Dad and the admiral are old friends. I think Dad and the admiral were officers on the same ship, or flew together . . . I don't really know. But they go back a good number of years."

Boxer was too surprised to answer. He wondered how much the senator knew about the *Shark*. How much was he responsible for getting Tom the command of the strike force?

"Do you know the admiral?" Sue-Ann asked.

Rather than lie, Boxer answered, "We've met recently." Then to explain a bit more, he added, "Because of the accident between the *Sting Ray* and the *Mary-Ann*."

"Good," Sue-Ann responded. "I'll take you to them now. Tom said he wanted to see you as soon as you came in."

"Lead the way," Tracy said. "I just adore meeting admirals!"

A few moments later, Boxer, Tracy and Sue-Ann were holding drinks and chatting with Stark, the senator and Tom. Most of the conversation was inconsequential. Stark seemed to be taken with Tracy and when she asked how he knew the senator, he said, "I know you'll find this hard to believe young lady, but when Sam and I were young, even younger than you are now —"

"Nobody can be that young," Tracy quipped.

"People were and still are," Stark answered with a smile. "Anyway, when we were that young, Sam was my wing man. We flew twenty-two combat missions off the carrier *Nimitz*. But Sam was smart, he got out of the Navy and became a politician."

"I didn't know you actually flew combat missions, Daddy," Sue-Ann said, her face suddenly going white.

"They weren't called 'combat missions' then," Stark said. "They were called other things, like reconnaissance flights. Those were troubled times in the Middle East."

"You see Tracy," the senator added, "we go back a long way."

"Now young woman," Stark said, "you mustn't use anything you hear tonight in one of your columns."

Tracy smiled. "I had no idea you knew who I was."

"I recognized the name," Stark answered. "But I'm pleased to see that you and Commander Boxer have, so to speak, buried the hatchet."

"We've buried more than that," Tracy answered with a smile.

Knowing exactly what Tracy meant, Boxer could feel the heat come into his cheeks.

Stark smiled and gave a slight nod.

Tom said, "I could use another drink. What about you, senator?"

"Why not?" the senator answered.

"I'll have one too," Stark said.

"And while all of you are enjoying yourselves," Sue-Ann told them, "I'll go see how dinner is coming along. We should be ready to serve very soon."

Boxer was quiet. Stark and the Senator were occupied with Tracy, who was being her most witty and engaging self.

Suddenly, there was a tinkle of the dinner bell and a servant in the doorway announced, "Dinner is being served. Dinner is being served."

The guests began to move toward the doorway.

"Please excuse me," Redfern said, "but I had better go and help Sue-Ann with the seating arrangements."

Tracy entwined her arm with Boxer's. "I'm starved," she commented. "What about you?"

Boxer put his empty glass down on the bar. "Now that you

143

mention, I guess I'm starved too."

The four of them ambled slowly out of the living room, across the foyer and into the dining room, where there was an enormous table laid out for dinner.

Boxer quickly counted thirty settings.

"Aren't those flowers beautiful," Tracy exclaimed, referring to the three floral displays on the table.

"The flowers come from Sue-Ann's own greenhouse," the senator said with pride. "That girl has a green thumb."

Boxer was seated close to the head of the table. Tracy was on his right. Stark sat across from him. The senator three places to the left of Stark.

"And this," Sue-Ann said, leading a slightly built gray haired man, who looked like a college professor, to the empty chair on Boxer's left, "is Mister Thomas W. Williams."

Boxer almost bolted up, instead he rose slowly. "Jack Boxer," he said, offering his hand.

"A pleasure to meet you, Commander," Williams said.

Boxer introduced Tracy.

"Miss Kimble, I'm one of your devoted readers," Williams said. "When the senator mentioned to me that you and Sue-Ann were friends and that you would probably be here tonight, I said, 'I must meet that woman and tell her how much I enjoyed her writing." Then with a quick glance at Boxer, he said, "And so must you, Commander, or you wouldn't be here with her, isn't that so?"

"I don't read her stories," Boxer answered.

"Oh?"

Tracy leaped into the breach. "That's why we're good friends, Mister Williams, he doesn't criticize how I write and what I write about."

"Obviously a good working arrangement," Williams said.

The servants began to serve the appetizer.

Several times Boxer tried to catch Redfern's eye. But the man was always looking somewhere else. He looked across the table at Stark, who was involved in a conversation with the woman on his right.

Over the soup, Tracy turned to Williams and asked, "Are you in government? Most of the people here are."

He gave her an avuncular smile. "Try to guess what I do?"

"Well, you are like a college professor, but somehow I don't think you are . . . . I'd guess you're either a lawyer, or perhaps a psychiatrist."

"Neither," Williams answered with obvious pleasure.

Trying hard not to pay too much attention to Tracy's conversation with Williams, Boxer continued to spoon up the soup.

"One more try?" Tracy asked.

"Please do," Williams responded.

"A minister!" Tracy exclaimed.

"No," Williams answered. "I am hardly the type. I am a government agent."

Boxer gaped and began to choke; then cough. "I'm terribly sorry," he said, feeling foolish that he had drawn everyone's attention to himself. "I'm all right."

"You're joking!" Tracy exclaimed, looking at Williams.

"CIA," he said.

Tracy began to laugh. "You're really a very funny man."

Williams laughed too. "So I have been told," he said.

"Now really, what are you into?" Tracy asked.

"I'm into, as you so quaintly put it, shipping," Williams answered. "I own and operated the Thomas W. Williams Shipping Company."

"Now that's more like it," Tracy said. "Jack, what do you think?"

He was tempted to say, 'you can't judge a book by its cover.' Instead, he managed a smile and said, "Now that Mister Williams told us, I'd have to say he looks as if he owns a shipping company."

"Okay," Tracy said. "Okay, I guess I deserve that."

Williams patted her hand. "It is all right, dear," he told her, "most people don't know the truth even when they're told it."

For the main course, the guests had a choice of roast venison, rack of lamb or steak.

Tracy asked for the lamb and Boxer, the venison.

The conversation at the table was either about politics, or about the social life of the city. Neither one interested Boxer, though he was more conversant with some aspects of the political situation than he was with the social.

Dessert was Flaming Alaska, which was followed by coffee and brandy for those who wanted it. After dinner the guests left the table and returned to the living room, where there were trays of various cheeses and crackers laid out and a servant behind the bar was ready to serve whatever a guest might want to drink.

After awhile, Sue-Ann came over to Tracy and said, "Some one wants to meet with you. Do be a dear and come with me."

"Mind?" she asked Boxer.

He shook his head. "Have to meet your public," he said.

As soon as Tracy left, Stark came up to him. "Go to the foyer, up the steps and into the third room on the right. Leave now. I'll follow in two minutes."

Boxer obeyed and found Redfern, the senator and Williams in what was obviously either the senator's or Redfern's study. "The admiral will be along shortly," he said.

Redfern offered him a cigar.

"I'll stay with the pipe," Boxer said, taking it out of his jacket pocket.

Stark entered the room and closed the door behind him. "This dinner was at my request," he said. "I wanted you, Boxer, to meet Williams. He's top man at the Agency for this project."

"I don't like being set up," Boxer said, blowing smoke from the bowl of the pipe. He figured it was best to let Stark know where he was coming from.

"It was the best way to handle the situation," the senator said.

"And I wanted to meet you in unofficial surroundings," Williams said.

"Did you know about all of this?" Boxer asked Redfern.

"Not a smidgin more than you did," he answered. "About five minutes ago the senator told me to go up to the study and he'll join me. I found Williams already up here."

"If you're concerned about the major having inside information," Stark said, "I can assure you he doesn't, or if he does, it concerns him and not you."

Boxer nodded. He was somewhat mollified.

"The reason for all of this," Stark said, "is that we've moved the timetable ahead. Jack, you'll resign from the Navy, as of Wednesday of this coming week; then I want to get the word out to the press that you went on vacation for a few days. Say three days somewhere in the Virgin Islands. Take that Tracy woman, or anyone else to make it look good. When you return, you will apply for the captaincy of the *Tecumseh*. A week or so later, the Williams Company will send out a press release to the effect that you are now associated with the company and will captain the *Tecumseh*."

"Why the speedup?" Boxer asked.

"We have good reason to believe that the Russians are contemplating a boat very similar to the *Shark*."

"We want to be able to exploit whatever lead we have over them," Williams added.

"Then that means the *Shark* will go downriver soon," Boxer said.

"She'll be ready about the time you come back from your vacation," Stark responded.

"With me and my crew aboard?" Boxer asked. "We're going to need all the on the job training we can get."

"Yes," Stark answered.

Boxer looked at Redfern again. "What's your cover, Tom?"

"I put in my resignation this morning," Redfern answered. "My men are already out of their respective branches and have been in training for the last month at various locations. All are going to be employed by the TW Oil Exploration Company, with headquarters in New York, and branch offices in Cairo, Rome and Tokyo."

"I didn't know you were so talkative," Boxer laughed.

"And I didn't want you to think —"

"The admiral settled that question," Boxer said.

"Good," Stark said. "Now is there anything else either you Jack, or Tom want to bring up?" he asked.

"I have nothing," Redfern said.

Boxer dug into the note he had scribbled in the hotel room. "Can you have this run down?" he asked, handing the piece of paper to Stark. "That report was about interviews with Soviet submarine captains. I want to know the name of the one who told him about the research mission in the Arctic."

"Why?" Stark asked.

"Because, sir, that's going to be where I'm going to put the *Shark* through the grinder."

"But —" Williams began.

"There aren't any buts," Boxer said, looking at Stark. "If the *Shark* is really what she was designed to be, then she'll do what she's asked to do. But if there are any flaws, the one place in the world where they'll show up is in the Arctic. I've been up there three times and let me tell you, it's the best place to test her."

"If that's what you think," Stark said, "then that's what you'll have to do."

"Thank you, sir," Boxer responded. Again he looked toward Redfern and said, "Tom, you and your men will have to be part of this shakedown cruise."

"That's okay with me," Redfern answered.

"I think we had better rejoin the rest of the company," Williams suggested, "or your lady friend, Commander — oh I forgot, you're really a captain now, aren't you?"

"Yes," Boxer said. "And yes, I think Tracy will become suspicious about an overlong absence."

"I'll return first," the senator said. "Williams, follow me."

"Jack and I can mosey on down after the admiral," Tom said. "If there are any questions, I can always say I was showing you some books and maps that Sam had stashed away in the library."

There was a round of handshakes and they wished each other good luck.

"How do you think the shakedown will be?" Redfern asked, when he and Boxer were finally alone.

"Under the best of conditions up in the Arctic, it's hard," Boxer said. "But I'm going to take the *Shark* up there just at the end of winter, when some of the worst weather occurs."

"You're the skipper," Redfern answered.

Boxer nodded. He had made his decision; now he'd have to carry it out and be responsible for its success or failure. . . .

On Tuesday, Boxer flew up to New York on the first shuttle flight out of Washington. The night before he had called his parents and Gwen and told them he was coming in to tell them something very important. He had arranged to see his parents in the morning and Gwen in the afternoon.

Gwen had been cool on the phone but had agreed, telling him

148

that she'd be working at home.

He had asked if anything was wrong.

"Just a bit more tired than usual," she had answered. "I'll see you tomorrow. . . ."

Boxer cabbed it from LaGuardia to his parents' home. His mother had a breakfast of sausage, eggs, and home baked coffee cake to go with the coffee.

There was no easy way for Boxer to say what he had come to say. He waited until after breakfast; then he said, "Mom, please sit down, I have something important to tell you."

She sat down.

Boxer plunged to the core of the matter. "Tomorrow, I'm resigning from the Navy."

His father's jaw went slack.

"I knew it," his mother said in a low moan. "As God is my judge, I told your father that you were coming to tell us that."

The pain on their faces knotted Boxer's stomach and forced him to clear his throat before he spoke. "I was given the choice of resigning or facing a court-martial, which I was told would most probably find me guilty of dereliction of duty. For that the penalty could be much worse, especially since it supposedly resulted in the death of five crewmen."

For a long time no one said anything.

Boxer listened to the sound of his own breathing and watched the second hand sweep around the face of the clock on the wall above the sink.

"You're not going to fight it?" his father asked, in a tremulous voice.

Boxer shook his head. "No point to it."

"What will you do?" his mother questioned.

Boxer managed a smile. "I'm going to be the master of the super-tanker, *Tecumseh*. It's owned by a shipping company and I'll—"

"Is that what you want?" his father asked.

Boxer looked straight at him. "Yes, Dad, it's what I want."

Again there was a period of silence, but not as long as the first.

"Maybe if the Kimble woman hadn't gone after you, things might have been different," his father said.

"I don't think so," Boxer said, wondering what his parents

149

would think if they knew he was sleeping with Tracy?

"What about your pension?" his mother asked.

"That's one of the reasons I'm resigning now," Boxer answered. "I don't want to risk losing any of the benefits that would have been mine under normal conditions."

The conversation drifted a bit longer and then changed to family matters, with Boxer asking after several of his relatives, all of whom he hadn't seen in several years.

Boxer left his parents' home at eleven o'clock. His father walked him to the subway station. When it came to say goodby, Boxer said, "You'll see, Dad, it won't be so bad."

"You don't have to convince me," his father answered. "You have to convince yourself."

"I've already done that, Dad," Boxer said. "It really wasn't as hard as you seem to think. The Navy no longer wants me. The reason doesn't matter. But it is the bottom line. I've found a place for myself that will give me a very good income and keep me at sea. It's a good combination."

His father accepted the explanation with a nod; they shook hands, embraced and Boxer hurried down the steps to the subway platform. The charade was so real, he was beginning to believe he had indeed let his parents down. . . .

Boxer found Gwen in a violet dressing gown, with her hair held back by a simple white ribbon. As soon as he had his coat off, he asked, "How is John doing at school with the other students?"

"Since you're not in the news any more, they seemed to have forgotten all about it," she answered, leading the way into the living room and sitting down on the couch with her feet curled under her.

Boxer settled in the easy chair opposite Gwen and said, "I've already seen my mother and father and told them what I'm about to tell you."

"You're not going to marry—"

"Absolutely not!" Boxer exclaimed, waving the question aside. He forced himself to keep a straight face, though he very much wanted to laugh.

"I thought you told me you weren't sleeping with her?"

150

"Gwen," Boxer said, "I didn't come here to discuss my sex life with you. I'm resigning from the Navy."

"Oh!" she exclaimed, standing up and going to the window, where she remained silent for several moments. Then slowly turning toward him, she said, "Is that what you really want to do?"

Boxer made an open gesture with his hands. "I don't have a choice." And he told her about the probable outcome of a court-martial. "This way I have my pension and all the other benefits that go with retirement."

"You're not just going to sit back and let the world go by, are you?"

He explained that he would soon be captain of the super-tanker, *Tecumseh*.

"So you'll still be at sea a good part of the time?"

"Yes, I suppose so," he answered.

Gwen laced her fingers and let them hang down in front of her. She went back to the couch and resumed her former position.

"You know I'm furious with you," she said.

"Don't you think that's kind of foolish?"

"You just flaunted that Kimble woman in front of me. How long have you been sleeping with her?"

Boxer shrugged. "Not long."

"Are you in love with her?"

"No."

"That night was one of the worst in my life," Gwen told him. "I wound up having a ferocious row with Paul. I haven't seen him since."

Boxer remembered what Tracy had said would happen between Gwen and her doctor friend. She had certainly called it accurately. He was finding it very hard to be sympathetic.

"He hasn't called," Gwen went on, "and I'll be damned if I'll call him."

Boxer felt like slapping his knee and saying, "Stick to your guns." But instead he very calmly suggested, "Perhaps you're being too harsh? Too stubborn?"

Gwen rose to her feet. "You don't understand," she said, pacing back and forth. "You don't understand. I was ready to make a commitment to him. I was ready to live with him."

"Do you love him?" Boxer asked.

151

Gwen stopped pacing. "Do you love that woman you were with?"

Boxer shook his head.

"I don't know," she said. "I don't really know if I love him. We've been good for each other, up until now that is."

"I can understand that," Boxer said, standing.

"Is that Kimble woman good for you?" Gwen asked.

Boxer avoided posing that question to himself before. But now that Gwen had done it for him, he felt bound to answer. "Sexually, probably. She uses me and I'm learning to use her."

"That's almost sick," Gwen said with disgust.

"Not as long as the two of us know what the score is," Boxer answered. "We don't love each other. I don't think we ever could."

"Isn't there any woman you love?" she asked.

"You, Gwen . . . I love you," he said, going up to her and putting his arms around her.

She nestled against his chest. "I can't be the wife you want and should have," she said.

Boxer nuzzled her hair. It smelled clean. He knew if he wanted her, he could have her. She was defenseless.

"Here I am going on about my problems," Gwen said, "and you have a few of your own."

"Mine are all solved," Boxer answered.

She looked up at him. "You know the real reason why I stayed home today?"

"Tell me?"

"To try and think everything through," she said. "I want some sort of life. I'm tired of the singles scene. Paul said he felt the same way." She pursed her lips and tears started to flow out of her eyes. "I'm really sorry . . . I shouldn't be laying this on you."

"What are ex-husbands for," he chuckled.

She started to speak; then stopped herself.

"Say it," Boxer urged.

"Are ex-husbands also there to make love to their ex-wives?" she asked in a whisper.

Boxer held her tightly. He could feel her breasts against his chest. He desperately wanted to lift her in his arms and carry her into the bedroom. He couldn't begin to remember the number of times he fantasied about doing just that. But now that he had the opportunity, he couldn't. "I'd just be taking advantage of a situation," he said, caressing her back. "Afterwards you'd be angry with yourself and with me."

She reached up to his face and touched his lips with her fingers. "Sometimes," she said, "for what it's worth, I love you too."

"Thanks," he said, kissing her on the forehead. He let go of her and stepped back. "You tell John I was here and I'll see him soon."

"Yes, I'll tell him," Gwen said. "If you want to stay for lunch—"

"No thanks," Boxer said. "If I were to stay, we'd be sorry afterwards." He went to the closet and got his coat and hat.

She started for the door.

"No, stay where you are," Boxer said. "I'll see you soon," he opened the door and let himself out. His heart was beating very fast and he was sweating profusely. With his gloved forefinger he stabbed viciously at the elevator button. . . .

The next few days went very quickly. He spent four of them with Cynthia on the island of Antigua. And the last morning there, after they made love, Boxer said, "I put my resignation in before I left."

Cynthia moved her hand ove his bare chest. "I thought you'd do something like that."

He told her about the *Tecumseh*.

"Then you'll be going to sea soon?"

"Yes, very soon."

"My offer still stands," she said. "You may stay at my place whenever you're in town. By the way, what city will be your home port?"

That was a question he hadn't even thought of asking Williams and no one, up until now, had asked him.

"You do have a home port?"

"It might be Baltimore," he lied. "The company is waiting to hear because of the size of the ship."

She accepted the explanation without additional comment.

When he returned to his office the next morning at BuPers, he found one of Quinn's aides waiting for him. "Don't tell me,"

153

Boxer said with a smile, "you're my personal escort to his office."

"You got it," the aide answered.

Quinn was in high dudgeon. He jumped to his feet as soon as Boxer entered his office and waving Boxer's letter of resignation in front of him, he shouted, "You're not going to get away with this, mister. You're not going to slink away and collect a pension for the rest of your life."

Boxer felt a sudden rush of anger. But as quickly as it came, it vanished. He wasn't going to make any reply. Not even raise an eyebrow.

"Something stinks here," Quinn ranted, "and I'm going to make it my business to find out what it is. I too have friends in high places and if it takes a congressional investigation to uncover the . . . the—"

Boxer couldn't resist. "The plot, sir."

A look of astonishment came across Quinn's cherubic face.

"Obviously there must be a plot," Boxer said with a straight face.

Quinn switched gears. He stopped shouting, took a deep breath and said, "I'm going to disapprove it."

Boxer shrugged. "As long as you send it forward and we both know you must do that, then I don't really care what you do or don't do, sir."

"We'll see," Quinn said. "Which one of us will have the proverbial last laugh on the other . . . Dismissed."

Boxer did his snappy about-face, marched to the door and left Quinn's office.

Later in the afternoon he received a visit from Courtney, who closed the door of the cubicle and sat down on the top of the desk before he said, "Quinn has called the CNO and said he'd go to the SECNAV if he can't stop, or at least delay your resignation."

"Can he do any harm?" Boxer asked.

"Raise some dust, probably . . . But real damage, no. Before he does that someone from the Company will be down to see him. By the way, have you seen the morning paper?"

Boxer shook his head.

"I thought you might be interested in this," Courtney said, taking a clipping out of his pocket and placing it on the desk in front of Boxer.

Boxer looked up at Courtney. "Luckily, I could prove I was in Antigua at the time."

"You'll probably be getting phone calls from some reporters," Courtney said. "Don't make any comments, other than to repeat what you just said to me. Remember nothing that could be construed as judgmental."

Boxer nodded.

"You don't have to read the rest of the story," Courtney said. "It goes on to describe what the New York police think happened."

"I had no intentions of reading it," Boxer said. "I don't go in for that kind of stuff."

Courtney launched himself off the desk. "See you around," he said and opening the door, he left the office.

The first reporter called twenty minutes later and asked him if he had any comments about the killings.

Boxer followed Courtney's instructions.

"Let me put it another way," the reporter said, "do you think those two men deserved to be killed?"

"That's something you'll have to decide for yourself," Boxer answered. "Now if you'll excuse me, I have important work to do." And he hung up.

In the space of an hour four more reporters called; then for the rest of the morning it was quiet. Boxer used the time to think about the coming trip down the Mississippi and the beginning of the *Shark*'s sea trials. He figured that the *Shark* wouldn't be moving more than five, possibly six knots an hour. Throughout the river trip, she'd be under tow and he'd have whatever time the voyage took, to drill the crew so that once they put to sea, every man would be thoroughly trained. Boxer figured he'd run the first tests in the Caribbean, off Antigua. And—

The phone rang.

Boxer was tempted not to answer it. But he picked it up. Before he could speak, Tracy said, "I want to have dinner with you,

Jack."

He decided to play with her a bit. "Well, I don't know."

"It's important," Tracy said.

"Important, according to Tracy, or important by broader standards."

"Do we meet or don't we?" She demanded to know.

"Say when and where?"

"The Black Swan," she said, "it's an English style pub near the Capitol. At seven."

"I'll be there," Boxer told her.

This time she hung up before he did.

Boxer took his pipe out, filled and lit it. He was just settling down to enjoying a good smoke, when the same officer he found waiting for him in the morning put his head into the open doorway and said, "The admiral wants to see you again."

"I hope his temper has improved," Boxer said, setting his pipe down in the ashtray. "By the time I come back, most of the tobacco will have burned and I'll have to dig it out, clean the stem and start all over again."

"Yes, sir," the young officer said.

Boxer smiled. He somehow couldn't picture himself ever having been that young, or that fearful of anyone with a higher rank. Yet he knew he was exactly like that. Only he wasn't an admiral's aide. He applied for and got submarine duty immediately after he graduated from Annapolis. "All right Ensign—" He looked at the man's name tag. "Ensign Grant is it?"

"Yes, sir."

"Lead me to the admiral's den," Boxer said. A few minutes later, he was again standing in front of the admiral.

"Sit down," Quinn ordered.

Boxer nodded and sat down.

"I've just come from a meeting with SECNAV and the CNO," Quinn said.

Boxer remained expressionless, though he guessed what would be coming next.

"I'm not the kind of man who's afraid to say he was wrong," Quinn told him.

"Sir, there's no need for you to say anything," Boxer said. "I enjoyed the role I played."

"You played it very well indeed," Quinn responded.

The two men faced each other across the desk and Quinn offered his hand. Boxer shook it and in a low voice, he said, "Better start shouting at me as soon as I start for the door, otherwise the rest of the staff out there wouldn't think our relationship was normal."

Quinn nodded. "I'll start now," he said and immediately shouted, "Get out of my office . . . Get out." Then in a low voice, he said, "Good luck, Jack, to you and all your men."

Boxer did a smart about-face, walked to the door, opened it, and paused to let everyone hear Quinn bellow, "I'm going to break you, Boxer, remember that!"

With a pained expression on his face, Boxer walked back to his cubicle. He felt the weight of every eye in the room on his back. Before he reached the cubicle, he decided to go down to the cafeteria and drown his sorrow in a cup of coffee.

When Boxer stepped through the doorway of the Black Swan, he felt as if he had stepped back in time at least two hundred years. The bar was dimly lit, with a huge teak counter. The walls were covered with darkly stained wainscoting and in the main dining room several logs were burning in a huge hearth. Boxer handed his coat and hat to the woman in the cloakroom. Then he went to the maitre d' and asked, "Has Miss Kimble arrived?"

The man nodded and in an English accent, he said, "Yes, if you will please follow me, sir."

Tracy was at a table that was situated catty-corner to the fireplace. She wore a black jersey dress that hugged every curve of her body.

Boxer sat down.

"Have any trouble finding the place?" she asked.

"None."

A waiter came to the table and asked if they wanted cocktails.

"A Gibson," Tracy said.

"Glenlivet, neat," Boxer ordered. "Now what's so important?" he asked, as soon as the waiter left the table.

"We'll talk about it later," she answered.

Two possibilities jumped into Boxer's mind: she was pregnant, or she wanted to get married. The first could easily be the reason

157

for the second, or each could be independent of the other.

The waiter brought their drinks.

"You didn't tell me you were going away for a few days," Tracy said. "I called your hotel several times."

Boxer downed his drink. He didn't care for her attitude. But he said nothing.

"After the last weekend at the Redferns—"

"Tracy, tell me what you want to tell me, or ask me what you want to ask. But don't beat around the bush."

"Why didn't you tell me you were resigning?"

"Oh that!"

"Yes that," she said. "Some other reporter got wind of it and did the story."

"Is that what you think is important?" Boxer asked.

Tracy lit a cigarette. "Yes, at least to me. I could have written a damn good piece about that, especially since those two men from the *Mary-Ann* were killed."

Boxer smiled. "Luckily I can prove I was in Antigua."

"I know," Tracy said.

"You know?" Boxer questioned, trying to keep the edge out of his voice.

"I also knew you were there with a woman," Tracy said with a catlike smile on her lips.

Boxer shook his head. "I don't like being spied on . . . I don't like it at all."

"Sue-Ann called me," Tracy said, "all in tears because Tom just resigned from the Corps."

Boxer looked down at his glass; he was sorry it was empty. And he didn't want to call attention to his anxiety by ordering another one.

"Now wouldn't you call that a coincidence?" Tracy asked.

Boxer ignored the question. "What would you recommend to eat here?" he asked.

"I know something is happening, or going to happen," she said.

"If you know that," Boxer answered, "then why don't you find out what it is."

"I promised not to write—"

"Tracy, you can promise what you want. I don't know what you're talking about."

She nodded. "Okay, I didn't think you'd tell me anything. But you can't blame a woman for trying, can you?"

Boxer relaxed. "Yes, I can blame her, when she begins to make connections that don't really exist. There are enough problems without creating more of them."

"Shall I consider myself reprimanded?"

"Yes," Boxer answered. "Now will you tell me what the specialty of the house is?"

"Roast prime rib of beef," Tracy answered.

Suddenly Boxer felt his right leg clamped between her two.

She smiled at him. "Any objections?"

"None," he answered.

"I don't know why," Tracy said, "but when I'm with you I want to do the most outrageous things."

"Am I supposed to have an answer for that?"

She shrugged. "I thought you might."

"I don't," Boxer said with mock seriousness. "But I have thought about it and attribute it to my magnificent sexual prowess, coupled to your insatiable appetite."

"And I thought the two of us just enjoyed fancy fucking."

"That too," Boxer said with a broad grin. "That too!"

10

Boxer went aboard the *Shark* at 1100.

The crew was in formation on the after deck.

Boxer stood in front of them and said, "Welcome aboard men. All of us are here because we want to be here. Except under certain conditions we'll dispense with the usual military formalities. Any questions?"

There weren't any.

"All right men, fall out and let's get this boat ready to move," Boxer said.

Harris, Pierce and Monty followed Boxer down to his quarters.

"What's this for?" Boxer asked, looking at a small computer console.

"It's called a System Test Net. It'll give you a system by system evaluation of every system on the boat and if there's a malfunction it will tell you where it is and the component that malfunctioned."

"Can it do anything else?" Boxer asked, expecting a negative response.

"If you press that red key there," Monty said, "you'll receive the same image pattern that CIC has."

"I can practically run the *Shark* from here," Boxer commented. He sat down at his desk and told the other men to sit on his bunk. "Now down to business. When are we due to leave here, Pierce?"

"Tonight, about eighteen hundred," Pierce said. "But we're not just going to be towed down between the barges. Everything is going with us. The entire facility goes."

"I don't understand," Boxer said.

Monty explained, "We're only going to travel at night."

"Christ," Harris exclaimed, "that'll take us several weeks to get all the way down river."

"On a good night's run," Pierce said, "we'll average about seventy-two miles."

"Why the turtle's pace?" Boxer asked, filling his pipe and lighting it.

"To the Ruskie spy satellites we'll look like a very large tow at night and during the day we'll be part of the river bank. The top is well camouflaged and has special materials to give a typical picture of a river bank."

Boxer looked at Harris. "The men could use the time to become more than just familiar with the equipment. We'll schedule every kind of drill we can think of between us from straight forward operating procedures to the improbable kind of an emergency. If we can think of it, chances are it probably can happen."

Harris agreed.

Boxer turned his attention to Pierce again. "The captain and the crew of the tug are the Navy or—"

"They're Company men," Pierce answered. "But the tug is rented. They have strict orders not to leave the tug, unless you order them to."

"I'll want to speak to the captain before we shove off," Boxer said. "I'll go aboard about fourteen hundred."

"I've organized the watches," Harris said, "as if we were at sea."

"Very good," Boxer responded. "And when we tie up for the day, I want to put out an armed guard say about two hundred feet out from where we are. The men are to be armed and have a clip of ammo in their weapons. I want all of them in radio contact with our COMOROOM."

"Yes, sir," Harris answered.

"Put two dinghies with two men in each on the river side," Boxer said.

"Will do," Harris responded.

"Redfern and his men will be coming aboard by thirteen hundred. Split the guard detail between his men and the crew. Now is there anything else?"

"Two things," Pierce said. "First has to do with the river. Because of the early thaw, the river is rising rapidly and that could mean changes that might delay us."

"What kind of changes?" Boxer asked.

"Sand bars where there was supposed to be a clear channel," Pierce answered. "We're going to have to pick our way very carefully."

"The gear we have on board should help solve that problem," Boxer said. "It'll give us a chance to test it before we get out to sea."

"Can't use it," Pierce said. "Once we turn any of those systems on the spy in the sky will have us on camera before you can say Moscow."

"Then we'll have a lead," Boxer said with a smile. "By the way how many feet of water do we need beneath us to stay afloat on this river."

"Fifteen feet all the way down to Baton Rouge where the river becomes more saline. Our daily anchorages have all been dredged out and for each there's an alternate one halfway betwween every two scheduled stops. The dredge works a day in front of us."

Boxer glanced at Harris.

"We could be lucky," Harris said.

"If we are," Boxer responded, "we'll need a string of luck a thousand miles long." He looked back at Pierce and asked, "What's the second problem?"

"It's not really a problem," Pierce said. "But during the day the tug won't be with us."

Boxer bolted up. "Why the hell not?"

"Tows usually don't tie up along the river," Pierce explained. "A tug sitting with us would look peculiar to everyone on the river and to anyone looking at photographs of the river."

"That means for twelve hours we'll be without power to move us in case of an emergency," Boxer fumed.

Pierce nodded.

"I don't like it one bit," Boxer said. "Not one fucking bit!"

"The Company has worked out these procedures to give us maximum security," Monty said.

"Maximum security of a damaged or wrecked sub is maximum security of nothing," Boxer answered. He didn't like the plans but he knew he had to live with them. It was just too late to do anything else. Not without causing a furor in Washington between Stark, who would certainly understand his reaction to leaving the *Shark* without any means to move, and the Company, who'd see security as their main objective. "I'm not angry at you," he told Pierce. "I'm just pissed at the idiots who come up with these dumb ideas that we're supposed to follow. Okay, we'll live with it. Harris, pass the word that I'm going to inspect every inch of this boat before we shove off."

"There's one more thing I think should be brought up," Harris said.

"Shoot!" Boxer answered.

"Our men do not know about the strike force that's coming aboard," he said. "I think you have to make it clear to them that the *Shark's* main mission is to carry the strike force wherever it is needed. Some of the men think they're still aboard the *Sting Ray*, at least part of their heads are still there."

"Will do," Boxer said. "But I want Redfern's men here when I do it. I want to make it clear to both groups that any sort of fighting — of the kind that usually takes place between Marines and sailors — will be severely dealt with."

"That's fine with me," Harris responded.

"I'll see all of you later," Boxer said. The men filed out of his quarters, leaving him alone. He took time to change into the white coveralls the officers wore and then he went on an inspection tour of the *Shark*. He saw every section, examined the status reports of each piece of equipment. He even checked the operating condition of the bilge pumps.

At 1300 Harris came to him and said, "The major is here."

Boxer hurried topside and greeted Redfern with a hearty handshake. "My man," he said proudly, gesturing to the five ranks of twenty men, all of whom were dressed in combat fatigues, carrying their M-22 rifles, knapsack and duffle bag. "Men, the skipper of the *Shark*, Captain Jack Boxer."

"Welcome aboard!" Boxer called out; then to Redfern, he said, "Get them settled in and give them a Cook's tour of the boat; then I have something to say to them and to my men."

Redfern started to salute.

"Stow it, Tom," Boxer said. "Aboard the *Shark* we don't have to go in for that kind of window dressing. The men know who we are and what we are."

"I knew I'd like this man," Redfern commented, "the very moment I saw him."

Boxer smiled and hurried down below to continue his inspection. He paid particular attention to the mess, where every man was given the kind of food he wanted but always the exact number of calories he needed to maintain his optimum weight.

"You know, Skipper," one of the bakers said, "if I didn't see this place with my own eyes, I'd think I was dreamin! There's everything a man can want here . . . Meats, vegetables, soups . . . They're all here. And there aren't any knives and forks. We were issued chopsticks, a spoon for soup, or ice cream and knife. Not a butter cutting knife, but a real knife." He drew it out of its sheath. "For cutting meat and other stuff."

This was something new for Boxer. Neither Pierce or Monty had mentioned anything about the chopsticks, the spoon or the knife.

"And there are no dishes to wash, or trays. Everything we throw away gets ground up and when we empty our slop tanks into the sea this stuff goes too. But everything disintegrates or can be eaten by fish. I never thought a boat would be like this."

"She's unique," Boxer said. "There's only one like her and we're aboard her."

At fourteen hundred Boxer went aboard the tub, the *Billy Dee*, and up to the bridge to meet its captain, a bullnecked man with a two-day growth on his chin and an unlit cigar stub in his mouth. "Name is Conway, Lewis Conway," he said.

Boxer introduced himself.

"I know who you are," Conway said. "And before we get off on the wrong footing, let's get one thing straight from the very beginning: this is my tow. That means, Mister, I'm the boss of what happens when we're underway. You understand that and everything will be just peaches and cream from here all the way down to the Gulf."

Boxer smiled. "Now if you don't mind I want to see your river charts for the next thirty miles downstream."

"What charts?"

"The navigation charts," Boxer said.

Conway rolled his cigar from one side of his mouth to the other. "Charts, sheet! Fuckin' pieces of paper. All my chart's up here." And he tapped the right side of his head.

Boxer took a deep breath. "I'll ask you once more, Captain, to show me the charts."

"And if I don't, what do you think you're going to do about it?"

"Mister," Boxer said, "I don't have time to play fucking games with you. This is your tow, all right, but all this including you are under my command." He opened one of the forward windows and shouted down to one of *Shark's* sailors, "Tell Major Redfern to come aboard the tug on the double with four armed men."

"Aye, aye, sir," the man answered.

Conway glared at him.

"They should be here," Boxer said, "in two minutes. That's as long as you have, Mister, to make up your mind to two things: who's in command and whether you have any brains between your ears or just plain stupidity."

"No one tells Lew Conway what to do."

Boxer glanced down to the deck of the *Shark*. Redfern and four men were running toward the tug. "You don't have much time," Boxer said.

"The charts are down there," Conway said, "in that closet."

"Get them and put them out on the chart table," Boxer said. "From now on until the *Shark* is no longer your tow, I expect to see the correct chart for the particular section of the river that we'll be traveling on. And Mister, make no mistake about it, if the correct chart isn't there, you're in, as the expression goes, 'deep shit.' You understand that?"

Redfern and his four men suddenly burst onto the bridge. "What's wrong, Skipper?"

"Mister Conway is about to give me an answer," Boxer said. "If he gives me the right answer, you and your men will return to the *Shark* with me. But if he gives me the wrong answer, place him under arrest and bring him to the *Shark*."

For a moment Conway's eyes looked as if they'd pop out of his skull. "You don't give a fuckin' inch, do you?"

"No," Boxer said quietly, "I don't."

Conway nodded.

"Not enough," Boxer said, "I want to hear it and I want Major Redfern to hear it too."

Grudgingly, Conway said: "You're in command."

"And the charts?"

"The right one for the night's run will be on the chart table," Conway said.

"Major, you and your men return to the *Shark*," Boxer said, "I'm going to remain here for a while."

"Aye, aye, sir," Redfern answered, giving Boxer a smart salute and he and his men left the *Billy Dee*'s bridge.

"Now, Captain, let's go over the chart for tonight's run," Boxer said.

An hour before sunset the sky clouded over and by 1800 the night was pitch black. But fifteen minutes after the hour the *Shark*, enveloped inside four enormous barges, began to move slowly downriver.

Boxer was on the bridge of the *Billy Dee* and with a radio no larger than a cigarette pack maintained communications with every officer on the *Shark*.

Conway worked the tow into midstream; then took time to light his stubby cigar. "Black as a witch's cunt," he commented. "Only thing you can see is the runnin' light of other tows and none of them, unless you're too close for comfort." He switched on the radar, looked at the screen for few moments, nodded and said, "nothin' for five miles above or below us."

Boxer went to the screen and looked at it. From the markings on the scope, he could tell that the river was three miles wide where they were: wide enough to give any other tow lots of room to pass them. "I'm going aboard the *Shark*," he said.

Conway nodded and continued to steer the *Billy Dee*.

A cold drizzling rain started to fall at 0100 when Boxer was making the fourth check of the lines that secured the tow to the *Billy Dee* and the barges to the *Shark*. He had never been in a situation even vaguely similar to this one and it made him uneasy. Should any of the lines part, the damage to the *Shark* could take weeks, if not months to repair. . . .

Boxer reentered the *Shark* and passed through the CR, where Harris and Cowly were going through a dry run dive.

"How's it going?" Boxer asked.

"So far, a piece of cake," Cowly said. "Less to worry about here. Everything is automatically checked and rechecked. The real problem is to get yourself and the men to trust the machines."

Harris agreed with Cowly on that point.

"How much longer are you going to go?" Boxer asked.

"Another hour," Harris said. "The next few dives will have some surprises."

Boxer smiled. "Let's hope we don't ever have those kinds of surprises."

Both Harris and Cowly nodded.

"Tom told me you had a bit of a problem with the captain of the tug," Harris said.

"He tried to push me a bit and discovered not only that he couldn't but that I could push a lot harder," Boxer said.

"Hell, he could have saved himself all that trouble just by asking any member of the crew," Harris said.

The three of them laughed and Boxer continued to walk through the boat, observing what each section was doing and taking time to chat with the officers and men.

His last stop as the area assigned to the strike force. Though its men ate in the same mess as the boat's crew and at the same time, they occupied the large space just forward of the after torpedo room. Even with a hundred men and their personal equipment there was room to spare. The area included sleeping space and a large open space for exercise, which was what they were doing when he entered.

Boxer watched them do two-hundred pushups and then started to run around the perimeter before he returned to his own quarters, where he made a taped log entry; then he dropped down on his bunk and closed his eyes. Already, he realized, the men were settling into a routine that they would hold until the *Shark* could move under her own power, which was at least three weeks away. Then he drifted off to sleep.

Boxer slept two hours and after having coffee in the galley, he checked the lashings again; then went through the boat once more. All stations, except the COMMO ROOM were secure.

Just before 0600, Boxer crossed over to the *Billy Dee* and went up to the bridge.

Conway looked at him, rolled his cigar stub to the left side of his mouth and said, "We're about two miles from where I drop you off."

Boxer nodded, went to the chart table and saw the position marked with a penciled in X.

Conway looked over at the radar and eased the wheel over a few degrees; then he rang up the engine room and reduced power to a third. "Could come in full power and swing into reverse," he explained. "But I like to let the river do some of the work. We got a four knot current going, be foolish not to use it."

"I'd do the same thing myself," Boxer commented.

Conway looked at him and smiled.

By 0610, the tow was tied up and the *Billy Dee* moved off.

The guards were posted and the men aboard the *Shark* were put through more dry runs.

Boxer took a particular interest in the DCC, the Damage Control Center. Short of total disaster, he wanted to make sure that the Damage Control Personnel would be able to keep the *Shark* underway and get it to the surface, where it might be able to rendezvous with the *Tecumseh*. It was his plan never to have the *Tecumseh* more than a thousand miles away, or something in the order of three and a half days sailing time.

All of the damage control information was in the Damage Control Computer and in a fifteen volume set of manuals that covered every system and every part in every system.

Boxer asked the Damage Control Officer to recreate the damage suffered by the *Sting Ray*.

"I've already done that, sir," the man said. "With what we have aboard the *Shark*, we could have brought the fire under control in two minutes and saved—"

"Run it," *Shark* said.

The officer turned the computer switch to simulator, typed in the description of the type of damage sustained, including the section of the hull damaged, followed by two sets of numbers.

Boxer asked what the numbers meant.

"They're coordinates. Each section of the *Shark* has two sets of numbers that define it for the computer."

A three dimensional picture came up on the screen.

"Watch this," the officer said with some pride. He pressed a key marked DAMAGE and immediately the picture on the screen changed to reflect the damage; then he pressed a third key, marked "EXECUTE." Instantly the following readout on the screen appeared: BLOWERS STOPPED. NITROGEN INTRODUCED. FIRE SUPPRESSED. SUFFICIENT OXYGEN AVAILABLE FOR BREATHING. COMPARTMENT CAN BE ENTERED TO

REMOVE INJURED PERSONNEL.

"You mean that's all there would have been to it?" Boxer asked, stunned by what he had just seen.

"Yes, sir."

"What about the necessary repairs?"

Again the officer typed in a description of the various kinds of damage sustained by the *Sting Ray*. This time he asked the computer to recommend repair procedures. They immediately came up on the screen. "You see, sir," the officer said, "it's almost like magic."

Boxer nodded. He wanted to say, Too bad we didn't have that kind of magic aboard the *Sting Ray*. But he checked himself and said, "I want every man in your section to be able to work that computer."

"Yes, sir. I've already started a training program."

Boxer left the DCC and toured the guard posts; then he returned to his cabin to make another taped log entry.

The days and nights on the river passed slowly and without incident. But just about the time they were going to pass Memphis, the weather worsened and a blizzard came roaring out of northern Canada into the Mississippi valley.

Boxer was on the bridge of the *Billy Dee* with Conway. The snow was coming down so fast and so thick, he couldn't see the running lights of the barges in front of him.

"What do you think, Captain," Boxer asked, "do we keep going, or do we pull over and wait this out?"

"I'd guess most other tows have decided to put in for the night," Conway answered. "We keep moving we'd have the river all to ourselves. But there's always the danger that another cap'in is going to feel the same way. Know what I mean?"

Boxer nodded and checked the ship's radar. It wasn't much good in that kind of weather. "I'll be back," he said and hurried aboard the *Shark*. He went straight to the COMMO ROOM and said to the duty officer, "I want to know if any Ruskie spies in the sky are due to pass over this area in the next ten to twelve hours. Radio Washington. I want an immediate reply."

Boxer summoned Pierce and Monty. "I'm waiting to hear from Washington if there are any spies in the sky tonight," he told them. "If the answer is negative; then we're going to raise the *Shark*'s sail

169

just enough to allow the radar to scan for us so we can tell Conway what's ahead of us."

"I'm against it," Monty said, "especially in this weather."

"The sail could freeze into its position," Pierce offered.

"It's better that it does it now, than when we go into the Arctic for the final phase of the shakedown," Boxer said.

"Message from Washington, sir," the COMMO officer said, "coming over the teletype now."

Boxer leaned over the machine and read aloud: "ANS TO YOUR REQUEST NEG. NEXT DUE 0645. Okay, that's it. Get that sail up and establish radio contact between our radar officer and me. I'll be on the bridge of the *Billy Dee*."

The *Shark*'s sail went up easily and Boxer relayed the position of any target picked up by the radar. They passed three other moving tows, all going upriver. But there were at least twenty tied up along the west bank of the river.

Pierce informed Boxer by radio that, "Ice has formed around the base of the sail and along the deck."

"Tell Mister Harris to get a work detail out there to chop away the ice," Boxer answered.

"Passing Memphis," the radar officer announced.

Boxer told Conway.

"In weather like this," Conway answered, "I wouldn't know if I was passin' myself, let alone a city."

"How would you like to come down and take a look at some of our gear?" Boxer asked.

Conway rubbed his hand over his stubble. "Might be somethin' to see at that," he said.

"Just tell me when," Boxer said, "and I'll take you around myself."

"Thanks, I'll take you up on it," Conway said.

Boxer took out his pipe, filled it and lighting it stood at the window, looking out at the snow falling through the blackness. He found himself thinking about his last visit with Gwen. He wanted her then as much as he had ever wanted any woman and wondered if he had done the right thing? Maybe if he had made love to her, it would have provided a bond —

"Skipper, target bearing twenty five degrees . . . Range five thousand yards."

170

Boxer repeated the bearing and range.

"That's about where we should be putting in," Conway said.

Boxer went to the chart, checked the location of the next stop and working backwards, plotted the position of the *Billy Dee*.

"Target twenty six degrees . . . Range four thousand eight hundred yards . . . Target stationary."

"We've got a problem," Boxer said to Conway. "There another tow in our spot."

"It's twenty miles to the alternate one," Conway said, rolling the cigar form the right side of his mouth to the left.

"I can't keep the *Shark's* sail up too much longer."

"Why the hell not?"

"A spy satellite is going to pass over this area soon," Boxer explained.

"Fuck'im'," Conway answered, "it won't be able to see nothin' in this storm."

"I can't count on that," Boxer said. "I have to protect the *Shark*."

"Tell me how we going to keep movin' an' at the same time protect your boat? That's like havin' your cake and eatin' it too and damn few ever get to do that."

Boxer didn't answer. He looked out of the side window. If anything the storm seemed to be worse, or the wind was and was blowing more snow around than before. "Twenty more miles," he said aloud, though he was really talking to himself, "in this weather and no guarantee that another tow wouldn't be there."

"That's right," Conway said.

Boxer looked at him; then called Monty on the radio. "What is your best guess about the storm providing a shield for us from the Ruskie?"

"I don't know," Monty said. "The new ones have the equipment to penetrate it. The older ones don't."

"We don't have time to find out what kind it is. We got a tow sitting in our spot; that means we have to go to the alternate and that's twenty more miles."

"I can't tell you something I don't know," Monty answered.

"Thanks," Boxer answered. "Out." He walked back to the window and looked at his watch. "That spy in the sky is due over in another forty minutes."

"Skipper," the radar officer said, "target bearing three hundred and twenty degrees, range six thousand yards . . . Speed five knots."

Boxer gave Conway the information.

"That's way over on the east bank," Conway said. "She's just crawling upstream."

"I'm going to chance it," Boxer said. "We can't risk a grounding or a collision." He radioed the radar officer. "Keep the gear operational until further orders." A half hour later Boxer looked at his watch. "The Ruskie is over us now!"

"Worried?" Conway asked.

Boxer shrugged. "Whatever happens happens. . . ."

"How about breakfast?" Conway asked. "I got me a good chef."

"That would be great," Boxer answered. "Really great!"

Boxer watched the lights of New Orleans slide by. It was three o'clock in the morning and there were still people on the levee.

"That's where I'm goin'," Conway said, "after I drop you off."

"Enjoy," Boxer said. "You and your crew deserve it."

"We'll be out in the Gulf by 0700," Conway told him. "It's been a long three weeks."

"Where do you go from here? I mean after you stop at New Orleans?"

"Bring the *Billy Dee* back to the people who own her and then I go home myself."

Boxer didn't ask where Conway's home was, or whether he worked for the Company. He figured that if the man wanted him to know, he'd tell him.

"How are things aboard your *Shark*?" Conway asked.

"Everything is ready for the big cutaway," Boxer answered. "I'm anxious to put to sea and so are the men."

Conway nodded, rolled the cigar from the right side of his mouth to the left, looked as if he were about to say something, but remained quiet.

There was heavy traffic on both sides of the river. Many of the tows were either heading out or returning from the oil rigs in the Gulf and there were freighters from as far away as India moving on the river.

Soon they were below New Orleans and into the estuary leading

172

into the Gulf of Mexico.

"What happens to the barges?" Conway asked, after a long period of silence.

Boxer shrugged. "My orders were to only destroy the top covering. But I was going to open the seacocks and sink the barges as well."

"They'd bring a good price down here, or even back up the river," Conway said.

Boxer didn't react immediately. He took time to light his pipe and smoke it a few minutes before he said, "I'll make a deal with you, Captain. You stay with us for another twelve hours, or so; that'll be until eighteen or seventeen hundred and the barges are yours to do what you want with."

Conway looked at him. "That's about fifty or sixty miles out, at the speed we're going."

Boxer nodded. "I want to be as far away from any of the shipping routes as possible."

"The *Billy Dee* ain't no ocean going tug. We can take some deep water but not much. We get caught there in a squall and more than likely we'll go over."

"I also want the cover of darkness," Boxer said. "The way things stand now, I'll have less than forty five minutes of it after we part company."

Conway rolled the cigar to the other side of his mouth." Suppose we just dawdle along the coast, say four, maybe five miles out. We'll go west. After a while we'll be off Texas. Come darkness, you can turn south and run on the surface if you like. I'll put you between nowhere and nowhere."

"It's a deal!" Boxer said, shaking Conway's strong, callused hand; then he returned to the *Shark* and over the MC system, announced the change of plans to the crew. "We want as much darkness as we can get. I want to stay on the surface for as long as we can to test our gear while underway. . . ."

Throughout the day, the crew was busy checking hundreds of operational details.

Boxer stood by and put the entire complement on a NUKALERT, while the engineering officer pushed the reactor up to its maximum operating condition; held it there for as long as the operating manual said it was safe, giving DMC the necessary time to check the entire system before it was brought down to its normal condition.

All communications and radar and sonar gear were checked out. The propulsion system was run up without the drive shafts being engaged.

The glitches that occurred were minor and were quickly repaired.

At 1500 Harris reported to Boxer that all systems were operational.

Boxer entered the report in the taped log. Then he said to Harris, "Send a work detail topside to strip off the covering. Have it tied in bundles and drop it over the side."

At 1700 Boxer gave the order to prepare for night vision. The white lights dimmed as the red lights came on, filling the interior of the *Shark* with a red glow.

Ten minutes later, he gave the order to raise the sail. Within fifteen seconds it was up and locked into position.

Immediately the radar officer and his men were at their stations, putting the air and sea acquisition radars into operation.

"Report all surface targets beginning at five thousand yards and all approaching aircraft," Boxer told the radar officer, as soon as he reported his system operational.

COMMO reported a message for Boxer.

"Read it," Boxer said over the phone.

" 'From Williams . . . Report you requested . . . Name Igor Borodine . . . Your rank . . . Former naval attache, Washington.' End of message, sir."

"Thanks," Boxer said.

At eighteen hundred, Boxer boarded the *Billy Dee* for the last time. The four barges that had shielded the *Shark* for so long had been eased away from her and realigned for the *Billy Dee* to take back in tow.

"I was wonderin' what your boat look like," Conway said. "It's big all right . . . Bigger than the one I served on."

Boxer raised his eyebrows.

"That surprised you, didn't it?" Conway chortled. "Yeah, I was on the *Tang*, one of the first atomic attack subs . . . Back in the seventies."

"You never did come aboard," Boxer said.

Conway shook his head. "No real reason to, skipper." And he offered Boxer his hand. "Good luck!"

"Good luck to you," Boxer said, shaking Conway's hand. "Keep clear of the sandbars." He turned, left the bridge, leaped back onto the deck of the *Shark* and hurried up the narrow stairwell to the bridge on the sail, where Cowly and Mahony were waiting for him.

"All hands," Boxer said over the MC, "Prepare to get under way." He looked down at the control console. All the switches, keys and dials were bathed in a soft red glow, making them visible.

One by one, Boxer touched a particular key or sets of keys that gave the *Shark*'s present position, instantly determined by radio signals to the orbiting navigational satellite. This information automatically activated the navigational computers. Boxer chose a course that would take the *Shark* to an area in the South Atlantic, where it could dive to its maximum operating depth.

He keyed the engine room and then punched in a speed of 20 knots.

The *Shark* gave a slight shudder and she began to move, slowly at first; then with increasing speed.

"A piece of cake," Cowly commented.

"A piece of cake," Boxer repeated. It felt good to be back at sea again, very good.

"Skipper," Mahony said, "I'd like to get the feel of the helm."

Boxer reached over to the console, flicked a switch to the right, "You have her now, Mahoney. Keep her on the same compass heading."

"When you put back on AUTONAV will you have to reset the course?" Mahony asked.

"No," Boxer said. "The computers keep going until the entire NAV system is shut down. That means even in port, or wherever we are , . . that NAV system operates."

"What would happen if you ordered a different heading and we went on that heading for hours or even days?"

"The NAV system would continue to function, making allowances for the new heading and the distance traveled; then if I put it back on AUTONAV, it will plot a new course from where we are to the original destination."

Mahony gave a long low whistle.

"All stations," Boxer said over the MC, "report operating status."

One by one the reports came in. All of them were positive.

Boxer keyed the engine room. Punched in FLK SP. The digital readout on the small video screen turned red. Boxer checked his watch. The numbers began to change on the screen. Twenty seconds passed and the *Shark* was making thirty knots on the surface.

"Any trouble with helm?" Boxer asked.

"Negative," Mahony answered.

Harris called and said, "Pierce would like to join you on the bridge?"

"Send him up," Boxer answered; then he asked, "how do things look down below."

"Couldn't be better," Harris answered.

"How's it up there?" Harris asked.

"The night is beautiful. We'll dive at zero five three zero," Boxer said, "unless something unexpected happens, release as many men as possible."

"Aye, aye, sir."

"I'll take the aye, aye. But not the sir," Boxer said.

"Aye, aye," Harris answered.

Boxer put the phone down and looked up. The night was very clear and the sky was filled with stars. The Big Dipper dominated the sky and in the south east Orion's Belt was clearly visible.

Boxer took several deep breaths and felt as if the salt air was purging his body of the events of the last few months.

Harris came on to the bridge. "We still at flank speed?" he asked.

"Yes."

"You're pushing her hard and fast" Pierce said.

"I know I am," Boxer said. "But we can't diddle around. I'm going to test dive her for maximum depth within the next four days; then after that we head for the Arctic, unless, of course, we get other orders."

Pierce said nothing.

"Aircraft," the radar officer announced. "Bearing two seven zero degrees . . . Range ten zero zero zero yards . . . Altitude fifteen zero zero zero feet . . . Speed five zero zero knots . . . ID Tom-Tom fighter bomber."

176

Boxer picked up the phone and signaled COMMO. "Can you pick up transmission from target bearing two zero zero seven zero degrees . . . Range ten zero zero zero yards, Altitude fifteen zero zero zero feet?"

Several seconds passed.

The radar officer reported another series of readings. The range had decreased by a thousand yards, the bearing and altitude remained the same.

COMMO came back on. "Routine recon flight, skipper. They haven't spotted us yet."

"Signal them we're here," Boxer said. "Transmit the following: safe play one. Tell them to check their home base for a reading on that."

"Roger, skipper,"

Less than two minutes passed when radar reported, "Target changing heading to one eight zero degrees, maintaining altitude and speed."

"I bet that pilot is wondering why he was ordered to change course," Boxer commented.

"How long do you think the *Shark* can remain under wraps?" Cowly asked.

"Not too long," Boxer answered. "But the longer the better, at least that's what I was told by the CNO."

Lieutenant Kenneth Dwight, Senior EO, called. "Skipper, we're getting some smoke in the main bearing of drive shaft number two. Looks like the packing is beginning to go."

Boxer reported the condition to Pierce.

"How long to repair?" Boxer asked.

"An hour at the most," Dwight said. "I already checked with the DCO, he's here now with the part and the repair crew."

"Okay, shut number two drive," Boxer said. "We'll be okay with what's left. I'm reducing speed now to one five knots. One five knots coming up on the screen."

"I had better go down and see what's going on," Pierce said, with an I-told-you-so- look on his face.

Boxer nodded and reported the problem to Harris. "Have the DCO keep the packing. I don't want to have that kind used aboard the *Shark* again."

"Aye, aye."

177

Boxer put the phone down.

A half hour later, Dwight phoned the bridge. "Skipper, the bearing has been repacked and number two drive is operational."

"Very good," Boxer said.

"Engaging propeller shaft now," Dwight reported.

A slight tremor passed through the *Shark* as she picked up additional thrust.

"Number two drive shaft in operation" Dwight said.

"Okay, let's see how the boat handles in reverse," Boxer said, putting instructions into the computer.

The *Shark* continued to slide forward through the water; then suddenly she seemed to hesitate; then she moved backward.

"Hold the helm steady, Mahony," Boxer said. "Now give me a full three six zero turn."

Harris was on the phone. "What's going on?"

"What does our OPS board say?"

"You're making big circles in the sea," Harris answered.

Boxer typed in a change of direction to move the boat forward again.

"Wow," Harris exclaimed, "some of the gear down here, including some of the men are getting bounced around."

"All stations," Boxer said over the MC, "report any damage."

"Tom here, skipper," Redfern said, "next time let me know in advance what you're going to do. One of my men was thrown in one direction and wound up going in another."

"Sorry about that," Boxer answered with a laugh. "Okay, no more rough stuff. We'll just cruise along. Harris, have Pierce go over the tapes of those last maneuvers for the propulsion systems."

"How detailed?"

"I want a record of every stress and strain that was the slightest bit abnormal," Boxer said.

"Will do," Harris answered.

Boxer ordered Mahony to bring the *Shark* back to its original heading. "I'm putting her back on AUTONAV," he said. "You can go below and get some sack time before we dive."

Mahony started to salute.

"Not aboard the *Shark*," Boxer said.

Mahony grinned. "Aye, aye, skipper."

"We've got the best damn crew in the service," Boxer said, "even

"That's a very valuable submarine to risk."

"It was designed for just this type of mission," Kinkade said.

"How much time do we have before it becomes critical?" the president asked.

"Three months but not more than five," Kinkade answered. "We'll continue to send overflights to keep up with the progress of the construction. If we do hit them, the best time to do it would be when the missiles are there but have not yet been put in their silos."

"I'd like to think about this one for a while," the president said. "By the way where is the *Shark* now?"

"Having her sea trials," Stark answered. "They began last night."

"How long will they take?"

"A month to six weeks," Stark answered. "Boxer is going to take her up into the Arctic for the final round."

The president nodded. "That's about what it'll take for me to make up my mind," he said.

"Suppose Kinkade and I put our collective heads together and come up with some sort of operational plan," Stark offered.

"No," the president said. "I don't want this to be so far along that I can't stop it. I'll think about it."

"Yes, Mister president," Kinkade answered.

Stark nodded.

"Now if you two gentlemen will excuse," the president said, "I have a meeting with the Secretary of State, who by the way would be totally against the idea of sending any kind of force against the island."

"Mister president —" Kinkade began.

"Don't worry," the president said. "I won't tell him anything until we meet to make the final decision."

Both men nodded.

The president stood up, came around to the front of the desk, shook their hands and walked as far as the door with them. "I'll let you know as soon as I've made my decision," he told Stark and Kinkade, as the two of them left the office.

Boxer was back on the bridge at the end of two hours. He had taped his log, slept for an hour and half, showered and put on clean

181

clothes.

"I'm going to take a stroll through the boat," he told Dwight, "and stop for coffee and cake along the way. While he spoke, his fingers went over the keys of the master computer, asking it for a status report of all systems.

System check In Progress. . . .
All systems positive.

Moving slightly to his left he asked the NAVCOMP to give the exact time of sunset.

Sunset will be at 1650

"Gentlemen," Boxer said, "we'll surface at seventeen hundred." He looked at his watch and checked it against the digital readout on the NAVCLOCK. Both read the same. "We have five more hours to go before surfacing. Sufficient time to run through several drills. Mister Dwight, take her down to four hundred feet."

"Aye, aye, skipper."

Boxer moved away from the Command Computer and Dwight took his place.

"Take her down," Boxer said.

"Bridge to all hands . . . Bridge to all hands," Dwight said over the MC, "stand by . . . Making new depth . . . Four zero zero feet . . . Helmsman maintain same heading."

Boxer watched Dwight manipulate the DC control.

Dwight began to read out the changing depths as the numbers came up on the screen. There was a slight tremor in his voice. "Reaching four zero zero feet," he announced. "Dive complete." He took a deep breath; then said, "Helmsman hold your course."

Boxer frowned.

Harris was about to step up to the console.

Boxer caught his eyes and motioned him back.

Several more seconds passed; then Dwight announced, "Reactuating stabilization system . . . Bubble centered." He took time to dab a handkerchief over his brow.

"Well done," Boxer said.

"I could have been faster on the —"

"You did it," Boxer said, "that's what counts. Now I'm off for my stroll."

Boxer went directly to the mess. He was ravenous and using his plastic ID card, he choose ham and sausage. The food came frozen. He placed it in one of the microwave ovens and in less than two minutes it was ready to eat, complete with toast, butter and jelly. He got his coffee from a large urn, with a predetermined amount of cream and sugar. Like all the other men, he had to adjust to eating everything with chopsticks, a spoon and knife. The eggs proved to be the most difficult. But the food tasted good and from what he could see, as he looked around him, the men enjoyed the food.

Boxer took time to drink his coffee. He lit his pipe and began to plan ahead. Part of what he'd be doing would be strictly by the book. Every system had been driven up to its maximum operating capabilities and held there for a predetermined period of time to check if the system could function under extreme conditions. Then there were the deep dives and the launching and retrieval of the two undersea craft: first while stationary then while underway. The second would be a tricky and dangerous procedure. But one which would have to become routine. Then there would be the rendezvous with the *Tecumseh* and the responsibility of bringing the *Shark* inside of her. That's something he and Harris would have to master. . . .

Redfern entered the mess area and came straight to where Boxer was sitting. "I have two men who are having some difficulty with being closed in," he said.

"How bad?"

"Just over jumpy," Redfern answered.

"Send them over to the bridge later," Boxer said, "and either I or Harris will give them a Cook's tour of the boat. Once they find out how safe it is, they'll never want to travel any other way."

Redfern laughed.

"An idea just popped into my head," Boxer said. "Suppose my men train your guys and your men train my guys? That way your men will have something to do beside running around a room and doing other exercises?"

"I like it," Redfern said. "When do I get to be captain?"

"In about a hundred years," Boxer said. "Well, I want to take a

183

look see around the boat. I'll notify my men that the training will begin as soon as we surface. That'll be at sixteen fifty."

"I'll pass the word to my men," Redfern responded.

The two of them left the mess area together and then separated.

Boxer toured the *Shark* and when he returned to the bridge, he announced over the MC that he had the con; then he summoned Monty to the bridge and told him, "Let's see how much we can see down here." He pointed to the 3D display on the CIC control board. "There are two hundred feet of water below us. According to what sonar is picking up, there are some ridges three thousand yards to our portside. Let's see what we get."

"At that range they should come in very clear," Monty said.

Boxer switched on the sonar imaging device. Instantly the screen was filled with crazy patterns. Boxer keyed in the portside scanner, adjusted for distance; and then for resolution. The ridges came into view. "Beautiful," Boxer exclaimed. "Just beautiful!" A school of barracuda swam into view. "Harris, Cowly, Dwight come take a look see at this!"

The men crowded around the console.

Boxer did a 360° take; then one directly below the *Shark*; they were traveling over a very flat plain. "It won't be like this when we're out in the South Atlantic."

"Won't matter," Monty said. "You'll see whatever is there."

"Is that a shark?" Cowly asked.

Boxer adjusted the focus.

"It sure as hell is," Dwight said. "It looks like fifteen feet long."

"I've seen them nine, ten feet," Harris said. "But never that big."

"What about you, skipper? Have you seen them that big?" Dwight asked.

Boxer shuddered, as the memory of the sharks circling him and Redfern filled his brain. "Not that size," he managed to say. "But a shark is—"

"That mother is coming straight toward us!" Cowly exclaimed.

"Holy Christ, look at those teeth," Monty said.

"He's going to try to take a bite out of the hull," Harris laughed.

The shark threw himself against the hull, bounced off and tried again.

"He's had it," Cowly commented, as the shark turned and swam off.

"Is there any way of hooking this system into the Command Console?" Boxer asked.

"Maybe," Monty answered. "But it would take some redesigning."

"Give some thought," Boxer said switching off the system. "It would be easier if I could view everything on one control screen."

"I'll give it some thought," Monty said.

The men returned to what they were doing and Boxer stayed on the bridge. For the next few hours several tests were successfully completed, including a simulated fire in the COMMO room and a shut down of the air purification system.

Several times during the day, Boxer scanned the immediate vicinity in which the *Shark* was moving. Twice he spotted what appeared to be wrecks of tankers that were probably sunk by German U boats during World War Two.

Just before the *Shark* was scheduled to surface, Boxer announced the joint training program, which was to go into effect immediately after the *Shark* surfaced.

At precisely 1530, Boxer said to Cowly, "She's yours. Take her up." And he moved aside to let Cowly at console.

"I'm going to take her up on manual," Cowly said.

Boxer nodded.

"Bridge to crew. Prepare to surface . . . Planesmen stand by."

"Planesmen standing by," the diving officer repeated.

"AUTOPLN off," Cowly said. "MANSYS ON."

"MANSYS ON," the diving officer said.

Cowly keyed the engine room. "Reduce speed to ten knots."

"Speed reduced," the EO reported.

The *Shark* slowed.

"Diving planes up one five degrees," Cowly ordered.

"Diving planes up one five degrees," the diving officer reported.

"Target," the SO reported. "Bearing, six six degrees . . . Range, twenty thousand yards . . . Speed one two knots. . . ."

Cowly put the sonar on his monitor. The target was moving away from the *Shark*. "Switch to night vision," he said.

"Five zero zero feet," the diving officer reported.

Cowly checked the digital readout of the depth: it matched. "Blow forward ballast," he ordered.

The sudden hiss of air filled the *Shark*. Its bow rose.

"Maintain one five degrees on the diving planes," Cowly said.

"Steady at one five degrees," the diving officer said.

The *Shark*'s bow eased down slightly.

Cowly watched the digital readout; they were going through the three hundred foot level.

Boxer watched him closely.

Cowly listened to the diving officer calling out the various depths, waiting until he reached the hundred foot level. Then he ordered, "Blow all main ballast!"

Another hissing noise, only louder than the first.

"Main ballast blown," the diving officer reported.

The *Shark* was rising very fast now.

"Raising sail," Cowly announced, pushing the control button. "Bridge detail ready!"

"Ready," Harris answered.

"Twenty feet," the diving officer reported.

A few seconds later the readout on the console went from red to green and the word SURFACED came up on the screen.

"Surfaced," the diving officer said.

"Return diving planes to normal position and secure," Cowly said.

"Diving planes in normal position and secured," the diving officer reported.

The bridge detail was already topside and the RO and SO were reporting their equipment operational.

Cowly keyed the engine room. "Increase speed to one eight knots." He checked the readout. One eight came up on it. He keyed Harris.

"I have the con," Harris said.

"Topside bridge has the con," Cowly announced over the MC.

"By the book," Boxer said coming over to him and shaking his hand.

"Thanks skipper," Cowly answered.

"But why did you do it the hard way, when you could have done it automatically?"

"I guess I wanted you to know I could do it in an emergency," Cowly said, looking straight at him.

Boxer nodded: he understood.

"Okay, if I go topside?"

186

"Sure go ahead," Boxer said.

"So, Comrade Boris, tell me what's so important that I had to come down to the Navel Ministry in the middle of the night," Rear Admiral Pavel Golovin asked.

Boris Donskoi was a civilian photogrammetrist, possibly the best in the Soviet Union, possibly in the world. He was a short, plump man with a penchant for young, beautiful women, whom he photographed in every conceivable erotic pose. Portfolios of these pictures brought a good price in the West, where Donskoi was considered by many to be an artist.

Donskoi took time to light a cigarette and blow smoke through his nose before he said, "Comrade Pavel, life has many strange and mysterious turns, much like the big rivers of the world."

Golovin, who was still wearing his heavy blue coat and gloves heaved a weary sigh, nodded and asked, "Are you in trouble with the authorities again? How many times do I have to tell you not to use girls under eighteen for your photographs?"

"If I were in that kind of trouble, do you think the police would allow me to speak to you here?" Donskoi asked, with a twinkle in his pale blue eyes.

"Then what kind of trouble are you in?" Golovin asked, removing his gloves and opening his coat. He often wondered why nature made such talented men so damn foolish? In his position as Chief of Navel Technology, Donskoi was not the only foolish genius with whom he had to deal; indeed, often he'd be father and confessor to them.

"Rivers," Donskoi said, "are symbolic of so many things in life. Literature makes full use of them in that way. We have for example, Quiet Flows The Don and the sequel The Don Flows To The Sea."

"I've read them," Golovin said, knowing nothing he could do or say would hurry Boris to his point.

"Perhaps the greatest books on the role of river in the lives of a people was written by an American," Donskoi said.

"Oh, I wasn't aware —"

"Mark Twin's Tom Sawyer and Huckleberry Finn."

"Aren't they on the forbidden list of books?" Golovin asked, guessing that Boris had been caught reading the book, or turned in to the KGB for possessing them.

Donskoi waved the question aside. "Forbidden list phooh!" he exclaimed. "No such list exists for me. The authorities know it and I'm surprised that you, one of my most . . . most intimate friends should not have known that the forbidden list means nothing to me."

Golovin threw up his hands. "I am sorry, Comrade Boris, truely sorry." He was afraid that Donskoi would either go into the sulks, or launch into a monologue on friendship before he'd finally get to the reason why he called him to the Ministry at eleven thirty at night.

"I accept your apology," Donskoi said. "I accept because I know you have a lot on your mind; and remembering whether I care or don't care about the list of forbidden books is not as important to you as it is to me."

Golovin nodded his head. "Thank you."

"But I have something important to show about a river," Donskoi said, going around the laboratory table. He dimmed the light, switched on a projector. On the far wall appeared a map of the United States. "This is the Mississippi River," he said, using an electronic pointer. "It starts up here in Lake Itasca and flows all the way to the Gulf of Mexico. It was the main waterway in the United States and because it is, I have been making various measurements of it daily."

"I'm aware of that," Golovin said.

Donskoi turned on another machine. "What do you see?"

"A composite satellite photograph superimposed on the map."

"Now what do you see?" Donskoi asked, pushing a button.

"A detailed view of a particular section of the river."

"Yes, an area fifty kilometers north of the city of St. Louis," Donskoi said. "Look closely at the left side of the photograph. What do you see?"

"Nothing . . . Wait . . . There's a small bulge in the bank."

"Yes . . . Now look at this." Another photograph came up on the screen.

"It's gone!" Golovin said. "It's no longer there."

"Now look at this," Donskoi said.

"It's come back again!" Golovin explained.

"But not in the same place," Donskoi exclaimed triumphantly.

"The photograph you're looking at is not the original. It's one hundred and twenty kilometers south of the first one. And this is still further south. But if we go back one photograph, we see the object is no longer there. The object moves all the way down the river. We lose it for twenty-four hours because of a blizzard; then it comes back. Now what does this suggest to you, Comrade Admiral Golovin?"

"Something is being moved down river that the Americans want to hide from us."

"Exactly!"

"I was able to follow it out into the Gulf. Here are photographs of the tug and its tow moving west in the Gulf at about five knots an hour. And that's the end of it. The tug is gone and so is the tow by the time our satellite returns the following morning."

"Remarkable," Golovin said.

"The new Oricom camera made it easy to identify. The camera remembers the pictures it takes. If there is the slightest discrepancy between two photographs it marks the two with a red dot in the upper right corner. All of the photographs came to my laboratory marked that way; then it was up to me to make the necessary photogrammetric analysis and what you have just seen is the result of that work."

Golovin left the stool on which he had been sitting. "What do you think it could have been?" he asked.

Donskoi shook his head, "Guessing is not my department," he answered. "But you have enough here to bring it to Naval Intelligence, or even to the Admiral of the Fleet, Gorshkov. I'm sure he'd be able to make some good guesses about what the Americans have hidden from us."

"When can you have all this in report form?" Golovin asked.

"It's ready now," Donskoi said, handing him a folder.

Golovin nodded. "You think it's that serious?"

"I think it's very serious," Donskoi answered, "if I didn't I wouldn't have dragged you away from the pretty ballerina you were with. I think you should take the matter up with the proper people first thing in the morning, or even now."

"Thank you," Golovin said, patting the folder. "You've done your country a service . . . possibly a great service!"

189

11

Boxer held the *Shark* on a course that would take her out of the Gulf of Mexico, through the Yucatan Channel into the Caribbean Sea. Then he planned to run east until he reached the Anegada Passage, where he'd turn north to enter the Puerto Rico Trench. There he'd put the *Shark* through a series of deep dives.

Three days after the *Shark* left the *Billy Dee,* she was scheduled to enter the Yucatan Channel at 1400 hours. But because Cuban gunboats and Russian ASW aircraft made frequent sweeps of it, Boxer wasn't going to risk an encounter with the Ruskies or their Cuban puppets, who would probably shoot first and make apologies later, especially if the *Shark* were sunk or damaged. They'd go through the channel submerged and stay submerged until they were clear of Cuban waters and out of range of its aircraft. He put the *Shark* down in 600 feet of water and waited until darkness to go through the channel.

"Rig for silent running," Boxer ordered, as the *Shark* got underway again.

Harris passed the order to the crew.

"Going to five zero zero feet," Boxer said, adjusting the EPC.

The *Shark* responded immediately

"Five nine zero," Boxer said, reading the digitally displayed numbers. "Five eight zero. Five seven zero . . ." He continued to read off the numbers at ten foot intervals. "Reaching five zero zero . . ." He touched the stabilization control. "Depth five zero zero feet." He checked the stabilization bubble. It was centered.

Boxer switched on the UWIS. Below the *Shark* was a deep channel that dropped steeply off to the port side. A myriad of brightly colored fish passed in front of the *Shark*.

"Target . . . Bearing four four degrees . . . Range six thousand yards . . . Speed two zero knots."

"ID?" Boxer requested.

Before the SO could answer, the entire crew of the *Shark* could hear the pinging sound of the target's sonar.

"Destroyer Kotlin class. Specific ship: the *Skoryy*."

Boxer punched in the name of the ship into the COMCOMP and asked for the ship's armament.

Main Armament: 2 twin 130mm DP gun mounts
4 twin 25mm gun mounts
4 quad 45 mm AA gun mounts
2 6 - barrel ASW rocket launchers
10 torpedo tubes

"Target bearing four four degrees . . . Range five thousand five zero zero yards."

The pings became louder.

Boxer hit the GQ button.

The men of the *Shark* responded instantly.

Boxer dialed in a change of speed from twenty to ten knots.

"Target bearing four four degrees . . . Range five thousand . . . Speed now two zero knots."

Boxer pursed his lips. The captain of the *Skoryy* would in a matter of moments decided to attack, or turn away.

"Two ASW rockets launched," the SO reported. "Four four degrees speed five zero knots."

"AUTO NAV off," Boxer said. "Helmsman come to course three zero zero." He spun the electronic speed selector to twenty five knots.

The *Shark* slashed through the water.

Boxer glanced over to the men at the CIC. Grim faced, they studied the GDT, fixing the position of the target as the SO called out its bearing, range and speed.

Suddenly the muffled sound of two explosions rolled over the *Shark*.

"Target bearing forty seven degrees . . . Range three thousand two five zero yards . . . Closing fast."

Boxer guessed that the skipper of the destroyer wasn't about to break off contact, even though for the time being, his sonar had lost the *Shark*. If he were in his place, he wouldn't. He'd call for aircraft and another ship. He may have even done that. If he had and they arrived before the *Shark* could get out of the channel, then they'd have a damn good chance of sinking, or damaging it. Either way, Boxer would lose. And he wasn't about to let that happen.

"Ready aft torpedo tubes five and six," Boxer ordered. "SO set target bearing into range computer."

"Target bearing set," the SO answered.

Boxer turned on the Fire Control Computer, coupled it to the range computer.

"FCO set torpedoes five and six for electronic control," Boxer said.

"Torpedoes set for electronic control," the Fire Control Officer reported.

Boxer touched a key. "Torpedo tube door opened," he said.

"Target bearing four six degrees . . . Range two thousand five zero zero yards . . . Speed two five knots . . ."

"Arm torpedoes," Boxer ordered.

"Torpedoes armed," the FCO responded.

Boxer touched two keys on the console. "Firing mechanism activated . . . Three zero seconds to firing," he said, his eyes riveted to the torpedo firing clock.

"Target bearing four eight degrees . . . Range two thousand five zero zero years . . . Target changing course . . . Speed two zero knots . . . Range increasing."

Boxer stabbed the abort control. "Fire mission aborted," he said with relief. "Fire mission aborted."

Harris repeated the command.

"Closing torpedo doors," Boxer said, touching the control that would accomplish the task and also vent whatever water was inside the tubes.

"FCO secure torpedoes," Boxer ordered.

"Torpedoes disarmed," the FCO reported.

"Returning to AUTONAV system," Boxer said.

The *Shark* turned back to her former heading.

"Secure from the GQ," Boxer announced over the MC. "Secure from GQ." He took a deep breath and turning away from the

COMCOMP, he stood up and stretched. Suddenly he felt very tired. "I'm glad I didn't have to fire those torpedoes," he said.

"I think everyone aboard the *Shark* feels the same way," Harris answered.

"I wonder what the hell made that Ruskie break off contact?" Boxer said.

"Maybe he figured that since he lost us on the sonar, he'd have to do a bit of searching before he'd locate us again and just didn't feel like it. Maybe he had one of those black-haired, black-eyed beauties waiting for him in port. Whatever it was, I'm damn glad he responded to it."

"So am I," Boxer answered. "So am I!"

In less than three hours, the *Shark* was out of the Yucatan Channel and Boxer headed her south. At 16° N. Lat., 85° W. Long., he turned the *Shark* east.

The remainder of the run to the dive area was uneventful. Though it was night, they were submerged when they went through the Anegada Passage. Exactly six days after they had left the *Billy Dee*, they entered the Atlantic Ocean.

Boxer held a meeting with his officers in the wardroom. He had also asked that Monty and Pierce attend. When everyone was seated, Boxer said, "Smoke if you wish gentlemen, I asked that you be here because I have a few things I want to say to all of you regarding your past and future performance.

"First, I think we all agree that the *Shark* has functioned magnificently and that the two engineers aboard deserve our thanks and appreciation.

A burst of applause followed.

"Secondly, I want to congratulate all of you and through you, the rest of the crew for their performance and above all for their performance in what could have been an extremely difficult situation. I am, of course, referring to our encounter with the Ruskie destroyer. This time we were lucky. Next time—well, we can only hope that we'll be as lucky.

"The third item has to do with our deep dives, the launching and retrieval of our two undersea recon craft. These craft will be used during our deep dives and retrieved at our maximum operating depth.

"Our area of operation will be in a box formed by one nine degrees north latitude on the southern edge, two zero one degrees north latitude on the northern edge and between six three degrees west longitude and six six degrees west longitude. That puts us in water whose maximum depth is four thousand feet and deeper in some places. I don't have to tell you that at those depths, strange things happen to equipment that functions perfectly well at six hundred feet. Glitches develop and it will be your responsibility to minimize them and more important to either overcome or correct them. For what it's worth gentlemen, we are going to dive deeper than any submarine has ever gone and we're going to operate at that depth for an extended period of time and, as I said before, launch and retrieve our recon craft. To answer the question uppermost in your minds, the *Shark* will begin her test dives at three thousand feet and go to four."

Several of the men gave long low whistles.

"Any questions?" Boxer asked.

"Skipper," Dwight began, "when do we begin the test dives?"

"Zero eight hundred," Boxer answered. "That gives us about twelve hours. Alert all sections to the situation. I'll speak to the crew just before we begin the dive."

"How long will we stay at maximum depth?" Redfern asked.

"At least thirty-six hours," Boxer said.

"Skipper," Pierce asked, "why that long?"

"To make sure that equipment won't fail if subjected to pressure for an extended period of time. Thirty-six hours should be long enough for any failures to show up. Any other questions?"

"Just one," Harris said.

Boxer nodded.

"Who will be going out in the recon craft?" Harris asked.

"I'll take the first one," Boxer said. "On the second launch Cowly will go with me."

"Skipper," Harris responded, "may I suggest I go in your place. The *Shark* needs you more than it needs any one of us."

"Request denied," Boxer answered. "Harris, you'll be in command of the *Shark* in my absence. If something happens to me, continue the deep dive tests; then when you surface notify the proper authorities."

"Skipper," Monty said, "I think you should give some thought to Harris' suggestion before you reject it out of hand."

"It has been rejected," Boxer answered. He was not going to risk Harris's life before he'd risk his own. The recon craft were untried. When he was satisfied with their performance, he'd let his other officers operate them.

"If there aren't any more questions," Boxer said, "you men can return to your duties."

The men stood up and filed out of the wardroom, leaving Boxer alone.

"Now hear this . . . Now hear this," Boxer said. "We are at a depth of one thousand feet. From this depth we will commence our deep dive. We will go to three thousand feet and continue to operate at that depth for three six hours before we surface."

Boxer put the MC mike down, set the EPC for twenty degree angle and maintained the *Shark*'s speed at fifteen knots.

The *Shark*'s bow began to sink; then the entire boat pitched forward.

The digital depth readout changed rapidly.

"Switching to MANDIV control," Boxer said. "DO keep two zero degrees."

"Two zero degrees on diving planes," the DO answered.

"Switching to MANNAV . . . Helmsman maintain indicated course," Boxer said.

"Course two seven zero degrees," Mahony answered.

Boxer keyed the engine room. "Going to manual control," he told the EO. "Maintain one five knots."

"One five knots," the EO answered.

"Depth one thousand five zero zero feet," Boxer said.

The *Shark* continued to descend.

Boxer checked the outside temperature. It was thirty-six degrees. Inside the *Shark,* despite the automatic heat adjustment system, it was only fifty-five degrees . . . Cold enough for Boxer to feel it in his fingers and toes.

"CIC reports bottom now in view of your GDI, skipper," Harris reported.

Boxer switched on his GDI. A sonar configuration of the bottom came up on the screen. "Deep trench below three thousand foot level."

"Depth of trench," Harris said, "five thousand feet."

Boxer checked the digital depth read out. "*Shark* at three thousand two five zero feet."

"Skipper," the DCO reported, "I have an indication of a forward ballast pump malfunction. Switching to secondary pump."

Boxer removed the GDT image from the COMMCOMP and keyed in the DCC. The pump was inside the ballast tank.

"DCO, can you get a reading on the cause of failure?" Boxer asked.

"Negative."

"Watch the other ballast pumps carefully," Boxer told him. If he had another failure, he'd be forced to abandon the dive, surface, pull the pumps and replace them before attempting another dive.

"Target bearing seven zero . . . Range ten thousand yards . . . Speed three knots."

"ID?" Boxer asked.

"None."

"What?" Boxer asked.

"Skipper, it's probably a whale," the SO said with a chuckle. "It can probably hear our sonar and is curious —"

"Skipper," the DCO reported, "failed pump started to operate again. Removed back from operation."

"No indication of cause?" Boxer asked.

"None."

"SO where's our curious whale?" Boxer asked.

"Bearing seven zero degrees . . . Range nine thousand one zero zero yards . . . But still coming toward . . . No, target has changed course to four five degrees and range is increasing. Maybe his girlfriend signaled to him. Hey, I was just kidding."

Suddenly every man in the *Shark* heard the sounds of two whales "singing" to one another.

Boxer smiled, glanced at the Digital Depth Readout and announced to the crew, "We are passing through two thousand five zero zero feet. Helmsman, come about to course one eight zero degrees."

"Coming about one eight zero degrees," Mahoney responded.

"DO bring planes up to one zero degrees," Boxer ordered.

"Planes at one zero degrees," the DO responded.

The *Shark* rose slightly.

Boxer keyed the engine room. "Give me two zero knots," he said.

Twenty knots came up on the screen.

"Two zero knots," the EO said.

Boxer watched the Digital Depth Readout. "Three thousand feet coming up . . . DO bring planes to neutral position."

"Diving planes in neutral position," the DO reported.

Boxer checked the bubble indicator. The *Shark* was level. "Skipper to crew," Boxer said over the MC, "we have reached our maximum rated depth . . . All systems go."

The crew cheered.

"Now," Boxer said, "let's stay down here for awhile and see how things are. All training programs are to continue."

Harris came up to the console. "Skipper, something must be wrong with the DCC, and the automatic temperature control. It's less than fifty-five degrees now."

Boxer looked up at the thermometer. It registered forty degrees.

"DCO get a reading on the auto-temp control system," Boxer said.

"Looks good," the DCO said.

Boxer keyed into the DCC. No malfunction was shown. "DCO we've got a problem: inside temp is four zero degrees; that's one five degrees less than minimum standard. Run a full check on interior heating system."

"Aye, aye, skipper."

Boxer signaled COMMCOMP, asking it to display all temperature variations throughout the *Shark*.

```
forward torpedo room .............................40°
midships ........................................40°
bridge ..........................................40°
missile well ....................................38°
aft torpedo room ................................40°
```

"Skipper," the DCO said, "DCC shows no malfunction in boat's heating system."

"Keep trying to find out what's going on," Boxer said. "Something is wrong."

"Will do, skipper."

"Mister Harris have all the men put on extra clothing and gloves. We're going to be down here for awhile and I don't want anyone sick."

"Aye, aye, skipper," Harris answered.

Boxer had hoped to launch the recon craft almost as soon as they reached the three thousand foot level. But now he was too concerned about the temperature control inside the *Shark* to consider launching the recon craft.

He was feeling the cold as keenly as anyone else and sent one of the crewmen to his quarters to bring him two sweaters and a pair of gloves.

He keyed the DCO. "Any luck?" he asked.

"Nothing yet, skipper."

"Mister Harris have the section officers send their men in shifts to the galley for hot food and coffee," Boxer said.

"Do you want anything?" Harris asked.

"Coffee would be fine," Boxer answered.

The minutes passed slowly.

One of the men brought coffee to Boxer and Mahony.

"Skipper," the DCO said, "I can't find anything."

"There must be something out of whack," Boxer said, looking at the thermometer. He frowned. The temperature had gone up to forty-eight degrees. "Check your thermometer," he told the DCO.

"Forty-eight degrees, skipper," the DCO answered.

Within five minutes the temperature climbed five degrees.

"DO," Boxer said, "standby . . . Switching on EPC system . . . EPC on . . ." The level bubble shifted slightly; then steadied.

"Skipper," the DCO said, "temperature up another five degrees."

"Pierce, what the hell is going on?" Boxer asked.

"One of the thermostats isn't reading the temperature correctly. But we don't know which one."

"Goddamn it, find it!" Boxer exclaimed angrily. "First we freeze our balls off and in not too long a time, if the temperature continues to rise, we're going to sweat them off."

The temperature went up. Within a half hour it was up to eight five degrees. Several of the men stripped to their undershirts.

Boxer ordered the ship's medical officer to give each man two salt tablets.

Suddenly Boxer got a red signal. Immediately he sounded the fire alarm.

"Skipper, fire is in the main electrical junction box," the DCO said.

Boxer pressed several keys on his COMMCOMP. A visual of the main electrical junction box came up on the screen.

The DCO said, "Nitrogen introduced . . . Smoke main problem . . . Exhaust system working."

Boxer's own computer gave him the same information.

"How much damage?" Boxer asked, realizing that some of the vital parts of the boat could have been damaged by the fire.

"Running system check now," the DCO said.

Boxer looked at his screen.

ALL SYSTEMS FUNCTIONING

"That's impossible," Boxer shouted. "Get a repair party to that junction box. I want Pierce and Monty with them. Not only do we have a goddamn malfunctioning heating and cooling system, we have a DCC that's not picking up the malfunction." Boxer was angry. The dive would have to be aborted. He'd have to surface and run a complete check to make sure that every system was tied into the DCC.

"Skipper, it will take three to four hours to make the repairs," the DCO said.

"None of us are going anywhere," Boxer answered. "Mister Harris, take the conn."

"Aye, aye, skipper."

Boxer left the bridge and went directly to where the repair party was working.

"The fire didn't do as much damage as it might have," Monty said, looking up at him.

"I want a full report about this on my desk by 0800 tomorrow," Boxer said. "And I want recommendations on how something like this could—no, must be prevented in the future." Without waiting for an answer, he stalked off and went straight to his quarters, where he dropped down into a chair and for a few moments pressed his face against the palms of his hands. He was angry at himself for taking his frustration out on the DCO and Monty. Neither man was responsible for the malfunction. But it was the kind of glitch that could easily develop into a major catastrophe.

"Skipper?" Harris called over the intercom.

"Yes," Boxer answered.

"We've reached a temp of ninety five degrees," Harris told him.

"I'm on my way to the bridge," Boxer said. He took a moment to check the *Shark*'s operation on the MINCOMMCOMP. All systems were functioning normally.

By the time Boxer reached the bridge, Pierce was there too.

"Captain," Pierce asked, "is there somewhere we might be able to speak privately?"

The distraught look on the man's face disturbed Boxer. He looked at Harris. "My exec is second in command," he said.

Pierce nodded. "The problem is more serious than just making electrical repairs. We can jury rig that but there's no guarantee that we won't have another fire."

Boxer frowned.

"Once we're on the surface, we can complete the repairs and hook in the DCC."

"I was prepared to surface," Boxer said, "as soon as you had the thermostats working."

"They're burned out," Pierce said. "They overloaded. I don't know why, but they did."

Boxer's stomach tightened. "Can we surface?" he asked.

"We should have no difficulty," Pierce answered. "But —"

"I want the bottom line," Boxer said, looking at Harris.

"The air scrubbing system will have to be turned off," Pierce said. "The trouble we're having with the temp controls seems to be tied to that system."

"How the hell could that have happened?" Harris asked.

Pierce shook his head. "I don't know. But that's the way Monty, I and your DCO see it."

"That means all of us will be on the emergency air system until we open the hatches," Boxer said, frowning.

"We'll have to take oxygen out of our water supply and vent the hydrogen," Harris said.

Pierce shrugged.

"When can we start to surface?" Boxer asked.

"As soon as word comes from the DCO that the repair party is finished with the rewiring."

"Let me know as soon as it's done," Boxer said.

Pierce nodded and left the bridge.

"Bill," Boxer said, "once we start making our own oxygen we're going to have a real problem. There's no way that we can stop either the oxygen or hydrogen from leaking out into the boat but we can minimize the chances for an explosion. All communication between myself and the other officers will be passed by you. No radios, telephones or computers will be used. Wherever possible all operations will be done manually. Make sure all devices in the mess are turned off. Before any electrical device is used, each section officer is to make absolutely sure that it must be used. I'll get on the MC and explain the situation to the crew. For the next few hours we're going to be between—" He looked up.

"A rock and a very hard place," Harris said.

"With no room for error," Boxer responded. A moment later he was on the MC. After he explained the situation and the danger of a possible explosion, he said, "Remember to breathe as normally as possible. Do not . . . I repeat do not exert yourselves in any way." Boxer put the mike down and wiped the sweat from his brow with his sleeve. "Cowly," he called.

"Aye, aye skipper," Cowly answered, running to him.

"You're in charge of oxygen generation. Make sure you vent as much hydrogen as possible. You're going to lose some of both gases. Try to cut your losses as much as possible."

Cowly nodded.

"I'll pass the word when you're to start generating the gases," Boxer said. "Just stand by the equipment until then."

The DCO came to the bridge. "You can start to surface now, skipper," he said. "I've already cut out the air cleaning system."

"Harris, pass the word to the crew; begin using their air masks." Boxer attached his to the outlet port just to the left of his monitor. "Better get to your station;" he told the DCO.

"Skipper, I want to stay close to the main junction box," the DCO said.

Boxer nodded. "Pass the word to the DO, diving planes up twenty degrees. Move planes into position slowly. Blow forward ballast."

Each of Boxer's commands were repeated until they reached the DO and he immediately executed them.

As soon as the forward ballast was blown, the bow of the *Shark* rose sharply up.

"Hold twenty degrees," Boxer ordered.

The *Shark*'s bow settled down again.

Boxer looked at the standard depth gauge. The *Shark* was rising at the rate of ten feet every minute. At that rate it would take five hours to bring her to the surface. Five long hours. The time could be shortened if he blew all ballast. But then the rapid ascent might damage some of the equipment, especially those with diaphragms.

"Skipper," Harris asked, "shall I pass the word to start generating oxygen?"

"Yes," Boxer answered. He looked over to the CIC; the men sat very still. In front of them was the blank GDT.

"Skipper," Harris said, "Cowly reports oxygen generation started."

Boxer nodded and said, "Bill you take the conn for a few minutes . . . I want to walk through the boat."

Harris stepped up to the bridge. "Don't go too long with out air," he cautioned.

Boxer detached his airline from the port and walked quickly down to the CIC area, where he plugged into an available air supply. He looked at the faces of the men. Fear was etched into every one of them. He went from station to station and into the the area occupied by Redfern and his strike force. It was the same everywhere. Fear, like an insidious disease, had struck at the men of the *Shark* and was slowly making zombies of them.

"I want you on the bridge with me, Tom," Boxer said.

"I think it would be better if I stayed with my men." Redfern answered.

"That's not a request," Boxer snapped. "It's an order."

"Aye, aye Captain," Redfern answered, saluting him.

"The bridge in three minutes," Boxer said, turning around and walking swiftly out of the area. He had to do something to help the men control their fear. He didn't have any less fear than any of them. But he fought it down. Maybe it was easier for him to do it because he had to be concerned about everyone else. But all of

202

them still had four hours to go before they'd be able to believe that they weren't going to die.

Boxer reached the bridge short of air. He was having difficulty breathing.

Harris helped him plug his line into an air supply port. "Like the rest of us, skipper, you need air," he said

Coughing, Boxer nodded.

Redfern came to the bridge. "Reporting as ordered, sir," he said

Boxer took several deep breaths. "Attach your air line to supply port, Major," Boxer said. "Maybe between the three of us we'll be able to think of something to help our men cope with what is happening to them."

"They're doing as well as can be expected," Redfern answered.

"That's not enough," Boxer said, scanning the depth gauge. They were passing through the twenty-two hundred foot level.

"You can't expect them to —" Redfern began.

"Tom, some of them look as if they're ready to crack wide open," Boxer said. "We don't want that to happen. The men on the *Shark* must be able to take whatever comes their way. No one wants something like this to happen but the men must be able to deal with it. Most of them are just sitting in one place, waiting to die."

"They know what the odds are," Redfern answered.

Boxer pointed to the depth gauge. "We're a thousand feet closer to the surface than we were when we started to go up."

"The skipper is right," Harris said. "So far we're doing okay. But as far as the men go, I don't have any ideas."

Boxer took another deep breath. "Maybe not this time," Boxer said. "But we have to think ahead to other times. If the Ruskie destroyer had called for air support and another ship, we would have stayed on the bottom for a couple of days. Maybe longer, if it meant not getting blown apart or damaged. The men would have been in the same fix. We've got to come up with something."

Redfern nodded. "I'll think about it," he said.

"So will I, skipper," Harris told him

"Now may I go back to my men?" Redfern asked

Boxer nodded.

"What was that all about?" Harris asked. "I thought the two of you were friends."

"We are . . . only he doesn't know it yet."

Harris looked up at the depth gauge. "We still have a way to go."

"But we are going," Boxer answered.

For awhile, the two men stood silently on the bridge; then Harris suggested that he walk through the *Shark*. "Just to make us more visible to the men," he said.

"Good idea," Boxer responded and repeated the caution Harris had given him about not going too long without air.

"Don't worry, I won't," Harris answered with a smile.

Boxer nodded and as soon as he was alone, his eyes went back to the depth gauge. The *Shark* was still going up, but at an excruciatingly slow rate, considering what was happening to the men and to himself. He was painfully aware of his fatigue, physical and psychological. The experience might have cost him his friendship with Redfern. He lowered his eyes and looked at the dead COMMCOMP. Without it and all the other electronic devices, he had no more knowledge of what was happening inside the vitals of the *Shark* than the lowest rate aboard.

"Mister Harris, pass the word we have just gone through the thousand foot level," Boxer said. He wanted very much to walk through the boat again, but somehow couldn't muster the strength. His legs felt heavy and his head throbbed.

He looked up at the gauge. It showed they were almost at the six hundred foot level. He felt the presence of danger more keenly than when they were the three thousand feet down. Something was happening to him. Suddenly he found himself looking at Cowly.

"Skipper," Cowly said, "we're not generating any more oxygen."

Boxer nodded. Damaged equipment was better than a dead crew. "Pass the word to blow all ballast," Boxer said. He waited to feel the sudden upward movement of the *Shark*.

It came!

"Cowly stand by the deck party to open number one hatch," Boxer said, realizing his speech was very slow. He squinted up at the gauge. The *Shark* was at two hundred fifty feet. Her bow would shoot out of the water; the rest of her would come up like a breeching whale.

The *Shark* broke water and came down hard, throwing several of the men off their feet.

"Open hatch!" Boxer ordered.

It took three men to move the dogged latch and push the hatch open. A rush of fresh air exploded into the *Shark*.

"Open all deck hatches," Boxer said, removing his breathing mask, and taking several deep breaths.

Water began to spill into the *Shark*.

Boxer climbed out on the *Shark*'s deck. They had surfaced into the middle of a thunderstorm. Despite the heavy sea and the lightning, the sea never before looked so good. Boxer was happy to be alive. He and his crew had come very close to death. He filled his lungs with the sharp salt air of the sea; then he went below. "Mister Harris, I want every man on deck, regardless of the weather, for at least five minutes."

"Aye, aye, skipper," Harris answered.

"Mister Cowly," Boxer said, "vent all gases. We want to raise our sail as quickly as possible." Within a few minutes he had given dozens of commands. The repair party was at work on the connections in the main electrical junction box that controlled the heating and cooling systems. Another party was working on the gas generating system. There was activity everywhere. The *Shark* and her crew were functioning.

As soon as Boxer could spare the time, he sent a coded message to Williams, explaining the situation. Then he ordered a change of course that would bring the *Shark* back to where she had started to dive.

An hour after the *Shark* had surfaced, Boxer ordered the sail up and gave Harris the conn, while he made a complete taped log of the dive.

The repairs took ten hours to complete and necessitated the replacement of all the thermostatic controls in the heating and cooling systems and connecting the DCC to monitor those systems. The oxygen generating system simply required new electrodes.

The storm continued during the time the *Shark* was forced to remain on the surface and acted as a shield for her. According to the barometer, they were actually sitting in the midst of a tropical depression.

Boxer was busy with hundreds of details, including the testing of recon craft's controls and communication equipment. Everything aboard the two crafts checked out. But because of Boxer's experience with the *Shark,* he ordered the tests run a second time. But the results were the same.

205

For the ten hours, Boxer sailed the *Shark* in a figure eight pattern that was never more than ten miles long and three miles wide. Part of the time, he was on the bridge, But for most of it, Cowly and Dwight spelled each other, taking two hour shifts on and two hours off.

After they were on the surface for five hours, Boxer was in his quarters lying down in an attempt to get some sleep when Redfern asked to see him.

"Sure Tom," Boxer said. "Com' on in . . . Sit down and tell me what I can do for you."

Redfern looked at the chair at the desk but didn't sit down. " I came," he said, "to offer my resignation."

Boxer pushed himself back against the wall. "What the hell for?"

"Com' on, Jack, you know why?"

"No I don't," Boxer answered. "If you mean because of your attitude down below, forget it!"

"I was no help and I should have been," Redfern said. "You and Harris and the rest of your officers, did the things you asked them to do, regardless of how bleak the outcome looked. Maybe I just don't have it for this kind of an assignment."

Boxer stood up, went to his desk and filled the pipe John had given him with tobacco. "You're not a submariner," Boxer said, lighting up. "You're on the *Shark* for the ride this time and should we be called upon to perform a mission, my job and the job of the *Shark*'s crew is to get you there. We're your transportation, that's all."

Redfern shook his head. "You bailed me out of one bad situation and I was too damn frightened to help you in another bad one."

"To tell you the truth," Boxer said, "I was scared shitless. But I'm the boat's captain and if I showed just how frightened I was, I'd have never been able to bring the *Shark* to the surface."

"I couldn't have done what you did," Redfern said.

Boxer put his hand on Redfern's shoulder. "No one would ever ask you to," Boxer said. "But I surely can't do what you can in the field."

Redfern pursed his lips.

Boxer put out his hand and said, "I don't want your resignation

Tom. I want you to continue to command your men. Now let's go get some chow. I'm starved."

Redfern shook Boxer's hand. "If you should ever have second thoughts about me, I want you to promise me that you'll ask me for my resignation."

"I absolutely promise," Boxer said. "Now let's go to the mess."

"Aye, aye, skipper," Redfern said with a smile.

At 0300 Boxer sounded the klaxon twice and the *Shark* began its second deep dive. Boxer took the boat to three thousand feet. All the equipment functioned without any problems.

For thirty six hours Boxer, held the *Shark* at its maximum depth; then he surfaced and sent a coded message to Williams that the second deep dive was successful. During the second dive to three thousand feet, he went down in stages of a thousand feet and spent ten hours at each level going through various drills with the crew. Emergency situations were created, and ways to cope with them were worked out. Entire sections of the *Shark* were theoretically damaged and the crew was trained to handle the situation. Short of major internal explosion that would flood more than half of the *Shark,* or a direct hit, as a result of enemy action, the operational procedures were developed to bring the *Shark* to the surface.

On the third deep dive, Boxer began the testing of the recon craft, which were delta wing shaped and driven by an electric motor that could deliver enough power to give the craft a speed of fifteen knots under water and four at the surface. They were equipped with a sufficient air supply to sustain two men for six hours and they were armed with four mini torpedoes, each of which had an effective operating range of four thousand yards.

Boxer and Cowly wore wet suits for the first dive. They climbed into the cockpit and closed the hatch above them.

"Begin to flood," Boxer said over the radio.

Moments later water surged into the recon craft bay.

"Switch on air supply," Boxer said.

"Air supply on," Cowly answered.

Boxer made a last minute check of the ballast and the dive controls.

"Bay flooded," Harris reported.

"Open bay doors," Boxer said.

"Bay doors opened," Harris reported.

"Drive power on," Boxer said, pushing a toggle switch forward. A humming sound filled the cabin. "Setting diving plane for three degrees."

The recon craft responded: its bow tipped slightly forward and it moved out of the *Shark*.

"UWIS on," Boxer said.

"System on," Cowly reported.

They were directly below the *Shark*'s hull. Boxer took the recon craft down ten feet, moved it to the port side and circled the *Shark*, which was being held almost stationary for the test.

"A piece of cake!" Cowly said with a smile.

"A chocolate cup cake," Boxer answered, making several turns around the *Shark*. "It's like flying in the water."

"*Shark* to recon, report your status," Harris said.

"A one," Boxer answered.

"Recon we have you on the UWIS," Harris said. "Looks like you're having fun."

"Roger that," Boxer answered.

For two hours, Boxer and Cowly moved around the *Shark* but never more than a thousand yards from her.

"Recon to *Shark*," Boxer said, "Recon returning, stand by." He brought the craft directly under the *Shark*.

"Have you on the screen," Harris said. "Drop twenty feet."

"Cowly," Boxer said, "you have the conn, bring her in."

Cowly reached over to the EPC and dialed in the additional twenty feet. "Down two zero feet," Cowly said.

The recon craft eased down.

"Good," Harris said. "Now hold your position."

"Position being held," Cowly answered.

"Doors opening," Harris reported.

"See them on the UWIS," Cowly said.

"Bring her in," Harris told him.

"Coming in," Cowly responded. "Blow outer ballast," he said.

Boxer moved a control wheel. There was the sudden hiss of escaping air. "Outer ballast blown."

The *Shark* started to rise.

Cowly switched on the outer sensors.

"One zero clearance on starboard side," Boxer said. "Two zero clearance on port side."

"Recon to *Shark*," Cowly said, "project guide beam."

A diamond shaped cursor came up on a small round screen on which there were two cross hairs. The cursor was diagonally off to the left.

Cowly moved the rudder control and the EPC until the diamond was exactly centered on the cross hairs. "Like riding a landing beam," he commented.

"You're in," Harris said.

"Switch off power," Cowly ordered.

"Power off," Boxer answered.

"Closing door," Harris said.

It took ten minutes to pump the bay clear of water. But as soon as Harris notified them the water was below the level of the hatch, Boxer reached up, undogged the hatch and pushed it open. Then he climbed out and leaped onto the catwalk.

Cowly followed him.

"You go down with Harris next time," Boxer said. "Then with Dwight."

"That's fine with me, Skipper," Cowly said. "I kind of like it out there."

"Just don't get too playful," Boxer said. "When we're in shallow water, I want you to try some escape techniques."

Cowly nodded.

When they returned to the bridge, Boxer resumed the conn. Two hours later, Cowly and Harris made another successful test of the recon craft and two hours after their return, Cowly and Dwight made the third test run.

"Now hear this," Boxer said over the MC, "Now hear this. The deep dive tests of the *Shark* and the two recon craft have been successfully completed. We are heading to the surface."

The men cheered.

Boxer gave control of the entire surfacing operation to COM-MCOMP, while he sat down and watched the readout on the monitor, as the computer went through each of the sequences.

He called Harris to the bridge and said, "This damn device not only tells the other controls what to do, but it also checks to see if they're doing it, or if it wants to alter its original instructions."

"It can do all that," Harris said, "but it can't examine a situation with the same insight that you can."

"That's probably why I'm feeling so superior to it," Boxer laughed.

"Oh I wouldn't let myself get carried away," Harris answered. "You never know what a man like Monty will think up next."

"And you want to know something," Boxer said, "I'm glad I don't know." Then he asked, "How about something to eat?"

"Good idea," Harris responded.

"Cowly," Boxer said, "you take the conn. Harris and I are going into the mess."

A few minutes later, Boxer was enjoying a bowl of beef barley soup and Harris settled on a bowl of chili.

"How did your wife take the change," Boxer asked.

"Not very well," Harris answered.

Boxer nodded.

"What about Gwen, how did she react?"

Boxer shook his head. "About the same as your wife did. But even if I could have told her what this was all about, I don't think it would have changed her point of view."

"Peggy thinks I'm crazy for leaving the Navy," Harris said; then with a laugh, he added, "she should see me now."

"I guess most of the men have had similar problems with their wives or family," Boxer commented.

"I think so," Harris answered.

Boxer finished his soup, put the paper bowl in the disposal unit and then sat down to smoke his pipe. He was at peace with himself.. . .

The *Shark* surfaced at 2230 and Boxer immediately went to the bridge on the sail, where he set a new course on the AUTONAV and NAVCLOCK systems that would bring the *Shark* into the vicinity of Caicos Islands. He decided to let Redfern give his men a landing exercise on West Caicos, off which there was 1800 feet of water, where the *Shark* could hide during the day.

The plan was to put Redfern and his men ashore at night; then move inland and be on the opposite side of the island the following night to rendezvous with the *Shark* and be withdrawn.

Redfern asked Boxer if he'd like "to come along for the hell of it?"

Boxer's first reaction was to say, "No . . . I don't like walking that much." But the more he thought about it, the more he realized that there might be times when some knowledge of land tactics would be helpful and he changed his mind.

But on this particular night, Boxer wasn't thinking of the coming landing. He had slipped into a reverie about Gwen, remembering how much they had loved and laughed when they had vacationed at Caneel Bay. Then it had seemed to both of them that nothing could ever come between them. . . .

"Skipper," Dwight said, "Mister Redfern requests permission to visit the bridge."

"Granted," Boxer answered. "But only if he promises not to talk shop."

"Will you look at those stars!" Redfern exclaimed, as he came up on the bridge. "Almost seems like you could reach up and grab a handful."

Boxer agreed, filled his pipe and started to smoke it.

"Sometimes I think that me and Sue-Ann will just chuck the fancy life and find a small island—"

"Com on, Tom, you know you'll never do anything like that, at least not with Sue-Ann. She's a society woman the way some women are career women."

"Guess you're right," Redfern admitted.

"I know I am," Boxer said. "I've been there with a career woman."

"Tracy is certainly that type."

"I didn't mean her," Boxer said. "I meant my ex-wife."

"Oh!"

Boxer puffed on his pipe and the smoke was immediately carried away. "She wanted freedom to become something more than just my wife . . . Well, now she is something more and—Well, I don't think she's happy being what she is."

Redfern didn't comment.

"All your men briefed about the operation?" Boxer asked.

"I thought you didn't want to talk shop?"

"I don't," Boxer answered. "But it's better than talking about women, especially out here."

"Guess you got something there," Redfern answered; then he

said, "The men are briefed. Rudy will coordinate the ops; Wild Bill and Hellwig will lead the two assault teams; Link and Ross will stay close to us. If any man gets hurt, I'll dispatch one or the other of them. But we don't anticipate any trouble. We're using the map on the island as shown on your NAVY chart. It gives just enough detail to make it interesting. We're going to land on the south side, hump it over the mountain, which is fifteen hundred feet high; then come down the other side and meet up with the *Shark* in a cove. By the way that's the only good harbor on the north side of the island. According to the map, that coast has cliffs going down to the ocean."

"Go over the pick-up with Harris," Boxer said. "He'll have command of the *Shark*."

"Already done, skipper," Redfern answered.

"You better plan on doing something similar when we're up in the Arctic," Boxer said. "I'll find you a nice barren piece of land and you men can run all over it."

"Thanks . . . You're all heart!"

Boxer laughed and said, "Sure I am. But don't let it get around."

"You can be damn sure I won't," Redfern said.

"I'm going below for some sack time," Boxer said. "We should be off the island by sixteen hundred hours. But if we reduce speed we could arrive by eighteen hundred and your guys will get off immediately."

"Doesn't matter," Redfern said. "If we come in close during the late afternoon, we'll get a chance to take a look at the beach. But any way you want to do it, skipper, will be okay with me."

Boxer nodded. "We'll come in at sixteen hundred. See you in a few hours." Then turning to Dwight, he said, "Take the conn until Cowly comes up."

"I'm going to stay here awhile longer," Redfern said.

"Cowly," Boxer said, "don't let Redfern tell you what a simple Indian he is, because, take it from me, he's not."

A few minutes later, Boxer was in his quarters. He made a last minute system check with the MINICOMMCOMP. All systems were functioning normally. Satisfied, he pulled off his shoes and jumpsuit and dropped down on his bunk. Within moments, he was asleep.

"Stand by to surface," Boxer said over the MC. "Deck party stand by. Mister Harris stand by to raise sail." Boxer watched the digital depth readout. "Coming up to five zero feet," he announced. "RO prepare to activate ATI."

"ATI systems on standby," the RO answered.

Boxer reduced the *Shark's* speed to ten knots. "Mister Harris, sail up!"

"Sail going up," Harris answered.

"Surface . . . Surface," Boxer said over the MC.

"ATI operating," the RO said.

"Full surface display on the CIC board," Dwight announced.

"Diving planes in neutral," Boxer said, reading a null on the EPC.

"Deck party on bridge," Cowly reported.

"Redfern," Boxer called, already moving away from the COMMCOMP and toward the access door of the sail, "let's go top side and get a look at the beach."

As soon as Boxer reached the bridge, he keyed the engine room. "I want just enough power to hold steerage way," he told the EO.

"Aye, aye, skipper," the man answered.

Boxer turned his field glasses on the island. The beach was white, a few hills covered with scrub gave way to a steep rise.

"This is the dry side of the island," Redfern said. "The other side must get most of the rain. "It's probably like PR's rain forest. The men will have to cut their way through."

"When is rendezvous time with the *Shark*?"

"Oh five thirty," Redfern answered. "About twenty five minutes before sunrise."

Boxer nodded approvingly.

"Target bearing two eight zero degrees," the RO announced. "Range twenty five thousand years . . . Altitude three thousand feet . . . Speed two zero zero per."

"What the fuck is he doing here?" Boxer questioned, as he turned around and examined the piece of sky where the target was located.

"Target two eight degrees . . . Altitude three thousand feet . . . Range twenty three thousand yards . . . Speed two zero zero per."

Boxer continued to watch the target, trying to decide whether he should give the order to dive.

"Target bearing two eight degrees . . . Altitude two thousand feet . . . Range twenty thousand yards . . . Speed two five zero."

Boxer realized the plane was coming straight at them. He hit the klaxon twice . . . "Diving . . . Diving," he announced over the MC and followed Redfern off the bridge, securing the hatch after him.

At the COMMCOMP he flooded all ballast and increased the *Shark*'s speed to fifteen knots.

In less than a minute, the *Shark* went down to seventy feet.

Boxer switched on the GDT. There was only another eight feet below the *Shark*. "Going all the way down," Boxer said. He reduced speed to zero. "Prepare for hard landing," Boxer said. Ordinarily, he would have blown some of the ballast to slow the rate of descent but now he didn't want to have that pilot looking down on a trail of bubbles.

Boxer switched on the UWIS. The bottom was full of rocks.

Within moments, the *Shark* ground down on them.

"DCO," Boxer said, "report."

"All systems functioning normally," the DCOP answered. "Hull normal."

"The pilot had to have seen us," Boxer said to Harris. "And came down to get a better look."

"No doubt about that," Harris answered. "But what the hell was he doing here in the first place?"

Boxer shrugged. "Out for a joy ride," he answered.

The *Shark* remained on the bottom until eighteen hundred; then it surfaced and Redfern began landing the strike force. The men went ashore in rubber assault boats. Each man carried his M-22 rifle, a hundred rounds of ammo for it, a trench knife, a machete, and four fragmentation grenades. Several of the men carried special weapons to give their assault teams more fire power.

Boxer, Redfern and the two medics, Link and Ross reached the beach behind the main assault teams.

Redfern was in radio contact with Rudy. The force was divided into four groups and these were spread along a front of five hundred yards. Each group covered the other as they made their way slowly up the fifteen hundred foot ridge that divided the two sides of the island.

Crossing the foothills in front of the ridge was easy. But when the men got to the base of the ridge, they found the rock face steep and treacherous. Often it was hand over hand. The men lifted one another from one ledge to another.

Boxer, Redfern and the two medics were having as much difficulty as anyone else.

"When does the moon rise?" Boxer asked, stopping on a narrow ledge to catch his breath.

"By the time it does," Redfern said, "we'll be in the rain forest on the other side."

Suddenly Redfern's radio began to beep and a red light flashed.

"Rudy is coming in on the scrambler," Redfern said, adjusting his radio to receive the message.

"Indian, this is Chico," Rudy said, "better take looksee from ridge line down."

"What's sailin'?" Redfern asked.

"Small sea bird next to big fish," Rudy answered.

"Roger," Redfern answered. "Rudy says a seaplane and a yacht are sitting in the cove."

Boxer immediately placed his scrambler on and keyed the *Shark* with his handset. "Harris," he said, "do not approach rendezvous point . . . Return to landing position . . . Repeat . . . Do not approach rendezvous point . . . Return to landing position . . . Acknowledge that?"

"Roger that," Harris responded.

"Let's get up to that ridge and have a look," Boxer said. A short while later, he was looking down at the cove through his field glasses. "That's the *Mary-Ann*," he said to Redfern. "Sanchez's yacht. She—"

"I know what she did," Redfern told him. "But what is she and that seaplane doing here?"

"Probably a cocaine pickup or dropoff," Boxer said. "I don't give a fuck what they're doing here . . . I don't want the seaplane to take off tomorrow."

"No problem," Redfern said.

"We can't have any shooting," Boxer told him, "though to tell

215

the truth I'd like to blow the plane and the *Mary-Ann* out of the water." Then suddenly he realized that Tracy might be aboard the *Mary-Ann*.

"Are you thinking what I think you're thinking?" Redfern asked.

"About Tracy."

"You should speak to her about the company she keeps," Redfern said.

"It wouldn't do much good," Boxer answered. "But next time I see her, I will. Now how do we stop that seaplane from flying?"

"Listen," Redfern said. "Chico, this is the Indian. Stop the seabird from flying. No bangs. A couple of holes would do fine."

"Fun . . . fun!" Rudy answered. "I'll go with Yellan."

"Negative. Stay with the men. Send Yellan and Wild Bill."

"You're one mean Indian," Rudy responded.

"Roger that," Redfern answered and turning to Boxer, he said, "Now we wait."

Boxer contacted Harris. "Stay off the landing beach . . . Will reboard before dawn."

"Will be there," Harris answered.

Boxer gave his attention to the cove. The *Mary-Ann* was all lit up and now and then Boxer caught the sound of music.

"The men are just to the left of the seabird," Rudy said over the radio. "They're going into the water now."

Boxer switched his glass to infra red for night use. He saw the two men moving through the shallow water and begin to swim toward the seaplane.

"So far so good," Boxer said, feeling his heart skip a beat and start to race.

Suddenly a searchlight on the *Mary-Ann* came on and began to sweep the water.

"Chic," Redfern said, "take the light out."

Two shots were fired.

The light went out.

Two other lights came one.

"Throw some stuff at the *Mary-Ann*," Boxer said. "I want our men covered."

"Chico," Redfern said, "this is Indian, let them know we're here."

216

"Roger that," Rudy answered.

Four seconds later, a half a dozen M-22 were firing down on the *Mary-Ann*.

Boxer watched the seaplane. It was slowly settling in the water.

"Indian, our men are clear," Rudy said.

"Cease firing," Redfern said.

The M-22s fell silent.

"As soon as Yellan and Wild Bill rejoin us," Boxer said, "move everyone back to the beach. I want to reboard the *Shark* as soon as possible."

"There'll be people up here looking for us in the morning," Redfern said.

"Too bad we can't wait around to greet them."

"I could leave a few men," Redfern offered. "They could do the job."

Boxer shook his head.

"It's not the time or the place," Boxer said. "But someday, I'll get Sanchez." He switched off the infrared vision and looked down at the cove.

"Well, what do you know," Boxer exclaimed with a smile, "the *Mary-Ann* is weighing anchor and leaving. Tom, have Rudy fire a few rounds of heavy stuff around her."

"You sure you want to do that?"

"Now that they're running, why not? I just didn't want any sort of a confrontation."

Redfern gave the order and Rudy had two of his men with 20mm weapons peper the water alongside and to the stern of the *Mary-Ann*.

"Enough," Boxer said. "Enough. You know that really gave me a kick. I feel great." He took out his pipe, filled it with tobacco and lit up. . . .

"Skipper," Harris said, as soon as Boxer made his way to the bridge, "you have a message from the Williams Company. It's marked urgent for your eyes only. That's why I didn't decode it."

"I'll get to it as soon as all of Redfern's men are aboard and we're underway."

"What happened to change the original plan?" Harris asked.

"I'll tell you about it later," Boxer answered. He looked down from the sail.

Redfern was still getting his men on board.

"Move it, Tom," Boxer shouted. "Ten more minutes and we'll have the sun on us."

Redfern waved to him but continued to count the men as they came on board the *Shark*. Finally he shouted. "All present and accounted for, skipper."

"Get those rubber boats deflated," Boxer yelled back.

"Just about done," Redfern answered.

The boats were finally on board and stowed in their special lockers built into the deck, just forward of the sail.

"Ready to move, skipper," Redfern shouted.

Boxer hit the klaxon twice; then scrambled down the hatch, securing it after him. "Harris, you have the conn, take her down to six zero feet and bring her around to the north side of the island. I want to take a look at that cove. I'll be in my quarters."

"Aye, aye skipper," Harris answered.

Boxer went to his quarters and immediately began to decode the message.

SHARK RENDEZVOUS WITH TECUMSEH. NOW HEADING TO 27° N. LAT. 60° WEST LONG. PROCEED FROM TECUMSEH TO WASH. D.C. FOR MEETING W/STARK ON FRI. 13.

Williams

Boxer jotted down the coordinates; then he shredded the message. He guessed the *Tecumseh* probably had a 'copter aboard that would able to fly him to Washington with no trouble at all. He'd set a course into the NAVCLOCK and the NAVCOMP to meet the *Tecumseh*, as soon as he looked at the cove. He was certain that the *Mary-Ann* would be back there.

Boxer keyed Harris. "I'm going to take some time to clean up and get a couple of hours sack time. Pass the conn to Dwight. Have him wake me in three hours, if I'm not up before."

"Sweet dreams, skipper," Harris answered.

Boxer smiled. Harris would have never dared to say that aboard a regular sub. But the *Shark* wasn't a regular sub. It wasn't even carried on the roster of active ships. It didn't exist and the men aboard her didn't exist. Maybe it was this condition that made it possible for them to be informal with one another and yet function with absolute military precision when the circumstance demanded it? Maybe — Boxer suddenly remembered that he wanted to commend Wild Bill and Yellan for their work. He jotted down their names and then went to shower.

Boxer was on the bridge when the *Shark* reached the cove. He was at the periscope. "She's there," he said. "The *Mary-Ann* is there and there are men swarming all over the sunken plane." He wasn't in the least bit surprised to see the *Mary-Ann*. He would have been surprised if she wasn't there.

Satisfied that he had been right, Boxer lowered the periscope and set the destination coordinates into the NAVCLOCK and NAVCOMP. Then he asked the COMMCOMP to display course options. A map came up on the screen showing three course lines to the destination point. There was much difference between them, with the exception that one would take them through a deepening tropical depression. He chose the most direct course.

Fifty hours later, the SO picked up a target moving at ten knots an hour in north north westerly direction. The *Tecumseh* was on station.

"Going to forty feet," Boxer announced over the MC. He adjusted the EPC and the AUTOBALCONTL to hold the *Shark* at forty feet. "Raise radio antenna."

"Antenna up," the COMMO officer reported.

At that depth only a foot of the antenna was above the surface of the water and the antenna itself was so slender it hardly caused a wake.

"COMMO send the following message," Boxer said. "Captain Nemo will board at your time. Send it in the two by two code."

"Message sent," the COMMO officer said. "Reply coming . . . I'll have it decoded in a minute. Okay, here it is: Ready now to have Captain Nemo board. Depth five five feet. Dead in the water. Current from two zero zero degrees, speed two knots. Surface wind from two nine five degrees, speed eight knots."

"Roger that," Boxer said, dialing the parameters just given to him by the *Tecumseh*. He moved to the periscope and looked at the *Tecumseh* for almost a minute. She was big, a fourth of a mile long. He brought the periscope down. "Lower radio antenna," he ordered.

"Antenna down," the COMMO officer reported.

"Now hear this," Boxer said, over the MC, "now hear this . . . We're going to rendezvous with our mother ship, the *Tecumseh*. We're going under her; then up inside of her, just the way our recon craft reenters the *Shark*. Going down to six zero feet. Manual Diving Control Section stand by."

"Diving Control Section standing by," the DO reported.

"Helmsman standby," Boxer said.

"Standing by," Mahoney answered.

Boxer slowed the *Shark* to five knots; then he keyed the EO. "When I tell you," he said, "two knots in reverse, followed by zero."

"Aye, aye, skipper." the EO responded.

The *Shark* was approaching the *Tecumseh*.

Boxer turned on the UWIS. He could see the ship's hull. The huge doors were already open. "Going to sixty five feet," Boxer said, adjusting the EPC to bring the *Shark* to that depth. He aligned the *Shark* with the *Tecumseh*. "Stand by, DO . . . Stand by helmsman, we're going over to manual control . . . On manual."

"Depth six five feet and holding," the DO said.

"Course three zero zero degrees," Mahony reported.

Boxer felt the sweat skid down his back. "We're coming in under her," he said, looking at the picture on the monitor. "EO, two knots reverse."

The *Shark* hesitated.

"Zero speed," Boxer said. "Five degrees on diving planes."

"Diving planes five degrees," the DO said.

"Blow forward and aft ballast," Boxer ordered.

The sound of hissing air filled the *Shark*.

"Forward and aft ballast blown," the DO reported.

The *Shark rose slowly into the hull of the Tecumseh.*

"Diving planes neutral," Boxer said, *watching the progress of the Shark* on the UWIS. Despite the fact the bay was filled with water, it was brilliantly illuminated. "Doors closing," Boxer announced. "We're in! All stations secure from surfacing procedure. Now we have to wait until the water is pumped out." He switched off the UWIS and patting the control, he said, "I couldn't have done it without you."

Boxer came down from the bridge and walked through the boat. He talked and joked with the men and when he visited Redfern's men, he asked to meet Wild Bill and Yellan.

Boxer shook their hands and said, "I can't write you up for any medals, but I can thank you for the job you did."

Both men seemed genuinely embarassed to be singled out by Boxer and each of them said that what they did "wasn't really much."

Boxer nodded and said, "Not much to you guys but a hell of a lot to me."

He left the area with Redfern walking beside him.

"You have good men," Boxer said.

"The best," Redfern answered.

Boxer returned to the bridge

Thirty minutes after the *Shark* had entered the *Tecumseh,* sufficient water had been pumped away to allow the *Shark*'s main hatch to be opened.

Boxer was the first man to come out the *Shark* and came face to face with a tall man, with a round red face and a bull neck.

"Rugger," he said, offering his hand. "Martin—" He smiled. "Marty Rugger, captain of the *Tecumseh*."

Boxer shook his hand and introduced himself.

"That was one fucking great bit of ship handling," Rugger said. "I thought I was good bringing this baby into port now and then. But you're something else!"

Boxer felt the color rise in his cheeks.

"My crew—"

"Sure, your crew," Rugger said. "But without you, well—let's just say that I know good seamanship when I see it. I'd have shit in my pants to do what you just did."

"I almost did," Boxer said.

Harris, Cowly, Dwight and Redfern came on deck.

Boxer was glad to have the opportunity to introduce them to Rugger.

"You and your men have the run of the ship," Rugger said. "We have accommodations for everyone and for dinner tonight, we have fresh turkey with all the trimmings."

"Sounds good to me," Boxer said.

Rugger escorted Boxer, his officers and crew across a gangway, through a tunnel-like structure, which, Rugger informed them, went through the oil storage area; then up a long flight of steps and finally into the stern area of the ship, where the crew lived.

It took four days for the *Tecumseh* to get within range of Washington D.C. On the morning of the fourth day, Boxer was airlifted by 'copter from the *Tecumseh* to Washington's International Airport, where Stark was waiting for him in a limo.

"I hope you've brought some clothing with you," Stark said.

"Just what I'm carrying in the suitcase," Boxer said. "Enough for a day or two. Why, how long am I going to stay?"

"The man I wanted you to meet is out of town now; he'll return at the end of the week. Friday we'll have our conference. Until then your time is your own."

"After the conference?" Boxer asked.

"You have the weekend; then you rejoin your ship," Stark answered.

Boxer thought that he was being driven to a hotel in the city, but he soon realized they were leaving Washington. "Where are we going?" he asked.

"To the Redfern's house. Don't worry, you won't be tied there. You have the use of this car and should you want to fly to New York for any reason, the Williams Company has put a 'copter at your disposal." Stark handed Boxer a piece of paper. "Dial that number and the 'copter will be waiting for you either at the International Airport, or come down to the Redfern's place to pick you up."

"That's really service," Boxer said with a smile.

Stark nodded. "Better in some ways than I have."

"Will the senator be at the house?" Boxer asked.

"He's back in New Mexico. Sue-Ann will be there, assorted house guests and the servants."

Boxer wondered if Tracy was one of the house guests.

"How did she handle?" Stark asked.

"Better than any boat I ever served on," Boxer answered.

Stark nodded, but didn't say anything, or ask any more questions for the remainder of the ride to the Redfern's house.

Boxer looked out of the window and realized there was snow on the ground and the sun's light was pallid. "When did it snow?" he asked.

"Two, three days ago," Stark answered. "It has been too cold and damp for my old bones."

"It's going to damn cold where I'm going," Boxer said.

Stark made a coughing sound and with his head, gestured toward the driver.

"When I go skiing," Boxer said.

"I don't like skiing," Stark responded. "And never did. By the way, when did you start growing a beard?"

"It goes with my new position."

"I don't like beards," Stark said.

The conversation between the two of them lapsed and before it could start again, they turned into the Redfern's long driveway.

At the door they were received by a butler, who took Boxer's suitcase and directed another servant to bring it up to the "guest bedroom in the right wing." Then turning to Boxer and Stark, he said, "Will you please follow me into the drawing room. Madam will be down shortly."

"I have to shove off," Stark said. I'll send the car back to you. Thursday night I'll give you a call and tell when."

Boxer almost forgot himself and was about to say, "Aye, aye, sir." But he fought down the words, extended his hand and said, "I'll see you soon."

Stark shook his hand and left the room.

Boxer went to the fireplace and warmed himself. He could hear a woman's and a man's voice coming from the foyer. He assumed Sue-Ann had met Stark. He was right. A few moments later, she came into the drawing room.

"You look wonderfully healthy," Sue-Ann said, sailing into his arms and giving him a hug and a kiss. "Where have you been?"

"Sailing the oceans blue," he answered, aware of her perfume and the way the green velvet jump suit fitted her.

"I was happy when Dad called and said you'd be spending a few days with us. Especially glad, since I'm giving a little something tonight to raise some money for our local library."

Boxer nodded. "It was kind of you to put me up," he said.

"Nonsense," Sue-Ann answered. "I have this big house and with Dad and Tom away — well, that's why I decided to have a few house

223

guests over."

Boxer nodded.

"Too bad Tracy won't be here," Sue-Ann said.

"Where is she?"

"Off on somebody's yacht," Sue-Ann said, with a shrug. "She wrote an absolutely wonderful story the other day about how they were attacked by modern day pirates. Would you believe that?"

Boxer suppressed a smile. "I would indeed."

"At the end of the story she intimates that the pirates may have been Cuban, or possibly Russian sailors off a submarine that apparently was anchored off the other side of the island."

"What an amazing story!" Boxer exclaimed.

"Tracy is an amazing woman, don't you think?"

"Absolutely," Boxer answered. "One of the most amazing women I have ever met."

"I cut the story out. If you'd like to read it — "

"I most certainly would," Boxer answered.

Sue-Ann smiled knowingly at him. Then she said, "The beard you're growing makes you look positively . . . like a seaman."

"But I am," Boxer laughed. "I'm captain of the super tanker *Tecumseh*."

"Well, Captain, some of the other guests are already here and several more will arrive within the next hour, so I have to leave you on your own until this evening."

"Black tie for dinner?" Boxer asked.

Sue-Ann shook her head. "This is Wednesday night. A suit, or a sports jacket and tie would be fine. Tonight we're casual."

Boxer nodded.

"See you for cocktails around six," Sue-Ann said, turning and walking toward the door.

Boxer enjoyed watching the gentle roll of her buttocks; then he turned back to the fireplace, extended his hands and warmed them.

In addition to Sue-Ann, there were fifteen people at the fund raising dinner for the local library. The women were either beautiful, or very attractive. Three of them were house guests. Two of them were with their husbands and the third was alone. She was a redhead. Her eyes were green and her body womanly with high breasts, a narrow waist and flaring hips. She sat next to Boxer at the table and except for telling him her name was Kathy Tyson, she didn't say much.

Most of the conversation at the table was about politics or business, or took the form of gossip about which congressman or senator had changed his mistress. None of the three subjects interested Boxer and he allowed his thoughts to move to his forthcoming voyage to the Arctic. . . .

Boxer was actually relieved when the guests started to depart. After the third couple left, he went up to Sue-Ann and said, "Would you excuse me? I'm really very tired."

"Of course," she answered. "Of course. Don't wait on me for breakfast. I'm a late sleeper."

"Goodnight," Boxer said, kissing the back of her hand. "And thank you for a lovely evening."

"You were bored to tears and don't tell me you weren't."

Boxer smiled and again he said, "Good night." He went straight to his room, showered and, getting into bed, he switched off the light. Tomorrow he planned to call his parents and Gwen. He hoped to see all of them over the weekend. Maybe he and John would be able to spend part of Saturday together. He felt himself drift off to sleep and let himself go. . . .

Boxer was suddenly aware that someone else was in the room. The lilac scent of perfume was in the air. He awoke and for a few moments, he thought he had been dreaming. But when he realized the lilac scent was still there, he opened his eyes.

Kathy Tyson stood at the window looking at him. She was wearing a diaphanous white nightgown and negligee. Drenched in moonlight, every curve of her body was clearly visible.

Boxer pushed himself up on his elbows. "Have you decided?" he asked.

She didn't answer immediately and when she did, she came slowly toward the bed. "I have been divorced for six months," she said. "And tonight —" She reached the bed and paused.

Boxer made room for her and threw back the blanket.

She opened the bowed ribbon that held the negligee closed and let it drop to the floor; then she slipped off the shoulder straps that held her gown and let it also slip to the floor. Naked she stood very still. Her nipples were hard from the cold.

"Come into bed," Boxer said gently.

Trembling, she lay down next to him.

Boxer took her in his arms.

"Tonight, sitting next to you at dinner," she whispered, "I felt as if I would explode. I want to be fucked so badly, so very badly!"

Boxer kissed her forehead, her eyelids and then her mouth.

She pushed her tongue against his and then moved it over his and against the roof of his mouth with exquisite, feathery light touches.

He caressed her breasts.

She reached down, took hold of his penis and rubbed over her kinky love mound. "It's hot," she whispered. "So wonderfully hot!"

Boxer took a few moments to strip off his skivvies and buried his face in the hollow of her stomach; then he swirled his tongue against her clitoris.

Pushing against him, she moaned with pleasure. "I'm going to come," she said in a throaty whisper. "I'm going to come." Her body tensed and then shook with delight. "Oh . . . Oh . . . Oh!" she cried out.

Even though she had come, Boxer continued to caress her vagina. He looked down at her. Her eyes were closed and her naked breasts rose and fell with her breathing. She was still aroused.

Slowly she pushed herself up and said, "I want to suck you. Lie back."

"Sixty nine," Boxer said, lying down and positioning her directly above him.

She took his penis in her mouth and caressed it with her tongue; then she moved lower and tongued his scrotum.

Boxer responded by working his tongue into her vagina and over her anus.

She stopped and caressing his scrotum, she asked, "Do you want to come this way?"

"I wanted to be inside of you," he said, intuitively knowing that was what she wanted.

"Oh yes!" she exclaimed, moving to face him. She put her naked thigh over his to make it easier for him to enter her and when he did, she uttered a soft cry of pleasure. "That feels so good, so very good."

Boxer began to move and at the same time he moved one hand over buttocks and down to her vagina.

She caressed his balls.

Boxer plunged into her and she met every one of his movements. The spasms in her vagina were strong. His own passion was beginning to boil. He could feel it in his toes and then it began to move up through his body.

"I'm almost there," she said in a whisper. "Almost there!" Then shuddering, she grasped him by the shoulders and pressed her lips against his, forcing her tongue into his mouth. . . .

Boxer's ejaculation poured out of him and swept by an enormous wave of pleasure, he pressed her to him.

When it was over, neither of them spoke. He held her in his arms and they slept. Boxer awoke at first light.

Kathy was nestled against him. The lilac scent still clung to her. She was really a lovely looking woman.

Boxer wondered what happened to her marriage? Was she or her husband at fault? Were they both at fault? Sometimes a marriage just falls apart; then neither the wife nor the husband are at fault. People change. A man or a woman starts out wanting one thing at twenty five and by thirty they might want something completely different. It happened that way between him and Gwen. . . .

"How long have you been looking at me?" Kathy asked.

"Not long," he answered.

She glanced at the window; then looked back at him. "It's gray again."

"Can't really tell yet," Boxer answered. "The sun hasn't come up yet."

"Oh!"

"Why don't we go back to sleep," he said, realizing that since he had boarded the *Shark* on the Mississippi some four weeks before, he hadn't really slept one night through. He slept when he was tired, when he could and always in cat-naps. To sleep a night through was a luxury!

"Are you telling me to go?" Kathy asked, moving away from

227

him.

Boxer threw his muscular arm around her bare stomach. "If I wanted you to go," he said, "that's what I'd have told you."

She took a deep breath and relaxed.

"How long will you be here?" Boxer asked.

" 'Till Sunday night."

"I'll be around until Friday," he explained. "Friday I have some ship business to take care of; Saturday I'll probably go to New York to see my parents, my ex-wife and my son. I go back to my ship Monday morning."

"Why did you tell me all that?"

"Because, if we're going to sleep with each other a few times," Boxer said, "I think you're entitled to know something about my schedule. I don't want you to think that when I'm not around, or in bed with you, that I'm sending secret messages to you to get lost, go home, find another bed companion, or all three."

She laughed.

"That's the first time I've heard you laugh, or smile," he said.

"It's hard to smile or laugh when you feel gray inside; when you feel as if you're drying up and never feel like a woman again."

Boxer put his hand on her breasts. "Did you feel like a woman last night?" he asked.

Kathy put her hand over his and pressed down. "Yes," she whispered. "Oh yes! More womanly than I have felt in years." Then she added, after a pause, "It wasn't easy for me to come to you. During the evening I was hoping you'd show some interest in me."

"I did," he answered. "But you didn't seem to be aware of it, or didn't seem interested. I wasn't going to force myself on you."

"Would I be in bed with you now, if I wasn't interested?"

"No," Boxer answered, "you wouldn't."

"And," she said, "would I be doing this?" She moved his hand from her breast to her crotch.

It was already warm and moist. Boxer inserted his forefinger into her vagina.

Kathy trembled. "Would I ask you to fuck me?" she whispered.

"I'm going to make love to you," Boxer said, covering her naked body with his and bending over Kathy, he kissed her on the lips; then he began to move.

She put her arms around his neck, closed her eyes and said, "I'm glad I decided to come to you."

"So am I," Boxer responded. "So am I!"

They climaxed quickly and together; then they fell asleep again.

When Boxer awoke again, Kathy had just gotten out of bed. "My God, you are a real redhead!" he exclaimed, reaching up and caressing her love mound.

Kathy laughed. "I thought you'd never notice."

"I like it," Boxer said. "It's kind of sexy looking."

"Is that all you have to say?"

"No, I'd also say it's kind of cute looking. Certainly adds color to your body."

"And —"

"And it's the first time I ever made love to a real redhead."

And how did the experience compare to making love to a blonde or a brunette?"

"I'm impressed," he answered. "But I'd need more first hand experience with a real redhead before I could make any valid comparisons."

"Are you sure that's what you want?" Kathy asked, her voice turning serious.

"Yes."

She took hold of his hand and kissed it. "I better go back to my room now."

"See you," Boxer answered.

The next few days turned out to be gray and cold. But Sue-Ann managed to keep her house guests occupied with everything from hiking in the woods in the morning to bridge games in the afternoon. She was a born organizer.

During this time, Kathy was discreet, never showing Boxer any more attention than the social situation demanded. But when she came to his room, she was an ardent and skilled lover.

On Thursday evening Stark phoned and told Boxer that he'd be flown by 'copter the following morning to Langley.

12

The 'copter flight from the Redfern's to Langley lasted twelve minutes. As soon as the 'copter was on the ground, Boxer was met by a young, gray business suited man, who politely asked, "Will you follow me, sir?"

Boxer nodded and was escorted through a warren of corridors, ushered into and out of an elevator and finally into a nondescript room, where Stark, Williams and a third man, whom he did not know, were sitting around a highly polished, oak wood conference table.

None of them rose when he entered.

"Your coat and hat, sir,?" his escort asked.

Boxer handed them to him.

As soon as the young man left the room, Stark said, "Jack Boxer, Bruce Kinkade."

Boxer nodded and the man nodded back.

Stark gestured to one of the empty chairs at the head of the table.

Boxer sat down and said, "I hope, Admiral, I'm not going to be grilled because you don't like beards."

Stark did a double take; then chortled. "That's not a bad idea. But now we have more important things to do than cater to my likes or dislikes."

"I'm glad," Boxer answered.

Williams laughed and Kinkade said, "We want to know the results of your shakedown cruise."

"Half of the *Shark*'s shakedown," Boxer corrected. "The second half will take place in he Arctic."

Kinkade didn't acknowledge the correction.

"The *Shark* performed beautifully," Boxer said. "We had two incidents that could have caused—" He paused and started over again. "One put us out of action for several hours and the other could have killed everyone on the boat."

The last statement made Stark lean forward. "We want all the details, Jack."

Boxer described the situation with the burnt-out bushing and the fire that followed. "I don't want to use parts—any parts—from that manufacturer again."

Stark wrote a few notes down and said, "I'll take care of it. Now tell us about the other difficulty."

"I'd much rather explain what happened sequentially."

"All right," Stark said.

Boxer told them about his encounter with the Russian destroyer.

"We monitored the Russian radio communications," Kinkade said. "The captain's base commander is a Cuban. He wanted the captain to continue the search and destroy mission and was ready to order out two more ships and an ASW plane . . . but Moscow cancelled it."

"Good for Moscow!" Boxer exclaimed. "I wouldn't have wanted to bet on the *Shark* coming out of a coordinated attack, if she came out at all. Any guesses why Moscow did that?"

"None," Kinkade answered. "They often do things like that . . . things that really can't be explained rationally by a Westerner. It has something to do with their mind-set."

Boxer told them about the near disaster during the first deep dive. "The problem is solved and will never happen again," he said. "But when we return from the Arctic, I'm going to want some changes made in the design of those two systems and I want fail safe controls on each of them."

"You've got it," Stark said, writing a few more notes.

Boxer explained his visit to Caicos Island. "The *Mary-Ann* was there too," Boxer said. He told them about the unexpected arrival of the seaplane, but made no mention of his orders to stop it from flying.

"Seems Miss Kimble was aboard the *Mary-Ann* at the time," Williams said, speaking for the first time. "We were wondering who the pirates might have been.".

"You ordered your men to fire at the *Mary-Ann*?" Kinkade asked.

"Around it," Boxer explained. "If I had ordered them to fire at it, the *Mary-Ann* would be at the bottom of that cove."

"What about shooting out the searchlights?"

"A precautionary measure," Boxer answered. "My men were up on the ridge and those lights were sweeping the north side of it," Boxer answered.

"Please continue," Stark said.

Boxer explained how well the recon craft handled. "It's almost like flying," he said, borrowing Cowly's description, "but only you're under the water."

"No trouble putting the *Shark* inside the *Tecumseh*?" Stark asked.

"None," Boxer answered. Then he said, "The *Shark* is everything her designers wanted her to be and maybe more."

"Will she be able to carry out any covert mission that might be assigned to her?" Kinkade asked.

"Short of taking on a whole ASW squadron, I have no doubt that she can."

"What about your crew?" Stark asked. "How did they shape up?"

"As well as they did on the *Sting Ray*," Boxer answered. "They're the best we have, Admiral."

"Is your opinion of the strike force the same?" Kinkade asked.

"From what I have seen, yes," Boxer answered. "But the real test of my crew, the strike force and myself will come in the Arctic. There the sailing conditions, even under the sea are impossibly difficult. And as for the strike force, I have already informed Redfern that I'm going to put his men ashore and let them run around a bit. In other words, they'll be carrying out landing exercises under the most difficult conditions."

Kinkade nodded.

"Now will you please tell me what this is all about?" Boxer asked.

"Just routine." Williams answered.

"Everything I told you," Boxer said, "is on tape. You didn't have to bring me in to hear it from me."

"There are times," Kinkade said, "when a personal touch is needed, a face to face briefing. All of us believed that this was one of them."

Boxer felt like answering, '*bullshit*'. But he smiled and said, "I don't mind coming in. I'm having a good time."

"Well then nothing was lost by it," Kinkade responded. "And you're having a good time."

Boxer nodded.

"That's it for now," Stark said. "You return to the *Tecumseh* on Monday. Arrangements will be made to fly you out to her. She'll be off the southern tip of Greenland by then."

Boxer stood up.

Kinkade got to his feet and walked to where Boxer was. "It's been a real pleasure to meet you, Captain," he said, shaking Boxer's hand.

"The same," Boxer said, suddenly realizing he was speaking to the top man in the Company. Kinkade was second only to the president in the amount and kind of power he wielded.

Kinkade walked him to the door, opened it and called to the young man. "Please escort this gentleman back to the 'copter," he said.

"Yes, sir," the young man answered. Then turning to Boxer, he said, "Will you follow me, sir."

Kinkade stepped back into the room and closed the door.

"Here's your coat and hat," the young man said, producing them from a hall closet.

"Thank you," Boxer said, following the young man. He was back at the Redferns in time for a late morning cup of coffee.

"How did your ship business go?" Kathy asked, as she sat down at the dining room table next to him.

"I'm not sure," Boxer answered.

"Nothing serious?"

"I'm not sure of that either," Boxer said. "It's something I have to think about."

"One of those meetings, eh?" Kathy asked with a smile. "God, how I hate those kinds of situations, where you leave more perplexed than when you entered."

Boxer suddenly realized that Sue-Ann had come to the table and was staring at them.

"I had no idea that the two of you knew each other," Sue-Ann said.

Kathy answered, "Mister Boxer—I mean—Jack, happened to mention his meeting to me last night at dinner."

"I was kind of dreading it," Boxer said, hoping to reinforce what Kathy said.

"I don't think you dread anything, Jack," Sue-Ann said. "You're not the dreading type."

The red flag went up in Boxer's mind. Sue-Ann suspected something was going on between him and Kathy and wanted to protect what she thought was Tracy's proprietary hold on him. "I have to go to New York later today," he said.

"Tracy will be here tomorrow," Sue-Ann said.

"I must be in New York for a couple of days," Boxer responded.

"Tracy will be terribly disappointed that she missed you."

Boxer suddenly realized that, though Sue-Ann was well meaning, she was interfering in his life and he had better put a stop to it. "Kathy," he said, "why don't you come to New York with me?"

Sue-Ann choked on what she was swallowing and began to cough. Boxer immediately started to stand.

"Please, I'll be fine," Sue-Ann said.

"Are you sure?" Boxer asked.

She nodded, but continued to cough.

"What about it Kathy, will you go with me?" Boxer asked.

"Yes, I think I will," Kathy said. "I think it would make for a nice change."

"Please excuse me," Sue-Ann said. "No don't get up." And she hurried away from the table.

"Do you really want me to go?" Kathy asked.

He leaned forward and hoping she'd remember, he whispered into her ear. "Would I have asked you if I didn't want to fuck you?"

"No," Kathy answered with a smile, "I don't suppose you would have."

"Then it's settled," Boxer said. "I'll make arrangements for the 'copter to pick us up in an hour." Then he added, "I guess Sue-Ann doesn't have any doubt that we've been sleeping with each other."

"Does that bother you?"

234

Boxer shook his head. "Not in the least."

On Monday morning Boxer boarded a VTOL and was flown from La Guardia Airport in Queens, New York directly to the *Tecumseh,* which was one hundred and fifty miles south of Nanortalik, Greenland. The flight took three and a half hours, giving him time to think about his weekend with Kathy. He did something with her he didn't expect to do; he took her to meet his parents. It was either that, or leave her alone to wander around the city while he visited them. To his absolute surprise, his mother and father immediately took to her and assumed something more to their relationship than existed. . . .

Boxer looked out of the window. From twenty thousand feet the ocean looked smooth, but he was sure it wasn't. There was a band of dark clouds to the west that were mountainous and stretched from north to south as far as he could see.

Leaning back in his eat, Boxer filled his pipe with tobacco and lit up. He spent Saturday afternoon with Gwen and John, taking them skating at the Rockefeller Center rink and then to a shushi bar, where they all enjoyed raw fish. It was a good visit. Gwen had even invited him to stay for dinner. He refused, telling her he was dining with the president of the company for whom he was now working. Had he told her the truth, it would have spoiled the day for all of them. Sunday he and Kathy had completely to themselves. They spent most of the morning in bed, had a late brunch and went to see a film. When they returned to the hotel, they made love, napped and then went to dinner. . . .

All in all, Boxer thought, it was a very good weekend. Kathy turned out to be more than just a bed companion. He actually enjoyed being with her. But though he knew everything about her physically, he really didn't know anything more about her when they parted, than the night she came to his room. She was divorced. He had no idea where she worked, or if she worked, or even where she lived. She gave him a telephone number and told him it was an answering service and that she could be reached at that number any time and —

235

The pilot buzzed him.

Boxer picked up the phone. "Yes," he answered.

"I have the *Tecumseh* on the radio," he said. "The weather is beginning to turn. The landing is going to be tricky. Do you want me to try it or land in Greenland?"

"Go for the *Tecumseh*," Boxer said.

"I'll tell them we're coming in. We should be over them in about fifteen minutes."

Boxer knocked the ashes out of his pipe, ran a pipe cleaner through it and put it back in his pocket. He felt the plane descend. The red seat belt sign came on.

The pilot came back on the phone. "We'll be guided down by instruments," he said. "It won't be as difficult to land as I had thought."

"Thank you. I appreciate you telling me that," Boxer said, realizing that the pilot didn't have the slightest knowledge of who he was and why he was going to the *Tecumseh*.

The plane banked to the left and lost altitude so rapidly that Boxer's ears popped. He looked out of the window. He could see the white tops of the waves and then the *Tecumseh* came into view. They dropped lower, leaving the *Tecumseh* behind them.

A few moments later, the pilot made a 180° turn and came in low over the water.

Boxer found himself looking directly down at the *Tecumseh;* then the plane seemed to stall and hover over the ship's deck. It dropped lower and with a tremendous roar touched down. The next instant it was silent. The red seat belt sign went off.

Boxer unbuckled, stood up, put on his coat and hat and, taking his suitcase out of the race went to the door of the aircraft.

The pilot and copilot came out of the cockpit.

"Thanks for the ride," Boxer said, as the pilot pushed the control that opened the aircraft's door and automatically extended a flight of steps.

"No sweat," the pilot answered.

"Why not stay for dinner," Boxer suggested.

"The weather is turning real mean," the pilot said. "I'll take a rain check. All I want to do is refuel and get into the air before it gets too rough for a take off."

"You guys are welcome to dinner any time," Boxer said, as he left the plane.

A strong, cold wind blew across the deck. The sea was more roiled than it seemed to have been when he had looked down at it from the plane.

Suddenly he saw Harris and Redfern coming toward him. He quickened his pace and they fell in alongside of him as the three of them entered the *Tecumseh*'s deck house.

"Have the *Shark* ready to get under way as soon as possible," Boxer said to Harris.

"She's ready and waiting," Harris answered.

"Your men ready?" Boxer asked Redfern.

"Packed and waiting," Redfern answered.

Boxer looked at his watch. It was 1400. "I want to be free of the *Tecumseh* by sixteen hundred," he said.

"I'll get my men aboard now," Redfern said.

"Do the same with the *Shark*'s crew," Boxer told Harris. "I'll have Captain Rugger begin flooding the bay as soon as I collect my gear from my cabin."

"How did your visit to D.C. go?" Harris asked.

"Damned if I know why I was called there," Boxer answered; then to Redfern, he said, "I stayed at your place for a few days."

"How's Sue-Ann?" Redfern answered.

"She's probably angry at me, Tom," Boxer said. "I'll tell you all about it once we're underway."

"She didn't try to get you and Tracy together?" Redfern asked.

"Tracy wasn't there. But that's another story," Boxer said, stopping at the elevator that went to the bridge. "I want to see Rugger for a few minutes. I'll see you aboard the *Shark*."

"Aye, aye, skipper," Harris said.

Boxer pressed the elevator button, the doors opened and he stepped into the car. It was good to be at sea again; it would be even better once he was back on the *Shark*. . . .

Boxer's course for the *Shark* took her along the reverse route sailed by the *Nautilus* in the summer of 1958, when it sailed under the arctic ice and surfaced at the North Pole.

At a depth of a hundred feet and speed of fifteen knots, the *Shark* moved north through the Davis Strait and into the Greenland Sea. Outside the *Shark* the water temperature was thirty-five degrees; cold enough to kill a man in three minutes. Above them, on the surface, a fierce storm wracked the sea with such force that now and then the *Shark* momentarily would lose headway, or be moved slightly off course.

During this time, Boxer ran drill after drill, bringing his crew to the peak of proficiency. Since his meeting with Stark, Williams and Kinkade, the idea formed in the back of his head that unless they were planning to use the *Shark* for a particular mission, the meeting absolutely made no sense. Everything he told them he had faithfully recorded on tape. But hearing something on tape could never give the listener the tone of the *Shark*'s readiness. To get that, they would have had to hear and see him.

Three days after leaving the *Tecumseh,* the *Shark* was a few miles west of Spitsbergen. Boxer went to periscope depth and looked at the island's coast. It was mountainous and barren. Even when he zoomed in on a particular area, he saw nothing. He wondered how people could live in such an inhospitable place? Yet they did. Not too many miles from where he was lay the northernmost town on earth.

Several times Sonar made contact with a pod of whales and if they were close enough, Boxer would watch them on the UWIS. But for the most part everything was routine.

Pierce and Monty continually checked every system on the boat and each of them spent long hours discussing engineering changes with Boxer and the other officers.

Between Spitsbergen and Franz Josef Land, Boxer brought the *Shark* to the surface. Though it was only 1300, he ordered the lighting in the *Shark* altered for night vision. When he and other members of the deck party reached the bridge it was night, very cold and a strong north wind was blowing, pushing the sea over the *Shark*'s bow.

Almost immediately, ice began to form on the deck and around the base of the sail. Boxer pointed to it and said to Harris, "Have the EO switch on the deicing system. When we dive, I don't want that extra weight on us and I don't want to risk having the sail being jammed halfway down in its well."

For several minutes Boxer occupied himself with making special optical sightings of the north star and correlating them with signals from a secret navigational satellite that remained in orbit over the pole. Later he'd translate the results of the findings into code and send them to Williams.

Then he set a new course into the NAVCLOCK and the NAV-COMP that would take the *Shark* to Kvitoya, an island just a few miles above 80° north latitude. It was remote enough for Redfern and his men to make a landing without fear of being seen, except, perhaps by a whale, or a polar bear.

"You take the conn," Boxer told Harris and he went down into the *Shark* to discuss the landing with Redfern, who was drinking coffee with Rudy in the mess.

Boxer drew a coffee for himself and sat down at the table with them. "It's cold up on the bridge," he said.

"Anyone who goes out in weather like this is nuts," Rudy said.

Boxer agreed, took a sip of his coffee and said, "Tom, in five hours we'll be off the coast of the island of Kvitoya, where I want you and your men to land."

"I guess we're nuts," Rudy commented.

"I guess," Boxer answered with a smile.

"The way I'd like to see it done is to put ashore half your men and have them be the defending force; then the other half will be the attacking force. The island isn't much but it's enough for our purposes."

"How long do you figure the exercise to last?" Rudy asked.

"I'll leave that up to Tom," Boxer answered. "But a lot will have to do with the weather. It changes very fast up here and if a blow begins it can last for days and you and your men would have to stay on the island until it was over."

"What's the weather look like now?" Redfern asked.

"Stable," Boxer answered, taking another sip of coffee.

"Maps?" Rudy asked.

Boxer was about to answer, when the SO began calling him on his handset.

He flicked the switch to its ON position and said, "Boxer here."

"Skipper, I think you should come down to the station," the SO said. "I got something coming in on the ACU that's weird."

"You sure you're not listening to a lovesick whale?"

"Well, if it is, it's making sound like—"

"Like what?"

"Music I think," the SO answered.

"Bearing and range?" Boxer asked.

"Bearing two seven zero. But I can't get a range on it, at least not one that I can read."

"I'll be with you in a couple of minutes," Boxer said.

"Okay, skipper," the SO answered.

Boxer switched off the set. "You heard it," Boxer said, looking at the two smiling men seated across from him.

"I think your SO has had it," Rudy commented. "Next thing you'll be hearing from him is that he's picked up dancin' whales."

"Why don't you guys come along," Boxer said. "As soon as we ID this music, we'll go take a look at a map."

"Fine with me," Boxer answered.

"Me too," Rudy said. "I want to hear a mermaid sing."

"Singing mermaids," Boxer laughed. "I never thought it could be that."

The three of them laughed, disposed of their paper cups and left the mess. A few minutes later they were at the Sonar station.

"What have you got?" Boxer asked the SO, whose name was Keith Rogers.

"Listen to this, skipper," Rogers said. "I'll put on the ACU on audio."

"Why I'll be dipped in shit!" Redfern exclaimed.

"It's not a whale," Boxer said, "that's for sure."

"Did you send for Mister Monty?"

"Yes skipper," Rogers answered.

"Did I hear my name?" Monty asked, joining them. "What the hell is that?"

"That's what we'd like to know," Redfern said.

"Sounds like music," Monty said, "though I would be hard pressed to say what kind."

"I did some rough triangulation," Rogers explained, "and what I came up with was that it's moving too, somewhere around eight five degrees north latitude and twenty four degrees east longitude."

"That's under the ice," Boxer said, recalling the latest satellite photograph of the area which he overlaid on his chart.

"We might get better sound," Monty suggested, "if we taped it; then ran it faster than normal, or if that didn't work, slower than normal."

Boxer nodded. "How long would it take you to do it?" he asked.

"Five minutes at the most," Monty answered.

"While he's setting that up," Boxer said, looking at Rogers, "I want you to key the ARCSOSUS and find out what it's picking up." Then he explained to the others that ARCSOSUS is the acronym for the Arctic Sound Surveillance System.

"Skipper," Rogers said, "I'll need your ID number."

Boxer leaned over Roger's control console and jotted the number down on a piece of paper.

"Got it," Rogers, said and immediately began keying.

Boxer tore the paper into small pieces and dropped them into the section's shredder. Then he keyed Harris. "Bridge stand by for a change of course," he said.

"Standing by," Harris answered.

"ARCSOSUS should be answering," Rogers said.

Boxer turned to the monitor.

"Here it comes!" Roger exclaimed.

SOUND NOT ID . . . SOUND NOT KNOWN . . . SOUND MOVING AT 10 KNOTS . . . BEARING 85° N. LAT; 22.5° E. LONG.

"I have the tape ready," Monty said.

Boxer keyed Harris. "Come about to course two seven two degrees," he said.

"Coming about to course two seven two degrees," Harris answered.

"Let's hear the tape," Boxer said.

"At half normal speed," Monty told them playing the tape.

"Sounds like moaning," Rogers offered.

"Twice the normal speed," Monty said.

"Just noise," Rudy commented.

Boxer rubbed his hand over his beard. "We'll wait on that landing exercise," he said to Redfern. "I want to know what the hell is causing that sound. Can you make an analysis of it?" he asked, looking at Monty.

"Probably, but it'll take time," Monty answered. "Maybe a few hours or days."

"A few hours, okay," Boxer said. "But we don't have days." He saw the questioning look on each of their faces. "Suppose you wanted to get through the ARCSOSUS and didn't want the sound of your engines ID by the system, you'd try to mask their sound and how would you mask their sound? By overlaying it with a louder one. A sound that can't be ID by the system."

"But who—" Rudy began.

"A smart Ruskie sub," Boxer said.

Redfern gave a long low whistle.

"We'll be diving in a few minutes," Boxer said. "Let's keep this under wraps for now. I'll tell everyone what's happening once we're down. Monty, let me know as soon as you have something."

"Will do, skipper," Monty answered.

"We'll make a sailor out of you yet," Boxer said with a smile.

"At least half a sailor," Monty answered sheepishly.

"Tom and Rudy go back to your area."

"Aye, aye, skipper," Tom answered.

Boxer went directly to his main control panel. "Now hear this . . . Now hear this . . . In five minutes we will be diving . . . Five

242

and we'll be diving."

"Roger that," Harris over the intercom.

Boxer set the NAVCLOCK and NAVCOMP for 85° N. lat; 22° E. long. He keyed Harris. "I have the conn," he said.

"It's all yours, skipper," Harris answered.

"Bridge party below," Boxer said, watching the clock. "T minus thirty seconds and counting until dive."

Harris came onto the bridge. "Am I ever glad to be down here," he said.

"Minus twenty seconds and counting," Boxer announced over the MC.

"All operational stations on automatic," Boxer said.

"Diving station on automatic," the DO responded.

"Helm on automatic," the duty helmsmen answered.

"Diving . . . Diving . . . Diving," Boxer announced, as he hit the klaxon button twice. "Going to five zero feet . . . Sail down."

"Sail down," Dwight answered from his station.

Boxer set the diving planes at five degrees and flooded the forward and aft ballast tanks. The digital depth readout began to show depth in increments of ten feet. "Coming to five zero feet," he said, adjusting the EPC control to move the diving planes to a null, as soon the *Shark* made fifty feet. "Five zero feet," he announced, pushing the ballast stabilization control buttons. The bubble came to dead center. "Dive complete," Boxer said, switching on the GDT system. Instantly a profile of the sea's bottom came up on the screen. The bottom was a flat, glacially scarred plain.

"One zero feet to bottom," CIC reported.

"In about an hour," Boxer said, "that should go to one thousand eight hundred."

"Skipper," the SO asked, "we still have the sound coming in."

"Let me know if there are any changes," Boxer answered.

"What's this all about?" Harris asked.

Boxer explained the situation. "Monty is trying to analyze it now," he said.

"And you think a Russian sub is trying to pass the ARCSOSUS?"

Boxer nodded. "Only we're going to find it and stop it," Boxer said.

"Skipper, the sound has stopped," the SO reported.

"Keep searching from two six zero degrees to two seven five degrees," Boxer said.

"Aye, aye," the SO answered.

"Attention all hands," Boxer said over the MC, "we have an unknown target somewhere ahead of us. I'm going to try and ID it. If it is a Ruskie sub, it has or is trying to break through our underwater surveillance system, ARCSOSUS for short. ARC because it's up here in the Arctic. You'll know what's happening by what we do." He switched off the system and said to Harris, "I have two choices: I can turn around and run. If I do that, then I keep the *Shark*'s security as tight as it has been. And if it is a Ruskie sub out there its skipper will have nothing to report to Moscow other than he was able to get through our ARCSOSUS. But if I stay and find him, well—"

"You only have one choice, Jack; to stay, find him and destroy him."

"That's the way I figure it," Boxer said.

Boxer was in his cabin. Ten hours had passed since the SO had reported the strange sound had stopped. Boxer had put the *Shark* on a course that would bring it to the point where the sound had originated.

He lay in his bunk, with his hands behind his head. That he was putting the *Shark* in the role of a killer submarine was uppermost in his thoughts. This cruise was supposed to have been the boat's sea trials. But circumstances were obviously going to determine whether the sea trials would also be the *Shark*'s baptism of fire. . . .

Boxer closed his eyes and imagined the map. Traveling at twenty knots the *Shark* would soon be approaching the icepack. Once they were under it, they'd only be able to surface in those areas where there was open water, or the ice was so thin that they could break through it without doing any structural damage to the *Shark*.

Forcing the immediate situation from his mind, Boxer thought of his meeting with Kathy. He still hadn't told Tom why Sue-Ann was angry with him. But he eventually would. As for Kathy, he really didn't expect to carry on any long term relationship. But he was curious about the circumstances of her divorce.. But only because, if he could believe her, it inhibited her from having sex with men until she made up her mind to come to his room at the Redfern's. He couldn't understand that, unless her ex-husband destroyed her image of herself as a woman. Some men will do that to protect their own image of themselves as a man. But he wasn't interested in really establishing a relationship with her. He preferred Cynthia. She was warm, tender and loving. And if he wanted a rough and tumble roll in the sack, he could always have Tracy. Suddenly he realized he had left the Redferns without having read Tracy's story of her encounter with the pirates, or Cubans, or Russian sailors off a submarine. He chortled. Knowing that when he saw her again, she would tell him all about it. And he would—

A knock on the door broke his train of thought.

"It's Monty, skipper," the voice announced.

Boxer sat up and planted his feet on the deck. "Come," he said.

Monty opened the door. "I have it," he said. He came into the cabin and put a small tape recorder down on Boxer's desk. "Listen," he said and pressed the button marked PLAY.

"It's a symphony!" Boxer exclaimed.

"Shostakovich's Seventh, sometimes called the Leningrad," Monty said, obviously proud of his knowledge. "My guess is that it was greatly amplified and played through special speakers several hundred miles from where we picked it up."

Boxer went to his MINICOMP, punched in data that brought a map of the Arctic to the screen.

"The water tends to spread the sound," Monty said. "It could have come from anywhere from one zero eight degrees to three six zero degrees and, as I said before, hundreds of miles from where we were."

"The ARCSOSUS runs in a rough line from across from one seven zero degrees west longitude to thirty degrees—

"Target bearing three zero zero degrees. . . . Range forty miles

245

. . . Speed twenty seven knots . . . Depth three zero zero feet."

"That's our sub!" Boxer exclaimed. He keyed Harris. "I'm coming to the bridge," he said. "But take us down to six zero zero feet. We want to stay below them." He glanced at the map on the monitor. "She's on this side of the ARCSOSUS."

Wide eyed, Monty asked, "Are we going after her?"

"Yes," Boxer answered, hurrying out of the door. As soon as he reached the bridge, he said over the MC," We have a Ruskie sub out there and we're going after it. She'll either turn and run, or fight. No matter what her captain chooses to do, we will try to destroy her."

The crew remained silent.

Boxer switched off the MC and keyed the SO. "Keep a close watch on the target. I want to know the moment she changes course. Give me bearing, range and speed when we're five miles away."

"Aye, aye, skipper," the SO answered.

Boxer brought the *Shark*'s speed up to its maximum.

The EO keyed him and asked, "How long are we going to run at flank speed?"

"Until we're in firing range of the target," Boxer said. "No more than two or three hours. Just keep things going. I don't want any malfunctions now."

"Do my best, skipper," the EO answered.

Boxer leaned back into the chair and watched the monitor. The Russian sub was on it.

Ten minutes passed.

"Skipper," the SO reported, "we're going under the ice."

"Roger that," Boxer answered.

CIC made the same report.

"How thick?" Boxer asked.

"Two to three feet thick," CIC responded.

"Roger that," Boxer said. The ice was too thick for the *Shark* to surface without suffering damage.

Thirty minutes passed. The target held the same course. Boxer wondered if the Russian sonar equipment was good enough to find them?

"Target NOVEMBER class attack submarine," the SO reported.

Boxer punched the information just given to him into the COM-MCOMP. Withinmoments the information came up on the screen.

NOVEMBER CLASS SUBMARINE
NUCLEAR POWERED
DISPLACEMENT ....4,500 TONS (ON SURFACE)
LENGTH ....360 FEET
MAIN ARMAMENT ....4 TORPEDO TUBES
SUBMARINES OF THIS CLASS USED FOR OPS
UNDER ARCTIC ICEPACK.

"Target changing course, going to three zero zero degrees," the SO reported.

"Target speed?" Boxer asked.

"Twenty knots," the SO reported.

"Skipper, target heading for Russian waters," Harris reported from the CIC.

"We'll follow," Boxer answered.

"Target using CM," the SO reported.

"Are we still locked on it?" Boxer asked.

"Affirmative," the SO answered.

Boxer hit the GQ button and over the MC, he said, "We're chasing the Ruskie sub."

"Target changing course," the SO said. "Bearing two nine five . . . Range twenty miles . . . Coming toward us at one five knots. . . ."

"Forward torpedo room, ready all tubes . . . Arm torpedoes . . . Set for guidance from CIC," Boxer ordered.

"Aye, aye, skipper," the FO answered.

More readings came in from the SO, indicating the target was attempting to take evasive action.

Watching it on the screen, Boxer realized he'd be doing exactly the same thing if he were the Russian captain.

"Contact broken," the SO reported.

"What?" Boxer shouted.

"Target blocked by a topographic feature," the SO answered.

"CIC," Boxer said, "give me a reading."

247

"A hill," Harris answered. "One five zero feet high."

Boxer swore under his breath.

"Skipper, the topographic feature is ten thousand yards long," the SO said.

"DO and helmsman stand by to go over to the manual control," Boxer said. "On manual control."

"Diving station on manual," the DO answered.

"Helmsman on manual control . . . Heading two seven three degrees," the helmsman reported.

Boxer changed the *Shark*'s course to bring her around the port side of the Russian submarine.

But just as the SO reported, "Target bearing thirty degrees . . . Range seven thousand yards . . . Speed zero knots . . . Correction speed increasing . . . Target bearing four five degrees and changing course . . . New course two six four degrees . . . She's coming back toward us."

Boxer ordered a new course of ninety four degrees; then changed to twenty two. He was taking evasive action. "CIC, activate CM system."

"New target . . . Bearing two seven two degrees . . . Speed fifty knots . . .Torpedo . . . Torpedo," the SO called out.

"Intercept target's guidance system," Boxer said coolly.

"Roger that," Harris answered.

"Target three thousand yards," the SO reported.

"Helmsman, come to one eight zero degrees," Boxer said.

"Guidance intercepted," CIC reported.

"Target changing course," the SO reported.

Boxer uttered a deep sigh of relief. He switched on the UWIS and framed the sub in the middle of the screen; then he activate the UTI and sighted on the sub. "Load torpedoes," he ordered.

"Torpedoes loaded," the TO reported.

Boxer centered the cursor on the sub; the TI was now reading through the UWIS.

"Target bearing two zero zero degrees . . . Range four thousand yards. Speed twenty knots and closing fast."

"Stand by to fire one," Boxer ordered. He depressed the red button on the side of the COMMCOMP. A red light flashed; then a green one came on. "Torpedo one fired . . . Stand by to fire torpedo two . . ." he said. He pressed the second firing button. The red light flashed and was immediately followed by the green.

Boxer watched the two torpedoes home in on the target. The first struck the forward part of the sub. The sound of the explosion filled the sea around the *Shark;* then came inside the *Shark,* while the shock wave rocked the boat back and forth several times. The second explosion tore the sail off the main deck and sent it tumbling over itself. A huge air bubble broke from it and started toward the surface. "My God," Boxer exclaimed, "someone is going to the surface on the air bubble!"

And then the AC system picked up the screams of the men trapped in the hull of the submarine as it settled on a ridge six hundred feet below the surface.

"SO shut down the AC system," Boxer ordered.

"Aye, aye, skipper," the SO answered.

"Secure from GQ," Boxer announced over the MC. "Secure from GQ." Drained he leaned back into his chair.

"Skipper," Harris said, coming up the bridge, "we better move the hell out of here . . . We're in Russian waters."

Boxer nodded. "Helmsman come about to one eight zero degrees," he said; the looking at Harris he added, "I don't think I've ever felt so tired, and something like sad. . . ."

13

Norfolk basked under a pale, early spring sun that held little warmth or promise. Brightly twinkling crystals of snow fell from a seemingly cloudless sky, a phenomenon that awakened memories of Jack Boxer's childhood. When the *Tecumseh* docked, Jack spent a long fifteen minutes on the wing of the bridge watching the spectacle of nature before he joined Tom Redfern and signed off the ship.

"*Tecumseh* can handle the minor repairs needed to the *Shark*," Jack told his friend. "Once your boys are off on leave, they'll put to sea and go to it."

"What are your plans?"

"I'm not sure, Tom. First thing, I'm going to call Gwen. After that . . ." He shrugged. "I have no idea."

"If you're thinking of Tracy, she'll probably be at her newspaper office."

Redfern grinned mischievously. "That's still one relationship that's hard to figure. It reminds me of the story of the wolf lying down with the lamb. Though I'm damned if I can figure out which of you is the wolf and which the lamb."

"There's a traditional Navy term that applies to you right now . . . *dork*."

Redfern rapped Jack lightly on one shoulder. "I know the word. If you're stuck for something to do, I'll be with Sue Ann and the kids. You're always welcome there."

"Thanks, Tom."

Boxer found a chargephone and inserted his Visa card. When the dial tone came, he punched out Gwen's apartment. A strange voice answered.

"Miz Holcomb, she ain't here right now. This is Bertha, de maid."

"Uh, Bertha, this is Miss Holcomb's former husband, Captain Boxer. Tell her that my ship just made port in Norfolk. I'd like to come up and see John and her some time this weekend."

"Yassah, Cap'n Boxer. I'll leave her a note. You might try her at the television studio, sir. She doin' a week's guest shot on that soap opera, *Another Universe*."

"Thank you, Bertha. That's, ah, CBC?"

"Yassah. That the one."

Jack hung up and called the network headquarters. After a five minute switching marathon, Gwen came on the line.

"I hope this is important, Jack. I have less than ten minutes before the taping begins," she started without preamble or greeting.

Jack's scowl could not be seen, but his tightened voice carried clearly from Virginia to Manhattan. "I wanted you to know the *Tecumseh* is back in port. I am healthy and alive, with no pieces missing. How's John?"

"He's . . . all right."

"How do you mean that?"

"He . . . we have had some words lately."

"About me?"

"Yes, if you must. About you. About how you disgraced your career and all and why you now command this super tanker and go about as though the Navy never existed."

"I'm supposed to wear black crepe and go around with a long face? Life goes on, Gwen. Look, we've been over this before. All this talk is wasting the ten minutes you limited us to. I . . . I want to see you and John this weekend, if that's possible."

"We finish taping the last segment on Saturday. It airs Monday afternoon. I, ah, had a sort of . . ."

"I'll make it easy," Jack interrupted, rising anger blurring his words. "Someone in the cast or the production staff has caught your eye as a potential step-father for John and you're spinning your web. Right?"

Why the hell did he have to keep on loving her so? The question echoed in Jack's mind, adding another dagger of pain.

"That's a rather cruel manner of putting it, Jack."

251

"It's the *female* Black Widow who kills her mate. Only you take a longer time at it."

"That's entirely uncalled for," Gwen snapped. "If you are so anxious to see your son, I'd suggest you show a bit more consideration for his mother."

"Forget it! I'll call you later."

"When?"

"When I feel like it." Jack slammed the handset into its cradle.

He took several deep breaths and reinserted his credit card. He fumbled the dialing twice before a perky female voice greeted him over the crackling line to Washington.

"Washington Globe, good morning."

"Miss Tracy Kimble, please."

"I'll ring her desk."

"Ms. Kimble, may I help you?"

"Tracy, it's Jack," Boxer said in a rush. "I jus got in and I very much want to see you. What are you doing tonight."

"Oh, Jack! I . . . I want to see you, too. I have nothing else planned," Tracy told him smoothly, thinking of the hard-won interview she would have to cancel with Senator Ruksa of the Armed Services Committee. "Where can we meet?"

"I can probably get a room at the Mayflower. Meet you in the lounge at six?"

"Fine."

Feeling somewhat better, Boxer went on to the offices of the Thomas Williams Shipping Company. He had expected an immediate summons to Williams' office, and puzzled over why it had not been waiting. In the small, though comfortable cubicle assigned to him, he relaxed and sat in a low-backed leather swivel chair behind a couple of yards of rosewood desk. Dark blue drapes bordered a large window, which framed the bustling harbor of Norfolk and the wide span of bridge that connected the city with Kiptopeke on Maryland's Eastern Shore. The strident buzz of the intercom interrupted his quiet contemplations.

"Message for you, Captain Boxer," a secretary informed him.

"Bring it in, will you?"

The envelope, a standard, over-large manila affair, yielded up a telex page filled with lines of five-letter code groups. From his safe, Boxer took a small crypto device and quickly broke down the letters into meaningful text.

"Effective immediately upon arrival. Stark, John Raymond, Captain USN, to report to Admiral Paul Kaiser, Chief of Naval Intelligence, Room 5035 S.W., the Pentagon."

Crisp and to the point. Jack ran the text and translation sheet through the shredder and made another phone call to Tracy, cancelling their rendezvous until further notice. He pleaded complicated repairs on the *Tecumseh* that required his presence. Next he had his secretary book him on the next Piedmont Airlines commuter flight to National Airport.

"The admiral is expecting you, Captain, go right on in," an attractive young female yeoman announced as Jack entered the office.

Beyond the reception area, an aide escorted Jack to the Admiral's door. Although big himself, Jack felt diminished beside this strapping, youthful lieutenant commander who had the appearance of a defensive tackle on a professional team. Inside, he saw that Tom Redfern had preceded him, along with Admiral Stark and a man in his early thirties whom Jack did not know.

"Come in, Captain. You know everyone here," Admiral Kaiser greeted. "Except for Marc, that is. Captain Jack Boxer, this is Marc Pottel from the Agency. Take a seat, Jack. We'll get coffee in and then we can begin."

Although not one to make snap decisions, Jack liked Marc Pottel on sight. He had rugged good looks that reminded Jack of the president who had been in office when he received his first submarine command. Pottel had short-cropped sandy hair and green eyes, a clear, healthy complexion and seemed every bit in control of himself.

"You're here to join the team?" Jack asked to make small talk.

Pottel smiled deprecatingly and made a small gesture with a blunt-fingered hand, then smoothed the knife-crease in his suit trousers. "I'm here to give the briefing and await you gentlemen for a decision."

"Oh?"

"Later, Jack," the Chief of Naval Intelligence prompted.

A white-coated steward rolled in an antique wooden coffee cart, complete with silver service and bone-thin china cups. He poured and departed.

"Now, then, Jack," Admiral Kaiser started. "We have been presented with a unique situation. One that would make an ideal first trial mission for *Shark*. Tell me first about the shakedown cruise."

Boxer took a deep breath and arranged his thoughts. "I've sent a report through to Admiral Stark's office, sir. Everything is there . . . including the sinking of the Soviet sub. Most of the tests went off routinely enough, we encountered the expected difficulties with electronic components, although we did develop a fire in the engine room that caused us to surface and make repairs at a small island off Puerto Rico. We, ah, were spotted there by a civilian seaplane that flew over the cove where the damage was being corrected. Also, the *Mary-Ann* was present in a small harbor on the opposite side of the island." Jack broke off his report and turned to Marc Pottel.

"I'm getting a little sick of continually running into *Senor* Sanchez. It seems a bit too convenient for him to be anchored in the same place at such a critical and arbitrary time as when we surfaced. The aircraft I mentioned had been alongside the *Mary-Ann,* of that I am certain. But what I would like to know was why Sanchez picked that particular location."

"Probably delivering a load of cocaine to the pilot of that plane," Marc Pottel surmised. "Although we have no proof of Sanchez's involvement in the drug traffic, and no way of checking that out. If that is the case, you can be sure that the presence of the *Shark* was a great deal more disturbing to him than his being there could be to you.

"I believe when you reported the incident to Mr. Williams, he made comment along the same line, right? It is unfortunate that anyone saw *Shark* before we were ready to have it known, but such things happen. I will see what can be done on closer observation of *Senor* Sanchez. With the influential friends he has on Capitol Hill, we will have to virtually catch him up to his elbows in white powder. Anything else?"

"Not really. The repairs were effected quickly and we continued without incident. On the forty-fifth day we went under the ice. Sonar made contact with an unknown sub and we began a game of cat and mouse. It turned serious when the stranger, we're now certain it was a Soviet submarine of unknown type, turned nasty. As a result, I ordered it destroyed to preserve security and protect the *Shark* and its crew."

"There'll be a hearing, of course," Admiral Stark inserted. "Somewhat more speedy than after *Sting Ray,* Jack. That can all be dealt with later."

"Yes," Admiral Kaiser agreed. "I think it's time Marc began the briefing."

Marc Pottel rose and went to a wall where he drew down a chart of the South Pacific. With a black rubber-tipped pointer he indicated a small chain of islands, strung along a crescent-shaped ridge of coral atoll. "The Soviets have succeeded in establishing an underwater base off the Nekor Islands. It is located on one of the small volcanic outcroppings associated with the Nekor Archipelago. Satellite photos and later overflights by U-Fours confirmed this.

"Only last week, this bit of information hotted up, as we say in the Company. A workman who defected provided rather startling information as to the composition of this site and its potential danger to the Free World.

"The base is at a stage where it will soon be operational."

"How soon is that?" Jack inquired.

"Give or take a week; two months from now. That means that within the near future, the base will be armed with long-range multiple warhead nuclear missiles. What with those in Central Europe, Siberia, Nicaragua and Cuba, it effectively rings North and South America with a circle of death." Marc paused and Jack raised a quizzical eyebrow. "Oh, the Cuban missiles? They never really took them out back in Sixty-three, you know, and have added more since. The current situation is different, though. Nikor is in international waters, claimed by no one. If the Russians establish a precedent there, they can seize any number of open spots and add still more bases. This cannot be tolerated."

"The final print-out is this, Jack," Admiral Kaiser took up the

255

briefing. "This base must be taken out, made entirely nonoperational. The Soviets know that we know about it. With their influence in the United Nations, any overt act to stop them would result in world-wide condemnation of the United States. Hell, every Third World, two-bit, cannibal country in the UN would be screaming for our guts for garters, with Uncle Anatole solidly behind them. Worse, the think-tank boys have come up with a scenario that shows the Russians feeling strong enough in world opinion and militarily, to start World War Three over it, with considerable justification."

A short, icy silence descended on the men in the room.

"It's the thinking of our people at Langley that since the island is volcanic, Mother Nature might be induced to take the base out. Of course she'd need some assistance in the form of a small nuclear bomb." Pottel nodded toward Jack. "That's where you and the *Shark* come into the picture."

Boxer swallowed with slight difficulty. "And you say that this would make an ideal *trial* mission for the Strike Force and *Shark?*"

Redfern beamed and spoke for the first time. "Why not, Jack? My boys are ready. Hot to go, in fact. Though, naturally, they have no idea a mission, particularly one of this nature, is in the offing."

"Christ!" Boxer looked from one man to the next, shook his head and raised both hands, palms outward in a gesture of warding off the inevitable. "We don't have all the bugs out yet. A two month shakedown cruise, interrupted by the battle under the ice cap, is hardly time enough. I have two requests for transfer to shore duty connected to the project and half a dozen crewmen who could benefit from a chat with a shrink. Don't get me wrong," Jack hastened to say. "They're all tough, professional and dedicated. It's only that . . . well, none of you gentlemen are submariners.

"With the sophisticated equipment aboard *Shark,* we heard that Ruskie sub break up. *Heard the screams of the dying crewmen.* 'There but for the grace of God go I,' is not a cliche in situations like that. My men felt those deaths as vividly as though it had been them. And, gentlemen . . . *it could have been,* had the other sub's commander enjoyed the fortunate position I possessed with *Shark*. I strongly suspect, and it's in my report, Admiral," Jack nodded toward Stark, "that I went up against the best the Russians had. The skipper of that boat could easily have been Igor Alexandriavich Borodine. He was too damned good to be a novice and it was only a week or so before I took the *Shark* out that French television indicated Borodine was going to engage in certain experiments under the arctic ice. Like the Sanchez incident, I'm a bit leary of coincidences of that sort."

"What do you suggest, then?" Marc Pottel asked.

"I strongly recommend that the *Shark* not be considered for an operation of this nature at this particular time."

Admiral Kaiser rose from behind his desk, his face screwed into a dark visage of thunderous decision. "I'm afraid this isn't a question of volunteering for a mission, Captain. Your orders have already been cut. It is my duty to inform you that as of this moment, you are ordered to make *Shark* ready for sea, familiarize yourself with the conditions and terrain around this Soviet base and proceed to the South Pacific to deliver the necessary nuclear device to terminate this installation. Mister Pottel here will be aboard the *Shark* and function as part of the landing party that places the bomb. He will have absolute control over its detonation."

He had to hand it to Jack, Redfern thought as he watched Boxer mentally change gears and accept this unalterable course, he was all pro. The other three in the office seemed unaware of the turmoil below the calm surface of Boxer's smooth face.

"Is the island well guarded?"

"We have to assume so," Pottel told him. "We can expect the presence of hunter-killer subs, destroyers and land-based ASW missiles. There will be nothing in the way of aircraft, because the island doesn't have sufficient land mass above the surface to support a runway capable of landing anything bigger than a single-engine, gasoline powered aircraft."

"What about troops?" Tom Redfern inquired.

"We have been informed by the defector that there are some five hundred crack Soviet troops, veterans of Afghanistan and more recent engagements, on the island as a security force. The construction people can all be assumed to be members of the Reserve," Pottel enlarged. "Armament consists of the new AK-SK

Five-fifty-six millimeter assault rifles, as primary arms. You can expect to encounter PDM anti-landing mines, at least ten gun sections with the AGS-17 Plamya, thirty millimeter automatic grenade launchers — though those are more a hazard to the troops who operate them than their targets, due to imperfect bore-safing. Also the usual infantry RKG-Three-M and RGD-Five hand grenades. About the heaviest artillery you can expect will be BRDM-Ones with the AT-Two Swatter missiles, the old stand-by RPG-Seven-V rocket launcher and three batteries of the new M-Ninety one-twenty millimeter mortars, that replaced the Nineteen Forty-three model."

"Is that *all?*" Redfern gasped.

"At the present, yes. When the missiles are in place, there will be some form of anti-aircraft and counter-missile protection. For the present, they have two ancient ZSU-Twenty-three-four self-propelled anti-aircraft gun units. They fire a quad system of ZU-Twenty-three millimeter guns. They can tear ass among infantry, so the landing force will have to keep low, move fast and get out with a minimum of engagement of the enemy."

"You make it sound so easy."

"Doubts, Major?" Admiral Stark asked icily.

"No, sir. Only trying for a lighter note. We can handle it all right."

"You will have two weeks to prepare *Shark* for this mission," Admiral Stark told Boxer.

"We'll make it, sir."

14

Tracy Kimble reached Jack at the Williams Company offices midmorning the next day. "Busy?" she inquired after their initial greetings.

"Me, busy? I'm up to my crotch in crocodiles and the lady wants to know if I am busy. But I can get free by evening. I'll fly up and we can take in dinner and the show at Kennedy Center."

"Don't let 'em bite, dear," Tracy returned throatily. "I'd miss something important that way. You won't have to go anywhere, though. I'm here in Norfolk. How about lunch?"

"And . . . ?"

"We don't have time for fucking in the middle of the day."

"Why not? I've always thought of it as romantic, sort of like out of a French movie."

"French postcard, more like it. It's . . . it's *decadent*."

"Then God knows that's for us," Jack quipped back.

"Be serious. Let's have lunch and then you can take me anywhere you want tonight and screw me crosseyed."

"I'm for that . . . all of that."

"Eleven-thirty, then? At the Oyster Shell? We can have a basket of Chesapeakes on the half-shell and their thick oyster chowder. That'll get your pecker up."

"I thought you were opposed to afternoon assignations?"

"You've made me see the light, Boxer. With you, all I want to do is fuck, fuck, fuck. I'll probably come sitting there at your side and slurping oysters. Hurry and meet me. My God, I'm getting all wet and sticky right now."

"Bye," Boxer said as he returned the handset to its place.

He beat Tracy to the Oyster Shell by three minutes. Already

seated, with a chilled glass of California chablis at his place, he gave her a warm smile of greeting as she slid into the booth and put aside her bulky purse.

"By God, they treat you well at that shipping company. You look good enough to eat."

"That comes later," Jack teased. He sensed something . . . intense about Tracy. She looked at him in that certain way, as though peering into his very soul, and her expression seemed rigid enough to have been frozen in place. She wet her vibrantly red lips and spoke in a husky hush.

"You have a place picked out?"

"I thought you would like to get it crouched on the top of my desk. Or in my swivel chair, while we spin around and around. Then with both feet in filing cabinet drawers."

Tracy began to laugh, deep gulps of glee that relaxed her previous rigidity. "Oh, my, my," she spluttered. "And here I thought an afternoon tete-a-tete was decadent. Will your secretary be there to record the strokes?"

"No. And you'll have to be quiet. She's very jealous and doesn't want to know if I'm screwing other women in the place where she's had so much fun and insured her job at the same time."

"Chauvinist pig! I should hate you for that. Of course it isn't true . . . is it?"

"Do I look like the office lothario type?"

"You look like a good fuck, darling, anywhere, anytime, any way."

"Thank you. I've ordered a dozen oysters on the half-shell."

"And some Marsala to go with them, I hope?"

The oysters arrived, and after them the heady oyster chowder for which the establishment was justifiably famous. Jack and Tracy shared a lobster salad and a crisp, icy cold '87 Chardonnay. Outside, feeling replete though the meal had been relatively light, Jack summoned a cab. It let them off outside the ancient, field-stone facade of the tidy rooming house where Boxer had taken quarters in keeping with his new role as captain of the *Tecumseh*.

Once behind the closed door of the spacious, tastefully decorated apartment, Jack took Tracy in his arms and kissed her with mounting desire. She responded in kind and when the embrace ended, they walked, hand-in-hand through the distinctly masculine quarters before stopping in the bedroom.

"I like your taste in decor," Tracy complimented him sincerely.

"Don't you think the brass bedstead was a, ah, bit too much?"

"Not at all. It fits you. All those years in the brassbound world of the Navy . . ."

"Please," Jack interrupted. "I don't want to be reminded of that."

Tracy made a small moue with her full lips. "Don't tell me you've gone liberal, Jack. Surely you can't have had that much change of heart that you now regret your dedicated service to extending American imperialism around the world by force of arms."

"I didn't think we came here to discuss politics," Jack suggested.

"No, we came to fuck." Tracy wriggled her shoulders and slid out of the mannishly-cut coat of her split-skirt suit. She hung it neatly over a chair back and smoothly pulled the zipper that released the lower portion.

As usual, Jack observed, she wore tall, sheer stockings and no underclothes. After frequent exposure to this practice, he considered, it tended to both excite and repel.

"Do the rest, darling," Tracy murmured and Jack responded with alacrity.

Only when she stood bronzed and bare before him did he remove his dark blue blazer with the Williams Shipping logo on the pocket, loosen his tie and draw his shirt from inside his trousers. While he manipulated the buttons, he found Tracy's fingers at his belt buckle. His shaft began to stir with increased vigor and pressed tightly against the cloth until she freed him. Tracy sank to her knees.

"Mummm. What a gorgeous cock you've got," she whispered throatily as her thin, firm fingers traced the network of bulging veins and began to tease the loose flesh sheath that bound it.

Jack shuddered with delight when her tongue flicked out to caress the sensitive tip. She inscribed spirals that worked ever lower onto the throbbing bulk of him, until she reached the thick base. Swiftly she rose to her feet.

"That was only a sample. We need something different." She

looked around the room and spotted a large, upholstered chair. "That isn't exactly a swivel chair, but . . . let's give it a try."

Tracy took his hand and led him. She turned Jack so that his back was to the aged Morris chair and pushed on his shoulders. He settled into it and reclined slightly so that his head rested half way down the backrest. Then Tracy straddled him and lowered herself until her moist, glistening mound made feather-light contact with his rigid manhood.

"Oh, I'm gonna like this," Tracy cooed. "Hang on, Buster, this is going to be the ride of your life."

With a hand made strong from years of typing, Tracy grasped his tingling organ and plunged it between the leafy fronds of her flowing canal. Once lubricated, she drove it with determined energy against the protruding button of her clit. Little shivers of ecstasy radiated through Tracy's body and her torrid humor transmitted itself to Jack. Then she adjusted her position so that when he penetrated her, the broad top of his slightly curved penis would rub firmly against the "rabbit's nose" bean buried in the upper arch of her passage in a manner she knew would bring delirious pleasure to her hungry body.

Of a sudden, Jack's desire took charge and he drove himself deeply into her pulsating membranes, spasmodic clenchings heightening his enjoyment with each inch that sped toward his goal.

"Oh . . . yes . . . that's . . . it! Tracy wailed. "Higher, deeper, harder!" she demanded in a voice turned strident by lust.

By conscious, careful control, Jack outlasted her and his flesh hummed with delight as she rose to a howling pitch and climaxed shudderingly, only to be driven upward again toward a mutual achievement like none either of them had experienced before.

When Jack's life-force at last burst forth, they jerked and pitched through to completion, then lay limp in the chair for a wondrous five minutes. Then Jack helped her to rise and led her to the bed.

"More?" Tracy asked in a little-girl voice. "I can't wait. I see what you mean. This daylight stuff is a real turn-on. Hurry, Jack."

Their second joining lasted ever so much longer, with gentle thrusts and counter-thrusts that inscribed indelible traces on their memory tracks. When the rosy veil rose to obscure reality for the celebration of the *petit mort,* their hearts beat a rhythm of mutual commitment and their lips fluttered with unspoken words of praise. Gradually the tide subsided and they parted, to lie at ease in the big brass bed.

"Jack," Tracy began lazily after Boxer had lighted her cigarette. "Do, ah, do you have any idea what Tom is doing? Sue Ann hasn't the slightest idea and it troubles her."

"Why do you think I should know anything about it?" Caution imperceptibly tightened the muscles of Jack's abdomen.

"Well, it seems he takes off on his 'job' at the same time you go somewhere on that big tanker."

"Coincidence."

"Sue Ann doesn't think so . . . and neither do I."

"What are you getting at?"

"Working for Williams Shipping isn't exactly a hush-hush matter, is it? I mean, darling, *you* got a big splash about being hired to handle their brand new tanker. So . . . Tom isn't seeing another woman, is he?"

"I hardly think so."

"You've both resigned your commissions, right? I've heard of that sort of thing before. Could it be that . . . that Tom is on some super-secret government assignment that he can't even tell his wife about?"

Jack felt a clutch at his heart and the warning bells went off in his head. He mustered his best acting ability and snorted derisively. "And the next logical thing is to say that I am, too, right? Horse pucky! I know Tom Redfern only slightly. I've been to his house. No big deal about that. As for what he is doing, I have no more idea than he probably has about my job."

Tracy affected a pout. "Jack . . . this is for a friend. Strictly off the record. Sue Ann is worried sick and I don't blame her. If you know anything . . . if you could help put this thing together, she'd be eternally grateful and so would I."

"I think you have your roles confused, lady." Jack shook his head, feigning sadness. "The hotshot investigative reporter, looking for a story, no matter who she tramples in the process, doesn't fit with the concerned sister seeking help and reassurance for poor Sue Ann. I don't know what Tom is doing, haven't seen him in a while. Whatever it is, I am sure he would confide in his wife if he could. That doesn't mean it's something military. It could be he is into something he doesn't feel totally confident in and doesn't want to get her hopes up before it becomes a real thing."

"Or he could be in training to enter the CIA."

"Don't look for spooks where there are none, Tracy."

"You're getting angry."

"I don't like being pumped. Not about me or about anyone I know."

"Goddamnit, you *are* angry. Here I screwed you until you're limp as a noodle and all you can do is be defensive."

"Pillow talk, humm?"

"Don't be nasty." Tracy rose and darted a hand for her clothing.

"Leaving mad?"

"You bastard!"

"Come on, Tracy, what is all of this about? Why the twenty questions after our rather delightful afternoon tumble?"

"Oh, shut up! Let . . . let me alone."

"You ask questions rather well. But I gather you're not so keen on answering them. Level with me, Tracy."

"You're a shit. Did you know that?"

"I've heard worse. Now come back to bed and let's make love again. You don't want to go away in a fury."

"I'll . . . go . . . when . . . and . . . how I want to," she grunted as she struggled into her clothes.

Jack leaned back, arms behind his head and watched her magnificent body disappear into the suit. They didn't speak again and Tracy gave only a perfunctory, glaring glance back at him as she went out of the room.

"Awh, shit!" Boxer declared to the slamming front door.

Eight men sat around an oval table in a special soundproofed room at Williams Shipping company. Tom Redfern, with Lt. Alvaro De Vargas to his left, followed by Wild Bill White, David Taylor, "Yellin' " Yellan and Peter Hellwig, looked attentively at a large section of corkboard where Jack Boxer stood, a pointer in one hand and a dozen glossy prints of a black, rock-strewn plain of sand. Nearly every shot showed a shoreline in a slightly different position, so that its identity as an island was not in doubt. Slouched slightly in one near corner, as though holding up the wall, stood Marc Pottel.

"While all of the craftsmen swarm over the *Shark*," Jack began, "we have a lot of work to do also. This is going to be Tom's show, and Marc's, so they should be up here. Let me go over the terrain features and details of the island first, then they can get into the operation." Jack tapped the first photo, at the top of a diamond shaped layout.

"This is the north end of the island. As you can see, there are a lot of rocks, coral reefs, natural obstacles that prevent a landing. Obviously the Ruskies have less in the nature of defenses here. It is currently our second choice for a landing spot. Here, to the right of it, is the next thirty degree slice of the pie. You'll notice the edges sligthly overlap. Wide angle lenses on the overflight plane's cameras.

"Now, there is a small cove here, and you can also see why it is out as a landing site. Two Soviet Z-Class frigates anchored there. This is also where the supplies and equipment are off-loaded. Lots of activity and a concentration of barracks and shops. I'm sure Tom will say to avoid this part of the island like a plague spot. The next portion contains one of the batteries of one-twenty millimeter mortars. The beach is extensive and the rise gradual. We could land and neutralize the gun crews and gain a double advantage, but they are suspected of being backed up by at least two companies of infantry."

"Question, Captain."

"Yes, Norm?"

Yellan rose on his slightly bowed legs. "Any evidence there of anti-landing mines?"

"Glad you asked that. Yes. The defector stated that there are at least three rows of twenty each laid out in criss-cross patterns to cover every approach to this beach."

"We could still do it with scuba."

Jack smiled. "It would take every member of all four teams to be sure and that puts too much in one basket. Ideally, we want to land in two sheltered places and move overland to the location of the hard-stand silos." Jack's pointer touched the three central photos. "They are along the spine of the island for maximum stability and to reduce the danger of collapse. Once our device is in place, that is negated. Correct me if I'm wrong, Tom. Moving a large force overland will attract too much attention. Two teams only will land, with a third in reserve and the fourth still aboard *Shark*. Now, let's look at the next segment of the island."

Ten minutes later, Jack finished and Tom rose. Marc came to stand beside him. Briefly, Tom outlined the operational mission of the two landing teams, indicated the preferred routes they would take to the target area and assigned all four team leaders the task of writing their own operations order and drawing a scenario of how they would conduct the covert assault.

"Based on the feasibility of your plans and ops orders, we will pick the teams to go in. From that time on, intensive training will begin on an isolated sand spit off the Carolina coast. It's not a perfect replica of the target, but it has several things to recommend it. There's no water, no vegetation and no suitable landing places. Therefore, no one visits the place. It is also off the regular shipping lanes and pleasure craft cruising areas. We will meet again two days from now and make the selection of teams. Any questions?"

"What's Mr. Pottel here going to be doing?" David Taylor asked, his gangly, lantern-jawed figure rising to address the briefers.

"He'll go along with the primary assault team to babysit the bomb. It will be his responsibility all the way. Only he can detonate it."

"Grim," Dave observed before sitting down.

"More?" Tom inquired of his audience.

Peter Hellwig rose, one strong hand to his firm jawline. "Any chance of some sort of air cover on this?"

"Not likely. This is a *covert* operation, remember? We get in and out with no chance of any proof our government was involved. Which reminds me, any wounded unable to walk or swim out have to be left behind. In a condition, naturally, where they cannot reveal any information to the enemy. Be sure you include this essential in your plans. We go in wearing our black jumpsuits. They're sterile, made in Taiwan and sold all over the world.

Also World War Two *Falshimjaeger* equipment harness. Every attempt must be made to recover any dropped weapons, though the M-Twenty-two and the civilian model, hand-crafted Sidewinders we carry are also available anywhere."

Peter's blond hair shone like strands of plastic under the harsh artificial lighting. His tense face revealed his feelings. No air support, or other involvement by his beloved Air Force went against the grain. Worse, the concept of leaving a buddy behind, of terminating him if necessary troubled him. Still, he made the best of it and asked another question.

"In our scenario, may we employ suppressed weapons?"

"Certainly. The M-Twenty-twos will be virtually worthless for suppressors, except for flash concealment. But the M-Eighty-eight Sidewinders are ideally suited. I recommend you double the number for each section in your fire team. Anyone else?"

No one made comment and the briefing was dismissed. Tom hung behind and, at a signal from Boxer, so did Marc Pottel.

"Marc," Boxer began without preamble. "I hate to mix my personal life with business, but I think this is important."

"What is it, Jack?"

"Yesterday, I got a rather thorough grilling on the 'coincidence' that Tom and I are always away from home at the same time. The person doing it could present a problem."

"Who is it?"

"Tracy Kimble. No matter what outrageous things they often write, reporters aren't dummies. She can add the same as anyone else, better even. We could have a huge compromise in security before we even get *Shark* and the Strike Force operational."

"Stop seeing her."

"It isn't that simple. She's a sorority sister of Sue Ann Redfern. The two girls are getting their heads together and asking the wrong sort of questions. If I drop Tracy and Sue Ann gets orders from Tom to do the same, it will only whet Tracy's interest. Then we can be in for a lot of deep shit."

"I appreciate that. Let me take it up with Williams and the people at Langley. It may be that we have to put her under wraps for a while."

"For the duration of *Shark*'s operations? For years, until the Soviets find out about it and it's not a secret any more?"

Pottel interrupted before Jack could say more. "Don't give me that song and dance about a 'free society,' and that 'laws to protect the citizens' crap. This is a highly secure situation, one so touchy that it could easily be declared illegal. Just the sort of thing these snoop reporters like to get their teeth into. Remember the mess in the Seventies? One asshole blowing his mouth in the daily press and we get two dozen deep cover agents compromised and at least three of them terminated for it by the KGB.

"Oh, I know all about the so-called free press and its supposedly sacred right to tell all no matter who is harmed. But even a priest is constrained by Church law from revealing what he hears in the confessional. Unless and until there are some curbs on these leftist sympathizing yellow journalists, we have no choice than to find some way of silencing those who threaten the security of this country."

"You figure to terminate Tracy with extreme prejudice?" Boxer snarled.

"Nothing so drastic, Jack. Just a friendly little talk. Tell her nothing, but let her think she's found out something highly important and so critical that we can appeal to her patriotism to not reveal it until we say she can. Put her on the inside, so to speak."

Jack snorted. "That won't work, my friend. The only patriotism Tracy feels is to her future as a big-time reporter. She'd sell her own mother for a headline."

"Then what are you screwing her for?" the CIA man snapped.

Jack thought a moment. In honesty he could not find any more motivation than before. They were good in bed. She used him and he used her.

"She's a good lay."

"Cold, Jack," Tom injected. "A real cold shot."

"But true."

"I'll take it up with Langley. Meanwhile, Jack, avoid her like she invented rabies."

15

"Listen up, people," Wild Bill White growled over the cries of gulls and the incessant roar of the salt-tang filled wind that blew across the sand of Ludlow Sprit. "This is the civilian model of the M-Eighty-eight Sidewinder submarine gun. It is in caliber Forty-five, ACP, convertible to Nine millimeter. It has a cyclic rate of fire of twelve hundred rounds a minute, with a three-stage progressive trigger that provides for single shot, three round burst a   n   d full auto. For the purpose of this exercise, you people will use Mode One or Mode Two only. Do not . . . I repeat, *do not* use full auto."

"What if we're up to our ass in Ruskie *Soldaty?*"

White gave his best gunnery sergeant scowl. "You do what you have to, Johnson. This is a fucking problem, an exercise, right? We are going through the approach, secure area, plant device and exfiltration step-by-step. It will be a live-fire exercise, so I am telling you how it will be done by the numbers. In combat, it's CYA and forget everything else. On the actual target island, your section leader or the circumstances will tell you when to go to full-auto. Am I understood?"

"Yes, Sergeant!" the twenty-three men chorused in a shout.

"Knock off that Sergeant shit. You know what the brass wants."

"Yes . . . Bill!"

Wild Bill winced but bore it. This goddamned new Strike Force took a bit of getting used to. "All right, you people. Assume the position as though you've just come in off your little rubber boats. Let's hit the objective and give it hell. Mr. Pottel,

269

you follow behind the first assault group. Ready, men?"

White blew his whistle and the seasoned combat troops moved out.

"We're ready," Alvaro De Vargas reported to Tom Redfern with considerable satisfaction three days later.

"No casualties? Not even a splinter? The morning report and sick call look like a week in garrison. You've done a fine job, Al," Redfern complimented over the steady pulsing of *Shark*'s turbines.

Small, neat, white teeth flashed in De Vargas' dark face as his lips spread in a smile. Seated beside Redfern in the captain's cabin of the submarine, Boxer could not get over the first impression he had of the young Puerto Rican. De Vargas still looked like he should be wearing a silly little waiter's jacket and a paper hat behind the counter of a fast food restaurant rather than be executive officer of the Strike Force. He should be thinking about high school ball games and the senior prom, not logistics and training schedules for a hundred men committed to do murder and mayhem among those designated by higher authority as enemies of the United States. He might be twenty-seven and the biggest cocksman Boxer had ever encountered, but it took only the least bit of squinting to blur the image and shave ten years.

"We've got a week to go," Tom went on. "When we get back to the mainland, give the boys three days leave, then into isolation at Quantico. Final briefing, weapons check and suiting up will go down there."

"Gotcha, boss," Alvaro replied. "Me, I'm headed for the Big Apple. There's a hot Trot contest that I'm gonna enter. Make me some real bucks for a change."

"Be careful you don't hit your chin," Boxer added dryly.

"What's with you, Jack?"

"All that wriggling and gyrations, the knees up by your shoulders. You don't seriously consider that dancing, do you, Al?"

"Hell, yes, Cap'n. I've been at it since I was eight. First disco, then Trot-rock. Hot stuff. Moves you inside."

"It moves me to want to puke," Redfern commented. "All these so-called Trotters have done is steal the rhythms and twist

270

the words of my people's music and turned it into a three-ring circus for . . . awh, fuck it. You like, you do it. Me, I'm too conservative. Give me Rock an' Roll any time. We rendezvous with the *Tecumseh* in an hour. Put our guys into their cabins on board and everyone stays below decks until dark tonight. You know the drill."

"On top, Kemosabe."

Redfern scowled. "Get hosed, Spick."

Al left the captain's cabin aboard *Shark* and returned to the troop bay. All the way he hummed a haunting melody from a Fifteenth Century Spanish romantic ballad. He'd have to work it out on the twelve-string on the cruise to the Pacific, he considered.

When the security duty officer authorized departure from the *Tecumseh* that night, Boxer went directly to the telephone he had used before. He managed to reach Gwen at home.

"Any, ah, complications this weekend?" he asked in a hopeful tone akin to that of a love-struck teenager.

"No. I'm still mad at you for the way you handled it last time."

"Sorry I didn't congratulate you on scoring another boyfriend."

"Jack . . . please. Let's don't, shall we? John is bursting at the seams to see you. Truth to tell, so am I. When will you be up?"

"We just pulled in from Aruba," he told her smoothly, the "professional" lies coming easier with passing time. "I'll catch a commuter first thing tomorrow morning. Be there in time for a late lunch."

"My place or . . .?"

"I thought we'd take John to Rockefeller Center. One of the little ethnic places around there."

"You want Italian? Jewish? Maybe corned beef and cabbage at Paddy Ryans?"

"Let John decide."

"Oh, foo. He'd opt for the Golden Arches, you know that."

"What's wrong with a hamburger?"

"If I want a hamburg, I sure as hell want it to be big, juicy and have something exotic on it. *Burger and Brew?*"

"If John's set on round sandwiches on a bun, yeah."

"God! We're talking like old married folks, Jack."

"Unh-unh. Like old, happily married folks. See you about twelve-thirty."

"We'll be here."

"The, ah, problems John was having before?"

"Dissolved away through the offices of a bloody nose."

"My kid getting clobbered at school?"

"No, the other boy's nose. John took a stand at last and really tore into this one kid. Offered to give a lickin' to any of the others who didn't think his Dad was a swell guy. Or words to that effect. The headmaster at his school nearly fainted over all that violence." From distant Manhattan, Gwen's titter of laughter sounded almost unforgiveably proud.

"That twit. I said it was a mistake sending John there."

"But, Doctor Leonard recommended it so highly," Gwen protested.

"There's another closet queen for you, if you ask me. See you tomorrow."

"Good-bye, Jack. Twelve-thirty. There's a segment of a talk show on at that time, interviewing me. Seems my appearance on *Another Universe* created quite a stir. The part may be expanded into a regular and I'll get the role."

"Congratulations, love. Now, I have to go, there's a whole day of paperwork to finish tonight if I can get away tomorrow."

"Where will you stay?"

"I thought maybe . . . no. Forget that idea. I'll try to get into the Taft, the company has a suite there."

"Ugh! Forty-second street. Repulsive."

"I'll defend my morals to the last drop of blood."

Boxer hung up and went directly to his rooming house. The phone was ringing when he inserted the key in the door. He hurried in and snatched up the handset. Tracy's voice came from the other end.

"There you are. Sometimes I get the feeling I'm being avoided. Are you busy tonight?"

"No. But I'm played out. Just docked and got off the ship. Tons of paperwork to deal with."

"Save it for tomorrow."

"Can't. I'm going to New York."

272

"The ex, huh?" A sour note had crept into Tracy's voice. "Some guys are suckers for abuse. You sure you're not a masochist? Maybe we should introduce the leather hot-pants and whips?"

"Get off it, Tracy."

"Sorry." She actually sounded contrite. "When you get back?"

"Don't know."

"If Tom's home, too, maybe we could take a couple of days on the beach?"

Would she never stop? Boxer stifled his irritation and thought of the men hunched over a small tape recorder in the basement of the building next door. They'd get another black mark for the book on Tracy Kimble from this call.

"We'll see," he replied tightly.

They said their good-byes and Boxer held down the plunger for a long moment. Then he dialed Cynthia's home number.

After fourteen unanswered rings, he gave up. Screw it all. That didn't detract from the fact he was hungry. He might as well go out to eat. Boxer took a quick shower, changed clothes and headed for the door.

In a quiet steakhouse overlooking the yacht harbor, Boxer accepted a crystal goblet half-filled with Glenlivet on the rocks and let the tension seep out of him. Looking out through the large plate-glass windows, he thought he recognized the bridge structure and fish tower of one large boat. No, he decided, it couldn't be. His clam cocktail arrived and he leisurely sipped the rest of his scotch before he began on it.

He had worked part way through an extra-large cut of very rare prime rib when a group of people appeared down the brightly illuminated pier, alighting from the gangway to the familiar-looking boat. The fork froze half-way to Boxer's lips.

Impossible. Yet, no one else had a body like that. It had to be Tracy. Had she said she was in Norfolk? No, they had only quarreled and she had hung up.

And beside her, *Senor* Julio Sanchez.

Boxer felt the fine hairs on the back of his head rise at sight of the man who had so plagued him. The party continued toward the short stairway that led to the yacht basin entrance to the res-

273

taurant. Boxer felt like growling. Determinedly, he placed the forkful of succulent beef in his mouth and methodically chewed. He'd be damned if he let Sanchez or Tracy ruin his meal.

Seven people accompanied Sanchez and they took places around a large, circular table near a window. It left no doubt that Tracy's escort was the sinister Colombian. Again, Boxer felt his blood heat toward the boiling point. Cut and chew, he reminded himself and put a pleasant smile on his face. Almost at once, after drinks had been ordered, Tracy nodded toward his table and Sanchez glanced that way. He nodded and summoned a waiter.

"Mister Sanchez's compliments, sir. He asked me to inquire if you would care to join them," the white-coated attendant asked Boxer a minute later.

"No, thank you. Tell Mister Sanchez that I am already engaged in my dinner and would hate to impose."

The waiter duly delivered the message. A moment of animated discussion and he returned. Boxer stifled a groan.

"Mister Sanchez extends an invitation for you to join them later for a drink, then."

Jack bit back a sharp retort and decided to do just that. He took his time finishing and rose after emptying the last from a bottle of excellent Napa Valley Pinot Noir. Then he crossed the short expanse of carpeted floor to the crowded table where Sanchez and his guests sat.

"I don't want to impose," Jack repeated his initial message.

"Not at all. It seems the oil tanker business has a salutary effect on you, Captain. You look in much better health than the last time I saw you."

"And when was that, *Senor* Sanchez?" Jack inquired. "I don't seem to recall."

Sanchez chuckled sardonically. "Surely you do. Not long after your unfortunate hearing in front of the Naval Board."

"Oh? I was certain we had met since then." Hell, he wasn't a spook, Jack chided himself. He should quit trying to be cute.

"Not to my knowledge. Do you know my guests?"

Introductions went the rounds.

"Rough place to do office work," Tracy said pointedly.

"Everyone has to eat. You didn't say you were in Norfolk."

"I wasn't. Julio informed me of a party tonight aboard the

274

Mary Ann and asked me to come along. We flew down in his Lear."

The small, dapper Latino leered at Boxer. How large an organization did Sanchez have in this country? Boxer considered it and another vexing question. How much did Sanchez know about his relationship with Tracy? More queries insinuated themselves in Jack's brain. Like, why did Tracy consent to come along? She was no longer assigned to the society column. A nagging suspicion began to grow in Boxer's mind. Sanchez spoke again.

"Why don't you join the party later on, Captain? I'd like to show I have no hard feelings."

"I'm afraid I have't a lady."

"You could always get hold of that dreary female sailor in the Pentagon," Tracy said in a nasty tone.

"Your claws are showing, Tracy," Boxer told her. *"Senor* Sanchez, may I speak to you alone?"

"But certainly. Excuse me, *senores, senoras."* Sanchez elegantly dabbed at his lips with a white linen napkin and left his place.

Together they walked out into the damp promenade that girdled the restaurant three steps below the second floor level. Boxer directed the way and Sanchez followed, apparently indifferent for once who gave the orders. Out of sight of the table, Boxer stopped abruptly and turned Sanchez with pressure on one elbow.

"I feel you have a few things to explain," Boxer growled.

"To you? Oh, no, *Senor.* I need account for nothing."

"Perhaps you can tell me why it is that you so frequently show up where I am or have just left?"

Sanchez shrugged. "Coincidence. You're a former Navy man," he tacked to change the subject. "Perhaps you could help me on a small matter, Captain. What do you know of a rather out of the ordinary submarine? One considerably larger than anything else known?"

Boxer forced himself to remain calm and betray nothing by his outward appearance. "I'm afraid I couldn't help you there. I was thrown out of the Navy, you remember? Thanks mostly to your efforts. If I knew of such a thing, I don't think I would tell you

275

about it."

"Come now, Captain. No need for hostilities. I figured it this way. Here you are, commander of the largest tanker permitted to dock on the East Coast and with at least some reliable contacts remaining inside the Navy. Word of something this large would have to reach you. I'm only curious, you understand."

"Where was it you saw this over-big sub?"

Again Sanchez hunched his shoulders in a typical Latin gesture. "Who is to say? I don't recall exactly right now. It was some time ago, you understand. Idle curiosity. I have other sources to satisfy my interest."

"I'm sure you do. I'd still like to know why it is you seem to dog my steps like this?"

"Believe me it is not the case, though I can think of a Colombian saying. 'Flies flock to *mierda.*' Oh? I see you are not familiar with the word. It is — how you say it in English? — shit."

Boxer fought for control and won. "Let's get back to these sources of yours. How is it you are so close to so many people in our government? Is it that you keep your lines out? Little lines of white powder perchance?"

Sanchez bristled. "Are you implying that I, of all people, am in the drug trade?"

"Sanchez, you are a drug-smuggling son of a bitch. You know it. I know it. And it won't be long before the Feds know it and put your ass away where it fucking well deserves to be. Tell me, how much coke and hash did you have on the *Mary Ann* the night you rammed the *Sting Ray?* And how much did you pay off to whom to get the evidence rigged against me like you did?"

A strangled deep gasp from Sanchez's lips before he clamped his jaw tightly. His overly handsome, almost effeminate face went white with fury and he balled one small fist.

Before he could swing, Boxer stepped in eagerly, smiling broadly, cocked a hard right and unleashed it below the Colombian's heart. Instantly he let go a solid left jab that caught Sanchez an inch behind teh point of his jaw.

Sanchez's eyes rolled upward, he sighed softly and, with a faint whimper, sagged to the salt-damp planking of the promenade. A second later, Boxer heard a scuffle of footsteps behind him.

"Julio!" Tracy's voice called. "Where . . . oh, there you . . ." Her eyes widened at the sight of Sanchez's recumbent, unmoving form. "Boxer, you crazy bastard, what did you do now?"

16

Even the thick greatcoat and warm, furry karakul hat he wore could not protect Captain First Class Igor Borodine from the biting cold that howled through the streets of Moscow. A sudden Arctic storm front had swept across the land and clasped the capital city in icy fingers with knife-edged claws. For a moment, Borodine harbored a decidedly revisionist thought. In Washington at this time of year, the cherry blossoms would nearly be in bloom along along the banks of the Potomac. Deep worry creases furrowed his brow. This summons to see the high command could result in a formal inquiry and perhaps a court-martial. He had, after all, lost his command, every single man and an unbelievably expensive submarine. He climbed the steps filled with concern for his future.

His mitten-encased hand barely returned the salute of the guard who held open the outer door and he paused in the marble-floored lobby to knock snow from his shoulders and hat. Then he sneezed.

"Your health," a young lieutenant in the uniform of the naval service announced as he walked toward Igor. "You are Captain First Class Borodine."

"*Spacibo, Tovarish.* Yes, I am Borodine."

"Come with me, please. Comrade *Admiral Flota* Gorshkov is waiting for you."

"This accursed storm has made travel across town impossible."

"I know," the lieutenant answered him. "I left half an hour early and still got to my post an hour late. It is like that for everyone."

In the admiral's office, no formalities interfered. The youthful officer led Borodine directly to the fleet commander's door and knocked diffidently.

At the command, Borodine entered. "*Dobroe ytro, Tovarish*

Admiral," Borodine greeted.

"Good morning to you, Igor Alexandriavich," Admiral of the Fleet, Sergei Gorshkov boomed, showing his approval of Borodine by use of his patronymic. "You know the members of my staff? Of course you do. Take a seat. There, at the end of the table. We were only now bringing up the matter of your miraculous escape from death in the Arctic. Perhaps you could better enlighten us than these dry reports?"

Borodine removed his heavy overcoat and took the offered chair. "*Spacebo.*" He offered his thanks to cover a second in which he once more rearranged the narrative he had prepared for this particular moment. Even captains first class had rivals, men ambitious and eager to rise at the expense of their fellows. What he said, what these men believed this morning in this room would determine the future of his career, if not his life.

""It's more than luck, Comrade Admiral. In many ways, I hardly know how it happened at all. Your choice of the word, 'miraculous' was a good one." Igor paused a moment and managed to half-stifle another sneeze. "Let me first retrace the entire action."

For the next ten minutes, Borodine held the rapt attention of the knowledgeable officers gathered around the staff table as he recounted the engagement with *Shark*. He freely admitted he had no positive identity for the other submarine, although he had his own speculations that it might be some new design of the Americans. He concluded with sincere praise for his opponent.

"Whoever commanded that vessel had iron control . . . remarkable tactical knowledge and . . . apparently a superior underwater weapons system to my own. That is not a deviant or revisionist opinion, comrades," he added in an aside. "I merely point out that the Americans have apparently developed a system, the properties of which we are as yet unaware. Suffice that no matter what countermeasures I employed, what electronic devices or decoy projectiles I utilized, it was all to no avail. At least . . . two torpedoes struck my boat.

"One with such force," Borodine went on, his mind mulling over each minute detail of the attack," and in exactly the right place that it blew the sail off the hull. Naturally it dropped a couple of fathoms immediately after it came free. I was at my duty station on the second deck of the sail."

"How then did you manage to escape?" *Vitse-Admiral* Vorshilov inquired testily. Although passed over several times for promotion, most of the staff deferred to the crusty old sailor's moods and peculiarities.

"That I can explain, Comrade Vice Admiral. The sail shifted . . . turned end over, so that the broken off lower section stood upright in the water. I had already put on my emergency escape gear and positioned myself at the edge of a hatchway. A great bubble of air was released, naturally, when the water poured into the sail. I rode that out . . . and it must have pushed me to the surface."

"Now you are under the ice, young man. What happened then?"

"The explosions . . . the tremendous turbulence had cracked the ice, Comrade Vice Admiral. I surfaced within waters fished by migratory esquimoux tribesmen. They launched an outboard motor skiff and hurried to where I floated, marked by orange smoke. They pulled me out and dried me as best they could. We traveled eastward until I contacted the first military outpost and had a message sent here to naval headquarters. The rest," he shrugged and emitted a third sneeze, "excuse me. The rest you know."

"You've taken cold, Igor?" Fleet Admiral Gorshkov asked kindly.

"It is close to pneumonia, Comrade Admiral."

"Could you provide more details about the engagement with the enemy boat," Admiral Novotney requested.

"*Da Tovarish Admiral.* At the time of the explosion, I had been engaging what sonar and other electronic instruments indicated was an American Trident-class submarine. Our sophisticated combat integration system electronics indicated that it was . . . a very different kind of Trident than the official identification book described. I am . . . positive it was larger."

"Oh? How so, Comrade Captain?" Novotney pressed.

"Longer . . . wider. And there was no indication of an external sail structure. In fact . . . no superstructure at all."

"How is that possible, Comrade Captain?" Vice-Admiral Vorshilov blurted. "Without a sail, or some form of conning tower, how did they control the boat?"

Borodine paused, one large, rough hand caressing his firm jaw. The thought had haunted him since the strained minutes of the engagement. He found it hard to put words to his thoughts.

"I . . . don't know, Comrade Vice-Admiral. How . . . how did they find me when all of our latest ECM equipment had been employed? How did they direct weapons at me when . . . when they couldn't see me?"

"This is not a formal hearing into the incident, Comrade Captain," *Admiral Flota* Gorshkov injected, as much to remind Vorshilov as to ease the tension of his number one submariner. "That will come later. For now, we only want a feel of this, ah, mystery sub."

"Yes," Admiral Dobriski added. "In which case, can you tell us something about the armament the American carried?"

"It had no nuclear missiles aboard. It could have been on a, ah, shakedown cruise as the Americans term it. An entirely new type of sub." Borodine smiled ruefully. "Believe me, if they have many like this, we could be in for a lot of trouble. The boat was lighter and much more maneuverable. My guess would be that she carried more men than the standard number of crewmen."

"For what purpose?" Fleet Admiral Gorshkov inquired.

For a second, Borodine felt an urge to laugh. "You understand, I hadn't the opportunity to inquire into that." His remark brought a chuckle from around the table. "I'm only speculating. If it's not an attack submarine, then perhaps the Americans are experimenting with, ah, troop transports. As I understand it, the Japanese had the idea in the last war."

"Right you are," Gorshov put in. "I had a chance to see one of those boats before the Soviet Union declared war on Japan. I think you've answered all our questions, Comrade Captain. Now for the reason I had you report here."

To his consternation and relief, Borodine saw the assembled officers of flag rank smiling at him. After losing his command, he felt certain of some sort of reprimand and had remained studiously formal. This had hardly been the reaction he had expected.

Admiral Gorshkov rose and spoke with a ringing voice he usually used only for ceremonies. "*Kapitan Pervogo Ranga* Igor Borodine it is my privilege to inform you that you have been selected for command of a radically new Soviet submarine, the Q-Twenty-one. Congratulations, Captain."

Not a reprimand, but a promotion. It staggered Borodine. He

blinked his dark eyes and slowly a smile spread on his broad, Tartar features. "I . . . I don't know how to express my pleasure and gratitude, Comrade Fleet Admiral. I . . . can only say . . . thank you. It is an honor beyond any expectations." Without a pause, the sailor in Igor took over. "What sort of boat is she?"

Gorshkov grinned like a proud father. "Like no other you have ever seen. With the, ah, possible exception of that American who sank the Z-Fifteen. The Q-Twenty-one is larger and carries even more sophisticated equipment than any of our hunter-killer submarines. It's not yet off the ways and the electronics haven't been installed. When she's outfitted, there will be nothing afloat that can harm her or that she can't successfully engage and sink."

"What about armament?" Borodine inquired, entirely taken up by his new command.

"The Q-Twenty-one will carry five intermediate range, multi-warhead missiles, three forward and two silos aft. She will mount the naval version of the hundred twenty-two millimeter gun on the forward deck. There will be two ZU-Twenty-three type anti-air-craft mounts, one in the sail and the other on the aft deck. In addition she has four torpedo tubes forward and two aft. They can handle every type torpedo we have in the fleet. And . . . I think you'll like this," the admiral went on. "There will also be a new type, electronically guided torpedo that will let you see your target, by way of sonar and television image. The sonar will be good up to five kilometers, the television resolution is good to five hundred meters."

"That's quite something for underwater cameras," Borodine observed.

"I'm not an expert on these things," Gorshkov admitted. "I've been told, though, that it has something to do with a process called fiber optics. Nevertheless, you will take command as soon as the hull comes off the ways. Until then, you are assigned to the Naval Intelligence section and will work closely with operatives of Department Six of the KGB."

Borodine's eyebrows rose. Department Six, *Mokkriye Della*, the "Wet Affairs" section of the Committee for State Security. Did it have something to do with the American sub that sank Z-Fifteen?

"I see that surprises you. The reason is simple. First of all the Committee for State Security requires a clear picture of this new

Trident submarine. They hope you can develop that for them. Also, the Q-Twenty-one will carry a complement of forty men and two officers, a special tactical force for conducting covert operations. They will, of course, be drawn for the most part from members of the 'Wet Affairs' section of KGB."

"Will I have the usual contingent of marines?" Borodine thought it prudent to make no comment on the KGB involvement in his new command.

"Yes. And your executive officer will be an old friend . . . Viktor Korzenko."

"Viktor Illyavich!" Borodine barked. "We were at the Academy together. This is . . . a real surprise. I thought he would have a command of his own."

"He did. When he learned of this new sub and who would command it, he requested a transfer from surface craft to be your second."

"That old *bubi*. I can't wait to beat hell out of him at chess."

"Well then, Comrade Captain," Gorshkov summed up. "I'm pleased you like your new command. This is, umm, Thursday. Report Monday to the Intelligence office downstairs. That is all for now."

"Thank you, Comrade Fleet Admiral. Thank you ever so much." Borodine wanted to reach out and wring the older man's hand in gratitude, but he restrained himself to a crisp salute. He made a smart about face and marched from the room.

"There goes the best man we have in the Soviet Navy," Gorshkov told the others.

Gwen met him at the door. "Jack, you look like that tanker job is agreeing with you."

"Funny," he returned after an exchange of kissed cheeks. "That's what Sanchez said."

"*Julio* Sanchez?"

"The same. He was at a restaurant I went to Friday night."

"He's a disagreeable person. What did you do?"

"I knocked him on his keester."

Gwen uttered a short laugh. "You didn't! Oh . . . well, I suppose . . ."

"I had no choice at the time, Gwen. He was trying to belt me one."

With all the aplomb of her acting talent, Gwen made quick recovery. "John's fidgeting waiting for you to get here."

"Traffic snarl coming in from Kennedy. We moved one mile in thirty minutes. Where is he?"

"In the living room reading to the accompaniment of the television. Come on in, my interview should be on in about five minutes. Do you want a drink?"

To Boxer, Gwen's words and actions seemed a bit forced, unlike her usual self. At least she wasn't bitching at him about one thing or another. He smiled and shook his head. "Not right now. Later maybe."

"This interview will drive anyone to drink. If you'll fix, I'll have a Perrier with a twist, no ice. I got a bottle of Glenlivet."

"Good girl. Maybe I will have one," Boxer enthused as he walked to the small built-in bar.

"Hi, Dad," John chirped from his deep chair. "I'm glad you got here."

"Hello, son. I feel better now that I am here. You want a soda?"

"Sure." John glanced at his mother, his eyes the same slate-gray as Jack's, though his fine, unruly blond hair he had inherited from Gwen. "Is it all right, Mother?" he amended.

"Yes, John. This is a special occasion."

The boy beamed. "Yeah. We're all together."

Jack located the bottles, poured and served his wife and son, then built his scotch on the rocks. He sat beside Gwen on the loveseat and took a long pull at the smoky-flavored liquor as a commercial faded to black and the face of talk show host Ed Sellers came on the big screen.

"Today we have with us a young actress whose face is becoming familiar to millions of loyal fans across the country. Ms. Gwen Holcomb."

"Ugh," Gwen expelled through a grimace. "I must be becoming a masochist to actually want to watch this. It's gruesome, believe me."

"You look pretty, Mom," John offered.

"I second my son's nomination," Jack added.

"You two. Really it's awful. I hate that dress and the camera was always at the wrong angle and the lights were too bright, they washed out my complexion entirely. I look like a vampire."

"No you don't, Mom," John countered. "Vampires look like this . . ." and he sucked in his cheeks and rolled his eyes up to show the whites.

"Jonathan Boxer," Gwen said in an admonitory tone.

"Yes, ma'am."

"Drink your soda."

As the interview wore on, Boxer had to admit that Gwen's evaluation had been accurate. The host had an uninspired delivery and his questions ran from the shallow to the trivial, hardly waiting for Gwen's responses. At last he felt compelled to make some comment.

"Don't tell me they put you on there to do you a favor."

"Yes, damnit. The producer thought it would help build viewer interest in the addition of my part as a permanent member of the cast. How were we to know that Ed's wife hates *Another Universe* and he thinks all soaps are trying, boring and juvenile?"

Boxer laughed. "Let's go eat. Where do you want to go, tiger?"

Young John affected an expression of concentration so like his father's that it gave Gwen a pang in her heart. Watching the two of them together she wondered how she could so love the boy and yet be content to divorce the man. There was, of course, her career. She had used that excuse a dozen times a hundred to other performers and to herself. No, that wasn't it, she was forced to admit. Not entirely. It was the Navy. The damned-blasted Navy.

After her years at Columbia and with the New York Repertory company, she considered herself as actively liberal as her peers. She had, as an undergraduate, participated in anti-war demonstrations during Vietnam. She seriously believed in peace. The military was not even human in her estimation. Then she had met Jack Boxer and all that went out the window. At least she thought it had. It had come back to nag her, though. Other officers' wives didn't think like she did. A lot of their comments sounded to Gwen like silly flag waving. She came to accept one thing, though. The Russians *were* the enemy. Ships that never came back, complete with pat stories of accidental sinkings, and the grief such incidents created among the families of officers and enlisted men made that fact certain enough. It drastically affected her liberal outlook. She no longer took at face value something someone said simply because he or she happened to be a current favorite of the liberal establishment. By the time she divorced Jack Boxer, Marxist-Socialism had become a monster, instead of an idealistic social experiment.

Or, she wondered, did that come with aging and the acquisition of a career, fame and money? With a start she realized her husband and son were continuing their conversation.

"I don't know, Dad. Where do you want to go?"

"It's your choice, son."

"Okay. I could sure go for a hamburger."

"Not the usual place."

"Uh . . . what then? We're going to Rockefeller Center, right? How about pizza?"

"Oh, John, you always get heartburn from pizza."

"Not this time, Mom. Promise."

"Let him have pizza," Boxer defended his son. "After all, like you said, this is a special occasion."

"I can see I'm outnumbered. But you are spoiling the boy, Jack."

"Every kid deserves a little of that."

Boxer finished his drink and three of them left the apartment.

Lunch went well and, with a little aid from Boxer, John managed an hour of skating on the outdoor ice rink. While he glided somewhat inexpertly around the arena, Jack and Gwen sat at a small round table and drank Irish coffee.

"What about this evening? Are we going to have dinner?"

"I'd like to, Jack. My place or would we go out?"

"I've had enough of going out in Manhattan for one day. What can we pick up on the way?"

"I have everything we'll need. There's some steaks in the freezer, nice thick sirloins. I have a broccoli casserole I can put in the microwave and hot rolls."

"I'll get us a good wine to go with it."

An amply padded woman in her mid-fifties bustled up to the table and cleared her throat to attract their attention. "Excuse me, but aren't you Miss Holcomb from *Another Universe?*"

"Why, yes I am," Gwen replied, flustered enough to bring color to her small, nicely shaped ears.

"I knew it. I told my husband 'Herman,' I said, 'that's Shanna

286

from *Another Universe.*' And here it is you are." She poked a crumpled cocktail napkin toward Gwen. "Could I have your autograph, Miss Holcomb?"

"Certainly." Gwen took the wrinkled paper and spread it smooth on the marble top of the table, then signed her name with a flourish. "There you are."

"Oh, thank you so much. I always watch my stories in the afternoon. You've become my favorite. Only . . . why do you have to be so scheming?" She gave a little wave of the napkin and walked away.

"Now that you're such a celebrity, I suppose I should make it *Mouton-Cadet.*"

Gwen laughed. "Can you believe it, I was embarrassed by that. She is such a sweet thing, though. Can you imagine someone actually watching that thing day after day."

"If you don't like soap opera, why do the role?"

"It's a big step up. Absolutely no one gets anywhere any more unless they've worked on the soaps. Speaking of careers, how is it on the *Tecumseh?*"

"Not like the Navy. I can tell you that. There's more paperwork, though only in duplicate. I get to see a lot of the Caribbean and the North Atlantic. May go to the Med later on. Or around Africa to the Middle East."

Gwen studied him through narrowed eyes. "You never get tired of traveling, do you? I'm . . . afraid John is going to inherit your wanderlust."

"Nothing to be afraid of. It's a great life."

"Never being home, never having time with your wife and family?"

"Gwen . . ." Boxer broke off. They had been through this argument too many times before.

For her own part, Gwen was glad enough to let it lie. "Do you have a room at the Taft?"

"Yes. Considering that the company rents a suite on a year-round basis, you'd think I had tried to steal someone else's reservation, the way the room clerk acted."

"Perhaps you did. It's not uncommon for hotels to rent out rooms they have on retainer. At least not here in New York."

Boxer smiled. "Washington is the same."

"Why I asked . . . I thought . . . perhaps . . ."

"I might stay at the apartment? I'd like that, Gwen."

"So would I, Jack. Will you then?"

"I'll drop by the Taft and pick up my suitcase."

Tinkling laughter rose in Gwen's throat. "They'll have a fit. First you are there, forcing them to cancel someone else, now you leave. You'd better tip big."

"I will."

Dinner went off as a big success. John plied his father with questions about the Caribbean and Jack hated having to invent lies for his son. He reconciled himself that some of the tales were true, only the events had happened years before. At last, the boy excused himself and went to his room.

"I'm shameless, asking you to stay here like this," Gwen told him.

"I'm glad you did. I would have asked if I was sure I'd get a yes answer."

"I . . . I want to make love to you. For some reason I feel as though it is very important right now to hold you in my arms and love you like we used to do."

Boxer felt his senses stirring. "Can we leave the dishes until tomorrow?"

"Bertha has the day off, but we can manage."

They undressed in a speedy hush. Boxer marveled at how well Gwen had kept her body. Taut and silky, not even stretch marks from the birth of John. Her flat tummy was hightlighted by the small indentation of her naval and luxuriously flared hips arrowed to the sparse thatch that covered her delightful mound. When Boxer turned from laying his trousers aside, he had a full, raging erection.

Gwen stepped to him and cupped his sack in one hand while the other encircled his cock and began to stroke it. "I love this wonderful old thing," she murmured.

"It's not all so old, you know. You smell sweet."

"A little something I picked out in case I needed help to seduce you."

"I rape easily, you should know that."

"Oh, God, yes. How well I know. Come to bed with me."

Boxer took her hand and they walked to a large, canopied affair with deep goose-down comforters. She lay on her back and wriggled into a comfortable position and Jack knelt beside her, kissing her ample, brown-tipped breasts. She murmured deep in her throat and reached out to stroke his back.

"You're a handsome devil, Jack Boxer."

Suddenly it was like always. Jack leaned forward and his lips gently nuzzled at the moist cleft of her womanhood. He bore in, tongue lapping, spreading the lacy fronds and plunging to her clit. Gwen suppressed a squeal of delight and sought his throbbing penis. With her tongue and lips she teased its sensitive tip and lavished affection on the rigid shaft. Jack straddled her and buried his face between her thighs. Gwen licked his scrotum and then sealed her vacuuming mouth over his burning hot cock.

From long experience they knew when each was about to peak. Slowly they subsided and Jack rolled over on his back.

"Oh, my wonderful man," Gwen cooed. She straddled him and let herself down ever so slowly, delighting both of them as she eased fractions of an inch at a time into her scalding passage. "It's so . . . good . . . Jack . . . so . . . very . . . good!"

Boxer wished it could be so good in all things between them, but his raging passion overpowered this moment's lapse. He arched his back and drove his length deep inside Gwen's pulsating cavern. Slowly, he began to swing his buttocks in a widening circle.

"Yes . . . Oh, yes-yes-yes! Harder, Jack. Fill me up. Push . . . push . . . push!"

Spectacular sunsets over Hawaii filled Jack's mind and he felt Gwen bursting apart with delirious completion while he churned in time with her own maddening bumps and grinds. Truly it had never been so good before. Their shared pleasure drove the dark thought from his mind that this might be the last time. That Nekor Island might spell the end of the *Shark* and of him.

17

Thick fog, in ragged-edged patches, covered the harbor when Boxer arrived at the gangway for the *Tecumseh*. Three men waited for him in a long, black car. First out of the back seat was Williams, followed by Admiral Stark, in civilian clothes. After a slight delay, a trim figure climbed from the front. It took Boxer a moment to place his name.

James Hicks.

He had first seen the tan, thin lipped man months ago at the Purple Onion with Tracy Kimble. His "something or other in government" Tracy had mentioned became clear in his present company. Where, Boxer wondered, was Marc Pottel?

"Good evening for this sort of thing," Admiral Stark observed as he shook Boxer's hand. "There's been a, ah, slight change in plans. Marc Pottel died suddenly last night. Good chance it might have been a KGB 'heart attack.' "

"That's bad news all around," Boxer commented.

"This is Jim Hicks, from the Company. He'll be taking Marc's place on this mission. Tom Redfern is already aboard. I'll let you and Jim get acquainted. We came down to wish you well."

"Thank you, Admiral. I have the feeling I'm going to need it." Boxer fixed Hicks with his eyes.

"Commander Boxer and I have already met," Hicks remarked with a sneer in his voice.

"A little arm wrestling at the Purple Onion," Boxer supplied. "And it's *Captain,* Mr. Hicks."

Hicks shrugged, his handsome features molded into an expression of disdain. "Have it your way, Captain."

Boxer and the new CIA man boarded the *Tecumseh* and headed

for the bridge. Unlike Marc Pottel, who kept to the background, Hicks stuck right to Boxer, peering over his shoulder as the ship prepared to get under way.

"Haul in the gangplank," Boxer commanded.

"Gangplank, aye," the seaman at the talker repeated.

"Bring turbines to five-seven-zero-zero revs."

The *Tecumseh* shuddered through her excessive length and the helmsman nudged the wheel slightly to keep the strain off the thick hawsers that held the super tanker to its berth.

"Cast off the stern line," Boxer ordered. "Cast off bow."

Gradually, the dock began to recede into the fog. Boxer took a deep breath and felt truly free for the first time in the two weeks the *Shark* had been outfitted for the mission.

"We'll cruise south until twenty-three hundred tomorrow, then the *Shark* will come out of the belly."

"We'll do that sooner, Captain. The *Shark* has a greater cruising speed under water than this tub has on the surface." Hicks' voice had a nasty tone to it.

"It's not wise to try to countermand a captain's orders, Mr. Hicks," Boxer told him warningly.

"You seem to forget, I am in complete charge."

"Wrong. Legally, I command both *Tecumseh* and *Shark*. All you have charge of, Mr. Hicks is the explosive device in my sub, its emplacement and detonation. Only the captain gives orders aboard his ship."

"We'll see about that." Hicks turned to the duty officer. "Where's the radio room? I want an immediate patch to Langley."

"You have been here a week, Comrade Captain," a fellow captain first class in Naval Intelligence remarked to Borodine. "How do you like our little cubbyhole?"

Borodine found it easy to smile. He knew Vassily Markov was an agent of the KGB and that his naval rank had been provided as a cover. All the same, he had found the challenges of piecing together data on the as yet unknown activities of the Americans to his liking.

"The atmosphere is a bit rarefied, compared to the submarine service, I'll admit. Between you and me, what does the admiral have that's so important to drag me away from the comforts of my bed at four in the morning?"

The intelligence captain handed Borodine a large manila file folder with a red and white striped tag on it. "These have come from our counterparts at Army Headquarters. Photo interp people have discovered a strange anomaly in the Mississippi River." He made a wry face and added in an aside, "Aren't these American names atrocious, Igor?"

"You get used to them. But then, Vassily, you've not been to America, have you? All it takes is practice."

"There's another bit of news, too. It seems that one of our 'Wet Affairs' teams has had to remove an American agent named Marc Pottel. This Pottel was reported by one of our reliables to be involved in some highly secret submarine mission. Our agents in place have been advised to increase surveillance on all American submarines."

"What has this to do with me and these, ah, photographs?"

Vassily smiled. "That is your job to analyze and give us some guidelines. After all, you had your sub blown out from under you by some unknown type of American submarine. The admiral thought you would be interested."

"I am." Borodine opened the folder and studied the series of satellite shots first examined by Boris Donskoi. He looked through them casually and then with greater care. Suddenly his innate sense of form and order signaled a warning. Absently he reached for a large magnifying glass.

"Hummm. Did you see these?"

"No I didn't Igor. What is it?"

"Look. Unless I am greatly wrong, a large chunk of the Mississippi River bank is moving southward in each twenty-four hour period between these satellite shots."

"How can that be?"

"If the Americans were to be moving something large and camouflaged down river, it would have to appear much like this." He laid out the glossy prints on his desk. "There you see it here, as it had been according to this report for some months. Now, it is gone and shows up . . . here. On the next day . . . here. And so on, right down past New Orleans."

"What would be that size and be moved by water?"

292

"Obviously something they didn't want us to know about. And equally, a type of ship, or boat that could float itself down the river. Add to that this CIA agent involved with a super-secret submarine mission." Borodine rose and started to the door.

"I'm going over to the computer room, Vassily. If anything more comes in, or if the admiral wants me, get word to me at once."

"Of course."

What the photos had revealed set Borodine's mind to working at a pace surprising even to him. By the time he reached the computer room, he had the rough parameters of what he wanted laid out. He quickly sketched his plan to the programming chief.

"I want a complete computer search for all officers and enlisted men assigned to United States submarines. On another machine, I want all data on our Z-Class submarines put in, along with the report of the description and tactics of the American vessel that sank the Z-Fifteen. You'll be going for a model of what sort of boat could have performed in the manner outlined."

"This will all take time, Comrade Captain," the programmer protested.

"Fine. We have a lot of that right now. Get someone on it . . . no, you handle the job yourself. I'll wait."

The expert gave Borodine a skeptical glance. "It could be hours . . . days."

"I'll be here, then."

Twenty minutes later, the phone emitted two short, strident rings. The technician who answered it indicated the call was for Borodine. He rose and took the handset.

"*Da*. Borodine here."

"This is Vassily. Another report has just been brought to us because it refers to a submarine. I thought you would like to see it at once."

"I'll be right back." He hung up and turned to the chief programmer. "Call me the moment you start getting some answers."

Back in the intelligence office, Borodine studied the flimsy sheets. "Is this accurate?"

"Highly reliable, I've been told. An agent of ours in Miami received the information from a part-time resource, a pilot in the drug trade, who claimed to have dived on this enormous submarine. Although bearing no regulation markings, he felt positive it had to be an American vessel. The pilot subsequently lost his aircraft and it was some time before he was able to make contact with our man."

"The submarine shot him down?"

"No. For some reason the pontoons flooded and it sank in ninety meters of water."

"Could the man be exaggerating the size?"

"I don't think so, Igor."

"What he describes here is colossal. There isn't a submarine anywhere in the world that size . . . except, maybe, for the one that sank the Z-Fifteen. I had suspected that the instruments aboard were affected by the cold water, the presence of our own countermeasure activity, something like that. They, too, recorded a Trident-class submarine but one decidedly larger than normal." Borodine stood and began to pace the floor.

After a few minutes, he paused beside a small side table. He picked up a white bishop and moved it three diagonal squares across the board. "Check," he said softly and made a notation of his move on a small postal card. He would send it to Priskin in Vladivostok. Let the wily cruiser captain figure his way out of that. Once more he started to walk about the room.

An American agent involved in a top-secret submarine mission, Borodine thought. The moving bank of the Mississippi, hiding something. A week after the bank section disappears entirely, the pilot spots a gigantic submarine off the shore of Puerto Rico. A month later the Z-Fifteen is blown to pieces. There had to be something in common between these widely separated incidents.

Nearly an hour went by in Borodine's silent contemplations before the phone rang. The chief programmer reported that the list of American submariners was printing out. Borodine hurried over.

"Let me see them."

"They're all on the list. Present and former submariners."

"Why *former,* Comrade?"

"Because we discovered a number of officers and men who, although still assigned to the submarine warfare service, are not posted to any specific sub."

"School?"

"The computer doesn't think so. There is also a list of officers of command rank who have left the service in the past year."

"Yes, yes. I can understand that. A discharge of convenience, eh?"

"Quite so. I'll start the profile on the Z-Fifteen sinking after lunch."

"Lunch!" Borodine declared with a snap of his fingers. "I am supposed to meet my wife in Gorky Park to eat at that new Ukranian place."

"Ugh! Ukranian food. Beets and onions, onions and beets. With potatoes for variety. How can you stand that?"

"Our cook on the Z-Fifteen was a Ukranian. I'm used to it, you see. Try cross-indexing these lists with regard to date of reassignment or discharge. I'm on to something, but I have to make certain before I take it to Admiral Gorshkov."

"I'll give it a try."

Hicks said nothing after a terse message came to him from Langley. But he appeared to sulk for the twenty-four hours until *Shark* came out of the belly of the *Tecumseh*. Once the cradle arms had released the submarine and it sped away from the mother ship, Hicks came to Boxer's cabin.

"Now we're in my part of the operation," Hicks declared firmly. "From this point forward, I give the orders."

Boxer suppressed a smile and shook his head. "I'm sure that was not in the message you got from Langley while we were still on the *Tecumseh,* Mr. Hicks. The boat is mine and you're only a passenger like Tom Redfern's Strike Force. Hell, you don't even command them. The only authority you have is to direct the placing of the nuclear bomb and when to trigger it."

"*I* decide what authority I have. I've been watching you, Captain. You are unstable, incompetent to command and decidedly dangerous on this sort of mission. You damaged one sub and got five men killed. Why in hell they ever let you take over a sensitive mission like this . . ."

"That's enough, Hicks. It should have been your neck I twisted, instead of your arm. It's plain enough that you have no more liking for me than I have for you. But I can't let that affect the mission. At least I appreciate your bringing this to me privately. In the future, however, you will keep in mind that I command here and keep your opinions to yourself."

Boxer rose to signal the conversation ended. Hicks held on, tenaciously. "Unless you relinquish command to me immediately, there is no way this matter can be kept private. I will be forced to have you arrested and placed under guard."

Boxer laughed out loud. *"You* will have *me* arrested? By whom?"

"By your executive officer if no one else. I was opposed to the Navy being brought into this from the first. It is an Agency task and should have been staffed entirely from Agency personnel. You submariners are too arrogant, over-confident and flamboyant to properly conduct covert operations."

"We're arrogant? You are a complete horse's ass, Hicks. You should have stuck with your forte; balling liberated lady reporters and making snotty remarks in restaurants." Without further comment, Boxer left his compartment and headed to the bridge.

Jim Hicks followed directly after him.

"I'll take the con, Mr. Cowly."

"Yes, sir."

Boxer reached for the MC microphone. "Now hear this . . . now hear this! This is the captain. Our course is set for east-southeast until we reach the coast of Africa. We will be running deep and at flank speed. We will have COMMCOP conning the boat, so everyone except routine duty sections get some chow and sack time and enjoy the ride. Major Redfern's men will continue their training activities and the map rehearsals for the objective. That is all."

"No it's not," Hicks said icily through clenched teeth as he came onto the second deck of the retracted sail. "Mr. Cowly, send for Lieutenant Harris. I am relieving the captain of command."

"I cautioned you, Hicks," Boxer growled.

"Also, rescind that order to head toward Africa. That is taking entirely too much time. We will go through the canal."

"You're fucking nuts, Hicks!" Boxer exclaimed as he took a step toward the deeply tanned CIA man.

"Have him restrained," Hicks hurriedly ordered.

"We can't go through the canal submerged, you ninny," Boxer said in a strangled voice. "You're risking discovery of the *Shark* when utmost secrecy is necessary for the mission to succeed."

"It's not your place to decide that any more, Captain. I have been clear enough on that before. From the time we left *Tecumseh,*

I was in command here."

"Bullshit!" Boxer roared. His astonished staff and the duty section in the con stood around in amazement. "If anyone is confined to his quarters in irons, it will be you, mister. Cowly, send for the CMA."

"CMA to the con," Cowly announced over the talker system.

"Disregard that!" Hicks shouted in a fury. "I'm giving the orders."

"Not to me you aren't," Cowly snapped loyally.

The disagreement, that had begun before the *Tecumseh* sailed had come to an impasse, Boxer saw. Hicks, whether power mad or glory seeking, would not back down. Neither, he realized, would he. The safety of the whole mission depended on the outcome. He could not, would not, let this incompetent pencil-pusher from Langley usurp his boat. At the same time, his own outburst must look unbalanced in the eyes of the officers and crew. He had to act decisively about this in no less manner than the crises of the past.

"I . . . ah, I'm sorry for this outburst, gentlemen," he apologized to his staff and crew. "It seems there is some question as to whose authority is to be accepted aboard the *Shark*. Mr. Hicks is not competent to make that decision, he's merely a passenger aboard. All considered, I don't think I am qualified either." At that point he paused when the Master at Arms arrived on the deck.

"Chief, for the time being, Mr. Harris is in command of the *Shark*. Mr. Hicks is under close arrest and confined to his compartment. See that a guard is detailed to keep him there until further notice from Mr. Harris or myself."

"You can't do that!" Hicks bellowed.

"Oh, yes I can. There will be a meeting of the staff in the officers' wardroom in five minutes. Please see to it that Major Redfern is present."

At a nod from Boxer, the burly Chief Master at Arms escorted a protesting James Hicks away to his quarters. Boxer left the con and went directly to the wardroom. When the others assembled, he faced them with a grim expression.

"Gentlemen, I find the situation aboard *Shark* to be intolerable. Since it results from a direct personality clash between Mr. Hicks and myself, I must step aside from making a final decision."

Quickly Boxer outlined Hicks' power play to take over operational control of the *Shark*. He went on to reveal part of the secret orders he had been delivered for his eyes only. "Mr. Hicks was a last minute replacement for Marc Pottel. Pottel was murdered by a team of KGB operatives. It is suspected that he had been targeted by a deep-cover mole inside the CIA. Hicks isn't even fully aware of the workings of the *Shark* or of the nature of this mission. For the security of everyone concerned, I cannot let him take over this boat. It will be up to you, then, to reach some determination."

Boxer paused to draw a deep breath and wipe one broad, hard hand over his lined face. He had not spoken so formally to anyone since his days as a midshipman at the Academy. Tension drained him of energy and hung heavily in the room. "After that little incident in the con, I feel it best if you take a secret ballot vote on whether I am still fit to command or whether I should relinquish my command to Lieutenant Harris, our executive officer."

"No!" Cowly exploded. "You're the skipper. There's no asshole spook going to take your place."

"Thank you for your confidence. But this is important. Find slips of paper and write your vote on it. I'll be back in one minute."

It took less than that for every officer aboard the *Shark* to write the name of Captain Jack Boxer on strips of napkin and put them together in an ashtray. Cowly quickly counted them and stepped into the passageway to summon Boxer back.

"It's unanimous, Captain. We're behind you in this."

Boxer breathed a sigh of relief, mixed with concern for what would come to pass during the long cruise to Torpy Island in the Nekor chain.

18

"Igor, you have paid no attention to me, or to the borsht, and now you ignore the lamb," Galena Borodinova gently chided her husband.

"I . . . have things on . . . my mind," Igor said through a mouthful of lamb and braised potatoes.

"You have been distracted for five days now. I think I liked you better as a big wooly bear submarine commander. You were gone a lot, but at least when you were home you had time for nothing but me."

"The service of our country is a harsh mistress," Borodine reminded his wife.

Galena looked around her own home as though suspecting hidden microphones. "A slut if you ask me."

"Galena! Such language. You talk like a fishwife."

They both laughed. It was an old story between them. About the time they had visited the Soho district of London during a layover on a flight to Washington. That had been back when Igor had first been assigned to attache duty at the embassy. The vociferous quarreling that passed for bargaining among the Cockney women cart peddlers of the area had reminded them both of the Shakespearian references to the foul-tempered fishwife in *King Lear*.

"Tell me what it is, darling," his wife urged.

"Sorry. I can't. All this secrecy involved with our intelligence service and the Committee for State Security. There is one thing, though, that has come up today. In some lists I'm going over it was discovered that one hundred twenty enlisted men and all five officers of the U.S. submarine *Sting Ray* left the service within an eleven day period."

"Isn't that the one that created such a stir, a collision or something?"

"Yes. Galena my pet."

"The incident caused the commanding officer to be disgraced, didn't it? What was his name?"

"Right again. Box . . . something. Commander Jonathan Raymond Boxer, that's it. He resigned after the inquiry board found against him. Strangely enough, he was given command of the largest American bottom on the seas, the super-tanker, *Tecumseh*. It flies the Williams Company flag."

Galena smiled impishly. "You've got all the facts and figures right at the tip of your tongue, don't you? Surely it must have something to do with what you're working on."

"No, I'm afraid it doesn't. Wait! . . . Damnit, wait a moment. Maybe it does. It just might be." Igor Borodine rose, wiping his lips with a linen napkin. "I'm sorry, dear. I have to go back to the office. I simply must get to the computer and find out if there are any satellite photos of the *Tecumseh*. I . . . I wonder where she's sailed since launching?"

Shark ran on the surface, plowing through a low, spume-topped chop in the Indian Ocean. Captain Boxer stood in the lee of the sail watching the moon make wavy yellow lines across the water. Crisp, clean air stimulated him and his thoughts ran to the days of his youth.

Sailing a twenty-one footer at the age of fourteen had been a big accomplishment. His father had absolute confidence in his son. "Jack was born with a spoked wheel in his hand and a brass Navy bell in his mouth," he had often remarked to guests in the Boxer home.

Boxer had loved the sea. He had a shaggy old mongrel dog that shared his romance and would sit on the bowsprit and bark joyously at sea gulls and sporting porpoises. Boxer never lost his passion for the sea, even though he discovered girls the next summer.

In the steamy little cabin of the twenty-one, he and Margaret Ann McMurtry had gone from necking to petting and then Boxer found her hot little hand on the painful bulge in his cut-off faded denims. She had quickly undone the brass buttons and exposed his

300

turgid flesh. Humming a dreamy little song, she had begun to expertly stroke him.

How much better, he thought, than when he did it for himself. In seconds she had wriggled out of her two piece swimsuit and lay, panting, on the narrow bunk. Boxer had gazed at her luscious body with the rapt attention of his first encounter. His mouth had gone dry and his throat ached as much as his throbbing penis. He knew what to do, at least intellectually. The boys at school talked about it incessantly. Only, he wondered in painful indecision, only how did he go about . . . asking?

"Stick it in me, Jackie," Margaret Ann had pleaded. "I'm so hot I'm going to burn up. Hurry. I want it all." She spread her legs and he climbed clumsily between them. "No, that's not the way. Get lower, rub the head in my juice. Yeah . . . ah, yeah, Jackie. That's it. Now, push. Hard. Harder! Oh . . . oh . . . *Now!*"

With a shudder, Boxer came back to reality. What the hell had caused him to think of Margaret Ann. Especially at a time like this.

His first piece of ass had been a disaster. He'd come before he had it half-way in. Margaret Ann had pouted until he had managed to get it up again and slide all the way into her slippery purse. Their coupling had lasted considerably longer that time and it quickly became clear that Margaret Ann had a great deal more experience and talent than he. Boxer had always been an apt and quick pupil, though. Over the delight-filled days of summer, he developed a technique that pleased both of them. By the time he had been graduated from prep school, he knew that his method pleased most every girl. But that was in the past and the future held a considerable amount of danger for Boxer and his crew.

Another message from Langley, addressed through the "Captain of the U.S.S. *Shark*." blunted Hicks' power grab. After two days, Hicks had put a good face on things and began to train with Redfern's troops. He made suggestions on how to handle the bomb and to implant it. All the same, he scrupulously avoided contact with Boxer when he could. The miles slid under the *Shark*'s hull and this short run on the surface had only been to provide a bit of luxury to the crew. Fresh air quickly became a premium on a sub.

Once, Boxer had been aboard an old pre-atomic era submarine and it took no more time than the closing of the hatches to know why they had been called "pig boats." Even the finest airscrubbing and replenishing equipment, like that aboard *Shark* could not replace clean, natural air. Another four days, Boxer figured. Then they would make their careful approach to Torpy.

Cowly turned his face from the softly glowing green screens of the sail con. "Captain, we've got the whole Indian Ocean to ourselves tonight. Radar shows nothing, sonar quiet, even the dolphins have stopped making love."

"That's strange. It's a full moon."

"Yeah." Cowley grinned. "I'd like to be back in Norfolk. My wife does the wildest things on a night like this. Will we, uh, be going straight back after the Island?"

"We're to cross the equator in a northerly direction and await messages with new orders."

"Unh-oh. Only, skipper, how many jobs can there be for an outfit like ours?"

"That's up to the brass. Remember the hostages in Iran? Or how about the pirates in the South China Sea? Someone might take it in his head to turn us loose on that sort of problem."

"Exactly who does run this boat?"

"From what I gather, the president and a select few men in NSC and DOD know the inside story and can propose employment of the *Shark*. Remember, Bud, we're a guinea pig. If the *Shark* works out there'll be more like us. Admiral Stark even hinted that we might be the only means to keep from having a hot war. Me, I like mine cold any day."

"You can double that for me."

"This is it!" Igor Borodine exploded with excitement even before he had finished viewing all of the satellite pictures taken of the *Tecumseh*. He turned to Vassily Markov and extended the picture he held in his left hand.

"I was right on this one. Here is the *Tecumseh*. This was taken from Suloz-Eight. See the ice. With the exception of the ice pack that is out of frame, the tanker is within eight hundred nautical miles of where I engaged the American submarine. What is a tanker doing there? To whom is he delivering oil? And this one. A thousand nautical miles from where the destroyer *Skoryy* made contact with an unidentified underwater vessel. A big one according to their sonar officer. And here. This is six hundred kilometers from where the agent reported his pilot resource dived on a giant submarine.

"The *Tecumseh* is big enough to be the mother ship for that mystery sub of the Americans. It has to be in fact. Who commands the *Tecumseh?* Captain Jack Boxer, an officer disgraced and resigned from the Navy because of an accident involving his Trident Class submarine." Borodine paused for emphasis. "What was it you said about a resignation of convenience? I'm taking this to Admiral Gorshkov at once."

The admiral saw Captain First Class Borodine immediately. After only the most perfunctory greetings, Borodine presented his case. He summed up with a strong insistence, based on his growing confidence.

"The Americans managed to build a superior new submarine type without any of our many agents discovering the fact. They launched it by taking it down the Mississippi at night, camouflaged to appear from the air as a piece of the landscape. It is serviced and tended by the Williams Company tanker, *Tecumseh*. In some manner, Captain Jack Boxer, USN, is involved. After the destruction of the Z-Fifteen, there is no doubt of the threat this new submarine has for the Soviet Navy."

"I agree, Comrade Captain. You were to take command of the Q-Twenty-one upon completion of its fitting out. The missiles are not aboard, nor many of the stores. I am putting a rush on completion of victualing and necessary chandlery services so men can live aboard. I want you to leave immediately for Rostov, take command and put the Q-Twenty-one to sea. Your mission is to find and destroy this American super submarine."

"It will be my greatest pleasure, Comrade Admiral."

19

Following his appointment, Captain First Class Igor Borodine had several thoughts he did not express to the admiral. First among them being that there was a lot of ocean out there and only one submarine he had to find. He possessed one advantage, though. Daily satellite photos of the earth's surface would provide him with the location of the super-tanker, *Tecumseh*. He had no doubt that the huge vessel, and its captain of record, Jack Boxer, were somehow mixed in with this new American underwater menace. Consequently, he ordered that each day's gathering be sent to him in Rostov and at sea throughout the search.

With that accomplished, he settled down to overseeing the outfitting of the Q-21. Considering his mission, he took delight in naming the vessel *More Dekar',* the Sea Savage. His crew began to report on the second day after his arrival in the Black Sea town of Rostov. To his pleasure, one of the first happened to be his old friend, Viktor Korzenko.

"Viktor Illyavich!" Borodine greeted his new executive officer, a slightly built man of his own age with blond hair and the patrician features of a Romanoff. Viktor's family had, in fact, been among the White Russian aristocracy before the revolution. It had not deterred his success in the naval service, however.

"What sort of impossible thing have you set out to do, Igor Alexandriavich?" Viktor countered as he seated himself in the shore-bound office provided for the officers of the Q-21.

"We are going to take that magnificent boat out there to sea. We are going to use it to hunt down a new American sub and destroy it. Our work will be in secret and, since the Americans are at great pains to hide the existence of our target, we can probably do the job and avoid any chance of open warfare between our countries."

Viktor only stared. The long, aesthetic fingers of one hand strayed to his left ear lobe and he stroked it. Igor Borodine recalled the habit from their days at the academy. At last the *More Dekar'* XO wet his lips and emitted a short whistle.

"You do go for the big ones, Igor."

"What can I tell you? I have been assigned this incredible mission instead of facing a formal hearing on the loss of my former command or . . . worse, a court-martial and visit to Siberia. Let me get you some vodka."

"What? No bourbon?" Viktor asked dryly. He recalled Borodine's preference for the American liquor from a visit he paid while Igor had been in the embassy in Washington.

"Not here, my friend. But . . . I have a case put aside that will go aboard the *More Dekar'*."

Viktor raised an eyebrow. "Sea Savage? Hummm. My idea of a name. When do we get to work?"

"It's already started. By the end of the week, the crew will be living aboard and we will be ready to sail."

"Good."

A young sub-lieutenant rapped at the open doorway. "Excuse me, Comrade Captain, another set of satellite photographs has arrived."

"Thank you, Comrade Lieutenant. Bring them in and we can have a look. You see, Viktor," he went on to his friend, "the Americans have been most clever in concealing their new menace. Only, perhaps, they have outsmarted themselves. I am certain that this ship, the Williams Company tanker, *Tecumseh,* is in fact on lease to the CIA and functions as mother ship to this submarine we are chasing. Thus, all we need do is keep track of the *Tecumseh* and we can find the sub. Ah! Here she is, headed along the east coast of South America . . . right there, off Brazil."

"Ten degrees down bubble," Boxer commanded.

"Ten degrees, aye," the DO repeated.

Seamen at the diving plane controls fed in the change and the *Shark* slanted downward, diving for two thousand feet. Only the soft hum of the air circulating system could be heard on the bridge.

Lieutenant Harris looked up from the chart table.

"We're seven hundred miles from Torpy Island," he announced.

"Right on course. We'll make our run-in from here. Silent and deep," Boxer added. "Take her down to two-five-zero-zero feet. You have the con, Mister Harris."

Boxer left the bridge to go to his compartment. There he found Jim Hicks waiting for him. "Problems, Mr. Hicks?"

"No, Captain. I . . . I wanted to have a short talk with you. The time is getting short and we will soon be entirely out of communication with Washington."

"Yes. Even with the miracle of squirt transmission and satellite relay, radio silence is a must," Boxer observed.

"That's why I wanted to get your opinion on how to proceed."

"Consulting, Mr. Hicks? All right, you can have it. Once we go under radio silence, at five hundred miles from Torpy, we are committed. There will be no way you can receive an abort command, if that's what is worrying you."

Hicks nodded. "It is, indeed. For my own part. I have no intention of aborting. I'm glad you see it the same way."

"I'm not so sure that I, ah, 'see it the same way.' I merely stated an unalterable circumstance that I and all of us will have to live with in the future. You see, I'm not a fire-eater like a lot of old-time naval officers. I would be perfectly content to keep the 'war' as cold as possible. We're in competition with the Russians. There's no doubt they are our enemy. But I respect them." Boxer paused. He wasn't accustomed to saying that much at one time. Nor to revealing his personal opinions.

"How deep does this 'respect' go?"

"Is that a question in your official capacity?"

For the first time in Boxer's presence, Jim Hicks relaxed a little and showed a smile. "Strictly off the record. You wouldn't be here if you weren't a hundred percent trustworthy."

"I've known a number of Russians, socially. We've never been at war with the Soviets. They were our allies in the past. Considering what we both have in the way of armament, it would be criminally irresponsible to actively seek an escalation that could result in total war."

"How so?"

"Neither of us would win. Only the so-called emerging nations in the southern hemisphere would have a chance at survival in some sort of marginal civilization. That is an unacceptable alternative to me."

"Then why don't you protest?"

"I don't indulge in politics. My thinking is a lot like the old soldiers from between the world wars. They considered it their duty to serve without comment or participation. After their term of service, that was the time to assume the duties, privileges and obligations of a citizen."

"A bit stuffy, isn't it?"

Boxer shrugged. "The alternative is to become an activist . . . and the very name turns my stomach." Then he got them back on the subject. "As regards this mission; I have a job to do and so do you. Let's try to do ours with the least amount of friction and the greatest amount of expertise. Let the pontificators in Washington do the talking. We are only here to carry out their wishes."

"I can live with that."

"I hope we all can."

After Hicks left, Boxer unrolled his own set of charts and studied the approaches to Torpy Island. He switched on the repeater of the COMMCOP and the other instruments mounted in the bulkheads and on precious table space. Then he bent low over the wiggly lines and fine-print numbers that outlined the ocean floor. He wanted to know every ridge and hollow, each seamount and coral reef in the event the *Shark* had to run for it.

At their present speed, they would reach the island in seventeen and a half hours. Add a little evasive action into their course, he reckoned, and make it twenty-two hours. Reconnaissance in depth with the mini-subs and visually by periscope, as well as electronic surveillance would consume another day. After that, the fireworks would begin. Better hold the final briefing two hours before jump-off. Boxer reached up and keyed a switch on his MC system.

"Have Major Redfern and Mr. Hicks come to my compartment in half an hour," Boxer ordered. That, he thought, would give him time for a short nap.

"What's up, Jack?" Tom Redfern inquired as he entered through the open hatchway.

"We're getting down to short numbers, Tom. I make it some twenty-one hours to the target. Five hours from now, we terminate

307

radio contact, I've gone over it with Mr. Hicks. After that, there's no turning back. Are your boys ready?"

"They could eat nails. From now on, I'm more concerned about over-training. They could go stale."

"Okay. Knock off the training sessions. One exception to that. The men who will go with Mr. Hicks will continue to make dry runs with him."

"They're pros. I feel confident of them as it is." An unexpected compliment from Hicks.

"The decision is yours, of course," Boxer told him dryly. "I'd feel better if they were kept at it until time to go out the tube."

"Everyone is a little keyed up, Jack," Redfern inserted.

"All right. One more go-around for everyone, then rest and eat until time to hit the target."

"You've just made a hundred men happy, Jack."

The MC system beeped at the three men. Boxer toggled the switch.

"Captain from the bridge. We have a target, bearing zero-five-zero degrees. Range, three-five-zero-zero yards. High-speed screws, closing fast."

"CIC have a make on it yet?"

"Negative, Captain. But they should have by the time you get here."

"On my way."

The Combat Information Center buzzed with incoming data. When Boxer reached the bridge, no formalities accompanied his taking command. He made an immediate check of the situation.

"Target, bearing zero-five-zero degrees. Range, three-two-zero-zero yards, closing fast. Speed, two-one knots."

"ID'ed it yet?"

"No, Captain. It's not one of ours or the Russians."

"I've a matched sonar profile, Captain," the SO announced from his computer console. "It's a Chinese Type-Fifty-six missile frigate. That's the one converted from the Soviet RIGA Class DE's."

"Shit! We're well clear of the South China Sea. What's he doing way the hell out here?" Boxer asked of no one.

The CIC operator punched up a series of numbers and the combat data scrolled onto the screen. Quickly he read it off.

"Dao-Lai class frigate, from her sonar profile, probably the *Yu-Kwai Chwan*. She has a twin five inch gun mount on forward deck, eight tube rank of the AT-Eleven ASW missiles forward, a four tube battery on after deck. Two torpedo tubes on main deck, anti-aircraft mounts fore and aft. A single, stern-ejecting depth charge rack."

"A lot of firepower," Harris observed to Boxer.

"Too damn much."

"Changing the revs, Captain. The *Yu-Kwai* has come to two-five knots, zero-five-zero degrees, range three-zero-zero-zero and closing."

"Captain to radio room," Boxer growled into the MC mike. "Is that target transmitting to anyone, Sparks?"

"Not on any frequency we normally monitor."

"She's Chinese."

"I'll try their usual channels."

A moment later, the radioman called the bridge. "Nothing so far, Cap'n."

"Get off a coded message to Admiral Stark. 'PRC frigate *Yu-Kwai Chwan* approaching *Shark* at high speed. Are we cleared to engage if threatened?' Flag it *most urgent*."

"Aye, aye, sir."

"Target has changed course to one-eight-zero, sir," the SO announced. "She's on an attack heading."

"Sparks, any transmissions to or from the target?"

"Negative, Captain," the radio operator returned.

"Well?" Harris inquired, tension beginning to line his forehead.

"We wait."

"What the hell is going on?" Hicks asked, his head poked through the hatch from the lower deck.

"We're under attack by a Peoples' Republic of China frigate," Boxer told him.

"Son of a bitch! That could blow the whole mission."

"Hang in there, Mister Hicks," Boxer advised.

On the bulkhead over the attack computer, the long red second hand seemed to creep around from twenty-five to forty-five. The SO switched on the sonar pickup speaker and everyone in the boat heard the distant sound of the frigate closing on their position.

"Bring course to one-eight-zero degrees," Boxer ordered.

"One-eight-zero, aye," the helmsman acknowledged.

"Cat and mouse?"

"More like cat and canary. You do know what a two hundred pound canary says?"

"Sure. 'Here kitty, kitty, kitty!' "

"Right. I'm only waiting for us to be turned loose to say it."

"Would you really fire on a Peoples' Republic of China vessel." Hicks asked in disbelief.

"Hell yes I would. If it threatened my mission."

"Target changing course accordingly, Captain, to one-nine-five degrees. Revs increasing. Speed now two-eight knots."

"Attack heading for fucking certain," Harris observed.

"Sound General Quarters. ECM on," Boxer ordered. "Stand by forward torpedo tubes one and two."

A klaxon sounded stridently through the boat.

"One and two standing by," the chief torpedoman reported a moment later.

"Stand by to launch decoy drones from aft torpedo tubes five and six."

"Drones ready," reached the bridge a minute later.

"Fire three."

A red light winked green on the console above Boxer's head.

"Three fired, sir," Harris announced.

Boxer made a long count, hoping.

"Target is not responding to drone, sir," the SO informed his captain. "Bearing remains one-nine-five degrees."

"Rig for depth charge, rig for silent running."

"Message coming in from NAVCOM, Captain," the radio room reported.

"Read it."

"Acknowledgement of our transmission. Uh . . . here's the response. 'Cleared to act on captain's initiative. Good luck. Stark.' "

"Range, two-seven-five-zero yards and closing, Captain."

"Bring her up to launch depth. Have non-nuclear warheads armed in torpedoes and missiles. If we have to hit her, I want to make it good and clean."

"All systems armed," the CIC informed Boxer.

"Come to zero-one-seven degrees. Stand by to fire."

"Four ASW missiles fired from forward deck of target. Running hot and straight," the SO declared. "Nineteen . . . eighteen . . . seventeen . . . sixteen . . ."

"Fire one," Boxer ordered. "Fire two. Right full rudder. Come to flank speed. Sing out when MGS locks on target."

Two seconds passed . . . three . . .

"MGS on target!" called a young petty officer at the console.

"Fire! Left full rudder."

The sensitive "ears" of the *Shark* picked up the splash-in of the Chinese missiles. A digital readout showed, comfortingly, that they struck at the anticipated position and nowhere near the racing submarine. An instant later, the crew cheered the sound of *Shark*'s missiles leaving the water and roaring to life.

"Target is transmitting in the clear, sir," the radioman informed the bridge. "Just their recognition signal, so far."

"T-O-T for missiles four seconds," The CIC announced. "Three . . . two . . . one . . ."

A second later, the automatic damper cut down the sound as the missiles struck the frigate in a roaring blast. A second later the first torpedo hit below the water line. Then the second projectile ripped out the Chinaman's bottom. As the shock waved radiated out the crew of the *Shark* heard the crackling and creaking noises as the *Yu-Kwai Chwan* broke up and settled to watery oblivion.

"Oh . . . fuck," Harris gasped in awe. "That bastard never had a chance."

Screams of the frigate's survivors filled the hull of the *Shark*. "Cut the squawk box," Boxer ordered in a gruff voice. "Secure from General Quarters. Return to cruise speed. Assume one-seven-four degrees."

White-faced, Cowly looked up from the console before him. "Skipper, I could sure use a drink."

"Come down to my compartment. In fact, let's have a medicinal dose for all hands. Mr. Harris, you have the con."

20

"Close," Boxer said for them all as he passed out special three-quarter ounce shot glasses of whiskey.

"Too damned close," Bob Cowly agreed.

"Will there be, ah, repercussions?" James Hicks asked as he accepted his glass.

"I doubt it," Boxer gave his opinion as he lighted his pipe. "He didn't send more than his registry number. The Chinese don't have enough naval forces or search-type aircraft to comb an area this size. The *Yu-Kwai* didn't even get off a position report. Just another of those mysteries of the sea."

Boxer was talking too much and he knew the reason why. He had just sent two hundred men to their deaths. Call it expediency, say it had to be done for the safety of the mission. No matter what, there was no war and no enemy. Scratch two hundred Chinese . . . and he'd done it.

"Everything is on full alert, Captain," Harris reported from the bridge. "Even with the men secured from General Quarters, we are ready for anything."

"How the hell did that one slip up on us like that?"

"We're replaying tapes now to find that out."

"Keep on it." Boxer turned back to the men in his compartment. "Now. We will dive to three thousand feet for the last five hundred miles in to Torpy. From that point on, we will maintain silent running rules. No shoes, no dangling objects on belts, no keys or change in pockets. No noise. That goes for all personnel. Mister Cowly, see to it that the cooks prepare enough cold food to last through five meals. Landing parties will assemble thirty minutes before evacuation from the boat."

The others marveled at the captain's coolness, his ability to calmly return to the subject under discussion when the Chinese frigate had been discovered. In his heart, James Hicks stored away another item of interest about one Captain Jack Boxer. When the right time came, he intended to use what he had learned to eliminate Boxer from the team. Not during this mission, of course, but when he saw fit.

"Sue-Ann didn't attach any importance to it," Tracy said as she raised her head from the pillow. "In fact, she seemed not to realize that Boxer and Redfern were always away at the same time."

"And that's the case this time?" Julio Sanchez inquired in a low, purring tone. He adjusted the angle of light from the small lamp that shone on his elaborate round bed in the suite he rented at the Watergate. Beside the lace-trimmed shade, a silver ice bucket collected beads of moisture. Two empty champagne bottles lay on their sides on the plush carpet and partly-filled glasses stood beside the lamp.

Before Tracy went on, Julio leaned casually over the glass top of the nightstand. He inserted a small silver funnel in one nostril and casually snorted a line of coke. Then he changed sides and inhaled the second file of crystalline powder. A warm glow filled his belly and he felt his cock begin to harden.

"Yes. Redfern left his home the day before Jack disappeared from Norfolk. The day after that, the *Tecumseh* sailed." Her reporter's curiosity roused and she spoke vehemently. "Goddamnit! There's a story in there somewhere and I want it."

Tracy went on as Julio began to knead the bright red buttons of her nipples. "What I wonder is your reason for all this interest?"

"He wrecked my boat. Is there any need for a purpose beyond that?" He bent and kissed one rigid nub, his warm breath fanning out over the darker aerola.

"Bullshit, Julio! You had a stoned junky at the helm that night. The *Mary Ann* rammed Boxer's submarine. You know that as well as I do."

"But the board of inquiry found otherwise."

"And . . . I wonder . . . why. You don't have that much influence. Not in the military at least."

313

"My interest is strictly academic. I consider Boxer a hazard to navigation, much like a hidden shoal or a rock. I certainly would not like to find he was still, somehow, connected to the Navy."

Tracy tried to examine Julio's words, but her rising passion prevented a clear-headed scrutiny. She began to stir and writhe as Julio's pencil-thin mustache ticked her hard, flat belly and his lips worked down to nuzzle her navel.

"Oh, God, Julio. I never thought I could come six times in one night."

Sanchéz lifted a long electric vibrator from a dish on the nightstand. With his other hand he lubricated it with vaseline. "It's this little instrument that lights your inner fires, my *chica*." he told her as he inserted the penis-shaped object in her anus and switched on its motor.

"Aiyyy!" Tracy cried. "Deeper, Julio. Shove it up my ass! Oh, Christ! Fuck me, baby! Fuck me . . . fuck me . . . *fuck me!*"

"Keep talking dirty to me, *chica*. I like that. Ummm. *Mi corazon,* I am going to fuck you until you want to die." Julio rose in the luxurious bed and exposed his hardened manhood. A black leather supporter cupped his balls and circled the base of his short, thick penis.

Tracy spread wide her legs and pulled him to her. "Stab me with it! Hard." She reached with one hand to manipulate the vibrating dildo and used the other to guide his slippery organ toward her dripping cleft.

"Poke me with it, baby. Poke me!" she cried.

"Only if you promise to tell me more about Boxer."

"I will!" Tracy pledged. "I will, soon as I find out more myself. Now fuck me you Latino son of a bitch. Split me apart!"

"What amazing speed!" Viktor Korzenko exaulted as the *Sea Savage* sped through the waters of the Mediterranean. He glanced toward the Combat Director console, where Vassily Markov stood watching the green lines unfurl on the screen. Viktor was fully aware that Markov was KGB, and his role as Combat Control Officer only secondary. Political officers came with the job. He neither respected the secret policemen nor feared him.

"Another three hours and we will be in the Atlantic," Igor Borodine declared from his position behind the helmsman. "Not like the old days. We'll make a submariner out of you yet, Viktor Illyavich. How are you doing, Vassily?"

Markov gave a sheepish smile. "At least down here you don't get seasickness."

"Don't count on it. Depends on the weather. Also the moon and tides."

"I went into intelligence work because the water had no mercy on my stomach," the KGB man went on. "Now here I am at sea again."

"The last satellite photos showed the *Tecumseh* nearing Cape Horn. We are going to have to run down the Atlantic at a hellish pace to catch her," Borodine observed. "Where she is, there we will find the sub."

"What could she be going into the Pacific for?" Vassily asked.

Markov shrugged. "Who knows? More shakedown cruise, perhaps."

"There aren't any targets in that area for them," Borodine offered.

"No, of course not. I would be more worried if the mother ship had been located in the Caribbean. Cuba is vulnerable to certain sorts of attacks. A submarine of this type might be able to carry it off." Markov bit at the inner side of his lower lip. He was letting the atmosphere of a submarine relax him too much. He should not confide such things to persons outside the Committee for State Security. For all he knew, Korzenko could also be from the KGB. Might be there to observe *him*. Or Captain Borodine. He would have to watch his thoughts and words.

"Tonight we have baked sturgeon in cream sauce, spinach souffle and *res Konstantin*. Potato-leek soup first and a salad of chilled cucumbers. Nothing too good for the officers of the *More Dekar'*."

"I suppose we'll have baluga caviar before that," Vassily joked.

"If you want. With freezer chilled *Komiskaya* vodka to please you, Prince Vassily Illyavich."

Both men chuckled, but Markov remained darkly silent. He stored a mental note of their frivolity.

"We have a contact, Comrade Captain, bearing two-three-nine degrees," a boyish looking seaman at the sonar console interrupted.

Markov studied his own instruments a moment, then announced. "A Greek cruise ship, filled with decadent American tourists. To-night we must let it go. But mark me, comrades, the day will soon come when with this very boat, we will blow such bourgeois capitalist scum out of the water."

Borodine and Korzenko looked at the KGB man with guarded concern.

"Underwater radar reports the Nekor Ridge ahead five thousand yards, Captain," the duty talker told Boxer.

"Reduce speed to ahead one-third."

"Ahead one third, aye."

"Captain to the crew," Boxer whispered to the man next to him, who would pass it along according to silent running procedure. "We're there."

"Sonar reports heavy twin screws, bearing three-two-two degrees. Range, three-nine-five-zero yards."

That would have to be from the island's lagoon, Boxer thought to himself. He walked cat-footed over to the CIC display. "Get a profile on that first thing," he ordered.

Fifteen seconds later the cursor began to sketch out the shape of a large, low-decked vessel of faintly foreign design. As details filled in, Boxer's eyebrows rose. He wished for his pipe, but the circulation system had been shut down to minimum.

"A Ruskie oil tanker," Boxer observed. "And a big one."

"What's it doing here?" Mark Bander inquired.

"I don't know. Mark, get your commo boys listening to all the Ruskie frequencies. They'll have to be using some voice transmissions and in the clear. Have someone who speaks Russian monitor those."

"Yes, sir."

"Aircraft noises from the location of the tanker, Captain," the SO informed Boxer.

"What type?"

"Choppers. Anti-Submarine Ka-Twenty-five Kamovs from the sound," the operator declared.

The Ka-25 Hormone-A, Boxer recalled from his storehouse of military hardware. It was powered by two 900hp Glushenkov

GTD-3 free-turbine turboshaft engines, with co-axial twin rotors. Lots of lift. Armament consisted of two 400mm anti-submarine torpedoes, with nuclear and conventional depth charges as backup. Fortunately they carried too much electronic gear to allow for other arms. And what electronic snoops, Boxer thought.

Each Ka-25 had a chin radar, a towed MAD — Magnetic Anomaly Detector — bird, a dunking sonar normally housed in its own rear compartment and an electro-optical sensor. Something the size of that tanker could haul fifty or more of them and keep them in the air around the clock. Boxer turned back to the other officers on the bridge.

"Nasty surprises. Helmsman, come to course zero-nine-zero. We'll put about twenty miles between us and that island and look things over with the mini-subs. In fact, we ought to launch one of them now, let it get up close and look things over from the bottom. See to it, will you, Mr. Harris."

"Yes, sir."

"Now, I wonder what other unpleasant things Ivan has added since our last information?"

The gathered officers and enlisted men looked at their commander. None of them seemed anxious to find out the hard way.

"Time to send the other mini out," Boxer observed six hours later. "Cowly, you'll command. I want everything, including the brand of toilet paper those Ruskies use, so be careful, but take what chances you must. I'll talk to Harris the moment he returns."

Boxer called Hicks in when Bill Harris reported after docking the mini-sub in its bay. "The place is crawling with ASW choppers," Harris began. "They fly spiral courses out to about ten miles. Use maximum time in air, just a shade over three hours. They go in to refuel and new ones are launched before the previous flight gets within five miles of the tanker.

"That tanker is sitting a thousand yards off the entrance to the lagoon. There's lots of bright lights inland and plenty of activity. The shore patrols are active, but not too alert."

"Damn!" Boxer exploded. "That must mean the missiles were delivered ahead of schedule. I can understand the guards, they've been patroling that beach for a long time with nothing exciting to report. But this increased air surveillance is bad."

"More the better," Hicks chimed in. "With the nuclear missiles here, our volcanic 'accident' will be all the more believable. Any radioactivity monitored in the atmosphere will be attributed to the warheads going off under the strain of natural forces. But, what does this do to our landing schedule, Captain?"

"Fucks it up, in simple words. That tanker has to go. But the destruction must appear to be an accident. With those choppers in the air twenty-four hours a day, we can't hope to move in close enough or provide support to the landing force. We need . . . we need to get to them from underwater approaches. At night, to prevent visual contact. We can use a UDT team. They can ride on the outsides of the mini-subs. Ah . . . six men. You know how the Russians are about having underwater safety teams in operations at all times.

"Four men to plant explosives, two to act as safety. If any Ivans discover them, they'll have to make it look like a shark attack. Messy, but we've got the boys with balls enough to do it. All right. Let's get it in the planning stage right now. By twenty-one-thirty tomorrow night I want that team on the way."

21

"You have made exceptional time, Captain," Vassily Markov remarked formally to Igor Borodine as the two men sat in the wardroom of the Q-21. "We had no idea the *More Dekar'* could reach such speeds." His concession to the use of the submarine's name encouraged Borodine.

"Thank you, Vassily. Yes, three days from sighting the Canary Islands to Cape Horn is spectacular. At flank speed, the engine room turned out nearly forty knots an hour. The *Tecumseh* can't be more than few hours ahead of us."

"The latest flimsies show her position as having rounded Tierra del Fuego and nearing Isla Hoste," Viktor Korzenko added. "At our speed, we will be in surveillance range by tomorrow morning."

"I admire your conviction, Igor," Markov went on, softening his tone and address. "Yet, I can't help but wonder at its accuracy."

"Believe me, the *Tecumseh* is somehow connected with this super-sub."

Markov's earlier formality, Borodine reflected, had come from a heated argument that had arisen when he and Viktor wanted to hold the traditional seaman's ceremonies while crossing the equator. Markov had revealed his position as the boat's political officer at the time and vehemently opposed the ritual.

"It is revisionist, a custom devised by the bourgeois capitalist captains of the past to enslave their ignorant seamen with superstitions and the opiate of religion," Markov had proclaimed.

"You sound like a textbook from the Lenin Institute, Vassily," Borodine had countered. "It's all just fun, some relaxation for the crew and a few drinks. Naturally, we can't dunk anyone, not under three hundred fathoms of water. But the new men, those who have

319

never crossed the equator before expect it."

"Definitely not," Markov held fast. "I forbid it."

"What's wrong with it?" Viktor had demanded. "We observe the practice in the surface fleet. The naval service of every nation does."

"I did it with all my former crews," Borodine added

Markov's eyes had narrowed and his voice grew cold. "So far, this discussion has been in the province of my own authority. If you persist, it will be necessary to make a report of the incident to Moscow."

Only too aware of the possible results of that, Borodine let the matter lie. It had taken two days for Markov to thaw enough to make a compliment regarding their progress. More than anything, the successful operation of a submarine depended on harmony. Borodine sought that with his next suggestion.

"It will be another hour until the evening meal. A game of chess, Vassily?"

Markov raised a hand, palm out in a gesture of surrender. "You're far too good for me, Igor. A Masters' player at the least, are you not? Now, with Viktor I have some chance to win. Perhaps you would be so kind as to play us both after we eat?"

"At the same time?" Borodine inquired, the idea appealing to him.

"Why not?"

"You're on, Vassily. It might prove a hard task, but I think I might beat you both."

"I . . . ah, have some vodka in my compartment," the KGB man offered, his doctrinaire rigidity softening a bit more.

"The offer is accepted . . . with great pleasure," Borodine agreed as they rose.

"Met report, Comrade Captain," a yeoman in utility trousers and dingy gray undershirt announced as he stood at the entrance to the wardroom.

"Let me see it. Hummm." Borodine expelled as he studied the flimsy sheets. "Gale-force winds throughout the area of Tierra Del Fuego, heavy squalls in the straits and a possibility of snow. Be glad we're down here, gentlemen. We'll ride out the worst of it, though we do have to rise to four hundred meters to navigate around the Horn."

320

"What does that mean?"

Borodine gave Markov a warm, sympathetic smile. "That you will probably have a battle with your stomach, Vassily. The weather report calls for surface swells of ten to fourteen meters. Even at four hundred, that will set us to rolling a bit."

At this gloomy prediction, Vassily Markov felt a prophetic twinge deep in his bowels.

". . . so, according to the ops order drawn up by Major Redfern, you five men, under Norm Yellan's command, will hitch a ride on 'Alpha,' while the *Shark* is maneuvered into position off the west coast of the island. There the first raiding party will go ashore and Lieutenant De Vargas will depart with Dave Taylor's team, towed on a sled behind 'Beta' to the north end of Torpy." Boxer paused a moment and consulted the fragmentary notes he had made to supplement the operations order written by Tom Redfern.

"When you reach the objective, place the charges as indicated and set the timers for thirty minutes. Then head out to rendezvous with the *Shark*. Meanwhile, the assault force will be in the process of landing. Lieutenant De Vargas, with Dave Taylor's team will land on Yellow Beach. The other team, with Mr. Hicks along, will land on Red. There is one last minute change in the orders.

"Major Redfern will remain aboard, as will Lieutenant Harris. I will lead the main assault force."

"What!" Redfern exploded. "Hey, that's my job, Jack."

"Not this time, Tom. I'm not casting any doubt on your abilities, but look at it this way. We're going out there with an American-made nuclear device. At the bottom line, it is the captain who is responsible to see it is not captured and that it goes off as expected. This is our first operational mission. I intend to see that it works. If something happens, you and Bill can bring the *Shark* out of here. No discussion, the decision is made."

"All right, people," the diving chief petty officer announced. "Line up for the ejection port. 'Alpha' crew to the access bay."

So excellently designed, the mini-subs left little torque in the water as they moved. Norm Yellan looked over his shoulder and marveled at the speed and efficiency of the little undersea vehicle. His intense green eyes glowed behind the scuba mask and he clung with little difficulty to the diver's ring on the round hull. A dim glow in the water ahead indicated that the drop-off point would come soon.

Beyond that hazy illumination hovered the bulk of the Russian tanker. Imperceptibly, the mini-sub designated "Alpha," slowed. At negative bouyancy, it slowly came to rest. Yellan tapped once on the hull to signal the crew, then kicked off, his five man team following. Guided by the increasing brightness, they soon reached the tanker.

Immediately, two men dived lower, heavy bags of explosives dragging at their waists. Yellan pointed to Tim Hardesty to take the far end of the vessel as look out. He hoped the young diver remembered to keep well away from the slowly revolving screws. Yellan made a lazy turn in the water, to take in a 360° view, then signaled the other two UDT men to move in and attach their magnetic-based limpet mines to the hull in line with the engine room. All he had to do now was wait and keep alert.

Down under the keel, the two demolitions men worked as a team. One held a thin wafer of styrofoam in place while the other nudged on top of it a large canvas satchel that contained a forty pound shaped charge of RDX. It would be set off by a fuse cap detonator, connected to an M-2 waterproof fuse igniter by a sufficient coil of time blasting fuse to last for thirty minutes. The plan called for all explosives to be attached to the ship before the strikers were pulled and the fuse trains set to sputtering. At a burning rate of forty seconds per foot, that made a length of forty-five feet. The charges they would place forward and aft of the engineering space would use this method.

A new, experimental electronic time detonator would be placed in the explosives directly under the huge turbines. Even from the other side of the island, the sensitive listening gear of the *Shark* would pick up and record if all three went off. When the first such charge had been positioned, the UDT man holding it twisted a small knob and activated the electro-magnet.

Despite the weight, the clamping process made only a soft whump, inaudible inside the tanker. Quickly the diver unrolled the fuse and the pair moved on to the next installation. While they worked, the other team attached their burdens to the outer bulkhead, well below the water line. These consisted of standard limpet mines, with a wind-up mechanical timer. They swiftly strung four of them along the area of the engine room.

Yellin' Yellan thought they had it made when all four of his divers appeared close at hand, moving languidly to maintain position. All six men, experienced in underwater demolition methods, felt the familiar pulsations from the living body of the ship and the constant surge created by the slowly turning propellers that kept the tanker in a relatively stable position. Anchor chains, like ghostly vines, angled out sharply at bow and stern. Thumbs up signals indicated all charges in place and timers running. Yellan made another quick look around and suddenly found their number had increased by four.

Russian divers.

Instantly the enemy frogmen shot through the water toward them. Two bore long poles with pronged tips. Yellan recognized them as a particularly nasty Soviet development, CO_2 powered underwater guns that had a range of fifty yards and could stop any shark, short of a great white. He darted to one side and pulled a wickedly sharp, ten inch knife from a scabbard affixed to his diving belt. A swirl of movement to his right caught his attention.

One of the Russians had fired his deadly weapon and Brent Powers, an American scuba diver, bent double, both hands wrapped around the shaft that protruded from his belly. With a powerful stroke of his flippers, Yellan moved in on the essentially unarmed Russian.

With one big, hard hand, Yellan reached for the Soviet sailor's facemask, which he knew also contained radio communications equipment to the ship above. He jerked it free as his other arm swung upward in a vicious arc.

The tip of his knife bit through the foam material of the wetsuit and burned into flesh. With a powerful yank, Yellan forced it upward, thrusting in and out with the rough saw teeth on the top edge. It ripped the Soviet UDT man open with a ragged wound like the razor jaws of a shark might do. He thrashed feebly and a black cloud of blood formed around the twisting combatants. Yellan pulled free and turned to gauge the fight.

Another servant of the Soviet slave state clutched desperately at his throat while his mouthpiece and mask sank to the bottom of the sea. The air hoses had been cut and trailed behind the drifting objects like fat, black snakes. Bubbles came from his mouth, and likewise from between his fingers. Someone had done good work. The Ruskie's windpipe had been slashed open. A short distance away, Tim Hardesty grappled with another enemy.

Two more of his boys had ganged up on the remaining Marxist minion. One wrested the mask and its important radio off the Russian's face while Yellan watched. The other industriously poked holes in the victim's exposed back, ruining both kidneys. Yellan decided to "dress up" the drowning Commie frogman.

He dived into the trail of bubbles the sinking man made and used his multi-purpose knife to messily hack out a large hunk of thigh. Then he gritted his teeth and decapitated the Soviet sailor.

For a moment, the world swirled for Norm Yellan and his stomach lurched. He pulled his own mouthpiece free and vomited profusely. Sickened by the grim necessity that faced them, he purged his mouth of sour bile and replaced the rubber teeth block. Drifting in the distance, he spotted the last Russian, his abdomen opened and his entrails streaming out like bloated black ribbons. Quickly his men assembled.

"Dive down and retrieve Brent," Yellan hastily scribbled on his white slate. Two men hurried to obey.

The moment they returned, the surviving five men struck out for their meet with mini-sub Alpha.

Only occasional soft splashes sounded from the low-profile rubber boats that took Boxer and the men of Wild Bill White's team in toward the thin crescent of beach on the west side of the island. Only fifty yards separated them from the landing point. Beside Boxer, James Hicks sat tensely over the wooden box containing the nuclear device. In dark clothing, faces blackened, the assault force remained nearly invisible against the gently rolling sea. Another moment passed, movement silenced in the soft hiss of the surf, then the CIA man pointed.

A nod of Boxer's head served for confirmation. He, too, had seen a lone sentry standing under a malformed palm, a cigarette cupped in one hand as he took a short break. Boxer tapped the sharpshooter in the bow and indicated the target.

The former Special Forces light infantry weapons specialist eased the stock of an old fashioned '03 Springfield to his shoulder and sighted through his advanced laser night scope. He timed his trigger finger to the rise and pitch of the boat, then squeezed the last fraction of an inch.

Sharp recoil rocked the trooper backward. The twenty-inch suppressor attached to the Springfield's muzzle effectively silenced the detonation. The Russian soldier slammed against the tree and slid to a sitting position. The soft-tip, expanding .30-06 bullet had nearly blown his head from his shoulders.

"Fuck a bunch of two-twenty-threes," Wild Bill whispered in Boxer's ear. "I always did like the bigger bullets. Bastards stay down that way."

Seconds later they landed. Boxer oriented himself on the dark mass of the volcano cone and led the way, with Red Simms as point man. Beside the *Shark*'s commander, James Hicks churned through the sand and started up a low rise that would connect with the slope of the dormant cinder pile. Four men to his left sweated and wrestled with the heavy container and its deadly bomb.

Luck held for the critical invasion force. They reached the base of the volcano without encountering any more enemy soldiers.

"Now comes the easy part," Boxer muttered under his breath to Hicks, who showed the strain of their progress so far.

Alvaro De Vargas grinned to himself. In his mind he ran over the intricate finger positions on the twelve-string that would produce the haunting gypsy music that accompanied a ballad composed by de Angrola in 1579. Adrenalin pumped through his system, charging him. He had been given a simple, though dangerous task.

Go ashore on the rocky north tip of Torpy Island, neutralize the guard posts there and then move inland to meet and reinforce Wild Bill's team for the exfiltration. A piece of cake.

They had surfaced from the sled towed by Beta and made their way rapidly in to a point where the shallow-sloping bottom gave them footing. Now he nodded as his twenty-three man team spread out. He watched from low in the surf as they moved in on the unsuspecting sentries. Then, directly ahead, he saw an erect and surprisingly alert figure. A sergeant, no doubt, he thought to himself. He suddenly realized that Taylor had gone on with his men. No one had been detailed to deal with the new arrival. De Vargas eeled through the water and rose as the Russian NCO turned and strode along the beach to where he had seen a dark figure come from the sea.

"Ostonovt' yeh yevoh!" the Soviet sergeant started to yell as Alvaro De Vargas slipped a wire garotte over his head. The former SEAL snapped it tightly around the Russian's throat and gave the strand a twist as he bent his knees and doubled over, jerking the man from his feet.

The warning to stop the man cut off into a guttural gargle that ended as the sergeant struggled feebly. The thin wire cut through his skin and severed the jugular vein, then the heavy-set NCO's bulk forced it through his larynx and carotid arteries. Blood cascaded over his body and Alvaro felt the warm, sticky syrup soak into his black sweater. He released the body and took quick stock of his men.

"Not a man lost, Lieutenant," Dave Taylor reported thirty seconds later.

"Then let's head for that volcano," De Vargas commanded. His dark black eyes twinkled and he felt the familiar thrill start in him that combat always brought on.

"Bridge, this is the security officer," the speaker crackled to life on the squat bridge of the oil tanker *Boris Paskov.*

"This is the captain."

"Comrade Captain, the divers we sent over the side have not returned to the surface. Their air supply is running short."

"Have you sent other divers to see if they encountered damage?"

"We are doing so now, Comrade Captain. Only . . . there has been no report over the communications net."

"Nothing at all?"

"N-no, sir."

"Then why have you waited so long? Is it possible that our defenses have been penetrated by an enemy?"

"What enemy, Comrade Captain?"

"The Americans, you congenital idiot!" the burly former commander of a Suslov Class heavy cruiser snarled. "You are the security officer and you have to ask me that? Get cracking on this."

"*Da*, C-Comrade Captain."

Hastily, six divers went over the side from the low hatchway amidships at the waterline. They sank in a welter of bubbles and slowly oriented themselves to the green-black environment of the tropic sea. The team leader gave directions by hand and arm signals, spreading his men out. Two of them dived deeply, talking as they descended so that their superior and the security officer aboard the *Boris Paskov* could follow their actions.

"Nothing so far."

"Down there," an excited voice broke in. "I . . . I think I see a . . . a diving suit."

"Go deeper," the petty officer in charge demanded.

Two of the men had spread out in opposite directions, working their way lower with each sweep of the area they had been assigned.

"I find nothing here," one reported.

"Nor I," his partner agreed. "Wait a minute. Down by the stern . . . it's . . . it must have been sharks. Hit them the second they got in the water. Terrible! All torn up. It could have been . . . Andreas. Or Misha."

"Make your report coherent, damnit!" the petty officer barked.

"Wait!" another voice broke in. "This is for the security officer, direct. I am under the keel. There are some sort of . . . it looks like . . ."

Brightness flashed along the side of the *Boris Paskov* and from under her keel. The explosions created enormous pressure under water, ripping the vulnerable flesh of the divers, blasting them to shreds with compression.

Aboard the stricken vessel, the captain felt a violent lurch and then heard the ominous rumble of the massive sub-surface detonation.

Then the *Boris Paskov* began to break up.

22

Another thirty feet and they would reach the top. Boxer looked upward at their goal and then at the struggling quartet who lugged the bomb. Bill White had spread his team out on the uneven surface of the volcano cone. He detailed six men to wait at the base as a rear guard and to link up with Dave Taylor's force when they reached the rendezvous. Not much left to do. Boxer checked his wristwatch. They had fifteen minutes, give or take five. Would it be enough?

As though reading his thoughts, Hicks forced his way forward and spoke softly in Boxer's ear. "It shouldn't take more than five minutes to lower the bomb into place."

"Oh?" Boxer returned.

"We had the compute do a holographic model of the volcano's caldera based on radar soundings. Only a hundred feet to the basalt cap. Four men can lower the container easily while I handle the antenna cable. The sooner we finish, the better." Then Hicks confided, "I feel sort of . . . exposed."

"I know what you mean," Boxer agreed.

At the lip of the caldera, the party halted. Stout nylon lines were affixed to the four handles on the sides of the wooden crate. Hicks slid back a small panel and threw a series of toggle switches, some up, others down in a sequence known only to him and the designers of the device. A small red light glowed on the spherical surface of the bomb.

"It's armed," the CIA man announced.

Next he took from his rucksack a long, thin cable, with a threaded coupler at one end. This he screwed into a protruding fixture on the bomb. One final check and he turned to the men on the lines.

"It will be smoother and faster if we put two on each rope," he told them. Unseen, the nautical men among the team winced at his choice of terms.

"You four," Wild Bill ordered. "Lend a hand."

Once the troopers had taken their places, Hicks nodded his head. "Lower away."

"At least he got that one right," Bill White muttered under his breath.

Slowly the powerful bomb began its descent into the heart of the inactive volcano. Boxer wordlessly counted off the seconds. Beside him, Hicks paid out the antenna cable as the men lowered the crate hand over hand. At last the count reached five minutes. Still the lines fed out.

Another twenty seconds and the five cords went slack.

"Bottom," Hicks declared. "Throw what remains over the side." He used rocks to secure the antenna. "Now we can get out of here."

Off to the left, toward the north end of the island, a short, staccato burst of gunfire sounded. An instant later a geyser of water rose beside the oil tanker outside the cove and the team on the volcano heard the dull thuds of a series of explosions.

"There goes the ballgame," Boxer remarked.

An instant later, sirens went off at several points on the island. Whistles began to shrill and powerful batteries of lights flared to illuminate large portions of the bare ground.

Her keel cracked, holed in bottom and side, the *Boris Paskov* began to settle toward the bottom. Water hit the boilers and another explosion savaged the stricken ship. The deck canted and unsecured helicopters slid toward the rail. Men began to leap over the side, fearful of being taken down with the doomed vessel.

"Let's make it fast," Boxer told Wild Bill.

Descending the sloping cone took decidedly less time than the laborious climb upward. At the base of the small mountain, Wild Bill made a quick head count and signified that all were present. Immediately the team assumed a loose diamond formation and headed toward the beach. Boxer felt concern for the men in Dave Taylor's team. Their suppressed weapons, of course, could not have been heard from a half mile's distance. And there had been only one burst of fire from a Russian AK-SK. Could they have been trapped and captured without a fight?

A hundred yards along the volcanic rubble-strewn plain, dark figures materialized out of the sparse vegetation on their right. Instantly the men halted, weapons aimed toward the newcomers.

"Shark," a voice called in a soft whisper.

"Boxer," Wild Bill replied with the countersign.

Quickly the two teams mingled and started along the way. Ahead of them small shafts of light probed the beach and swung inland. Getting out wouldn't be so easy. Boxer worked his way toward Alvaro De Vargas.

"What was the shooting?"

"We ran into a pair of Ruskies with a dog patrol. One of them got off a burst before we finished them."

"Good thing it didn't happen sooner."

"You know it. What happened with the tanker?"

"She went down like a stone."

Out of the darkness ahead, a voice challenged. *"Kto tam eteny?"*

"Eto laytenant Kurbic," a Russian speaking trooper replied.

"Ogon'!" the challenger bellowed.

Tiny yellow blossoms flickered from several points and the thunder of gunfire rolled toward the exposed Americans.

"Must have been the wrong guy," Boxer said to no one as he brought up his Sidewinder and sped silent death toward their enemy.

To his right, a trooper went down, a trickle of blood accompanying a soft moan. Boxer turned in that direction and lit off a three-round burst. In the darkness a Russian soldier screamed and thrashed about in the underbrush.

"Keep moving! Keep moving!" Wild Bill White shouted over the tumult of battle.

A grenade crashed ahead, a U.S. made one from the sharp sound. More screams came out of the night. Dark shapes surged forward, six men running while the same number gave covering fire. Two hundred yards to the beach, Boxer figured. He stumbled over a corpse and sprawled face-first in the sharp-edged outfall from the volcano.

330

Blood trickled from a dozen cuts on Boxer's cheeks and forehead. His eyes stung from grains of volcanic sand. His ears rang from the constant detonation of grenades and bursts of fire from the Russian weapons. *Keep moving,* Wild Bill had said. From the best he could tell, they seemed to be surrounded now. How many out there?"

"This way!" a voice shouted in English.

"Vot on!" came in a gravelly Russian bellow. Then, *"Posmotret'yeh!"*

The cry to look out had done no good. Another hand grenade exploded and three Soviet soldiers died.

More fire came from the Russians.

"Oh, shit!" James Hicks yelled. "I'm hit."

Boxer turned back, only to see bits of clothing and a small spray of blood fly as Hicks took another stitching from a Soviet AK-SK. Dark forms moved in toward the wounded man and Boxer had to retreat. Before he left, he emptied his Sidewinder from the hip and two Ruskies folded with soft grunts, to hit head-first in the decomposing vegetation under the low trees. Head for the beach, his mind told him. While he ran, he changed magazines.

As he fired and worked his way forward, Boxer made a quick review of the events since the Russians had jumped them. No matter how he reconstructed it, it appeared as though Lt. De Vargas and fully half the members of Dave Taylor's team simply faded out into the darkness. Unfamiliar with land warfare tactics, Boxer could only wonder if they panicked and ran away. A few seconds later, as the Russians menaced the remaining Americans, Boxer found the answer.

A furious volley opened up from the right flank, sweeping across the upright Soviet troops, who sensing victory had abandoned their concealment and raced toward the trapped invaders. Now they died by the score.

Russian bodies spun, leaped and flopped on the ground while the dying shrieked, groaned or left the earth in silence.

"Kill! Kill! Kill!" De Vargas bellowed as his small force pushed forward. Then, in screeching Spanish . . . *"Matalo!"*

In thirty seconds the fight ended. An eerie silence clung to the stunted tropical growth that ringed the clearing where the Americans had been surprised. The stench of blood and death mingled with the sharp, pungent odor of burnt powder and TNT.

"Form 'em up, Gunny," Boxer heard De Vargas order.

"*Semper Fi,* Lieutenant," Wild Bill returned. "You SEALS are all right."

Seven men, besides James Hicks, had been wounded. Miraculously, only two Americans had died. Thanks to the training Redfern put them through, Boxer thought. They had responded with a ferocity unexpected or ever experienced by the Russians. Boxer went to where the medic, Sherman Ross, had propped Hicks against a squat palm.

"Is he able to travel?" the *Shark's* commander inquired.

"He'll have to be carried. Took some bad hits, Captain." Ross' usually boyish features had become gray and drawn. He looked bad enough to have been one of the wounded himself.

"Plug up the holes and drag him along," Boxer ordered.

"You're all heart, Boxer," Jim Hicks managed to gasp out. "Leave me behind with the other corpses."

"Who'll set off our little firecracker?"

"I'll give you the numbers."

"No. You're coming along. If you start to die for real, then you can tell me. Get some bearers over here."

"That firefight is going to attract some attention," De Vargas stated the obvious.

"All the more reason to haul out of here," Boxer declared.

As they neared the beach, more Russian soldiers appeared.

The suppressed weapons held all the advantage. Only three Soviets triggered their assault rifles before all seven lay dead on the sand.

"Wounded into the boats first," Boxer ordered.

"You, too, Captain," De Vargas urged.

"I'll take the last one."

"No, sir. You're too important. If Hicks buys it on the way out, only you have the authority to set off that bomb."

Boxer relented and climbed aboard the second rubber craft. Most of the weapons had to be abandoned, tossed into the sea, to make room. Even then, fifteen men had to cling to the sides. That made the paddlers' job doubly difficult as they labored to drive the boats through the choppy water and avoid striking their bud-

332

dies. Behind them, the Russian troops turned the island into a bedlam.

Tracer rounds streaked green through the sky. Mortars fired on suspected invaders, only to kill their comrades in fiery, shrapnel-laden blossoms of death. The sirens continued to wail, diminishing in volume as the escaping Americans put distance between them and the doomed atoll. Ahead, a low, dark shape rose from the sea.

Quite on his own initiative, Harris had ordered the *Shark* to surface, its sail retracted to present less of a silhouette. The overburdened landing boats steered in that direction, while hope grew larger in the breasts of all of the men.

"Good thinking, Bill," Boxer told his executive officer as he climbed aboard.

"I figured there might be some shooting, so I had to allow for casualties."

"Thanks, Bill. Get someone to give a hand with Hicks. He's shot up pretty badly. Maybe Link can do something for him."

Down on the bridge deck, Boxer gladly returned to his role as sub commander. "Take her down. Twenty degrees on the bow. Ahead one half. Blow all ballasts."

The klaxon sounded and a harsh voice, made rougher by relief, blared over the speaker system. "Dive! Dive! Dive!"

"N'yehvozmozhno!" General Vladamir Menchakov shouted, his florid face darkening to near purple as he pounded a fat fist on his desk.

"It is not impossible, Comrade General. Someone has sunk the *Boris Paskov* with underwater explosives," Colonel Arkady Glovnoski answered shakily.

"Sound all alarms. Alert all troops."

"It has already been done. There have also been reports of firing from the other side of the island. Also in the north."

"Get more patrols out at once. It has to be the Americans. If they blew up that ship it was to enable them to land on the island. Send two hundred men to the missile stands. Make it a wide perimeter. All lights to be turned on. Whatever you do, Comrade Colonel, get me some Americans, dead or alive, for proof. And

333

. . . get me a direct line, voice communication, with Moscow."

"It is being done, Comrade General. And I have ordered a loading area cleared to land the Kamovs caught off the ship when it sank."

"Get them refueled and send them out. There has to be a submarine out there somewhere. Sink it!"

"Yes. Comrade General."

Within half an hour, the two dead Americans had been brought to the low headquarters building. Menchakov left his office to view them. They were definitely not Chinese. Their hair styles, clothing, features . . . all pointed to the Americans. He would act on that assumption in any case. Grimly he returned to his office to place his call to Moscow. As he did, more reports came in.

A soft rap sounded on the door of the West Wing bedroom. A bedside lamp came on as the door opened.

A Secret Service man stood in the opening. Behind him, pressing forward, came the duty deputy from the State Department.

"Sorry to disturb you, Mr. President. It's the Soviet premier on the hotline."

The president sat up and his thin lips formed a tight smile. "By God, they did it!"

"I'm afraid so, sir. At least part of the job. The premier is pretty mad. Yelling about violation of sovereign Soviet territory, acts of international piracy, all that sort of thing."

"Give me two minutes and I'll talk with him from the Oval Office."

"He's such a dislikable man," the president's wife remarked as her husband shrugged into a dark maroon silk lounging coat and matching slippers.

"It is all part of the job, my dear." He glanced at his wristwatch. Ten of five in the morning. "I'll handle it quickly and we can still get a few hours sleep."

In the Oval Office, with representatives of State, Defense and the Pentagon at hand, the president lifted the handset of his red telephone. As he did, a quick glance at the clock on his desk gave him the time. Five a.m. That would make it afternoon of another day in Moscow.

"Dobree d'yen, Mister Premier," he began. "This is the president."

"Don't give me that 'good afternoon' stuff," the premier's voice growled, his anger so great he neglected the fiction of not speaking English. "You have gone too far this time."

"I'm not certain I know what you are talking about."

"I'm sure you do. This is an international incident of such great proportions that it can lead to war."

"Please, Mr. Premier. Can you at least be more explicit?"

"Your act doesn't fool me. You landed troops on Tropy Island."

"Where is Tropy Island?"

"Come, Mr. President, this could not have happened without your knowledge and consent. A legitimate Soviet scientific research base in the Pacific has been attacked by American forces."

"I have ranking representatives of the Departments of State and Defense here with me, along with senior officers of all services who have come over from the Pentagon. I categorically deny that the government of the United States has had anything to do with this incident. Likewise I have been assured that no active members of the armed forces could have been involved. What possible proof can your offer to refute that?"

"The of . . . er, the scientist in charge has assured me that some of the invaders have been killed and positively identified as American military personnel."

"Is that so? Who made the identification?"

"General Menchakov himself."

"I didn't know that old fire-breather had turned to the work of science," the president said mildly.

"That doesn't matter. Have your Secretary of State ready to receive my ambassador at eight in the morning, Washington time. The ambassador will be bearing an official note of protest. If any further acts of hostility are initiated by your country against mine, I will consider it to be warlike in nature. This unwarranted violation of international law will go before the Security Council at the United Nations first thing. That is all."

"I haven't had any opportunity to inquire or to make answer, Mr. Premier. At least allow me that time."

"The situation is critical. I warn you, we will not tolerate further interference. Good-by."

"He's hotter than a bear with a beaver biting his balls," the president told the other men in the room, after he hung up. "How soon now before she blows?"

"Any time now," Admiral Stark informed the president.

"It might be wise to prepare for a preemptive nuclear strike by the Soviets," the president said grimly, regretting for the moment that he had ordered the use of the *Shark* at all.

"You don't think . . .?" the Secretary of State blurted out.

"No. All initial Soviet protests are essentially a bag of wind. This time, though, they don't know all the hole cards. I don't want to be caught sitting here thinking about it if they do decide to retaliate after that bomb goes off."

"They are aware of our displeasure," the premier informed the gathered members of the Politburo. "Notify General Vorshov and the Defense Ministry that I want every available ship, submarine and aircraft to head into the vicinity of Torpy Island immediately."

"The Presidium is ready to vote for war, Comrade Premier," one of the members declared.

"That . . . can come later. If at all necessary. The fact is we have no definite proof that Americans are involved. That is why we must locate their means of arrival. A submarine, it must be. We have to force it to the surface, or damage it enough to capture it. Then we can see. In the meanwhile, let us be like the players of the American game poker. We will bluff for all we can get."

"Signal from Moscow Central, Comrade Markov," the junior officer of the Q-21 informed the KGB operative. "And here are orders for you, Captain, direct from Fleet Admiral Gorshkov."

Both men looked up from the wardroom table and reached for the communications. Markov read his hurriedly and a cynical smile touched his lips.

"We're in for an exciting voyage, Igor. I'm supposed to capture the crew of an unidentified American submarine. Alive, of

336

course. And to interrogate them."

"And I am to break off surveillance of the *Tecumseh*, rendezvous with a hunter-killer pack off the island of Torpy and locate that same unidentified submarine. Isn't it interesting that the *Tecumseh* is headed in the general direction of Torpy? What is so important about a volcanic atoll?"

"I haven't the slightest idea," Markov lied.

"One thing certain." Igor Borodine said with absolute certainty. "With this boat there isn't anything I can't track down and destroy."

23

James Hicks had turned gray. His face felt icy to the touch and the sucking wounds from the 5.56mm Russian bullets had only partly been closed. Master Sergeant Michael Link worked with all the skill his training at the Special Forces medical school had given him. Hicks' pulse dropped even as Link finished cleaning and started to suture another hole.

"Not good," the senior medic said over his shoulder to Boxer, who stood in the background.

"How much more do you have to work on?"

"The thigh wound. It was the least critical. He's going to go through a lot more blood than we have. We'll need live donors."

"I'll get on that."

Boxer left the small sick bay and removed his surgical mask. He started toward the nearest MC terminal to send his announcement through the boat. As he reached for it, a voice came from the metal speaker.

"Captain, this is the bridge. There's more electronic activity from the island and the ASW choppers are ranging out to forty miles."

"Keep her on the bottom for a while, Mr. Harris. At sixty miles away, we're safe enough."

After Boxer's announcement, five men showed up to volunteer their blood for James Hicks. "He had balls enough to handle that nuclear bomb," one of them explained.

Forty minutes dragged slowly past as Boxer worried about the safety of his command. At last Link tied the final knot and the operation concluded.

"He'll be out of it for at least two hours."

"We don't have that much time. I'll be on the bridge," Boxer told the medic.

Once in the con, Boxer ordered the *Shark* to fifty feet. He thought of the pain on James Hicks' face, his gasping, feathery voice as he insisted on giving Boxer the frequency and sequence of letters and numbers to be transmitted to detonate the bomb.

"I . . . trust you, Boxer. You can do it. You've got to. I . . . you saved my ass from the Reds. Now go up there and blow the . . . b-bastards to hell."

Link had waved the captain away then and in his inactivity Boxer set to brooding. His entire future depended on what he did. More so, perhaps the entire future of the human race. Hicks had put it right though. It was his duty. That was something he had never failed at.

Even now, though, as the *Shark* rose through the murky depths, he continued to think about it. Never in his career had Boxer fired or exploded a nuclear device. The enormity of doing so now weighed on him. He pulled the pipe John had given him from his pocket and sucked on it noisily. One bitterly cold fact faced him. He could not afford to delay any longer.

"Five-zero feet, Captain," the DO sang out.

"Hold steady at five-zero, same course and speed. Rig to crash dive." Boxer keyed the command microphone. "Captain to radio room."

"Radio room, aye."

"Raise the antenna, Sparks."

"Antenna going up, sir."

When the indicator light above his head winked green, Boxer took another deep breath. "Sparks, tune to one-one-seven-three megacycles. Transmit the following in the clear."

"Aye, aye, sir. One-one-seven-three megacycles."

"Quebeck-Delta-Bravo . . . One-nine . . . seven-zero . . . five-five . . . Hotel-Mike. . ." Boxer took a deep breath, his mind aflame at the incredible deed he had been chosen by fate to perform. "Six . . . three . . . eight."

The radioman repeated the series, ending with, "Message sent, sir."

"Thank you, Sparks. Crash dive!"

The klaxon hooted and the deck of the *Shark* canted radically.

Three hundred feet came on them swiftly.

"Leveling off at three-zero-zero feet, Captain."

"Very well. Hold her steady for ten minutes."

Time eked out on the digital readouts and the old reliable sweep-hand electric clock on the bridge. When the ten minutes had spent themselves into eternity, Boxer wiped his brow and prepared for the worst part.

"Stand by to surface. Blow main ballast. Blow forward and aft."

Swiftly the *Shark* rose in the water.

"Photographic party to the conning tower," Boxer ordered. "Raise the sail, Mr. Harris."

Boxer preceded the other crewmen to the small enclosed bridge on the sail. To the north, the night still glowed an ominous, sickly orange, tinged with long tongues of white and blue. Night had become day and the sensitive film of the photographers recorded the scene out of Dante with painful accuracy.

A thick mushroom cloud rose, boiling in flaming fury, above the spot where Torpy Island used to be. Nothing within ten miles of that blast could have survived. An immutable fact that nagged at Boxer's conscience as he gazed in awe at the fearsome power unleashed by man. By him.

"Oh . . . my . . . God," Bob Cowly gasped as he stood at Boxer's side and gaped at the awesome inferno.

"Not like on film, is it?" Boxer managed through a tight throat.

Hell continued to hold court on earth for another hour.

24

Admiral Gorshkov stood beside General Vorshov in the presence of the premier and the Council of Five of the Central Committee. The lavishly decorated office, deep within the Kremlin's walls, held a fortune in Czarist art treasures. It was, Gorshkov knew well, the premier's favorite office for use when he wanted the full weight of his position to be felt. Both men were pale and shaken. The premier had just asked a question, which neither of them wanted to answer, and now he repeated himself.

"What do you mean there is no evidence any more?"

"Ah . . . Comrade Premier," General Vorshov stumbled out. "We were receiving direct voice communication from the island until, ah. . ." He checked the large Regency clock on the ornate gold mantel. "Twelve-twenty-five this afternoon. That is, until ten minutes ago. General Menchakov was most meticulous. He even transmitted the results of the autopsy. Unfortunately, that alone is insufficient to prove, uh, anything. The two dead invaders wore a mixture of foreign-made clothing, sold anywhere in the world. Nothing to indicate American origin. Their weapons, the civilian model of the U.S. Army M-Eighty-eight submachine gun, are on sale at numerous places in the West. All of these factors, together with the autopsy report and their physical remains . . ."

"Get to the point, Comrade General," the premier demanded acidly.

"It is all useless now, because there is every good chance the island, *and everything on it,* is no longer there," Admiral Gorshkov stepped into the breach.

Stunned, the premier held in check a sharp retort, then asked

341

in a quiet, shaken voice, "Explain that, please."

"Suddenly, in mid-sentence," Vorskov rushed on, "the transmission stopped. There was a loud sound and enormous static. Then . . . nothing. The static continues."

"What could have caused that?"

"I suspect a nuclear device of some sort," the general stated firmly.

"One of the missiles, no doubt," Admiral Gorshkov hastened to clarify. "Within minutes following the break in communications, we began to receive reports from our seismographs, indicating an undersea quake in the vicinity of Torpy Island. It measured nine-point-two on the Richter scale. The island is little more than the outflow from a now-dormant volcano. If the quake set off the volcano, its eruption could easily account for the static. Tons of molten ferrous material, thrown into the atmosphere in the blast would account for that alone. If one or more of the missiles were detonated as a result of the natural disaster, the radiation would insure that. Worse . . ." Gorshkov hesitated.

"I understand. If our missiles blew, there went the island, too. Yes. It could have happened that way. Entirely plausible. Only, don't you gentlemen think that it is remarkably coincidental to the sinking of the *Boris Paskov* and an invasion by unidentified foreign soldiers?"

"Naturally, Comrade Premier," Vorskov blurted. "Only . . . now we have no way of proving it."

"The invasion force had to get there somehow. There was no radar contact with any aircraft, according to your earlier report. That leaves a submarine. It is absolutely vital that this sub be located and forced to the surface. It, or sufficient wreckage to prove that it was American. I must go before the Presidium in one hour. *If* we have proof, I am certain they will vote to go to war. It is up to you to get it, Comrade Admiral of the Fleet. See to it at once."

"Yes, Comrade Premier."

James Hicks opened his eyes to a fuzzy pink balloon, floating in some sort of limbo above him. He blinked and tried to rub his eyes, only to feel his arms restrained. He felt thick-headed and furry-tongued, the most horrendous hangover of his memory. Or . . . was this death?

"Are you an angel?" he croaked.

"Do I look like it?" Boxer growled goodnaturedly.

"Christ. Boxer? Is . . . am . . . I . . .?"

"You're all in one piece and aboard the *Shark*. You took some good hits there."

"I ache like hell, but I can't seem to feel anything below the neck."

"You're lucky. But that won't last. At least that's what Link tells me."

"How long since . . . ? You *did* set it off, didn't you?"

"Yes. Five hours ago. Torpy Island is no more. It's just a thousand foot hole in the ocean bottom. My guess is that the nuke missiles the Russians had in place went by sympathetic detonation. Our monitoring equipment indicates the water is over a hundred rads out as far as twenty miles."

"God! Uh . . . I . . . I owe you, Boxer. You . . . well, without you . . . I suppose I'd be a lot of basic, very radioactive elements right now. I . . . I told you thanks, didn't I? Uh . . . well, I meant it and I want to say it again. You . . . uh . . . saved my life out there. I . . ."

"Hell, Mike Link did the doctoring. All I did was see your carcass got hauled aboard. I didn't even row the boat."

Hicks tried to force a grin. "You're not going to get out of it that easily. I . . . *really* owe you."

"Captain, this is the bridge," the MC speaker interrupted.

"Captain here," Boxer spoke crisply when he keyed the device.

"Sir, sonar has contact with two targets, range five thousand yards. They are converging on our area."

"I'll be right up. Sound General Quarters. All ECM on, prepare to launch decoy drones."

"Aye, aye, Captain."

"The shit has hit the fan."

"You're a master of understatement, Hicks," Boxer replied.

On the bridge, Boxer made a quick up-date on the condition of the targets, determined their courses and mentally projected their intercept point. "Right full rudder," he ordered. "Come to course zero-five-zero. Take her down to two-zero-zero-zero feet."

The seconds ground on his nerves. He watched the green worms that represented the approaching targets inch across the GDT. At three thousand five hundred yards, the CIC spoke to him quietly.

"We have a profile on the targets, skipper. Two Zee Class Soviet hunter-killer subs. Bearing on the first is two-seven-zero degrees, course zero-one-zero. Second target is at zero-nine-five degrees, course two-seven-zero. They are at seven hundred feet, speed three-zero knots."

"Okay. Let's see how 'smart' they are. Set depth on two drones for one-two-zero-zero feet. Stand by to fire from aft tube seven and forward tube one."

"Aye-aye, Cap'n," the chief torpedoman sang out.

On the GDT, the glowing points progressed as before. "Tubes one and seven ready, sir," came from the squawk box.

"Open outer doors."

"Outer doors opened, sir."

"Open inner doors."

"Opened, sir."

"Stand by to fire."

"Standing by to fire."

"Ready on one . . . Fire one."

A hiss of compressed gas, barely audible through the thick insulation of the *Shark*'s triple hull, launched the first decoy drone.

"Engine running hot and smooth," sonar reported.

"Heater element operative," the IRS operator announced.

"Drone radio transmitting, sir," the radio room reported.

"Get the UWIS on," Boxer ordered.

Thirty seconds went by. "Got her on screen," came the report.

Boxer peered intently at the Underwater Image Screen. There it was. The sixteen foot drone that would show the same mass and infrared image to the Soviet hunter-killers as the *Shark* herself. It sped away from the sub's bow, at a ninety degree angle to the approach of one Russian submarine.

"Left full rudder, come to course zero-zero-five."

"Zero-zero-five, aye," the helmsman echoed.

When the compass and red LED readout agreed that the

Shark's nose pointed at five degrees east of due north, Boxer nodded with satisfaction.

"Stand by to fire seven."

"Seven ready," the after torpedoman fired back.

"Ready on seven . . . Fire seven."

The new drone showed up quicker. Again the monotone voices went through the start-up drill for the decoy.

"Right full rudder. Come to course zero-nine-zero."

Due east the *Shark* raced now at thirty-five knots.

"Sonar indicates torpedo fired from target number one at one second ago," the SO informed Boxer. "Running hot, straight and normal."

"Underwater radar reporting, skipper. Target's torpedo will intercept drone number one in sixteen seconds."

"Fine tune the UWIS on that drone," Boxer ordered.

As the countdown sped to zero, the command crew watched the screen. The torpedo became visible at the count of seven. It swelled to the same proportions as the drone by the count of three. Inexorably the two courses verged, became one in a bright flash.

"Conventional warhead, sir," the radiation station monitor declared. "No noticable increase in radiation."

"Good. They don't want to disintegrate us. Come to flank speed. Right full rudder to course one-seven-zero."

"Another target, sir. At extreme range," the SO called out. "Bearing one-six-zero. Course three-four-zero. Speed, three-seven knots." A long pause followed.

Boxer began to sweat. Three hunter-killers this close? The Russians must have called in all the dogs. They would panic over the loss of Torpy, all right. But how did they get here so fast?

"She's a big one, sir. Computer doesn't have any profile to match. A Q Class comes closest, only this thing is as much bigger than the usual Q-Boat as we are compared to the Trident."

"Damn!" Boxer swore aloud. "The Ruskies must have learned or guessed enough about *Shark* to make their own version. Fast building."

"Too damned fast," Bill Harris offered. "The must have had the same idea and only been a bit slower in completing the project. From its bearing and course, I would guess it came from the

Atlantic."

"Probably built in those underground pens at Riga," Boxer surmised. "Must have been on its shakedown cruise."

"That could explain it. Do you think it would be fully armed then?" Harris inquired.

"It's Russian, isn't it?"

"Any word from the *Shark?*" the president asked. He sa[t] tensely at his desk in the Oval Office, still wearing his lounging coat and slippers. "It's been nearly six hours since the monitoring stations recorded the nuclear blast."

"No, sir," Admiral Richard Stark replied.

The president sipped coffee from a Wedgewood china cup. I[t] had grown cold and tasted like dilute battery acid. "Where are they? Where is the *Tecumseh?*"

"We won't hear from the *Shark* until Captain Boxer determines it is safe to broadcast. The *Tecumseh* is approximately three hundred miles west of the coast of Chile, seven hours from the rendezvous point. Boxer will signal soon now, I'm sure."

An aide entered the room with a sheaf of papers he handed to Admiral Stark. The Chief of Naval Operations studied the computer-enhanced photographs with a growing scowl. He read the short text on the print-out and handed them to the president.

"Mr. President, our surveillance satellite have picked up three high speed surface vessels headed toward the area where the *Shark* must be. A Gorky Class heavy missile cruiser and two Petrov Class destroyers. The second set of photos shows deep penetration shots of underwater images. The first, the largest, has to be the *Shark*. It's the rest that worries me. Three Soviet subs. Two are the typical Z-Class hunter-killers. The third is of unknown type."

"What's the bottom line on that?"

"It means, sir, that if they can find the *Shark,* Boxer is in a lot of trouble. We might even lose the vessel."

"Nothing can be left for the Russians to find and analyse. You understand that?"

"Yes, sir. Boxer is unaware of it, but the reactors are rigged to reach critical mass in the event of serious damage to the two outer

346

hulls. I didn't used to be possible, but the engineers devised a method to use on *Shark* to prevent any possibility of identification in the event the crew was forced to abandon ship. Activating the escape system triggers the buildup."

"And then?"

"Boom. No more *Shark*."

"We have a satellite patch to Moscow, Comrade Captain," the radio room informed Igor Borodine.

"Good. I will take the call in my compartment."

"This is Gorshkov," the amazingly static-free signal informed Borodine when he settled in the privacy of his cabin, the hatch tightly dogged closed.

The captain first class knew the scrambler equipment would be in use and this was the secure line. "Captain First Class Borodine here, Comrade *Admiral Flota*. Go ahead."

"Captains Ivan Sobel and Ludor Parovik are patched in, too. I want them to hear this and offer their observations and suggestions. As of this moment, Captain First Class Igor Borodine is in complete charge of the chase and capture of the American submarine in the vicinity of Torpy Island. Your mission is to capture the craft itself, with crew intact, or parts of the vessel and bodies or survivors of its destruction."

"That may not be possible, Comrade Admiral," Borodine countered.

"You must make it so. Without that sub, we have no proof against the Americans. Since our last communication, Torpy Island has ceased to exist."

"How?" Borodine's keen mind did not waste time on expressions of surprise or doubts of such a statement.

"We don't know for certain. Either the Americans did it with a nuclear device of some sort or the missiles there went off as the result of an earthquake and volcanic eruption. In any case, the Presidium has voted for a preemptive nuclear strike against the United States. But . . . paranoid as they are, they have demanded absolute proof in some form of American involvement before they authorize the launching of missiles. That means, of course, the premier demands it, since he can authorize the attack with or without the consent of the Presidium."

"Then . . . we're going to war?"

"It looks that way. At least if you can give me that submarine."

"I shall do all I can. We are likely to lose a lot of men and ships, Comrade Admiral."

"Why is that?"

"My analysis of what has happened so far indicates this to be the mysterious super-sub that sank the Z-Fifteen. If that is the case, their capabilities, ah, far outstrip anything we can bring against them. Even with what we have aboard the Q-Twenty one."

"Go after him anyway, Igor Alexandriavich. I need some live sailors, bodies, wreckage . . . anything. Get it for me."

"I will, sir."

25

"High speed surface vessels approaching at five miles range, sir. Bearing, two-five-zero degrees. Course, two-zero-zero degrees."

"They're going to pass astern," Harris remarked.

"Too far away to make positive identification," Boxer observed. "But I get the feeling the Russians are trying to sew us into a sack."

"A . . . sack, sir?"

"Yes, Mister Cowly. An old naval expression that goes back to the days of wooden ships and iron men," Boxer explained. "After a battle in those days, the sailmaker would sew the KIAs into sacks made of sailcloth, weighted down with two roundshot between their legs and they'd be dumped over the side for burial at sea."

"Sort of a grim picture, skipper," Cowly opened."

"That it is."

"Sir, sonar reports surface targets changing course to zero-nine-zero."

"That'll bring 'em in closer. They must be taking orders from one of the subs. It would be nice to know who it is calling signals for the other side."

"Any ideas, Captain?"

"Nothing positive. The Ruskies had a hot-shot sub commander named Borodine. Admiral Kaiser's people made some inquiries at my request and developed that it *was* Borodine's sub we sank in the Arctic. The Soviets are bound to send their very best. If it wasn't for that, I'd suspect that unknown Q-Class out there was commanded by Borodine."

"Any chance he could have survived, sir?" Cowly inquired.

"Think about it, Bob. A man has how long? . . . Thirty, forty-five seconds to survive in Arctic waters. The GDT showed us a picture of the sail being blown off that Z-Boat and turning over. A lot of air escaped in the form of a bubble. It could be that several of the crew were blown free of the wreckage. But the chances of them surviving once they got to the surface are pretty slim."

"Captain, surface targets closing to two miles. Disturbance pattern on the screw revs indicate one Gorkey Class missile cruiser and two Petrov Class destroyers. Speed, twenty-two knots. Course remains zero-nine-zero."

"Gentlemen, it looks like we are going to have to shoot our way out. Bill, take the con. Ready nuclear torpedoes, all tubes, and conventional warhead surface to surface missiles."

"Aye, aye, Captain."

"I'm going to grab something to eat. The next few hours are bound to be busy."

"Voice radio for you, Comrade Captain. On the underwater net."

"Thank you, Signalman." Igor Borodine lifted the telephone type handset and spoke into the mouthpiece. "Borodine here."

"Ivan Sobel, Comrade Captain. My detection equipment has been tracking a remarkably 'empty' bit of ocean. It is about four thousand meters from my present location. Have you noticed it?"

"I'll ask Battle Information. Hold, will you?"

"*Da.*"

Borodine quickly got his answer. Infrared, sonar and magnito-meters all failed to penetrate a dense water layer at a bearing of 350 degrees, relative. The depth indicated lay at nearly 1500 meters. Range, 3,200 meters. Not all that strange, considering the volcanic upheaval, seaquake and detonation of one or more nuclear devices. Inversion layers were common enough without natural disasters and frequently baffled electronic instruments. He lifted the handset again.

"We have it, too. What is your bearing?"

"Zero-zero, relative, Comrade."

"Hummm," Borodine mulled out loud. "I want to contact Parovik. I'll get back to you." Borodine punched out the call signal for other Z-Class hunter-killer and asked for the captain.

"Ludor, this is Borodine. Do your detectors indicate an inversion layer at . . . ah, about three-zero-zero degrees? It would be below you by about a thousand meters."

"Let me check." Parovik came back on the radio after only a brief delay. "*Nechevo*, Igor. Nothing at all. We are getting a readin gof the bottom at only one thousand meters."

"That's odd. I'll get Sobel back on and we can discuss this."

In less than a second, all three Russian captains had been linked by radio. Borodine began with an unexpected question.

"In your remarks to the Comrade Admiral of the Fleet, Ivan, you mentioned firing at what you believed to be the American submarine. You said you definitely hit it but heard no sounds of breaking up. So, what did you hit?"

"I am prepared to state that it was a decoy drone torpedo, Comrade Captain."

Borodine made his voice light. "No need for all that formality, Ivan. We have all made that mistake before. Over the years we have fired how many torpedoes? If the Americans weren't so clever in the design of their decoys, by now they wouldn't have any submarines. What I am wondering is, where did this drone seem to come from? What was its bearing and course?"

Sobel pondered a moment, then asked over the internal communicator for the readout on the tracking recorder. When the figures displayed on his small screen he emitted a tight whistle.

"It must have come from that inversion layer."

"That, gentlemen, is where the American is hiding. It is either a real inversion, which the enemy captain is taking advantage of, or one electronically created. I experienced something much like that on the Z-Fifteen. At the time, and after, I credited it to the strange conditions in the Arctic. Now, I wonder. I want a report every five minutes, for the next twenty minutes, on the relative position of that inversion layer. Also an indication of its relationship to current and surrounding water. That's all."

Like a involved chess maneuver, Igor Borodine thought to himself while the other subs made reports he compared with his own. After the twenty minutes he beamed in satisfaction and summoned the other captains on a conference call.

"That 'inversion layer' *is* the American sub. It is moving contrary to all other known data and measures too small in size to remain stable in warm water. Ivan, you've had one shot at him. I want you take another. Dive to a reasonable level and close in to torpedo range. Try for a damaging hit to force him to the surface."

"Captain? Sorry to disturb you, sir. Target number one has descended a thousand feet and is closing on our position."

"I'll be right there." Boxer pushed aside his unfinished hot turkey sandwich and left the wardroom.

On the bridge, he quickly took in the situation. "Range?"

"Four-eight-zero-zero yards."

"Bearing?"

"Two-nine-five."

"Mark. Turn left to three-five-zero degrees. Open outer doors. Stand by to fire one and two."

"One and two ready, sir."

"Open inner doors. Bearing on target?"

"Zero-zero, sir."

"Fire one."

There was a slight whoosh and thump.

"One fired, sir."

"Track?"

"Running hot, straight and normal, sir. Indicates self-guidance system on and functioning."

"Get it on the GDT."

"Yes, sir."

The fish showed as a thin red line, streaking toward the green snake of the attacking Soviet sub. Boxer watched as the Russian captain's instruments indicated the approaching torpedo. He swerved.

The torpedo turned with him. A small television monitor showed the blurry sea ahead of the deadly nuclear projectile. Boxer clenched both fists.

A second later, the Russian sub tried another evasive maneuver.

352

Within a fraction of a second, the torpedo duplicated the change. A dark shape could now be seen on the screen.

Swiftly the bulk grew larger. It seemed to snap sideways and disappear from the frame. The television image whirled giddily and then centered once more on the target.

Suddenly the Soviet vessel turned bow-onward and fired two fish of its own. Self-guiding in a manner similar to the U.S. made torpedoes, they came on, at extreme range. Propellers churning, they sped past the hostile device that threatened their parent sub.

"Give those shots a Mode Three pulse," Boxer ordered the ECM operator.

"Mode Three on, sir."

First one, then the second torpedo veered off course and ran in wide, eliptical arcs. Boxer looked away from the activity on the GDT in time to see the self-guidance monitor flash white.

"Bullseye," the CIC officer called out.

"Give me a radiation count," Boxer ordered.

"Ten rads, sir. Now twenty . . . now fifty . . . now . . . eighty. Diminishing to seventy, sir. Sixty . . . fifty . . . thirty . . . holding steady at thirty rads, sir."

"Low enough. We can handle it."

"Surface targets two and three moving toward area of disturbance, sir," the SO announced. "Beginning standard sweep pattern."

"Change all ECM modes, ready three more drones. I'll take the con."

"Yes, sir," Harris readily agreed.

"Helmsman, come right to one-four-zero."

"Right to one-four-zero, aye."

"Reactor room, ahead two-thirds."

"Two-thirds, aye, sir."

Mentally Boxer ticked off the seconds, then announced, "Come left to zero-nine-zero. Stand by to fire drone from tube eight."

"Eight standing by, sir."

"Open outer doors."

Quickly the well honed crew went through the drill.

"Fire eight. Come left again to zero-one-zero. Reduce speed to ahead one-half. Stand by to fire drone tube three."

Again Boxer counted off the seconds. "Fire three. Right full rudder. Come to one-zero-zero. Ahead flank speed."

This time he let a full minute run by. "Fire four."

Another drone sped out, broadcasting to all the world that it was a full-grown submarine.

"A few more fancy maneuvers ought to stir things up a bit for our Russian friends," Boxer observed. "Load all tubes. Nuke torpedos."

"He got Sobel!" Igor Borodine shouted as he saw the display on the combat director. For a moment he wished he had been brought up as a believer. Then he could have the satisfaction of calling down God's wrath on the American captain. He reached for the handset of the underwater communicator.

"Ludor?" he inquired when the remaining Z-Class answered. "You saw that? A hundred and thirty men gone in a flash. Nuclear, of course. We are going to have to attack."

"I don't have the inversion layer any more, Igor. Everything on the screen is changed. We can't tell what or where the American is."

"I know we're blind. But we are both going to make a run on him. Load all tubes and fire a random pattern. Some of them will probably lock on drones. That's all right. What we have to do is make it too hot for the American. Force him to surface. Commence in three minutes. That is all." He put the phone set aside and reached for the microphone that would let him talk to the surface vessels.

"What does your combat director show? he asked the destroyer commanders.

"I have an underwater target, bearing zero-nine-zero. Speed three-two-knots, range five hundred meters."

"Commence depth charge run."

"Aye, aye, Captain."

"I have that target also," the other captain acknowledged. "And another one bearing two-zero-zero degrees."

"Commence depth charge run on it, too," Borodine told him. "Let them get the first salvo off then we'll fire into where that 'inversion layer' disappeared."

Two minutes passed and then sonar picked up the splash, double click of arming and boom of depth charges.

"Fire a spread of four, two degrees apart . . . beginning . . . now. Fire one," Borodine commanded. "Fire two . . . fire three . . . fire four. Stand by aft tubes. Helm, reverse course one-eighty degrees."

"Aye, aye, sir. . . . Course steady at one-seven-zero degrees."

"Fire five . . . fire six." Borodine drove one hard fist into the opposite palm. "We'll get that bastard. We'll get him."

"Torpedoes coming from everywhere, sir," the SO told Boxer.

"Too many for Mode Three to handle?"

"Yes, sir."

"Fire starboard counter battery."

"Aye, aye."

"Hedgehogs fired, sir."

Three seconds passed . . . four . . . five . . . *BOOM!*

The blast sounded through the *Shark* with no need of listening devices. Two seconds later another blast as an approaching torpedo had been homed in on and destroyed. Then a third. In the distance, the dampered sonar continued to record depth charge explosions on two of the drone locations.

Other torpedoes, deflected by electronic magic, swerved away from the position of the *Shark*. Suddenly the bridge lurched sideways and an ominous belling of metal rang through the boat.

"What the hell?" Cowly exclaimed.

"We've been hit. A fish at extreme range. Not enough to let it go off. Must have been a glancing blow," Boxer answered calmly. "Helmsman, come left to zero-one-zero. Maintain flank speed. We're going after that damned cruiser. Right now, he's the one who can cause us the most trouble."

Three minutes later, all systems agreed. "Launch surface to surface tubes one through six."

"Missiles fired, sir."

The short countdown sped by and then the sound pickups transmitted four powerful detonations as that many missiles made contact with the heavy cruiser *Beautiful Ukraine*. Internal explosions followed and the eerie sound of grinding metal as the ship started to break up.

"Now let's get the hell out of here. That will give them a fix."

He had only two choices, Boxer realized. He could go back to the water around Torpy and rely on the engineer's estimates of how much radiation the *Shark* could withstand. The sea was still so hot there that the Russian subs wouldn't dare follow, nor would it be safe for the destroyers. Or he could find a place and dive deeply, to a depth the Soviet equipment could never stand. For a long moment, Boxer mulled over each possibility. At last he went to the chart table and scanned the sea bottom in an area two miles around their present indicated position.

His finger fell on one series of closely set lines, wide at the outside, coming closer together as they merged on the paper. A deep trench with narrow, steep sides. Depth, three thousand five hundred feet. Pushing it, but he had faith *Shark* could endure the pressure. He fed the data to the computer and waited as the answer ground out. The depth sensors, echo sounding range finder and several sophisticated instruments he didn't fully understand all agreed. If anything, since the chart had been made, the trench had grown deeper.

"Helmsman, come right to zero-nine-zero. Put the EPC on manual and begin a descent to three-five-zero-zero feet."

Tension became a palpable thing throughout the boat as the crew and Redfern's Strike Force realized the strain to be put on the *Shark*'s hull. The drawn, pale faces of his men brought Redfern to the bridge.

"Well, Jack?"

"Yeah, Tom. Now we do some sweating."

"It's balls to the wall, huh? All right if I have De Vargas pipe some guitar music through the boat?"

"Sorry, Tom. I was just going to pass the word to rig for silent running. We'll have to get through this one without it."

"Damn!"

"I'll double that in spades."

26

Borodine paced the bridge of his *More Dekar'*. The torpedo attacks had failed. Another drone had been blown up. An unexpected and unknown type of counter fire battery had destroyed three more of his torpedoes. Time went on and, worse, they seemed no nearer to finding the accursed American than before.

"Comrade Captain, our sensors indicate launch of some type sub-surface missiles. Indicated target is the cruiser *Kraceve Ukran*."

"Damnit! Where is the point of origin?"

The operator quickly told him. Immediately Igor ordered his ships to converge on that point.

"We've got him," he exulted.

"Comrade Captain, there is no more indication of any nature on our detectors. The American has . . . has disappeared."

"Impossible. Sweep the area where the missiles were fired."

A pounding rumble, much like a distant thunderstorm sounded in the boat.

"Sonar contact to the north, at zero-five-zero degrees. It's our cruiser, Comrade Captain. She's breaking up. Sustained four direct hits."

Borodine, normally mild tempered and controlled, wanted to hit something. "Where is the American?" he demanded.

"Gone, Comrade Captain."

"That's not good enough. Find him."

He called Parovik and the two destroyers and got the same answer.

An intensive sweep, that occupied thirty minutes, produced no better results. Borodine put himself in the enemy commander's place. What would he do?

Borodine paced as he contemplated the alternatives. He might try reversing course and heading back toward the radioactive cauldron that had been Torpy Island. All that background emission would render electronic search equipment useless. Yes. A possibility. His own radiation monitor had indicated an impossibly high count. He doubted the Americans had come with better shielding. What then?

He could make a run for it. No. Simply out of the question. Even his 'not being there' left an indelible mark.

He could find someplace deep and lie on the bottom, low ECM profile and rigged for silence. Yes. That's what *he* would do. He had no doubt the American captain had ample intelligence to reach the same conclusion. So far his unseen enemy had performed brilliantly. A sudden insight hit him. That was exactly what had happened.

He felt certain that the American sub could go deeper than their own boats. Now he had to find a suitable spot, within two or three nautical miles of the place where the missiles had been fired. Borodine went quickly to the chart table.

His search produced three possibles. Which one?

The American's original course could be considered to be north by northeast. Fine. Only one submarine trench existed in that direction.

"Helm. Come to zero-one-zero degrees. Slow to half ahead. Rig all listening devices. Rig all electronic sensors."

"What is it, Igor?"

"I think I've found the American, Vassily."

"Good!" Viktor enthused. "Now we can smash him."

Time moved slowly by. The canyon began to appear on the bottom sounding simulator screen. At a creeping pace of minimal steerage way, Borodine brought his boat along the uneven gash in the sea floor. He made a long pass and turned back.

Two more sweeps made up his mind.

"He's there. He has to be. The configuration of the bottom is all too normal." Borodine strode to the surface communicator.

"Both of you are to home in on me," he informed the captains of the destroyers. "You are to systematically depth charge the canyon your echo sounders indicate at this location. I want the walls of that fissure on the floor of it within half an hour. Our American friend is hiding there."

"How will that provide us with the 'proof' the Comrade Admiral of the Fleet wants?" Markov inquired tartly. This sudden change in tactics had brought back his officious nature.

"Simple, Vassily. We can seal that sub in the canyon, then at our leisure come back here and send down divers to recover papers, uniforms, bodies . . . anything. Trust me in this. The simple fact remains that this American sub is something special. It can blow us all out of the water. Then simply sail on home. By this means we can insure it is here waiting when we return with diving bells and other specialized equipment."

Fifteen minutes later, the destroyers lined up astern and began their first run. Borodine held the Q-21 off at a safe range.

Set for maximum depth, the ashcans sank to eight hundred feet before detonating. The powerful explosive charges disrupted milleniums of debris. Boulders large as a modest house dislodged and rolled down the sandy slopes to the seabed. Aboard the *Shark,* men grew white-faced and drawn. Nerves began to snap and crackle.

The blasts seemed endless. Tons of rock cascaded down, striking the hull and causing men to jump and twitch with each tocsin impact. A crewman and two of Redfern's men secluded themselves in the heads and wept in secret. Settled on the sand, in absolute silence, with a minimum of air circulation and no outlet through smoking, the men listened to doom slide down on them.

"I don't know how those Ruskie bastards found us," Bill Harris observed.

"It's Borodine or his ghost leading this attack force," Boxer growled. "This has lasted too long to be a random thing."

"Can we make a run for it?" Tom Redfern asked, his own face a sickly yellow-green.

"Not now. We're trapped."

"God, don't say that word."

Nervousness became near terror when a large portion of the canyon overhang let go and rumbled down onto the forward deck of the *Shark.*

359

"Hail Mary, full of Grace . . . the Lord is with thee" a quiet voice prayed in one corner of the bridge.

"Who's saying that?" Boxer demanded.

"I . . . I am, sir," Mahony announced.

"Use a mike, then. It might do everyone some good," Boxer told him in a gravely unfamiliar tone.

The concussions had come so frequently that it took five minutes before the crew and officers of the *Shark* realized that the depth charge bombardment had ended.

"Thank God for that," Boxer breathed out. "Now comes the hard part."

"What's that?"

"Digging us the hell out of here, Tom."

"All firing is to cease," Igor Borodine commanded over the radio net to the surface. He turned to Vassily Markov with a wan smile. "They are sealed in. They will never be able to get out of that canyon and I doubt they are aware of our recent advances in underwater exploration equipment. Within three or so days, we can open that sub like a tin of caviar and feast on all the proof the Presidium wants." He reached for the bank of communications terminals.

"This is Captain First Class Igor Borodine, aboard the Q-Twenty-one." His voice was heard in far off Moscow with the same ease as the commanders of his task force. "The Americans are trapped in a deep sea canyon some eighty miles north-by-northeast of the site of Torpy Island. As of eight hundred hours this morning, I am ending the operation. That is all. Good work to all hands."

Divers, in special pressure suits, provided their own critical analysis of the situation as well as the data from the Damage Control computer. Closed circuit television cameras allowed additional points of view. None of it looked good to Boxer.

Their electronic listening devices indicated the Russians pulling off. Only one sub stayed anywhere within detectable range. After four hours, it, too, proceeded out of the vicinity.

"Picks and shovels?" Tom Redfern quipped as he stood at Boxer's shoulder.

"Don't I wish," Boxer retorted. He felt an additional sense of relief from the assured manner his friend Redfern had exhibited during the earlier attack and the frightening bombardment by the destroyers. He felt confident that never again would Tom doubt his ability to "tough it out." Boxer picked up the MC microphone. "Captain to the Reactor Room."

"Reactor aye."

"If we use small explosive charges to blast the rocks free of the stern, can you give me power?"

"Some. All we need to do is dislodge some more of this crap while the screws are turning and we can figure to spend the rest of our lives here."

"Put the air circulation on full and the other electrical equipment on line. Then we'll get started on the clearing job. I'll let you know."

"Even with the special gear, this depth is taking it out of the divers," Bill Harris advised Boxer.

"An hour's rest, then we go all out. Chow for all hands."

It took twenty minutes to probe, dig, tamp and rig the explosive charges. All personnel returned to the *Shark* and Boxer personally turned the crank.

Muffled blasts shook the sturdy triple-hulled vessel. Rock screeched and rumbled outside. A long five minutes went by as the water cleared of its silty clouds.

Television images showed the stern to be exposed and free of the welter of rubble.

"Wheew!" Bill Harris breathed out. "Can we haul all this weight, skipper?"

"No. What I want to do is set up a rocking motion, shake off a lot of it. Let's get to it right now."

At first the *Shark* only strained. Gradually the speed of revolutions increased. The incredible power of the twin reactors gave all the thrust to the propellers they could. Slowly, the stern lifted a fraction of a foot.

"Blow aft ballasts," Boxer commanded.

Compressed air drove the water from the ballast tanks and the scene disappeared in new clouds of silt and sand.

When they cleared, Boxer brought the *Shark* to half power. Metal beams shrieked in protest and rivets popped off the inner hull plates. They sang musically as they ricocheted off the inner bulkheads and zinged along passageways.

Still the *Shark* lay penned in its earthen prison.

"More power, Bill, try to raise the sail."

Rock and sand cascaded away as the powerful hydraulic rams drove the *Shark*'s sail upward.

"That's it! That's it! She's doing it," Boxer cried in delighted relief. Great streams of confining stone and silt rolled off the rounded foredeck and ran in muddy rivers from the stern.

"Blow main ballast!"

With a frightful groan and awkward wobbling attitude, the *Shark* began to rise at the stern. Slowly, ever so slowly, the heavy boat began to shake itself free of the encasement of mud and rock. Metal wailed at the strain and several steam lines separated, sending scalding white clouds through the engine room, forward torpedo room and up the tunnel to the bridge, now elevated to full height in the sail.

"Damage control to the bridge. Skipper we've got five men here scalded by steam."

"Get Link and Sherm Ross started treating them. How about other damage?"

"We're on it."

Boxer looked at the Damage Control computer. *Three broken steam lines, from main reactor, forward of number three bulkhead. Close valves and effect manual repair,* it told him. *Two broken steam lines in engine room, port side outer bulkhead. Valves already closed, repair under way.*

Not too bad.

with a sudden, violent lurch, the *Shark* came entirely free of the bottom and wallowed upward.

"Blow all ballasts! Boxer shouted.

Twenty minutes later, the *Shark* had risen half way out of the trench. Within two hours she hung at cruise depth and a grinning Boxer stood behind the helmsman.

"All ahead full. Helmsman, set course for zero-six-zero." Boxer reached for the MC mike and keyed the switch. "This is the captain. *Shark* is on her way home. All hands well done."

THE BLACK EAGLES
by Jon Lansing

#1: HANOI HELLGROUND   (1249, $2.95)
They're the best jungle fighters the United States has to offer, and
no matter where Charlie is hiding, they'll find him. They're the
greatest unsung heroes of the dirtiest, most challenging war of all
time. They're THE BLACK EAGLES.

#2: MEKONG MASSACRE   (1294, $2.50)
Falconi and his Black Eagle combat team are about to stake a claim
on Colonel Nguyen Chi Roi—and give the Commie his due. But
American intelligence wants the colonel alive, making this the
Black Eagles' toughest assignment ever!

#3: NIGHTMARE IN LAOS   (1341, $2.50)
There's a hot rumor that the Russians are secretly building a
nuclear reactor in Laos. And the Black Eagles are going to have to
move fast—to prevent the nuclear fallout from hitting the fan!

*Available wherever paperbacks are sold, or order direct from the
Publisher. Send cover price plus 50¢ per copy for mailing and
handling to Zebra Books, 475 Park Avenue South, New York, N.Y.
10016. DO NOT SEND CASH.*

ZEBRA WINS THE WEST
WITH THESE EXCITING BESTSELLERS!

PISTOLERO (1331, $2.25)
by Walt Denver

Death stalks the dusty streets of Belleville when a vicious power struggle tears the town in half. But it isn't until a beautiful rancher's daughter gets trapped in a bloody crossfire that someone with cold nerve and hot lead goes into action. Only who would've guessed that a stranger would be the one to put his life on the line to save her?

RED TOMAHAWK (1362, $2.25)
by Jory Sherman

Soon, deep in the Dakotas—at a place called Little Big Horn—Red Tomahawk will discover the meaning of his tribe's fateful vision. And the Sioux will find a greatness in his enduring legend that will last through all time!

BLOOD TRAIL SOUTH (1349, $2.25)
by Walt Denver

Five years have passed since six hardcases raped and murdered John Rustin's wife, butchered his son, and burned down his ranch. Now, someone with cold eyes and hot lead is after those six coyotes. Some say he's a lawman. Others say—in a low whisper—that it's John Rustin himself!

Available wherever paperbacks are sold, or order direct from the Publisher. Send cover price plus 50¢ per copy for mailing and handling to Zebra Books, 475 Park Avenue South, New York, N.Y. 10016. DO NOT SEND CASH.

OTHER BOOKS ON THE WORLD AT WAR
by Lawrence Cortesi

D-DAY MINUS 1	(1318, $3.25)
THE DEADLY SKIES	(1132, $3.25)
PACIFIC HELLFIRE	(1179, $3.25)
PACIFIC STRIKE	(1041, $2.95)
TARGET: TOKYO	(1256, $3.25)
VALOR AT LEYTE	(1213, $3.25)
VALOR AT SAMAR	(1226, $2.75)
THE BATTLE FOR MANILA	(1334, $3.25)

Available wherever paperbacks are sold, or order direct from the Publisher. Send cover price plus 50¢ per copy for mailing and handling to Zebra Books, 475 Park Avenue South, New York, N.Y. 10016. DO NOT SEND CASH.